SUNSET LIMITED

JAMES

SUNSET

DOUBLEDAY

NEW YORK

LONDON

TORONTO

SYDNEY

AUCKLAND

LEE BURKE

LIMITED

PUBLISHED BY DOUBLEDAY
a division of Bantam Doubleday Dell Publishing Group, Inc.
1540 Broadway, New York, New York 10036

DOUBLEDAY and the portrayal of an anchor with a dolphin
are trademarks of Doubleday, a division of
Bantam Doubleday Dell Publishing Group, Inc.

Book design by Claire Vaccaro

Library of Congress Cataloging-in-Publication Data
Burke, James Lee, 1936–
Sunset limited / by James Lee Burke. — 1st ed.
p.   cm.
I. Title.
PS3552.U723S86   1998
813'.54—dc21   97-23893
CIP

ISBN 0-385-48842-4
First Edition
June 1998
1   3   5   7   9   10   8   6   4   2

FOR BILL AND SUSAN NELSON

I would like to thank the following attorneys for all the legal information they have provided me in the writing of my books over the years: my son James L. Burke, Jr., and my daughter Alafair Burke and my cousins Dracos Burke and Porteus Burke.

I would also like once again to thank my wife Pearl, my editor Patricia Mulcahy, and my agent Philip Spitzer for the many years they have been on board.

I'd also like to thank my daughters Pamela McDavid and Andree Walsh, from whom I ask advice on virtually everything.

ONE

I had seen a dawn like this one only twice in my life: once in Vietnam, after a Bouncing Betty had risen from the earth on a night trail and twisted its tentacles of light around my thighs, and years earlier outside of Franklin, Louisiana, when my father and I discovered the body of a labor organizer who had been crucified with sixteen-penny nails, ankle and wrist, against a barn wall.

Just before the sun broke above the Gulf's rim, the wind, which had blown the waves with ropes of foam all night, suddenly died and the sky became as white and brightly grained as polished bone, as though all color had been bled out of the air, and the gulls that had swooped and glided over my wake lifted into the haze and the swells flattened into an undulating sheet of liquid tin dimpled by the leathery backs of stingrays.

The eastern horizon was strung with rain clouds and the sun should have risen out of the water like a mist-shrouded egg yolk, but it didn't. Its red light mushroomed along the horizon, then rose into the sky in a cross, burning in the center, as though fire were trying to take the shape of a man, and the water turned the heavy dark color of blood.

Maybe the strange light at dawn was only coincidence and had nothing to do with the return to New Iberia of Megan Flynn, who, like a sin we had concealed in the confessional, vexed our conscience, or worse, rekindled our envy.

But I knew in my heart it was not coincidence, no more so than the fact that the man crucified against the barn wall was Megan's father and that Megan herself was waiting for me at my dock and bait shop, fifteen miles south of New Iberia, when Clete Purcel, my old Homicide partner from the First District in New Orleans, and I cut the engines on my cabin cruiser and floated through the hyacinths on our wake, the mud billowing in clouds that were as bright as yellow paint under the stern.

It was sprinkling now, and she wore an orange silk shirt and khaki slacks and sandals, her funny straw hat spotted with rain, her hair dark red against the gloom of the day, her face glowing with a smile that was like a thorn in the heart.

Clete stood by the gunnel and looked at her and puckered his mouth. "Wow," he said under his breath.

She was one of those rare women gifted with eyes that could linger briefly on yours and make you feel, rightly or wrongly, you were genuinely invited into the mystery of her life.

"I've seen her somewhere," Clete said as he prepared to climb out on the bow.

"Last week's *Newsweek* magazine," I said.

"That's it. She won a Pulitzer Prize or something. There was a picture of her hanging out of a slick," he said. His gum snapped in his jaw.

She had been on the cover, wearing camouflage pants and a T-shirt, with dog tags around her neck, the downdraft of the British helicopter whipping her hair and flattening her clothes against her body, the strap of her camera laced around one wrist, while, below, Serbian armor burned in columns of red and black smoke.

But I remembered another Megan, too: the in-your-face orphan of years ago, who, with her brother, would run away from foster homes in Louisiana and Colorado, until they were old enough to finally disappear into that wandering army of fruit pickers and wheat harvesters whom their father, an unrepentant IWW radical, had spent a lifetime trying to organize.

I stepped off the bow onto the dock and walked toward my truck to back the trailer down the ramp. I didn't mean to be impolite. I admired the Flynns, but you paid a price for their friendship and proximity to the vessel of social anger their lives had become.

"Not glad to see me, Streak?" she said.

"Always glad. How you doin', Megan?"

She looked over my shoulder at Clete Purcel, who had pulled the port side of the boat flush into the rubber tires on my dock and was unloading the cooler and rods out of the stern. Clete's thick arms and fire-hydrant neck were peeling and red with fresh sunburn. When he stooped over with the cooler, his tropical shirt split across his back. He grinned at us and shrugged his shoulders.

"That one had to come out of the Irish Channel," she said.

"You're not a fisher, Meg. You out here on business?"

"You know who Cool Breeze Broussard is?" she asked.

"A house creep and general thief."

"He says your parish lockup is a toilet. He says your jailer is a sadist."

"We lost the old jailer. I've been on leave. I don't know much about the new guy."

"Cool Breeze says inmates are gagged and handcuffed to a detention chair. They have to sit in their own excrement. The U.S. Department of Justice believes him."

"Jails are bad places. Talk to the sheriff, Megan. I'm off the clock."

"Typical New Iberia. Bullshit over humanity."

"See you around," I said, and walked to my truck. Rain was pinging in large, cold drops on the tin roof of the bait shop.

"Cool Breeze said you were stand-up. He's in lockdown now because he dimed the jailer. I'll tell him you were off the clock," she said.

"This town didn't kill your father."

"No, they just put me and my brother in an orphanage where we polished floors with our knees. Tell your Irish friend he's beautiful.

Come out to the house and visit us, Streak," she said, and walked across the dirt road to where she had parked her car under the trees in my drive.

Up on the dock, Clete poured the crushed ice and canned drinks and speckled trout out of the cooler. The trout looked stiff and cold on the board planks.

"You ever hear anything about prisoners being gagged and cuffed to chairs in the Iberia Parish Prison?" I asked.

"That's what that was about? Maybe she ought to check out what those guys did to get in there."

"She said you were beautiful."

"She did?" He looked down the road where her car was disappearing under the canopy of oaks that grew along the bayou. Then he cracked a Budweiser and flipped me a can of diet Dr Pepper. The scar over his left eyebrow flattened against his skull when he grinned.

The turnkey had been a brig chaser in the Marine Corps and still wore his hair buzzed into the scalp and shaved in a razor-neat line on the back of his neck. His body was lean and braided with muscle, his walk as measured and erect as if he were on a parade ground. He unlocked the cell at the far end of the corridor, hooked up Willie Cool Breeze Broussard in waist and leg manacles, and escorted him with one hand to the door of the interview room, where I waited.

"Think he's going to run on you, Top?" I said.

"He runs at the mouth, that's what he does."

The turnkey closed the door behind us. Cool Breeze looked like two hundred pounds of soft black chocolate poured inside jailhouse denims. His head was bald, lacquered with wax, shiny as horn, his eyes drooping at the corners like a prizefighter's. It was hard to believe he was a second-story man and four-time loser.

"If they're jamming you up, Cool Breeze, it's not on your sheet," I said.

"What you call Isolation?"

"The screw says you asked for lockdown."

His wrists were immobilized by the cuffs attached to the chain around his waist. He shifted in his chair and looked sideways at the door.

"I was on Camp J up at Angola. It's worse in here. A hack made a kid blow him at gunpoint," he said.

"I don't want to offend you, Breeze, but this isn't your style."

"What ain't?"

"You're not one to rat out anybody, not even a bad screw."

His eyes shifted back and forth inside his face. He rubbed his nose on his shoulder.

"I'm down on this VCR beef. A truckload of them. What makes it double bad is I boosted the load from a Giacano warehouse in Lake Charles. I need to get some distance between me and my problems, maybe like in the Islands, know what I saying?"

"Sounds reasonable."

"No, you don't get it. The Giacanos are tied into some guys in New York City making dubs of movies, maybe a hundred t'ousand of them a week. So they buy lots of VCRs, cut-rate prices, Cool Breeze Midnight Supply Service, you wit' me?"

"You've been selling the Giacanos their own equipment? You're establishing new standards, Breeze."

He smiled slightly, but the peculiar downward slope of his eyes gave his expression a melancholy cast, like a bloodhound's. He shook his head.

"You still don't see it, Robicheaux. None of these guys are that smart. They started making dubs of them kung fu movies from Hong Kong. The money behind them kung fus comes from some very bad guys. You heard of the Triads?"

"We're talking about China White?"

"That's how it gets washed, my man."

I took out my business card and wrote my home number and the number of the bait shop on the back. I leaned across the table and slipped it in his shirt pocket.

"Watch your butt in here, Breeze, particularly that ex-jarhead."

"Meet the jailer. It's easy to catch him after five. He like to work late, when they ain't no visitors around."

. . .

Megan's brother Cisco owned a home up Bayou Teche, just south of Loreauville. It was built in the style of the West Indies, one story and rambling, shaded by oaks, with a wide, elevated gallery, green, ventilated window shutters, and fern baskets hanging from the eaves. Cisco and his friends, movie people like himself, came and went with the seasons, shooting ducks in the wetlands, fishing for tarpon and speckled trout in the Gulf. Their attitudes were those of people who used geographical areas and social cultures as playgrounds and nothing more. Their glittering lawn parties, which we saw only from the road through the myrtle bushes and azalea and banana trees that fringed his property, were the stuff of legend in our small sugarcane town along the Teche.

I had never understood Cisco. He was tough, like his sister, and he had the same good looks they had both inherited from their father, but when his reddish-brown eyes settled on yours, he seemed to search inside your skin for something he wanted, perhaps coveted, yet couldn't define. Then the moment would pass and his attention would wander away like a balloon on the breeze.

He had dug irrigation ditches and worked the fruit orchards in the San Joaquin and had ended up in Hollywood as a road-wise, city-library-educated street kid who was dumbfounded when he discovered his handsome face and seminal prowess could earn him access to a movie lot, first as an extra, then as a stuntman.

It wasn't long before he realized he was not only braver than the actors whose deeds he performed but that he was more intelligent than most of them as well. He co-wrote scripts for five years, formed an independent production group with two Vietnam combat veterans, and put together a low-budget film on the lives of migrant farmworkers that won prizes in France and Italy.

His next film opened in theaters all over the United States.

Now Cisco had an office on Sunset Boulevard, a home in Pacific Palisades, and membership in that magic world where bougainvillea and ocean sun were just the token symbols of the health and riches that southern California could bestow on its own.

It was late Sunday evening when I turned off the state road and drove up the gravel lane toward his veranda. His lawn was blue-green with St. Augustine grass and smelled of chemical fertilizer and the water sprinklers twirling between the oak and pine trees. I could see him working out on a pair of parallel bars in the side yard, his bare arms and shoulders cording with muscle and vein, his skin painted with the sun's late red light through the cypresses on the bayou.

As always, Cisco was courteous and hospitable, but in a way that made you feel his behavior was learned rather than natural, a barrier rather than an invitation.

"Megan? No, she had to fly to New Orleans. Can I help you with something?" he said. Before I could answer, he said, "Come on inside. I need something cold. How do you guys live here in the summer?"

All the furniture in the living room was white, the floor covered with straw mats, blond, wood-bladed ceiling fans turning overhead. He stood shirtless and barefooted at a wet bar and filled a tall glass with crushed ice and collins mix and cherries. The hair on his stomach looked like flattened strands of red wire above the beltline of his yellow slacks.

"It was about an inmate in the parish prison, a guy named Cool Breeze Broussard," I said.

He drank from his glass, his eyes empty. "You want me to tell her something?" he asked.

"Maybe this guy was mistreated at the jail, but I think his real problem is with some mobbed-up dudes in New Orleans. Anyway, she can give me a call."

"Cool Breeze Broussard. That's quite a name."

"It might end up in one of your movies, huh?"

"You can't ever tell," he replied, and smiled.

On one wall were framed still shots from Cisco's films, and on a side wall photographs that were all milestones in Megan's career: a ragged ditch strewn with the bodies of civilians in Guatemala, African children whose emaciated faces were crawling with blowflies, French Legionnaires pinned down behind sandbags while mortar rounds geysered dirt above their heads.

But, oddly, the color photograph that had launched her career and had made *Life* magazine was located at the bottom corner of the collection. It had been shot in the opening of a storm drain that bled into the Mississippi just as an enormous black man, in New Orleans City Prison denims strung with sewage, had burst out of the darkness into the fresh air, his hands raised toward the sun, as though he were trying to pay tribute to its energy and power. But a round from a sharpshooter's rifle had torn through his throat, exiting in a bloody mist, twisting his mouth open like that of a man experiencing orgasm.

A second framed photograph showed five uniformed cops looking down at the body, which seemed shrunken and without personality in death. A smiling crew-cropped man in civilian clothes was staring directly at the camera in the foreground, a red apple with a white hunk bitten out of it cupped in his palm.

"What are you thinking about?" Cisco asked.

"Seems like an inconspicuous place to put these," I said.

"The guy paid some hard dues. For Megan and me, both," he said.

"Both?"

"I was her assistant on that shot, inside the pipe when those cops decided he'd make good dog food. Look, you think Hollywood's the only meat market out there? The cops got citations. The black guy got to rape a sixteen-year-old white girl before he went out. I get to hang his picture on the wall of a seven-hundred-thousand-dollar house. The only person who didn't get a trade-off was the high school girl."

"I see. Well, I guess I'd better be going."

Through the French doors I saw a man of about fifty walk down the veranda in khaki shorts and slippers with his shirt unbuttoned on his concave chest. He sat down in a reclining chair with a magazine and lit a cigar.

"That's Billy Holtzner. You want to meet him?" Cisco said.

"Who?"

"When the Pope visited the studio about seven years ago, Billy asked him if he had a script. Wait here a minute."

I tried to stop him but it was too late. The rudeness of his having to ask permission for me to be introduced seemed to elude him. I saw him bend down toward the man named Holtzner and speak in a low voice, while Holtzner puffed on his cigar and looked at nothing. Then Cisco raised up and came back inside, turning up his palms awkwardly at his sides, his eyes askance with embarrassment.

"Billy's head is all tied up with a project right now. He's kind of intense when he's in preproduction." He tried to laugh.

"You're looking solid, Cisco."

"Orange juice and wheat germ and three-mile runs along the surf. It's the only life."

"Tell Megan I'm sorry I missed her."

"I apologize about Billy. He's a good guy. He's just eccentric."

"You know anything about movie dubs?"

"Yeah, they cost the industry a lot of money. That's got something to do with this guy Broussard?"

"You got me."

When I walked out the front door the man in the reclining chair had turned off the bug light and was smoking his cigar reflectively, one knee crossed over the other. I could feel his eyes on me, taking my measure. I nodded at him, but he didn't respond. The ash of his cigar glowed like a hot coal in the shadows.

TWO

The jailer, Alex Guidry, lived outside of town on a ten-acre horse farm devoid of trees or shade. The sun's heat pooled in the tin roofs of his outbuildings, and grit and desiccated manure blew out of his horse lots. His oblong 1960s red-brick house, its central-air-conditioning units roaring outside a back window twenty-four hours a day, looked like a utilitarian fortress constructed for no other purpose than to repel the elements.

His family had worked for a sugar mill down toward New Orleans, and his wife's father used to sell Negro burial insurance, but I knew little else about him. He was one of those aging, well-preserved men with whom you associate a golf photo on the local sports page, membership in a self-congratulatory civic club, a charitable drive that is of no consequence.

Or was there something else, a vague and ugly story years back? I couldn't remember.

Sunday afternoon I parked my pickup truck by his stable and walked past a chain-link dog pen to the riding ring. The dog pen exploded with the barking of two German shepherds who caromed off the fencing, their teeth bared, their paws skittering the feces that lay baked on the hot concrete pad.

Alex Guidry cantered a black gelding in a circle, his booted calves fitted with English spurs. The gelding's neck and sides were iridescent with sweat. Guidry sawed the bit back in the gelding's mouth.

"What is it?" he said.

"I'm Dave Robicheaux. I called earlier."

He wore tan riding pants and a form-fitting white polo shirt. He dismounted and wiped the sweat off his face with a towel and threw it to a black man who had come out of the stable to take the horse.

"You want to know if this guy Broussard was in the detention chair? The answer is no," he said.

"He says you've put other inmates in there. For days."

"Then he's lying."

"You have a detention chair, though, don't you?"

"For inmates who are out of control, who don't respond to Isolation."

"You gag them?"

"No."

I rubbed the back of my neck and looked at the dog pen. The water bowl was turned over and flies boiled in the door of the small doghouse that gave the only relief from the sun.

"You've got a lot of room here. You can't let your dogs run?" I said. I tried to smile.

"Anything else, Mr. Robicheaux?"

"Yeah. Nothing better happen to Cool Breeze while he's in your custody."

"I'll keep that in mind, sir. Close the gate on your way out, please."

I got back in my truck and drove down the shell road toward the cattle guard. A half dozen Red Angus grazed in Guidry's pasture, while snowy egrets perched on their backs.

Then I remembered. It was ten or eleven years back, and Alex Guidry had been charged with shooting a neighbor's dog. Guidry had claimed the dog had attacked one of his calves and eaten its entrails, but the neighbor told another story, that Guidry had baited a steel trap for the animal and had killed it out of sheer meanness.

I looked into the rearview mirror and saw him watching me from the end of the shell drive, his legs slightly spread, a leather riding crop hanging from his wrist.

Monday morning I returned to work at the Iberia Parish Sheriff's Department and took my mail out of my pigeonhole and tapped on the sheriff's office.

He tilted back in his swivel chair and smiled when he saw me. His jowls were flecked with tiny blue and red veins that looked like fresh ink on a map when his temper flared. He had shaved too close and there was a piece of bloody tissue paper stuck in the cleft in his chin. Unconsciously he kept stuffing his shirt down over his paunch into his gunbelt.

"You mind if I come back to work a week early?" I asked.

"This have anything to do with Cool Breeze Broussard's complaint to the Justice Department?"

"I went out to Alex Guidry's place yesterday. How'd we end up with a guy like that as our jailer?"

"It's not a job people line up for," the sheriff said. He scratched his forehead. "You've got an FBI agent in your office right now, some gal named Adrien Glazier. You know her?"

"Nope. How'd she know I was going to be here?"

"She called your house first. Your wife told her. Anyway, I'm glad you're back. I want this bullshit at the jail cleared up. We just got a very weird case that was thrown in our face from St. Mary Parish."

He opened a manila folder and put on his glasses and peered down at the fax sheets in his fingers. This is the story he told me.

Three months ago, under a moon haloed with a rain ring and sky filled with dust blowing out of the sugarcane fields, a seventeen-year-old black girl named Sunshine Labiche claimed two white boys forced her car off a dirt road into a ditch. They dragged her from behind the wheel, walked her by each arm into a cane field, then took turns raping and sodomizing her.

The next morning she identified both boys from a book of mug shots. They were brothers, from St. Mary Parish, but four months earlier they had been arrested for a convenience store holdup in New Iberia and had been released for lack of evidence.

This time they should have gone down.

They didn't.

Both had alibis, and the girl admitted she had been smoking rock with her boyfriend before she was raped. She dropped the charges.

Late Saturday afternoon an unmarked car came to the farmhouse of the two brothers over in St. Mary Parish. The father, who was bedridden in the front room, watched the visitors, unbeknown to them, through a crack in the blinds. The driver of the car wore a green uniform, like sheriff's deputies in Iberia Parish, and sunglasses and stayed behind the wheel, while a second man, in civilian clothes and a Panama hat, went to the gallery and explained to the two brothers they only had to clear up a couple of questions in New Iberia, then they would be driven back home.

"It ain't gonna take five minutes. We know you boys didn't have to come all the way over to Iberia Parish just to change your luck," he said.

The brothers were not cuffed; in fact, they were allowed to take a twelve-pack of beer with them to drink in the back seat.

A half hour later, just at sunset, a student from USL, who was camped out in the Atchafalaya swamp, looked through the flooded willow and gum trees that surrounded his houseboat and saw a car stop on the levee. Two older men and two boys got out. One of the older men wore a uniform. They all held cans of beer in their hands; all of them urinated off the levee into the cattails.

Then the two boys, dressed in jeans and Clorox-stained print shirts with the sleeves cut off at the armpits, realized something was wrong. They turned and stared stupidly at their companions, who had stepped backward up the levee and were now holding pistols in their hands.

The boys tried to argue, holding their palms outward, as though they were pushing back an invisible adversary. Their arms were olive with suntan, scrolled with reformatory tattoos, their hair spiked in points with butch wax. The man in uniform raised his gun and shouted an unintelligible order at them, motioning at the ground. When the boys did not respond, the second armed man, who wore a Panama hat, turned them toward the water with his hand, almost gently, inserted his shoe against the calf of one, then the other, pushing them to their knees, as though he were arranging manikins in a show window. Then he rejoined the man in uniform up the bank. One of the boys kept looking back fearfully over his shoulder. The other was weeping uncontrollably, his chin tilted upward, his arms stiff at his sides, his eyes tightly shut.

The men with guns were silhouetted against a molten red sun that had sunk across the top of the levee. Just as a flock of ducks flapped across the sun, the gunmen clasped their weapons with both hands and started shooting. But because of the fading light, or perhaps the nature of their deed, their aim was bad.

Both victims tried to rise from their knees, their bodies convulsing simultaneously from the impact of the rounds.

The witness said, "Their guns just kept popping. It looked like somebody was blowing chunks out of a watermelon."

After it was over, smoke drifted out over the water and the shooter in the Panama hat took close-up flash pictures with a Polaroid camera.

The witness used a pair of binoculars. He says the guy in the green uniform had our department patch on his sleeve," the sheriff said.

"White rogue cops avenging the rape of a black girl?"

"Look, get that FBI agent out of here, will you?"

He looked at the question in my face.

"She's got a broom up her ass." He rubbed his fingers across his mouth. "Did I say that? I'm going to go back to the laundry business. A bad day used to be washing somebody's golf socks," he said.

I looked through my office window at the FBI agent named Adrien Glazier. She sat with her legs crossed, her back to me, in a powder-blue suit and white blouse, writing on a legal pad. Her handwriting was filled with severe slants and slashes, with points in the letters that reminded me of incisor teeth.

When I opened the door she looked at me with ice-blue eyes that could have been taken out of a Viking's face.

"I visited William Broussard last night. He seems to think you're going to get him out of the parish prison," she said.

"Cool Breeze? He knows better than that."

"Does he?"

I waited. Her hair was ash-blond, wispy and broken on the ends, her face big-boned and adversarial. She was one of those you instinctively know have a carefully nursed reservoir of anger they draw upon as needed, in the same way others make use of daily prayer. My stare broke.

"Sorry. Is that a question?" I said.

"You don't have any business indicating to this man you can make deals for him," she said.

I sat down behind my desk and glanced out the window, wishing I could escape back into the coolness of the morning, the streets that were sprinkled with rain, the palm fronds lifting and clattering in the wind.

I picked up a stray paper clip and dropped it in my desk drawer and closed the drawer. Her eyes never left my face or relented in their accusation.

"What if the prosecutor's office does cut him loose? What's it to you?" I said.

"You're interfering in a federal investigation. Evidently you have a reputation for it."

"I think the truth is you want his *cojones* in a vise. You'll arrange some slack for him after he rats out some guys you can't make a case against."

She uncrossed her legs and leaned forward. She cocked her elbow on my desk and let one finger droop forward at my face.

"Megan Flynn is an opportunistic bitch. What she didn't get on her back, she got through posing as the Joan of Arc of oppressed people. You let her and her brother jerk your pud, then you're dumber than the people in my office say you are," she said.

"This has to be a put-on."

She pulled a manila folder out from under her legal pad and dropped it on my desk blotter.

"Those photos are of a guy named Swede Boxleiter. They were taken in the yard at the Colorado state pen in Canon City. What they don't show is the murder he committed in broad daylight with a camera following him around the yard. That's how good he is," she said.

His head and face were like those of a misshaped Marxist intellectual, the yellow hair close-cropped on the scalp, the forehead and brainpan too large, the cheeks tapering away to a mouth that was so small it looked obscene. He wore granny glasses on a chiseled nose, and a rotted and torn weight lifter's shirt on a torso that rippled with cartilage.

The shots had been taken from an upper story or guard tower with a zoom lens. They showed him moving through the clusters of convicts in the yard, faces turning toward him the way bait fish reflect light when a barracuda swims toward their perimeter. A fat man was leaning against the far wall, one hand squeezed on his scrotum, while he told a story to a half circle of his fellow inmates. His lips were twisted with a word he was forming, purple from a lollypop he had been eating. The man named Swede Boxleiter passed an inmate who held a tape-wrapped ribbon of silver behind his back. After Swede Boxleiter had walked by, the man whose palm seemed to have caught the sun like a heliograph now had his hands stuffed in his pockets.

The second-to-last photo showed a crowd at the wall like early men gathered on the rim of a pit to witness the death throes and communal roasting of an impaled mammoth.

Then the yard was empty, except for the fat man, the gash across his windpipe bubbling with saliva and blood, the tape-wrapped shank discarded in the red soup on his chest.

"Boxleiter is buddies with Cisco Flynn. They were in the same state home in Denver. Maybe you'll get to meet him. He got out three days ago," she said.

"Ms. Glazier, I'd like to—"

"It's Special Agent Glazier."

"Right. I'd like to talk with you, but . . . Look, why not let us take care of our own problems?"

"What a laugh." She stood up and gazed down at me. "Here it is. Hong Kong is going to become the property of Mainland China soon. There're some people we want to put out of business before we have to deal with Beijing to get at them. Got the big picture?"

"Not really. You know how it is out here in the provinces, swatting mosquitoes, arresting people for stealing hog manure, that sort of thing."

She laughed to herself and dropped her card on my desk, then walked out of my office and left the door open as though she would not touch anything in our department unless it was absolutely necessary.

A t noon I drove down the dirt road by the bayou toward my dock and bait shop. Through the oak trees that lined the shoulder I could see the wide gallery and purple-streaked tin roof of my house up the slope. It had rained again during the morning, and the cypress planks in the walls were stained the color of dark tea, the hanging baskets of impatiens blowing strings of water in the wind. My adopted daughter Alafair, whom I had pulled from a submerged plane wreck out on the salt when she was a little girl, sat in her pirogue on the far side of the bayou, fly-casting a popping bug into the shallows.

I walked down on the dock and leaned against the railing. I could smell the salty odor of humus and schooled-up fish and trapped water out in the swamp. Alafair's skin was bladed with the shadows of a willow tree, her hair tied up on her head with a blue bandanna, her hair so black it seemed to fill with lights when she brushed it. She had been born in a primitive village in El Salvador, her family the target of death squads because they had sold a case of Pepsi-Cola to the rebels. Now she was almost sixteen, her Spanish and early childhood all but forgotten. But sometimes at night she cried out in her sleep and would have to be shaken from dreams filled with the marching boots of soldiers, peasants with their thumbs wired together behind them, the dry ratcheting sound of a bolt being pulled back on an automatic weapon.

"Wrong time of day and too much rain," I said.

"Oh, yeah?" she said.

She lifted the fly rod into the air, whipping the popping bug over her head, then laying it on the edge of the lily pads. She flicked her wrist so the bug popped audibly in the water, then a goggle-eye perch rose like a green-and-gold bubble out of the silt and broke the surface, its dorsal fin hard and spiked and shiny in the sunlight, the hook and feathered balsa-wood lure protruding from the side of its mouth.

Alafair held the fly rod up as it quivered and arched toward the water, retrieving the line with her left hand, guiding the goggle-eye between the islands of floating hyacinths, until she could lift it wet and flopping into the bottom of the pirogue.

"Not bad," I said.

"You had another week off. Why'd you go back to work?" she said.

"Long story. See you inside."

"No, wait," she said, and set her rod down in the pirogue and paddled across the bayou to the concrete boat ramp. She stepped out into the water with a stringer of catfish and perch wrapped around her wrist, and climbed the wood steps onto the dock. In the last two years all the baby fat had melted off her body, and her face and figure had taken on the appearance of a mature woman's. When she worked with me in the bait shop, most of our male customers made a point of focusing their attention everywhere in the room except on Alafair.

"A lady named Ms. Flynn was here. Bootsie told me what happened to her father. You found him, Dave?" she said.

"My dad and I did."

"He was crucified?"

"It happened a long time ago, Alf."

"The people who did it never got caught? That's sickening."

"Maybe they took their own fall down the road. They all do, one way or another."

"It's not enough." Her face seemed heated, pinched, as though by an old memory.

"You want some help cleaning those fish?" I asked.

Her eyes looked at me again, then cleared. "What would you do if I said yeah?" she asked. She swung the stringer so it touched the end of my polished loafer.

M egan wants me to get her inside the jail to take pictures?" I said to Bootsie in the kitchen.

"She seems to think you're a pretty influential guy," she replied.

Bootsie was bent over the sink, scrubbing the burnt grease off a stove tray, her strong arms swollen with her work; her polo shirt had pulled up over her jeans, exposing the soft taper of her hips. She had the most beautiful hair I had ever seen in a woman. It was the color of honey, with caramel swirls in it, and its thickness and the way she wore it up on her head seemed to make the skin of her face even more pink and lovely.

"Is there anything else I can arrange? An audience with the Pope?" I said.

She turned from the drainboard and dried her hands on a towel.

"That woman's after something else. I just don't know what it is," she said.

"The Flynns are complicated people."

"They have a way of finding war zones to play in. Don't let her take you over the hurdles, Streak."

I hit her on the rump with the palm of my hand. She wadded up the dish towel and threw it past my head.

We ate lunch on the redwood table under the mimosa tree in the back yard. Beyond the duck pond at the back of our property my neighbor's sugarcane was tall and green and marbled with the shadows of clouds. The bamboo and periwinkles that grew along our coulee rippled in the wind, and I could smell rain and electricity in the south.

"What's in that brown envelope you brought home?" Bootsie asked.

"Pictures of a mainline sociopath in the Colorado pen."

"Why bring them home?"

"I've seen the guy. I'm sure of it. But I can't remember where."

"Around here?"

"No. Somewhere else. The top of his head looks like a yellow cake but he has no jaws. An obnoxious FBI agent told me he's pals with Cisco Flynn."

"A head like a yellow cake? A mainline con? Friends with Cisco Flynn?"

"Yeah."

"Wonderful."

That night I dreamed of the man named Swede Boxleiter. He was crouched on his haunches in the darkened exercise yard of a prison, smoking a cigarette, his granny glasses glinting in the humid glow of lights on the guard towers. The predawn hours were cool and filled with the smells of sage, water coursing over boulders in a canyon riverbed, pine needles layered on the forest floor. A wet, red dust hung in the air, and the moon seemed to rise through it, above the mountain's rim, like ivory skeined with dyed thread.

But the man named Swede Boxleiter was not one to concern himself with the details of the alpine environment he found himself in. The measure of his life and himself was the reflection he saw in the eyes of others, the fear that twitched in their faces, the unbearable tension he could create in a cell or at a dining table simply by not speaking.

He didn't need a punk or prune-o or the narcissistic pleasure of clanking iron in the yard or even masturbation for release from the energies that, unsatiated, could cause him to wake in the middle of the night and sit in a square of moonlight as though he were on an airless plateau that echoed with the cries of animals. Sometimes he smiled to himself and fantasized about telling the prison psychologist what he really felt inside, the pleasure that climbed through the tendons in his arm when he clasped a shank that had been ground from a piece of angle iron on an emery wheel in the shop, the intimacy of that last moment when he looked into the eyes of the hit. The dam that seemed to break in his loins was like water splitting the bottom of a paper bag.

But prison shrinks were not people you confided in, at least if you were put together like Swede Boxleiter and ever wanted to make the street again.

In my dream he rose from his crouched position, reached up and touched the moon, as though to despoil it, but instead wiped away the red skein from one corner with his fingertip and exposed a brilliant white cup of light.

I sat up in bed, the window fan spinning its shadows on my skin, and remembered where I had seen him.

Early the next morning I went to the city library on East Main Street and dug out the old *Life* magazine in which Megan's photos of a black rapist's death inside a storm drain had launched her career. Opposite the full-page shot of the black man reaching out futilely for the sunlight was the group photo of five uniformed cops staring down at his body. In the foreground was Swede Boxleiter, holding a Red Delicious apple with a white divot bitten out of it, his smile a thin worm of private pleasure stitched across his face.

But I wasn't going to take on the Flynns' problems, I told myself, or worry about a genetic misfit in the Colorado pen.

I was still telling myself that late that night when Mout' Broussard, New Iberia's legendary shoeshine man and Cool Breeze's father, called the bait shop and told me his son had just escaped from the parish prison.

THREE

Cajuns often have trouble with the *th* sound in English, and as a result they drop the *h* or pronounce the *t* as a *d*. Hence, the town's collectively owned shoeshine man, Mouth Broussard, was always referred to as Mout'. For decades he operated his shoeshine stand under the colonnade in front of the old Frederic Hotel, a wonderful two-story stucco building with Italian marble columns inside, a ballroom, a saloon with a railed mahogany bar, potted palms and slot and racehorse machines in the lobby, and an elevator that looked like a polished brass birdcage.

Mout' was built like a haystack and never worked without a cigar stub in the corner of his mouth. He wore an oversized gray smock, the pockets stuffed with brushes and buffing rags ribbed with black and oxblood stains. The drawers under the two elevated chairs on the stand were loaded with bottles of liquid polish, cans of wax and saddle soap, toothbrushes and steel dental picks he used to clean the welts and stitches around the edges of the shoe. He could pop his buffing rags with a speed and rhythm that never failed to command a silent respect from everyone who watched.

Mout' caught all the traffic walking from the Southern Pacific passenger station to the hotel, shined all the shoes that were set out in the corridors at night, and guaranteed you could see your face in the buffed point of your shoe or boot or your money would be returned. He shined the shoes of the entire cast of the 1929 film production of *Evangeline;* he shined the shoes of Harry James's orchestra and of U.S. Senator Huey Long just before Long was assassinated.

"Where is Cool Breeze now, Mout'?" I said into the phone.

"You t'ink I'm gonna tell you that?"

"Then why'd you call?"

"Cool Breeze say they gonna kill him."

"Who is?"

"That white man run the jail. He sent a nigger try to joog him in the ear with a wire."

"I'll be over in the morning."

"The morning? Why, t'ank you, suh."

"Breeze went down his own road a long time ago, Mout'."

He didn't reply. I could feel the late-summer heat and the closeness of the air under the electric light.

"Mout'?" I said.

"You right. But it don't make none of it easier. No suh, it surely don't."

At sunrise the next morning I drove down East Main, under the canopy of live oaks that spanned the street, past City Hall and the library and the stone grotto and statue of Christ's mother, which had once been the site of George Washington Cable's home, and the sidewalks cracked by tree roots and the blue-green lawns filled with hydrangeas and hibiscus and philodendron and the thick stand of bamboo that framed the yard of the 1831 plantation manor called The Shadows, and finally into the business district. Then I was on the west side of town, on back streets with open ditches, railroad tracks that dissected yards and pavement, and narrow paintless houses, in rows like bad teeth, that had been cribs when nineteenth-century trainmen used to drink bucket beer from the saloon with the prostitutes and leave their red lanterns on the gallery steps when they went inside.

Mout' was behind his house, flinging birdseed at the pigeons that showered down from the telephone wires into his yard. He walked bent sideways at the waist, his eyes blue with cataracts, one cheek marbled pink and white by a strange skin disease that afflicts people of color; but his sloped shoulders were as wide as a bull's and his upper arms like chunks of sewer pipe.

"It was a bad time for Breeze to run, Mout'. The prosecutor's office might have cut him loose," I said.

He mopped his face with a blue filling-station rag and slid the bag of birdseed off his shoulder and sat down heavily in an old barber's chair with an umbrella mounted on it. He picked up a fruit jar filled with coffee and hot milk from the ground and drank from it. His wide mouth seemed to cup around the bottom of the opening like a cat-fish's.

"He gone to church wit' me and his mother when he was a li'l boy," he said. "He played ball in the park, he carried the newspaper, he set pins in the bowling alley next to white boys and didn't have no trouble. It was New Orleans done it. He lived with his mother in the projects. Decided he wasn't gonna be no shoeshine man, have white folks tipping their cigar ashes down on his head, that's what he tole me."

Mout' scratched the top of his head and made a sound like air leaving a tire.

"You did the best you could. Maybe it'll turn around for him someday," I said.

"They gonna shoot him now, ain't they?" he said.

"No. Nobody wants that, Mout'."

"That jailer, Alex Guidry? He use to come down here when he was in collitch. Black girls was three dollars over on Hopkins. Then he'd come around the shoeshine stand when they was black men around, pick out some fella and keep looking in his face, not letting go, no, peeling the skin right off the bone, till the man dropped his head and kept his eyes on the sidewalk. That's the way it was back then. Now y'all done hired the same fella to run the jail."

Then he described his son's last day in the parish prison.

■ ■ ■

The turnkey who had been a brig chaser in the Marine Corps walked down the corridor of the Isolation unit and opened up the cast-iron door to Cool Breeze's cell. He bounced a baton off a leather lanyard that was looped around his wrist.

"Mr. Alex says you going back into Main Pop. That is, if you want," he said.

"I ain't got no objection."

"It must be your birthday."

"How's that?" Cool Breeze said.

"You'll figure it out."

"I'll figure it out, huh?"

"You wonder why you people are in here? When you think an echo is a sign of smarts?"

The turnkey walked him through a series of barred doors that slid back and forth on hydraulically operated steel arms, ordered him to strip and shower, then handed him an orange jumpsuit and locked him in a holding cell.

"They gonna put Mr. Alex on suspension. But he's doing you right before he goes out. So that's why I say it must be your birthday," the turnkey said. He bounced the baton on its lanyard and winked. "When he's gone, I'm gonna be jailer. You might study on the implications."

At four that afternoon Alex Guidry stopped in front of Cool Breeze's cell. He wore a seersucker suit and red tie and shined black cowboy boots. His Stetson hung from his fingers against his pant leg.

"You want to work scrub-down detail and do sweep-up in the shop?" he asked.

"I can do that."

"You gonna make trouble?"

"Ain't my style, suh."

"You can tell any damn lie you want when you get out of here. But if I'm being unfair to you, you tell me to my face right now," he said.

"People see what they need to."

Alex Guidry turned his palm up and looked at it and picked at a callus with his thumb. He started to speak, then shook his head in disgust and walked down the corridor, the leather soles of his boots clicking on the floor.

Cool Breeze spent the next day scrubbing stone walls and side-walks with a wire brush and Ajax, and at five o'clock reported to the maintenance shop to begin sweep-up. He used a long broom to push steel filings, sawdust, and wood chips into tidy piles that he shoveled onto a dustpan and dumped into a trash bin. Behind him a mulatto whose golden skin was spotted with freckles the size of dimes was cutting a design out of a piece of plywood on a jigsaw, the teeth ripping a sound out of the wood like an electrified scream.

Cool Breeze paid no attention to him, until he heard the plywood disengage from the saw. He turned his head out of curiosity just as the mulatto balled his fist and tried to jam a piece of coat-hanger wire, sharpened to a point like an ice pick and driven vertically through the wood handle off a lawn-mower starter rope, through the center of Cool Breeze's ear and into his brain.

The wire point laid open Cool Breeze's cheek from the jawbone to the corner of his mouth.

He locked his attacker's forearm in both his hands, spun with him in circles, then walked the two of them toward the saw that hummed with an oily light.

"Don't make me do it, nigger," he said.

But his attacker would not give up his weapon, and Cool Breeze drove first the coat hanger, then the balled fist and the wood plug gripped inside the palm into the saw blade, so that bone and metal and fingernails and wood splinters all showered into his face at once.

He hid inside the barrel of a cement mixer, where by all odds he should have died. He felt the truck slow at the gate, heard the guards talking outside while they walked the length of the truck with mirrors they held under the frame.

"We got one out on the ground. You ain't got him in your barrel, have you?" a guard said.

"We sure as hell can find out," the truck driver said.

Gears and cogs clanged into place, then the truck vibrated and shook and giant steel blades began turning inside the barrel's black-ness, lifting curtains of wet cement into the air like cake dough.

"Get out of here, will you? For some reason that thing puts me in mind of my wife in the bathroom," the guard said.

Two hours later, on a parish road project south of town, Cool Breeze climbed from inside the cement mixer and lumbered into a cane field like a man wearing a lead suit, his lacerated cheek bleeding like a flag, the cane leaves edged with the sun's last red light.

I don't believe it, Mout'," I said.

"Man ain't tried to joog him?"

"That the jailer set it up. He's already going on suspension. He'd be the first person everyone suspected."

" 'Cause he done it."

"Where's Breeze?"

Mout' slipped his sack of birdseed over his shoulder and begin flinging handfuls into the air again. The pigeons swirled about his waxed bald head like snowflakes.

My partner was Detective Helen Soileau. She wore slacks and men's shirts to work, seldom smiled or put on makeup, and faced you with one foot cocked at an angle behind the other, in the same way a martial artist strikes a defensive posture. Her face was lumpy, her eyes unrelenting when they fixed on you, and her blond hair seemed molded to her head like a plastic wig. She leaned on my office windowsill with both arms and watched a trusty gardener edging the sidewalk. She wore a nine-millimeter automatic in a hand-tooled black holster and a pair of handcuffs stuck through the back of her gunbelt.

"I met Miss Pisspot of 1962 at the jail this morning," she said.

"Who?"

"That FBI agent, what's her name, Glazier. She thinks we set up Cool Breeze Broussard to get clipped in our own jail."

"What's your take on it?"

"The mulatto's a pipehead. He says he thought Breeze was somebody else, a guy who wanted to kill him because he banged the guy's little sister."

"You buy it?" I asked.

"A guy who wears earrings through his nipples? Yeah, it's possible. Do me a favor, will you?" she said.

"What's up?"

Her eyes tried to look casual. "Lila Terrebonne is sloshed at the country club. The skipper wants me to drive her back to Jeanerette."

"No, thanks."

"I could never relate to Lila. I don't know what it is. Maybe it's because she threw up in my lap once. I'm talking about your AA buddy here."

"She didn't call me for help, Helen. If she had, it'd be different."

"If she starts her shit with me, she's going into the drunk tank. I don't care if her grandfather was a U.S. senator or not."

She went out to the parking lot. I sat behind my desk for a moment, then pinged a paper clip in the wastebasket and flagged down her cruiser before she got to the street.

ila had a pointed face and milky green eyes and yellow hair that was bleached the color of white gold by the sun. She was light-hearted about her profligate life, undaunted by hangovers or trysts with married men, laughing in a husky voice in nightclubs about the compulsions that every two or three years placed her in a hospital or treatment center. She would dry out and by order of the court attend AA meetings for a few weeks, working a crossword puzzle in the newspaper while others talked of the razor wire wrapped around their souls, or staring out the window with a benign expression that showed no trace of desire, remorse, impatience, or resignation, just temporary abeyance, like a person waiting for the hands on an invisible clock to reach an appointed time.

From her adolescent years to the present, I did not remember a time in her life when she was not the subject of rumor or scandal. She was sent off by her parents to the Sorbonne, where she failed her examinations and returned to attend USL with blue-collar kids who could not even afford to go to LSU in Baton Rouge. The night of her senior prom, members of the football team glued her photograph on the rubber machine in Provost's Bar.

When Helen and I entered the clubhouse she was by herself at a back table, her head wreathed in smoke from her ashtray, her unfilled glass at the ends of her fingertips. The other tables were filled with golfers and bridge players, their eyes careful never to light on Lila and the pitiful attempt at dignity she tried to impose on her situation. The white barman and the young black waiter who circulated among the tables had long since refused to look in her direction or hear her order for another drink. When someone opened the front door, the glare of sunlight struck her face like a slap.

"You want to take a ride, Lila?" I said.

"Oh, Dave, how are you? They didn't call you again, did they?"

"We were in the neighborhood. I'm going to get a membership here one day."

"The same day you join the Republican Party. You're such a riot. Would you help me up? I think I twisted my ankle," she said.

She slipped her arm in mine and walked with me through the tables, then stopped at the bar and took two ten-dollar bills from her purse. She put them carefully on the bar top.

"Nate, this is for you and that nice young black man. It's always a pleasure to see you all again," she said.

"Come back, Miss Lila. Anytime," the barman said, his eyes shifting off her face.

Outside, she breathed the wind and sunshine as though she had just entered a different biosphere. She blinked and swallowed and made a muted noise like she had a toothache.

"Please drive me out on the highway and drop me wherever people break furniture and throw bottles through glass windows," she said.

"How about home, instead?" I asked.

"Dave, you are a total drag."

"Better appreciate who your friends are, ma'am," Helen said.

"Do I know you?" Lila said.

"Yeah, I had the honor of cleaning up your—"

"Helen, let's get Miss Lila home and head back for the office."

"Oh, by all means. Yes, indeedy," Helen said.

We drove south along Bayou Teche toward Jeanerette, where Lila lived in a plantation home whose bricks had been dug from clay pits and baked in a kiln by slaves in the year 1791. During the Depression her grandfather, a U.S. senator, used dollar-a-day labor to move the home brick by brick on flatboats up the bayou from its original site on the Chitimacha Indian Reservation. Today, it was surrounded by a fourteen-acre lawn, live oak and palm trees, a sky-blue swimming pool, tennis courts, gazebos hung with orange passion vine, two stucco guest cottages, a flagstone patio and fountain, and gardens that bloomed with Mexicali roses.

But we were about to witness a bizarre spectacle when we turned onto the property and drove through the tunnel of oaks toward the front portico, the kind of rare event that leaves you sickened and ashamed for your fellow human beings. A movie set consisting of paintless shacks and a general store with a wide gallery set up on cinder blocks, put together from weathered cypress and rusted tin roofs and Jax beer and Hadacol signs to look like the quarters on a 1940s corporation farm, had been constructed on the lawn, a dirt road laid out and sprinkled with hoses in front of the galleries. Perhaps two dozen people milled around on the set, unorganized, mostly at loose ends, their bodies shiny with sweat. Sitting in the shade of a live oak tree by a table stacked with catered food was the director, Billy Holtzner, and next to him, cool and relaxed in yellow slacks and white silk shirt, was his friend and business partner, Cisco Flynn.

"Have you ever seen three monkeys try to fuck a football? I'd like to eighty-six the whole bunch but my father has a yen for a certain item. It tends to come in pink panties," Lila said from the back seat.

"We'll drop you at the porch, Lila. As far as I'm concerned, your car broke down and we gave you a lift home," I said.

"Oh, stop it. Both of you get down and have something to eat," she said. Her face had cleared in the way a storm can blow out of a sky and leave it empty of clouds and full of carrion birds. I saw her tongue touch her bottom lip.

"Do you need assistance getting inside?" Helen said.

"Assistance? That's a lovely word. No, right here will do just fine. My, hasn't this all been pleasant?" Lila said, and got out and sent a black gardener into the house for a shaker of martinis.

Helen started to shift into reverse, then stopped, dumbfounded, at what we realized was taking place under the live oak tree.

Billy Holtzner had summoned all his people around him. He wore khaki shorts with flap pockets and Roman sandals with lavender socks and a crisp print shirt with the sleeves folded in neat cuffs on his flaccid arms. Except for the grizzled line of beard that grew along his jawline and chin, his body seemed to have no hair, as though it had been shaved with a woman's razor. His workmen and actors and grips and writers and camera people and female assistants stood with wide grins on their faces, some hiding their fear, others rising on the balls of their feet to get a better look, while he singled out one individual, then another, saying, "Have you been a good boy? We've been hearing certain rumors again. Come on now, don't be shy. You know where you have to put it."

Then a grown man, someone who probably had a wife or girlfriend or children or who had fought in a war or who at one time had believed his life was worthy of respect and love, inserted his nose between Billy Holtzner's index and ring fingers and let him twist it back and forth.

"That wasn't so bad, was it? Oh, oh, I see somebody trying to sneak off there. Oh, *Johnny* . . ." Holtzner said.

"These guys are out of a special basement, aren't they?" Helen said.

Cisco Flynn walked toward the cruiser, his face good-natured, his eyes earnest with explanation.

"Have a good life, Cisco," I said out the window, then to Helen, "Hit it."

"You don't got to me tell me, boss man," she replied, her head looking back over her shoulder as she steered, the dark green shadows of oak leaves cascading over the windshield.

FOUR

That night the moon was yellow above the swamp. I walked down to the dock to help Batist, the black man who worked for me, fold up the Cinzano umbrellas on our spool tables and close up the bait shop. There was a rain ring around the moon, and I pulled back the awning that covered the dock, then went inside just as the phone rang on the counter.

"Mout' called me. His son wants to come in," the voice said.

"Stay out of police business, Megan."

"Do I frighten you? Is that the problem here?"

"No, I suspect the problem is use."

"Try this: he's fifteen miles out in the Atchafalaya Basin and snakebit. That's not metaphor. He stuck his arm in a nest of them. Why don't you deliver a message through Mout' and tell him just to go fuck himself?"

After I hung up I flicked off the outside flood lamps. Under the moon's yellow light the dead trees in the swamp looked like twists of paper and wax that could burst into flame with the touch of a single match.

. . .

A t dawn the wind was out of the south, moist and warm and checkered with rain, when I headed the cabin cruiser across a long, flat bay bordered on both sides by flooded cypress trees that turned to green lace when the wind bent their branches. Cranes rose out of the trees against a pink sky, and to the south storm clouds were piled over the Gulf and the air smelled like salt water and brass drying in the sun. Megan stood next to the wheel, a thermos cup full of coffee in her hand. Her straw hat, which had a round dome and a purple band on it, was crushed over her eyes. To get my attention, she clasped my wrist with her thumb and forefinger.

"The inlet past that oil platform. There's a rag tied in a bush," she said.

"I can see it, Megan," I replied. Out of the corner of my eye I saw her face jerk toward me.

"I shouldn't speak or I shouldn't touch? Which is it?" she said.

I eased back the throttle and let the boat rise on its wake and drift into a cove that was overgrown by a leafy canopy and threaded with air vines and dimpled in the shallows with cypress knees. The bow scraped, then snugged tight on a sandspit.

"In answer to your question, I was out at your brother's movie set yesterday. I've decided to stay away from the world of the Big Score. No offense meant," I said.

"I've always wondered what bank guards think all day. Just standing there, eight hours, staring at nothing. I think you've pulled it off, you know, gotten inside their heads."

I picked up the first-aid kit and dropped off the bow and walked through the shallows toward a beached houseboat that had rotted into the soft texture of moldy cardboard.

I heard her splash into the water behind me.

"Gee, I hope I can be a swinging dick in the next life," she said.

T he houseboat floor was tilted on top of the crushed and rusted oil drums on which it had once floated. Cool Breeze sat in the corner, dressed in clothes off a wash line, the wound in his cut face stitched with thread and needle, his left arm swollen like a black balloon full of water.

I heard Megan's camera start clicking behind me.

"Why didn't you call the Feds, Breeze?" I asked.

"That woman FBI agent wants me in front of a grand jury. She say I gonna stay in the system, too, till they done wit' me."

I looked at the electrical cord he had used for a tourniquet, the proud flesh that had turned the color of fish scale around the fang marks, the drainage that had left viscous green tailings on his shirt. "I tell you what, I'll dress those wounds, hang your arm in a sling, then we'll get a breath of fresh air," I said.

"You cut that cord loose, the poison gonna hit my heart."

"You're working on gangrene now, partner."

I saw him swallow. The whites of his eyes looked painted with iodine.

"You're jail-wise, Breeze. You knew the Feds would take you over the hurdles. Why'd you want to stick it to Alex Guidry?"

This is the story he told me while I used a rubber suction cup to draw a mixture of venom and infection from his forearm. As I listened on one knee, kneading the puncture wounds, feeling the pain in his body flicker like a candle flame under his skin, I could only wonder again at the white race's naïveté in always sending forth our worst members as our emissaries.

Twenty years ago, down the Teche, he owned a dirt-road store knocked together from scrap boards, tin stripped off a condemned rice mill, and Montgomery Ward brick that had dried out and crusted and pulled loose from the joists like a scab. He also had a pretty young wife named Ida, who cooked in a cafe and picked tabasco peppers on a corporate farm. After a day in the field her hands swelled as though they had been stung by bumblebees and she had to soak them in milk to relieve the burning in her skin.

On a winter afternoon two white men pulled up on the bib of oyster shell that served as a parking lot in front of the gallery, and the older man, who had jowls like a bulldog's and smoked a cigar in the center of his mouth, asked for a quart of moonshine.

"Don't tell me you ain't got it, boy. I know the man from Miss'sippi sells it to you."

"I got Jax on ice. I got warm beer, too. I can sell you soda pop. I ain't got no whiskey."

"That a fact? I'm gonna walk back out the door, then come back in. One of them jars you got in that box behind the motor oil better be on the counter or I'm gonna redecorate your store."

Cool Breeze shook his head.

"I know who y'all are. I done paid already. Why y'all giving me this truck?" he said.

The younger white man opened the screen door and came inside the store. His name was Alex Guidry, and he wore a corduroy suit and cowboy hat and western boots, with pointed, mirror-bright toes. The older man picked up a paper bag of deep-fried cracklings from the counter. The grease in the cracklings made dark stains in the paper. He threw the bag to the younger man and said to Cool Breeze, "You on parole for check writing now. That liquor will get you a double nickel. Your woman yonder, what's her name, Ida? She's a cook, ain't she?"

The man with bulldog jowls was named Harpo Delahoussey, and he ran a ramshackle nightclub for redbones (people who are part French, black, and Indian) by a rendering plant on an oxbow off the Atchafalaya River. When the incinerators were fired up at the plant, the smoke from the stacks filled the nearby woods and dirt roads with a stench like hair and chicken entrails burned in a skillet. The clapboard nightclub didn't lock its doors from Friday afternoon until late Sunday night; the parking lot (layered with thousands of flattened beer cans) became a maze of gas-guzzlers and pickup trucks; and the club's windows rattled and shook with the reverberations of rub board and thimbles, accordion, drums, dancing feet, and electric guitars whose feedback screeched like fingernails on slate.

At the back, in a small kitchen, Ida Broussard sliced potatoes for french fries while caldrons of red beans and rice and robin gumbo boiled on the stove, a bandanna knotted across her forehead to keep the sweat out of her eyes.

But Cool Breeze secretly knew, even though he tried to deny it to himself, that Harpo Delahoussey had not blackmailed him simply to acquire a cook, or even to reinforce that old lesson that every coin pressed into your palm for shining shoes, cutting cane, chopping cotton, scouring ovens, dipping out grease traps, scrubbing commodes, cleaning dead rats from under a house, was dispensed by the hand of a white person in the same way that oxygen could be arbitrarily measured out to a dying hospital patient.

One night she wouldn't speak when he picked her up, sitting against the far door of the pickup truck, her shoulders rounded, her face dull with a fatigue that sleep never took away.

"He ain't touched you, huh?" Cool Breeze said.

"Why you care? You brung me to the club, ain't you?"

"He said the rendering plant gonna shut down soon. That mean he won't be needing no more cook. What you gonna do if I'm in Angola?"

"I tole you not to bring that whiskey in the store. Not to listen to that white man from Miss'sippi sold it to you. Tole you, Willie."

Then she looked out the window so he could not see her face. She wore a rayon blouse that had green and orange lights in it, and her back was shaking under the cloth, and he could hear her breath seizing in her throat, like hiccups she couldn't control.

He tried to get permission from his parole officer to move back to New Orleans.

Permission denied.

He caught Ida inhaling cocaine off a broken mirror behind the house. She drank fortified wine in the morning, out of a green bottle with a screw cap that made her eyes lustrous and frightening. She refused to help out at the store. In bed she was unresponsing, dry when he entered her, and finally not available at all. She tied a perforated dime on a string around her ankle, then one around her belly so that it hung just below her navel.

"Gris-gris is old people's superstition," Cool Breeze said.

"I had a dream. A white snake, thick as your wrist, it bit a hole in a melon and crawled inside and ate all the meat out."

"We gonna run away."

"Mr. Harpo gonna be there. Your PO gonna be there. State of Lou'sana gonna be there."

He put his hand under the dime that rested on her lower stomach and ripped it loose. Her mouth parted soundlessly when the string razored burns along her skin.

The next week he walked in on her when she was naked in front of the mirror. A thin gold chain was fastened around her hips.

"Where you get that?" he asked.

She brushed her hair and didn't answer. Her breasts looked as swollen and full as eggplants.

"You ain't got to cook at the club no more. What they gonna do? Hurt us more than they already have?" he said.

She took a new dress off a hanger and worked it over her head. It was red and sewn with colored glass beads like an Indian woman might wear.

"Where you got money for that?" he asked.

"Mine to know, yours to find out," she replied. She fastened a hoop earring to her lobe with both hands, smiling at him while she did it.

He began shaking her by the shoulders, her head whipping like a doll's on her neck, her eyelids closed, her lipsticked mouth open in a way that made his phallus thicken in his jeans. He flung her against the bedroom wall, so hard he heard her bones knock into the wood, then ran from the house and down the dirt road, through a tunnel of darkened trees, his brogans exploding through the shell of ice on the chuckholes.

■ ■ ■

In the morning he tried to make it up to her. He warmed boudin and fixed cush-cush and coffee and hot milk, and set it all out on the table and called her into the kitchen. The dishes she didn't smash on the wall she threw into the back yard.

He drove his pickup truck through the bright coldness of the morning, the dust from his tires drifting out onto the dead hyacinths and the cattails that had winter-killed in the bayou, and found Harpo Delahoussey at the filling station he owned in town, playing dominoes with three other white men at a table by a gas stove that hissed with blue flame. Delahoussey wore a fedora, and a gold badge on the pocket of his white shirt. None of the men at the table looked up from their game. The stove filled the room with a drowsy, controlled warmth and the smell of shaving cream and aftershave lotion and testosterone.

"My wife ain't gonna be working at the club no more," Cool Breeze said.

"Okay," Delahoussey said, his eyes concentrated on the row of dominoes in front of him.

The room seemed to scream with silence.

"Mr. Harpo, maybe you ain't understood me," Cool Breeze said.

"He heard you, boy. Now go on about your business," one of the other men said.

A moment later, by the door of his truck, Cool Breeze looked back through the window. Even though he was outside, an oak tree swelling with wind above his head, and the four domino players were in a small room beyond a glass, he felt it was he who was somehow on display, in a cage, naked, small, an object of ridicule and contempt.

Then it hit him: *He's old. An old man like that, one piece of black jelly roll just the same as another. So who give her the dress and wrap the gold chain around her stomach?*

He wiped his forehead on the sleeve of his canvas coat. His ears roared with sound and his heart thundered in his chest.

．　．　．

He woke in the middle of the night and put on an overcoat and sat under a bare lightbulb in the kitchen, poking at the ashes in the wood stove, wadding up paper and feeding sticks into the flame that wouldn't catch, the cold climbing off the linoleum through his socks and into his ankles, his confused thoughts wrapped around his face like a net.

What was it that tormented him? Why was it he couldn't give it words, deal with it in the light of day, push it out in front of him, even kill it if he had to?

His breath fogged the air. Static electricity crackled in the sleeves of his overcoat and leaped off his fingertips when he touched the stove.

He wanted to blame Harpo Delahoussey. He remembered the story his daddy, Mout', had told him of the black man from Abbeville who broke off a butcher knife in the chest of a white overseer he caught doing it with his wife against a tree, then had spit in the face of his executioner before he was gagged and hooded with a black cloth and electrocuted.

He wondered if he could ever possess the courage of a man like that.

But he knew Delahoussey was not the true source of the anger and discontent that made his face break a sweat and his palms ring as though they had been beaten with boards.

He had accepted his role as cuckold, had even transported his wife to the site of her violation by a white man (and later, from Ida's mother, he would discover the exact nature of what Harpo Delahoussey did to her), because his victimization had justified a lifetime of resentment toward those who had forced his father to live gratefully on tips while their cigar ashes spilled down on his shoulders.

Except his wife had now become a willing participant. Last night she had ironed her jeans and shirt and laid them out on the bed, put perfume in her bathwater, washed and dried her hair and rouged her cheekbones to accentuate the angular beauty of her face. Her skin had seemed to glow when she dried herself in front of the mirror, a tune humming in her throat. He tried to confront her, force the issue, but her eyes were veiled with secret expectations and private meaning that made him ball his hands into fists. When he refused to drive her to the nightclub, she called a cab.

The fire wouldn't catch. An acrid smoke, as yellow as rope, laced with a stench of rags or chemically treated wood, billowed into his face. He opened all the windows, and frost speckled on the wallpaper and kitchen table. In the morning, the house smelled like a smoldering garbage dump.

She dressed in a robe, closed the windows, opened the air lock in the stove by holding a burning newspaper inside the draft, then began preparing breakfast for herself at the drainboard. He sat at the table and stared at her back stupidly, hoping she would reach into the cabinet, pull down a bowl or cup for him, indicate in some way they were still the people they once were.

"He tole me, you shake me again, you going away, Willie," she said.

"Who say that?"

She walked out of the room and didn't answer.

"Who?" he called after her.

It was the letter that did it.

Or the letter that he didn't read in its entirety, at least not until later.

He had driven the truck back from the store, turned into his yard, and seen her behind the house, pulling her undergarments, jeans, work shirts, socks, and dresses, her whole wardrobe, off the wash line.

A letter written with a pencil stub on a sheet of lined paper, torn from a notebook, lay on the coffee table in the living room.

He could hear his breath rising and falling in his mouth when he picked it up, his huge hand squeezing involuntarily on the bottom of the childlike scrawl.

Dear Willie,

You wanted to know who the man was I been sleeping with. I am telling you his name not out of meaness but because you will find out anyway and I dont want you to go back to prison. Alex Guidry was good to me when you were willing to turn me over to Mr. Harpo because of some moonshine whisky. You cant know what it is like to have that old man put his hand on you and tell you to come into the shed with him and make you do the things I had to do. Alex wouldnt let Mr. Harpo bother me any more and I slept with him because I wanted to and—

He crumpled up the paper in his palm and flung it into the corner. In his mind's eye he saw Alex Guidry's fish camp, Guidry's corduroy suit and western hat hung on deer antlers, and Guidry himself mounted between Ida's legs, his muscled buttocks thrusting his phallus into her, her fingers and ankles biting for purchase into his white skin.

Cool Breeze hurled the back screen open and attacked her in the yard. He slapped her face and knocked her into the dust, then picked her up and shook her and shoved her backward onto the wood steps. When she tried to straighten her body with the heels of her hands, pushing herself away from him simultaneously, he saw the smear of blood on her mouth and the terror in her eyes, and realized, for the first time in his life, the murderous potential and level of self-hatred that had always dwelled inside him.

He tore down the wash line and kicked over the basket that was draped with her clothes. The leafless branches of the pecan tree overhead exploded with the cawing of crows. He didn't hear the truck engine start in the front and did not realize she was gone, that he was alone in the yard with his rage, until he saw the truck speeding into the distance, the detritus of the sugarcane harvest spinning in its vacuum.

Two duck hunters found her body at dawn, in a bay off the Atchafalaya River. Her fingers were coated with ice and extended just above the water's surface, the current silvering across the tips. A ship's anchor chain, one with links as big as bricks, was coiled around her torso like a fat serpent. The hunters tied a Budweiser carton to her wrist to mark the spot for the sheriff's department.

A week later Cool Breeze found the crumpled paper he had flung in the corner. He spread it flat on the table and began reading where he had left off before he had burst into the back yard and struck her across the face.

I slept with him because I wanted to and because I was so mad at you and hurt over what you did to the wife that has always loved you.

But Alex Guidry dont want a blak girl in his life, at least not on the street in the day lite. I know that now and I dont care and I tole him that. I will leave if you want me to and not blame you for it. I just want to say I am sorry for treating you so bad but it was like you had thrown me away forever.

Your wife,

Ida Broussard

Cool Breeze lay on a row of air cushions inside the cabin cruiser, his arm in a sling, his face sweating. When he had finished speaking, Megan looked at me sadly, her eyes prescient with the knowledge that a man's best explanation for his life can be one that will never satisfy him or anybody else.

"Y'all ain't gonna say nothing?" he asked.

"Let go of it, partner," I said.

"The Man always got the answer," he replied.

"Your daddy is an honest and decent person. If you're still ashamed of him because he shined shoes, yeah, I think that's a problem, Breeze," I said.

"Dave . . ." Megan said.

"Give it a break, Megan," I said.

"No . . . Behind us. The G sent us an escort," she said.

I turned and looked back through the hatch at our wake. Coming hard right up the trough was a large powerboat, its enamel-white bow painted with the blue-and-red insignia of the United States Coast Guard. A helicopter dipped out of the sky behind the Coast Guard boat, yawing, its downdraft hammering the water.

I entered a channel that led to the boat ramp where my truck and boat trailer were parked. The helicopter swept past us and landed in the shell parking area below the levee. The right-hand door opened and the FBI agent named Adrien Glazier stepped out and walked toward us while the helicopter's blades were still spinning.

I waded through the shallows onto the concrete ramp.

"You're out of your jurisdiction, so I'm going to save you a lot of paperwork," she said.

"Oh?"

"We're taking Mr. William Broussard into our custody. Interstate transportation of stolen property. You want to argue about it, we can talk about interference with a federal law officer in the performance of her duty."

Then I saw her eyes focus over my shoulder on Megan, who stood on the bow of my boat, her hair blowing under her straw hat.

"You take one picture out here and I'll have you in handcuffs," Adrien Glazier said.

"Broussard's been snakebit. He needs to be in a hospital," I said.

But she wasn't listening. She and Megan stared at each other with the bright and intimate recognition of old adversaries who might have come aborning from another time.

FIVE

The next day at lunchtime Clete Purcel picked me up at the office in the chartreuse Cadillac convertible that he had bought from a member of the Giacano crime family in New Orleans, a third-generation miscreant by the name of Stevie Gee who decided to spot-weld a leak in the gas tank but got drunk first and forgot to fill the tank with water before he fired up the welding machine. The scorch marks had faded now and looked like smoky gray tentacles on the back fenders.

The back seat was loaded with fishing rods, a tackle box that was three feet long, an ice chest, air cushions, crushed beer cans, life preservers, crab traps, a hoop net that had been ground up in a boat propeller, and a tangled trot line whose hooks were ringed with dried smelt.

Clete wore baggy white pants without a shirt and a powder-blue porkpie hat, and his skin looked bronzed and oily in the sun. He had been the best cop I ever knew until his career went south, literally, all the way to Central America, because of marriage trouble, pills, booze, hookers, indebtedness to shylocks, and finally a murder warrant that his fellow officers barely missed serving on him at the New Orleans airport.

I went inside Victor's on Main Street for a take-out order, then we crossed the drawbridge over Bayou Teche and drove past the live oaks on the lawn of the gray and boarded-up buildings that used to be Mount Carmel Academy, then through the residential section into City Park. We sat at a picnic table under a tree, not far from the swimming pool, where children were cannonballing off the diving board. The sun had gone behind the clouds and rain rings appeared soundlessly on the bayou's surface, like bream rising to feed.

"That execution in St. Mary Parish . . . the two brothers who got clipped after they raped the black girl? How bad you want the perps?" he said.

"What do you think?"

"I see it as another parish's grief. As a couple of guys who got what they had coming."

"The shooters had one of our uniforms."

He set down the pork-chop sandwich he was eating and scratched the scar that ran through his left eyebrow.

"I'm still running down skips for Nig Rosewater and Wee Willie Bimstine. Nig went bail for a couple of chippies who work a regular Murphy game in the Quarter. They're both junkies, runny noses, scabs on their thighs, mainlining six and seven balloons a day, sound familiar, scared shitless of detoxing in City Prison, except they're even more scared of their pimp, who's the guy they have to give up if they're going to beat the Murphy beef.

"So they ask Nig if they should go to the prosecutor's office with this story they got off a couple of johns who acted like over-the-hill cops. These guys were talking to each other about capping some brothers out in the Basin. One of the chippies asks if they're talking about black guys. One duffer laughs and says, 'No, just some boys who should have kept practicing on colored girls and left white bread alone.' "

"Where are these guys out of?"

"They said San Antone. But johns usually lie."

"What else do the girls know?"

"They're airheads, Dave. The intellectual one reads the shopping guide on the toilet. Besides, they're not interested in dealing anymore. Their pimp decided to plea out, so they're off the hook."

"Write down their names, will you?"

He took a piece of folded paper from his pants pocket, with the names of the two women and their addresses already written on it, and set it on the plank table. He started eating again, his green eyes smiling at nothing.

"Old lesson from the First District, big mon. When somebody wastes a couple of shit bags . . ." He realized I wasn't listening, that my gaze was focused over his shoulder on the swimming pool. He turned and stared through the tree trunks, his gaze roving across the swimmers in the pool, the parents who were walking their children by the hand to an instruction class a female lifeguard was putting together in the shallow end. Then his eyes focused on a man who stood between the wire enclosure and the bathhouse.

The man had a peroxided flattop, a large cranium, like a person with water on the brain, cheekbones that tapered in an inverted triangle to his chin, a small mouth full of teeth. He wore white shoes and pale orange slacks and a beige shirt with the short sleeves rolled in neat cuffs and the collar turned up on the neck. He pumped a blue rubber ball in his right palm.

"You know that dude?" Clete said.

"His name's Swede Boxleiter."

"A graduate?"

"Canon City, Colorado. The FBI showed me some photos of a yard job he did on a guy."

"What's he doing around here?"

Boxleiter wore shades instead of the granny glasses I had seen in the photos. But there was no doubt about the object of his attention. The children taking swim lessons were lined up along the edge of the pool, their swimsuits clinging wetly to their bodies. Boxleiter snapped the rubber ball off the pavement, ricocheting it against the bathhouse wall, retrieving it back into his palm as though it were attached to a magic string.

"Excuse me a minute," I said to Clete.

I walked through the oaks to the pool. The air smelled of leaves and chlorine and the rain that was sprinkling on the heated cement. I stood two feet behind Boxleiter, who hung on to the wire mesh of the fence with one hand while the other kneaded the rubber ball. The green veins in his forearm were pumped with blood. He chewed gum, and a lump of cartilage expanded and contracted against the bright slickness of his jaw.

He felt my eyes on the back of his neck.

"You want something?" he asked.

"We thought we'd welcome you to town. Have you drop by the department. Maybe meet the sheriff."

He grinned at the corner of his mouth.

"You think you seen me somewhere?"

I continued to stare into his face, not speaking. He removed his shades, his eyes askance.

"Soooo, what kind of gig are we trying to build here?" he asked.

"I don't like the way you look at children."

"I'm looking at a swimming pool. But I'll move."

"We nail you on a short-eyes here, we'll flag your jacket and put you in lockdown with some interesting company. This is Louisiana, Swede."

He rolled the rubber ball down the back of his forearm, off his elbow, and caught it in his palm, all in one motion. Then he rolled it back and forth across the top of his fingers, the gum snapping in his jaw all the while.

"I went out max time. You got no handle. I got a job, too. In the movies. I'm not shitting you on that," he said.

"Watch your language, please."

"My language? Wow, I love this town already." Then his face tilted, disconcerted, his breath drawing through his nose like an animal catching a scent. "Why's Blimpo staring at me like that?"

I turned and saw Clete Purcel standing behind me. He grinned and took out his comb and ran it through his sandy hair with both hands. The skin under his arms was pink with sunburn.

"You think I got a weight problem?" he asked.

"No. 'Cause I don't know you. I don't know what kind of problem you got."

"Then why'd you call me Blimpo?"

"So maybe I didn't mean anything by it."

"I think you did."

But Boxleiter turned his back on us, his attention fixed on the deep end of the pool, his right hand opening and closing on the blue rubber ball. The wind blew lines in his peroxided hair, and his scalp had the dead gray color of putty. His lips moved silently.

"What'd you say?" Clete asked. When Boxleiter didn't reply, Clete fitted his hand under Boxleiter's arm and turned him away from the fence. "You said, 'Blow me, Fatso'?"

Boxleiter slipped the ball in his pocket and looked out into the trees, his hands on his hips.

"It's a nice day. I'm gonna buy me a sno'ball. I love the spearmint sno'balls they sell in this park. You guys want one?" he said.

We watched him walk away through the trees, the leaves crunching under his feet like pecan shells, toward a cold drink stand and ice machine a black man had set up under a candy-striped umbrella.

"Like the boy says, he doesn't come with handles," Clete said.

That afternoon the sheriff called me into his office. He was watering his window plants with a hand-painted teakettle, smoking his pipe at the same time. His body was slatted with light through the blinds, and beyond the blinds I could see the whitewashed crypts in the old Catholic cemetery.

"I got a call from Alex Guidry. You reported him to the Humane Society?" he said.

"He keeps his dogs penned on a filthy concrete slab without shade."

"He claims you're harassing him."

"What did the Humane Society say?"

"They gave him a warning and told him they'd be back. Watch your back with this character, Dave."

"That's it?"

"No. The other problem is your calls to the FBI in New Orleans. They're off our backs for a while. Why stir them up?"

"Cool Breeze should be in our custody. We're letting the Feds twist him to avoid a civil suit over the abuse of prisoners in our jail."

"He's a four-time loser, Dave. He's not a victim. He fed a guy into an electric saw."

"I don't think it's right."

"Tell that to people when we have to pass a parish sales tax to pay off a class action suit, particularly one that will make a bunch of convicts rich. I take that back. Tell it to that female FBI agent. She was here while you were out to lunch. I really enjoyed the half hour I spent listening to her."

"Adrien Glazier was here?"

It was Friday, and when I drove home that evening I should have been beginning a fine weekend. Instead, she was waiting for me on the dock, a cardboard satchel balanced on the railing under her hand. I parked the car in the drive and walked down to meet her. She looked hot in her pink suit, her ice-blue eyes filmed from the heat or the dust on the road.

"You've got Breeze in lockdown and everybody around here scared. What else do you want, Ms. Glazier?"

"It's Special Agent Gla—"

"Yeah, I know."

"You and Megan Flynn are taking this to the media, aren't you?"

"No. At least I'm not."

"Then why do both of you keep calling the Bureau?"

"Because I'm being denied access to a prisoner who escaped from our jail, that's why."

She stared hard into my face, as though searching for the right dials, her back teeth grinding softly, then said, "I want you to look at a few more photos."

"No."

"What's the matter, you don't want to see the wreckage your gal leaves in her wake?"

She pulled the elastic cord loose from the cardboard satchel and spilled half the contents on a spool table. She lifted up a glossy eight-by-ten black-and-white photo of Megan addressing a crowd of Latin peasants from the bed of a produce truck. Megan was leaning forward, her small hands balled into fists, her mouth wide with her oration.

"Here's another picture taken a few days later. If you look closely, you'll recognize some of the dead people in the ditch. They were in the crowd that listened to Megan Flynn. Where was she when this happened? At the Hilton in Mexico City."

"You really hate her, don't you?"

I heard her take a breath, like a person who has stepped into fouled air.

"No, I don't hate her, sir. I hate what she does. Other people die so she can feel good about herself," she said.

I sifted through the photos and news clippings with my fingers. I picked up one that had been taken from the *Denver Post* and glued on a piece of cardboard backing. Adrien Glazier was two inches away from my skin. I could smell perspiration and body powder in her clothes. The news article was about thirteen-year-old Megan Flynn winning first prize in the *Post*'s essay contest. The photo showed her sitting in a chair, her hands folded demurely in her lap, her essay medal worn proudly on her chest.

"Not bad for a kid in a state orphanage. I guess that's the Megan I always remember. Maybe that's why I still think of her as one of the most admirable people I've ever known. Thanks for coming by," I said, and walked up the slope through the oak and pecan trees on my lawn, and on into my lighted house, where my daughter and wife waited supper for me.

Monday morning Helen Soileau came into my office and sat on the corner of my desk.

"I was wrong about two things," she said.

"Oh?"

"The mulatto who tried to do Cool Breeze, the guy with the earring through his nipple? I said maybe I bought his story, he thought Breeze was somebody else? I checked the visitors' sheet. A lawyer for the Giacano family visited him the day before."

"You're sure?"

"Whiplash Wineburger. You ever meet him?"

"Whiplash represents other clients, too."

"Pro bono for a mulatto who works in a rice mill?"

"Why would the Giacanos want to do an inside hit on a guy like Cool Breeze Broussard?"

She raised her eyebrows and shrugged.

"Maybe the Feds are squeezing Breeze to bring pressure on the Giacanos," I said, in answer to my own question.

"To make them cooperate in an investigation of the Triads?"

"Why not?"

"The other thing I was going to tell you? Last night Lila Terrebonne went into that new zydeco dump on the parish line. She got into it with the bartender, then pulled a .25 automatic on the bouncer. A couple of uniforms were the first guys to respond. They got her purse from her with the gun in it without any problem. Then one of them brushed against her and she went ape shit.

"Dave, I put my arm around her and walked her out the back door, into the parking lot, with nobody else around, and she cried like a kid in my arms . . . You following me?"

"Yeah, I think so," I said.

"I don't know who did it, but I know what's been done to her," she said. She stood up, flexed her back, and inverted the flats of her hands inside the back of her gunbelt. The skin was tight around her mouth, her eyes charged with light. My gaze shifted off her face.

"When I was a young woman and finally told people what my father did to me, nobody believed it," she said. " 'Your dad was a great guy,' they said. 'Your dad was a wonderful parent.' "

"Where is she now?"

"Iberia General. Nobody's pressing charges. I think her old man already greased the owner of the bar."

"You're a good cop, Helen."

"Better get her some help. The guy who'll pay the bill won't be the one who did it to her. Too bad it works out that way, huh?"

"What do I know?" I said.

Her eyes held on mine. She had killed two perps in the line of duty. I think she took no joy in that fact. But neither did she regret what she had done nor did she grieve over the repressed anger that had rescinded any equivocation she might have had before she shot them. She winked at me and went back to her office.

SIX

With regularity politicians talk about what they call the war against drugs. I have the sense few of them know anything about it. But the person who suffers the attrition for the drug trade is real, with the same soft marmalade-like system of lungs and heart and viscera inherited from a fish as the rest of us.

In this case her name was Ruby Gravano and she lived in a low-rent hotel on St. Charles Avenue in New Orleans, between Lee Circle and Canal, not far from the French Quarter. The narrow front entrance was framed by bare lightbulbs, like the entrance to a 1920s movie theater. But quaint similarities ended there. The interior was superheated and breathless, unlighted except for the glare from the airshaft at the end of the hallways. For some reason the walls had been painted firehouse red with black trim, and now, in the semidarkness, they had the dirty glow of a dying furnace.

Ruby Gravano sat in a stuffed chair surrounded by the litter of her life: splayed tabloid magazines, pizza cartons, used Kleenex, a coffee cup with a dead roach inside, a half-constructed model of a spaceship that had been stuck back in the box and stepped on.

Ruby Gravano's hair was long and black and made her thin face and body look fuller than they were. She wore shorts that were too big for her and exposed her underwear, and foundation on her thighs and forearms, and false fingernails and false eyelashes and a bruise like a fresh tattoo on her left cheek.

"Dave won't jam you up on this, Ruby. We just want a string that'll lead back to these two guys. They're bad dudes, not the kind you want in your life, not the kind you want other girls to get mixed up with. You can help a lot of people here," Clete said.

"We did them in a motel on Airline Highway. They had a pickup truck with a shell on it. Full of guns and camping gear and shit. They smelled like mosquito repellent. They always wore their hats. I've seen hogs eat with better table manners. They're johns. What else you want to know?" she said.

"Why'd you think they might be cops?" I asked.

"Who else carries mug shots around?"

"Beg your pardon?" I said.

"The guy I did, he was undressing and he finds these two mug shots in his shirt pocket. So he burns them in an ashtray and that's when his friend says something about capping two brothers."

"Wait a minute. You were all in the same room?" Clete said.

"They didn't want to pay for two rooms. Besides, they wanted to trade off. Connie does splits, but I wouldn't go along. One of those creeps is sickening enough. Why don't you bug Connie about this stuff?"

"Because she blew town," Clete said.

She sniffed and wiped her nose with her wrist. "Look, I'm not feeling too good. Y'all got what you need?" she said.

"Did they use a credit card to pay for the room?" I asked.

"It's a trick pad. My manager pays the owner. Look, believe it or not, I got another life besides this shit. How about it?"

She tried to look boldly into my face, but her eyes broke and she picked up the crushed model of a spaceship from its box on the floor and held it in her lap and studied it resentfully.

"Who hit you, Ruby?" I asked.

"A guy."

"You have a kid?"

"A little boy. He's nine. I bought him this, but it got rough in here last night."

"These cops, duffers, whatever they were, they had to have names," I said.

"Not real ones."

"What do you mean?"

"The one who burned the pictures, the other guy called him Harpo. I go, 'Like that guy in old TV movies who's a dummy and is always honking a horn?' The guy called Harpo goes, 'That's right, darlin', and right now I'm gonna honk *your* horn.' "

She tried to fit the plastic parts of the model back together. Her right cheek was pinched while she tried to focus, and the bruise on it knotted together like a cluster of blue grapes. "I can't fix this. I should have put it up in the closet. He's coming over with my aunt," she said. She pushed hard on a plastic part and it slid sharply across the back of her hand.

"How old a man was Harpo?" I asked.

"Like sixty, when they start acting like they're your father and Robert Redford at the same time. He has hair all over his back . . . I got to go to the bathroom. I'm gonna be in there a while. Look, you want to stay, maybe you can fix this. It's been a deeply fucked-up day."

"Where'd you buy it?" I asked.

"K&B's. Or maybe at the Jackson Brewery, you know, that mall that used to be the Jax brewery . . . No, I'm pretty sure it wasn't the Brewery." She bit a hangnail.

Clete and I drove to a K&B drugstore up St. Charles. It was raining, and the wind blew the mist out of the trees that arched over the streetcar tracks. The green-and-purple neon on the drugstore looked like scrolled candy in the rain.

"Harpo was the name of the cop who took Cool Breeze Broussard's wife away from him," I said.

"That was twenty years ago. It can't be the same guy, can it?"

"No, it's unlikely."

"I think all these people deserve each other, Streak."

"So why are we buying a toy for Ruby Gravano's son?"

"I seldom take my own advice. Sound like anybody else you know, big mon?"

On Wednesday I drove a cruiser down the old bayou road toward Jeanerette and Lila Terrebonne's home. As I neared the enormous lawn and the oak-lined driveway, I saw the production crew at work on the set that had been constructed to look like the quarters on a corporation farm, and I kept driving south, toward Franklin and the place where my father and I had discovered a crucifixion.

Why?

Maybe because the past is never really dead, at least not as long as you deny its existence. Maybe because I knew that somehow the death of Cisco and Megan Flynn's father was about to come back into our lives.

The barn was still there, two hundred yards from the Teche, hemmed in by banana trees and blackberry bushes. The roof was cratered with a huge hole, the walls leaning in on themselves, the red paint nothing more than thin strips that hadn't yet been weathered away by wind and sun.

I walked through the blackberry bushes to the north side of the barn. The nail holes were sealed over with dust from the cane fields and water expansion in the wood, but I could still feel their edges with the tips of my fingers and, in my mind's eye, see the outline of the man whose tormented face and broken body and blood-creased brow greeted my father and me on that fiery dawn in 1956.

No grass grew around the area where Jack Flynn died. (But there was no sunlight there, I told myself, only green flies buzzing in the shade, and the earth was hardpan and probably poisoned by herbicides that had been spilled on the ground.) Wild rain trees, bursting with bloodred flowers, stood in the field, and the blackberries on the bushes were fat and moist with their own juices when I touched them. I wondered at the degree of innocence that allowed us to think of Golgotha as an incident trapped inside history. I wiped the sweat off my face with a handkerchief and unbuttoned my shirt and stepped out of the shade into the wind, but it brought no relief from the heat.

I drove back up the bayou to the Terrebonne home and turned into the brick drive and parked by the carriage house. Lila was ebullient, her milky green eyes free of any remorse or memory of pulling a gun in a bar and being handcuffed to a bed in Iberia General Hospital. But like all people who are driven by a self-centered fear, she talked constantly, controlling the environment around her with words, filling in any silent space that might allow someone to ask the wrong question.

Her father, Archer Terrebonne, was another matter. He had the same eyes as his daughter, and the same white-gold hair, but there was no lack of confidence in either his laconic speech or the way he folded his arms across his narrow chest while he held a glass of shaved ice and bourbon and sliced oranges. In fact, his money gave him the kind of confidence that overrode any unpleasant reflection he might see in a mirror or the eyes of others. When you dealt with Archer Terrebonne, you simply accepted the fact that his gaze was too direct and personal, his skin too pale for the season, his mouth too red, his presence too close, as though there were a chemical defect in his physiology that he wore as an ornament and imposed upon others.

We stood under an awning on the back terrace. The sunlight was blinding on the surface of the swimming pool. In the distance a black groundskeeper was using an air blower to scud leaves off the tennis courts.

"You won't come inside?" Archer said. He glanced at his watch, then looked at a bird in a tree. The ring finger of his left hand was missing, sawed off neatly at the palm, so that the empty space looked like a missing key on a piano.

"Thanks, anyway. I just wanted to see that Lila was all right."

"Really? Well, that was good of you."

I noticed his use of the past tense, as though my visit had already ended.

"There're no charges, but messing with guns in barrooms usually has another conclusion," I said.

"We've already covered this territory with other people, sir," he said.

"I don't think quite enough," I said.

"Is that right?" he replied.

Our eyes locked on each other's.

"Dave's just being an old friend, Daddy," Lila said.

"I'm sure he is. Let me walk you to your cruiser, Mr. Robicheaux."

"Daddy, I mean it, Dave's always worrying about his AA friends," she said.

"You're not in that organization. So he doesn't need to worry, does he?"

I felt his hand cup me lightly on the arm. But I said goodbye to Lila and didn't resist. I walked with him around the shady side of the house, past a garden planted with mint and heart-shaped caladiums.

"Is there something you want to tell me, sir?" he asked. He took a swallow from his bourbon glass and I could feel the coldness of the ice on his breath.

"A female detective saved your daughter from a resisting arrest charge," I said.

"Yes?"

"She thinks Lila has been sexually molested or violated in some way."

His right eye twitched at the corner, as though an insect had momentarily flown into his vision.

"I'm sure y'all have many theories about human behavior that most of us wouldn't understand. We appreciate your good intentions. However, I see no need for you to come back," he said.

"Don't count on it, sir."

He wagged his finger back and forth, then walked casually toward the rear of the house, sipping his drink as though I had never been there.

The sun was white in the sky and the brick drive was dappled with light as bright as gold foil. Through the cruiser's front window I saw Cisco Flynn walk toward me from a trailer, his palms raised for me to stop.

He leaned down on the window.

"Take a walk with me. I got to keep my eye on this next scene," he said.

"Got to go, Cisco."

"It's about Swede Boxleiter."

I turned off the ignition and walked with him to a canvas awning that was suspended over a worktable and a half dozen chairs. Next to the awning was a trailer whose air-conditioning unit dripped with moisture like a block of ice.

"Swede's trying to straighten out. I think he's going to make it this time. But if he's ever a problem, give me a call," Cisco said.

"He's a mainline recidivist, Cisco. Why are you hooked up with him?"

"When we were in the state home? I would have been anybody's chops if it hadn't been for Swede."

"The Feds say he kills people."

"The Feds say my sister is a Communist."

The door to the trailer opened and a woman stepped out on the small porch. But before she could close the door behind her, a voice shouted out, "Goddamnit, I didn't say you could leave. Now, you listen, hon. I don't know if the problem is because your brains are between your legs or because you think you've got a cute twat, but the next time I tell that pissant to rewrite a scene, you'd better not open your mouth. Now you get the fuck back to work and don't you ever contradict me in front of other people again."

Even in the sunlight her face looked refrigerated, bloodless, the lines twisted out of shape with the humiliation that Billy Holtzner bathed her with. He shot an ugly look at Cisco and me, then slammed the door.

I turned to go.

"There's a lot of stress on a set, Dave. We're three million over budget already. That's other people's money we're talking about. They get mad about it," Cisco said.

"I remember that first film you made. The one about the migrant farmworkers. It was sure a fine movie."

"Yeah, a lot of college professors and 1960s leftovers dug it in a big way."

"The guy in that trailer is a shithead."

"Aren't we all?"

"Your old man wasn't."

I got into the cruiser and drove through the corridor of trees to the bayou road. In the rearview mirror Cisco Flynn looked like a miniature man trapped inside an elongated box.

That night, as Bootsie and I prepared to go to bed, dry lightning flickered behind the clouds and the pecan tree outside the window was stiffening in the wind.

"Why do you think Jack Flynn was killed?" Bootsie asked.

"Working people around here made thirty-five cents an hour back then. He didn't have a hard time finding an audience."

"Who do you think did it?"

"Everyone said it came from the outside. Just like during the Civil Rights era. We always blamed our problems on the outside."

She turned out the light and we lay down on top of the sheets. Her skin felt cool and warm at the same time, the way sunlight does in the fall.

"The Flynns are trouble, Dave."

"Maybe."

"No, no maybe about it. Jack Flynn might have been a good man. But I always heard he didn't become a radical until his family got wiped out in the Depression."

"He fought in the Lincoln Brigade. He was at the battle of Madrid."

"Good night," she said.

She turned toward the far wall. When I spread my hand on her back I could feel her breath rise and fall in her lungs. She looked at me over her shoulder, then rolled over and fit herself inside my arms.

"Dave?" she said.

"Yes?"

"Trust me on this. Megan needs you for some reason she's not telling you about. If she can't get to you directly, she'll go through Clete."

"That's hard to believe."

"He called tonight and asked if I knew where she was. She'd left a message on his answering machine."

"Megan Flynn and Clete Purcel?"

I woke at sunrise the next morning and drove through the leafy shadows on East Main and then five miles up the old highway to Spanish Lake. I was troubled not only by Bootsie's words but also by my own misgivings about the Flynns. Why was Megan so interested in the plight of Cool Breeze Broussard? There was enough injustice in the world without coming back to New Iberia to find it. And why would her brother Cisco front points for an obvious psychopath like Swede Boxleiter?

I parked my truck on a side road and poured a cup of coffee from my thermos. Through the pines I could see the sun glimmering on the water and the tips of the flooded grass waving in the shallows. The area around the lake had been the site of a failed Spanish colony in the 1790s. In 1836 two Irish immigrants who had survived the Goliad Massacre during the Texas Revolution, Devon Flynn and William Burke, cleared and drained the acreage along the lake and built farmhouses out of cypress trees that were rooted in the water like boulders. Later the train stop there became known as Burke's Station.

Megan and Cisco's ancestor had been one of those Texas soldiers who had surrendered to the Mexican army with the expectation of boarding a prison ship bound for New Orleans, and instead had been marched down a road on Palm Sunday and told by their Mexican captors to kneel in front of the firing squads that were forming into position from two directions. Over 350 men and boys were shot, bayoneted, and clubbed to death. Many of the survivors owed their lives to a prostitute who ran from one Mexican officer to the next, begging for the lives of the Texans. Her name and fate were lost to history, but those who escaped into the woods that day called her the Angel of Goliad.

I wondered if Cisco ever thought about his ancestor's story as material for a film.

The old Flynn house still stood by the lake, but it was covered by a white-brick veneer now and the old gallery had been replaced by a circular stone porch with white pillars. But probably most important to Megan and Cisco was the simple fact that it and its terraced gardens and gnarled live oaks and lakeside gazebo and boathouse all belonged to someone else.

Their father was bombed by the Luftwaffe and shot at by the Japanese on Guadalcanal and murdered in Louisiana. Were they bitter, did they bear us a level of resentment we could only guess at? Did they bring their success back here like a beast on a chain? I didn't want to answer my own question.

The wind ruffled the lake and the longleaf pine boughs above my truck. I glanced in the rearview mirror and saw the sheriff's cruiser pull in behind me. He opened my passenger door and got inside.

"How'd you know I was out here?" I asked.

"A state trooper saw you and wondered what you were doing."

"I got up a little early today."

"That's the old Flynn place, isn't it?"

"We used to dig for Confederate artifacts here. Camp Pratt was right back in those trees."

"The Flynns bother me, too, Dave. I don't like Cisco bringing this Boxleiter character into our midst. Why don't both of them stay in Colorado?"

"That's what we did to Megan and Cisco the first time. Let a friend of their dad dump them in Colorado."

"You'd better define your feelings about that pair. I got Boxleiter's sheet. What kind of person would bring a man like that into his community?"

"We did some serious damage to those kids, Sheriff."

"*We?* You know what your problem is, Dave? You're just like Jack Flynn."

"Excuse me?"

"You don't like rich people. You think we're in a class war. Not everybody with money is a sonofabitch."

He blew out his breath, then the heat went out of his face. He took his pipe from his shirt pocket and clicked it on the window jamb.

"Helen said you think Boxleiter might be a pedophile," he said.

"Yeah, if I had to bet, I'd say he's a real candidate."

"Pick him up."

"What for?"

"Think of something. Take Helen with you. She can be very creative."

Idle words that I would try to erase from my memory later.

SEVEN

I drove back toward the office. As I approached the old Catholic cemetery, I saw a black man with sloping shoulders cross the street in front of me and walk toward Main. I stared at him, dumbfounded. One cheek was bandaged, and his right arm was stiff at his side, as though it pained him.

I pulled abreast of him and said, "I can't believe it."

"Believe what?" Cool Breeze said. He walked bent forward, like he was just about to arrive somewhere. The whitewashed crypts behind him were beaded with moisture the size of quarters.

"You're supposed to be in federal custody."

"They cut me loose."

"Cut you loose? Just like that?"

"I'm going up to Victor's to eat breakfast."

"Get in."

"I don't mean you no disrespect, but I ain't gonna have no more to do with po-licemens for a while."

"You staying with Mout'?"

But he crossed the street and didn't answer.

. . .

At the office I called Adrien Glazier in New Orleans.

"What's your game with Cool Breeze Broussard?" I asked.

"Game?"

"He's back in New Iberia. I just saw him."

"We took his deposition. We don't see any point in keeping him in custody," she replied.

I could feel my words binding in my throat.

"What's in y'all's minds? You've burned this guy."

"Burned him?"

"You made him rat out the Giacanos. Do you know what they do to people who snitch them off?"

"Then why don't you put him in custody yourself, Mr. Robicheaux?"

"Because the prosecutor's office dropped charges against him."

"Really? So the same people who complain when we investigate their jail want us to clean up a local mess for them?"

"Don't do this."

"Should we tell Mr. Broussard his friend Mr. Robicheaux would like to see him locked up again? Or will you do that for us?" she said, and hung up.

Helen opened my door and came inside. She studied my face curiously.

"You ready to boogie?" she asked.

Swede Boxleiter had told me he had a job in the movies, and that's where we started. Over in St. Mary Parish, on the front lawn of Lila Terrebonne.

But we didn't get far. After we had parked the cruiser, we were stopped halfway to the set by a couple of off-duty St. Mary Parish sheriff's deputies with American flags sewn to their sleeves.

"Y'all putting us in an embarrassing situation," the older man said.

"You see that dude there, the one with the tool belt on? His name's Boxleiter. He just finished a five bit in Colorado," I said.

"You got a warrant?"

"Nope."

"Mr. Holtzner don't want nobody on the set ain't got bidness here. That's the way it is."

"Oh yeah? Try this. Either you take the marshmallows out of your mouth or I'll go down to your boss's office and have your ass stuffed in a tree shredder," Helen said.

"Say what you want. You ain't getting on this set," he said.

Just then, Cisco Flynn opened the door of a trailer and stepped out on the short wood porch.

"What's the problem, Dave?" he asked.

"Boxleiter."

"Come in," he said, making cupping motions with his upturned hands, as though he were directing an aircraft on a landing strip.

Helen and I walked toward the open door. Behind him I could see Billy Holtzner combing his hair. His eyes were pale and watery, his lips thick, his face hard-planed like gray rubber molded against bone.

"Dave, we want a good relationship with everybody in the area. If Swede's done something wrong, I want to know about it. Come inside, meet Billy. Let's talk a minute," Cisco said.

But Billy Holtzner's attention had shifted to a woman who was brushing her teeth in a lavatory with the door open.

"Margot, you look just like you do when I come in your mouth," he said.

"Adios," I said, walking away from the trailer with Helen.

Cisco caught up with us and waved away the two security guards.

"What'd Swede do?" he asked.

"Better question: What's he got on you?" I said.

"What have I done that you insult me like this?"

"Mr. Flynn, Boxleiter was hanging around small children at the city pool. Save the bullshit for your local groupies," Helen said.

"All right, I'll talk to him. Let's don't have a scene," Cisco said.

"Just stay out of the way," she said.

Boxleiter was on one knee, stripped to the waist, tightening a socket wrench on a power terminal. His Levi's were powdered with dust, and black power lines spidered out from him in all directions. His torso glistened whitely with sweat, his skin rippling with sinew each time he pumped the wrench. He used his hand to mop the sweat out of one shaved armpit, then wiped his hand on his jeans.

"I want you to put your shirt on and take a ride with us," I said.

He looked up at us, smiling, squinting into the sun. "You don't have a warrant. If you did, you'd have already told me," he said.

"It's a social invitation. One you really don't want to turn down," Helen said.

He studied her, amused. Dust swirled out of the dirt street that had been spread on the set. The sky was cloudless, the air moist and as tangible as flame against the skin. Boxleiter rose to his feet. People on the set had stopped work and were watching now.

"I got a union book. I'm like anybody else here. I don't have to go anywhere," he said.

"Suit yourself. We'll catch you later," I said.

"I get it. You'll roust me when I get home tonight. It don't bother me. Long as it's legal," he said.

Helen's cheeks were flushed, the back of her neck damp in the heat. I touched her wrist and nodded toward the cruiser. Just as she turned to go with me, I saw Boxleiter draw one stiff finger up his rib cage, collecting a thick dollop of sweat. He flicked it at her back.

Her hand went to her cheek, her face darkening with surprise and insult, like a person in a crowd who cannot believe the nature of an injury she has just received.

"You're under arrest for assaulting a police officer. Put your hands behind you," she said.

He grinned and scratched at an insect bite high up on his shoulder.

"Is there something wrong with the words I use? Turn around," she said.

He shook his head sadly. "I got witnesses. I ain't done anything."

"You want to add 'resisting' to it?" she said.

"Whoa, mama. Take your hands off me . . . Hey, enough's enough . . . Buddy, yeah, you, guy with the mustache, you get this dyke off me."

She grabbed him by the shoulders and put her shoe behind his knee. Then he brought his elbow into her breast, hard, raking it across her as he turned.

She slipped a blackjack from her pants pocket and raised it over her shoulder and swung it down on his collarbone. It was weighted with lead, elongated like a darning sock, the spring handle wrapped with leather. The blow made his shoulder drop as though the tendons had been severed at the neck.

But he flailed at her just the same, trying to grab her around the waist. She whipped the blackjack across his head, again and again, splitting his scalp, wetting the leather cover on the blackjack each time she swung.

I tried to push him to the ground, out of harm's way, but another problem was in the making. The two off-duty sheriff's deputies were pulling their weapons.

I tore my .45 from my belt holster and aimed into their faces.

"Freeze! It's over! . . . Take your hand off that piece! Do it! Do it! Do it!"

I saw the confusion and the alarm fix in their eyes, their bodies stiffening. Then the moment died in their faces. "That's it . . . Now, move the crowd back. That's all you've got to do . . . That's right," I said, my words like wet glass in my throat.

Swede Boxleiter moaned and rolled in the dirt among the power cables, his fingers laced in his hair. Both my hands were still squeezed tight on the .45's grips, my forearms shining with sweat.

The faces of the onlookers were stunned, stupefied. Billy Holtzner pushed his way through the crowd, turned in a circle, his eyebrows climbing on his forehead, and said, "I got to tell you to get back to work?" Then he walked back toward his trailer, blowing his nose on a Kleenex, flicking his eyes sideways briefly as though looking at a minor irritant.

I was left staring into the self-amused gaze of Archer Terrebonne. Lila stood behind him, her mouth open, her face as white as cake flour. The backs of my legs were still trembling.

"Do y'all specialize in being public fools, Mr. Robicheaux?" he asked. He touched at the corner of his mouth, his three-fingered hand like that of an impaired amphibian.

■ ■ ■

The sheriff paced in his office. He pulled up the blinds, then lowered them again. He kept clearing his throat, as though there were an infection in it.

"This isn't a sheriff's department. I'm the supervisor of a mental institution," he said.

He took the top off his teakettle, looked inside it, and set the top down again.

"You know how many faxes I've gotten already on this? The St. Mary sheriff told me not to put my foot in his parish again. That sonofabitch actually threatened me," he said.

"Maybe we should have played it differently, but Boxleiter didn't give us a lot of selection," I said.

"Outside our jurisdiction."

"We told him he wasn't under arrest. There was no misunderstanding about that," I said.

"I should have used their people to take him down," Helen said.

"Ah, a breakthrough in thought. But I'm suspending you just the same, at least until I get an IA finding," the sheriff said.

"He threw sweat on her. He hit her in the chest with his elbow. He got off light," I said.

"A guy with twenty-eight stitches in his head?"

"You told us to pick him up, skipper. That guy would be a loaded gun anyplace we tried to take him down. You know it, too," I said.

He crimped his lips together and breathed through his nose.

"I'm madder than hell about this," he said.

The room was silent, the air-conditioning almost frigid. The sunlight through the slatted blinds was eye-watering.

"All right, forget the suspension and IA stuff. See me before you go into St. Mary Parish again. In the meantime, you find out why Cisco Flynn thinks he can bring his pet sewer rats into Iberia Parish . . . Helen, you depersonalize your attitude toward the perps, if that's possible."

"The sewer rats?" I said.

He filled his pipe bowl from a leather pouch and didn't bother to look up until we were out of the room.

That evening Clete Purcel parked his Cadillac convertible under the shade trees in front of my house and walked down to the bait shop. He wore a summer suit and a lavender shirt with a white tie. He went to the cooler and opened a bottle of strawberry soda.

"What, I look funny or something?" he said.

"You look sharp."

He drank out of the pop bottle and watched a boat out on the bayou.

"I'll treat y'all to dinner at the Patio in Loreauville," he said.

"I'd better work."

He nodded, then looked at the newscast on the television set that sat above the counter.

"Thought I'd ask," he said.

"Who you going to dinner with?"

"Megan Flynn."

"Another time."

He sat down at the counter and drank from his soda. He drew a finger through a wet ring on the wood.

"I'm only supposed to go out with strippers and junkies?" he said.

"Did I say anything?"

"You hide your feelings like a cat in a spin dryer."

"So she's stand-up. But why's she back in New Iberia? We're Paris on the Teche?"

"She was born here. Her brother has a house here."

"Yeah, he's carrying weight for a psychopath, too. Why you think that is, Clete? Because Cisco likes to rehabilitate shank artists?"

"I hear Helen beat the shit out of Boxleiter with a slapjack. Maybe he's got the message and he'll get out of town."

I mopped down the counter and tossed the rag on top of a case of empty beer bottles.

"You won't change your mind?" he said.

"Come back tomorrow. We'll entertain the bass."

He made a clicking sound with his mouth and walked out the door and into the twilight.

After supper I drove over to Mout' Broussard's house on the west side of town. Cool Breeze came out on the gallery and sat down on the swing. He had removed the bandage from his cheek, and the wound he had gotten at the jail looked like a long piece of pink string inset in his skin.

"Doctor said I ain't gonna have no scar."

"You going to hang around town?" I asked.

"Ain't got no pressing bidness nowheres else."

"They used you, Breeze."

"I got Alex Guidry fired, ain't I?"

"Does it make you feel better?"

He looked at his hands. They were wide, big-boned, lustrous with callus.

"What you want here?" he asked.

"The old man who made your wife cook for him, Harpo Delahoussey? Did he have a son?"

"What people done tole you over in St. Mary Parish?"

"They say he didn't."

He shook his head noncommittally.

"You don't remember?" I said.

"I don't care. It ain't my bidness."

"A guy named Harpo may have executed a couple of kids out in the Basin," I said.

"Those dagos in New Orleans? You know what they do to a black man snitch them off? I'm suppose to worry about some guy blowing away some po'-white trash raped a black girl?"

"When those men took away your wife twenty years ago, you couldn't do anything about it. Same kind of guys are still out there, Breeze. They function only because we allow them to."

"I promised Mout' to go crabbing with him in the morning. I best be getting my sleep," he said.

But when I got into my truck and looked back at him, he was still in the swing, staring at his hands, his massive shoulders slumped like a bag of crushed rock.

It was hot and dry Friday night, with a threat of rain that never came. Out over the Gulf, the clouds would vein and pulse with lightning, then the thunder would ripple across the wetlands with a sound like damp cardboard tearing. In the middle of the night I put my hands inside Bootsie's nightgown and felt her body's heat against my palms, like the warmth in a lampshade. Her eyes opened and looked into mine, then she touched my hardness with her fingertips, her hand gradually rounding itself, her mouth on my cheek, then on my lips. She rolled on her back, her hand never leaving me, and waited for me to enter her.

She came before I did, both of her hands pushing hard into the small of my back, her knees gathered around my thighs, then she came a second time, with me, her stomach rolling under me, her voice muted and moist in my ear.

She went into the bathroom and I heard the water running. She walked toward me out of the light, touching her face with a towel, then lay on top of the sheet and put her head on my chest. The ends of her hair were wet and the spinning blades of the window fan made shadows on her skin.

"What's worrying you?" she asked.

"Nothing."

She kicked me in the calf.

"Clete Purcel. I think he's going to be hurt," I said.

"Advice about love and money. Give it to anyone except friends."

"You're right. You were about Megan, too. I'd thought better of her."

She ran her fingernails through my hair and rested one ankle across mine.

．．．

Sunday morning I woke at dawn and went down to the bait shop to help Batist open up. I was never sure of his age, but he had been a teenager during World War II when he had worked for Mr. Antoine, one of Louisiana's last surviving Confederate veterans, at Mr. Antoine's blacksmith shop in a big red barn out on West Main. Mr. Antoine had willed Batist a plot of land and a small cypress home on the bayou, and over the years Batist had truck farmed there, augmented his income by trapping and fishing with my father, buried two wives, and raised five children, all of whom graduated from high school. He was illiterate and sometimes contentious, and had never traveled farther from home than New Orleans in one direction and Lake Charles in the other, but I never knew a more loyal or decent person.

We started the fire in the barbecue pit, which was fashioned from a split oil drum with handles and hinges welded on it, laid out our chickens and sausage links on the grill for our midday customers, and closed down the lid to let the meat smoke for at least three hours.

Batist wore a pair of bell-bottomed dungarees and a white T-shirt with the sleeves razored off. His upper arms bunched like cantaloupes when he moved a spool table to hose down the dock under it.

"I forgot to tell you. That fella Cool Breeze was by here last night," he said.

"What did he want?"

"I ain't ax him."

I expected him to say more but he didn't. He didn't like people of color who had jail records, primarily because he believed they were used by whites as an excuse to treat all black people unfairly.

"Does he want me to call him?" I asked.

"I know that story about his wife, Dave. Maybe it wasn't all his fault, but he sat by while them white men ruined that po' girl. I feel sorry for him, me, but when a man got a grief like that against hisself, there ain't nothing you can do for him."

I looked up Mout's name in the telephone book and dialed the number. While the phone rang Batist lit a cigar and opened the screen on the window and flicked the match into the water.

"No one home," I said after I hung up.

"I ain't gonna say no more."

He drew in on his cigar, his face turned into the breeze that blew through the screen.

B ootsie and Alafair and I went to Mass, then I dropped them off at home and drove to Cisco Flynn's house on the Loreauville road. He answered the door in a terry-cloth bathrobe that he wore over a pair of scarlet gym shorts.

"Too early?" I said.

"No, I was about to do a workout. Come in," he said, opening the door wide. "Look, if you're here to apologize about that stuff on the set—"

"I'm not."

"Oh."

"The sheriff wants to know why the city of New Iberia is hosting a mainline con like your friend Boxleiter."

We were in the living room now, by the collection of photographs that had made Megan famous.

"You were never in a state home, Dave. How would you like to be seven years old and forced to get up out of bed in the middle of the night and suck somebody's cock? Think you could handle that?"

"I think your friend is a depraved and violent man."

"*He's* violent? Y'all put him in the hospital over a drop of sweat."

Through the French doors I could see two dark-skinned people sitting at a glass table under a tree in the back yard. The man was big, slightly overweight, with a space between his front teeth and a ponytail that hung between his shoulder blades. The woman wore shorts and a tank top and had brownish-red hair that reminded me of tumbleweed. They were pouring orange juice into glasses from a clear pitcher. A yellow candle stub was melted to the table.

"Something bothered me the last time I was here. These photos that were in *Life* magazine? Y'all caught the kill from inside the drain-pipe, just as the bullet hit the black guy in the neck?"

"That's right."

"What were you doing in the pipe? How'd you know the guy was coming out at that particular place?"

"We made an arrangement to meet him, that's all."

"How'd the cops know he was going to be there?"

"I told you. He raped a high school girl. They had an all-points out on him."

"Somehow that doesn't hang together for me," I said.

"You think we set it up? We were *inside* the pipe. Bullets were ricocheting and sparking all around us. What's the use? I've got some guests. Is there anything else?"

"Guests?"

"Billy Holtzner's daughter and her boyfriend."

I looked out the French doors again. I saw a glassy reflection between the fingers of the man's right hand.

"Introduce me."

"It's Sunday. They're just getting up."

"Yeah, I can see."

"Hey, wait a minute."

But I opened the French doors and stepped outside. The man with the ponytail, who looked Malaysian or Indonesian, cupped the candle stub melted to the table, popping the waxy base loose, and held it behind his thigh. Holtzner's daughter had eyes that didn't fit her fried hair. They were a soapy blue, mindless, as devoid of reason as a drowsy cat's when small creatures run across its vision.

A flat, partially zipped leather case rested on a metal chair between her and her boyfriend.

"How y'all doing?" I asked.

Their smiles were self-indulgent rather than warm, their faces suffused by a chemical pleasure that was working in their skin like flame inside tallow. The woman lowered her wrist into her lap and the sunlight fell like a spray of yellow coins on the small red swelling inside her forearm.

"The officer from the set," the man said.

"It is," the woman said, leaning sideways in her chair to see behind me. "Is that blond lady here? The one with the blackjack. I mean that guy's head. Yuck."

"We're not in trouble, are we?" the man said. He smiled. The gap in his front teeth was large enough to insert a kitchen match in.

"You from the U.K.?" I said.

"Just the accent. I travel on a French passport," he said, smiling. He removed a pair of dark glasses from his shirt pocket and put them on.

"Y'all need any medical attention here?"

"No, not today, I don't think," the man said.

"Sure? Because I can run y'all down to Iberia General. It's no trouble."

"That's very kind of you, but we'll pass," the man said.

"What's he talking about?" the woman said.

"Being helpful, that sort of thing, welcoming us to the neighborhood," the man said.

"Hospital?" She scratched her back by rubbing it against her chair. "Did anybody ever tell you you look like Johnny Wadd?"

"Not really."

"He died of AIDS. He was very underrated as an artist. Because he did porno, if that's what you want to call it." Then her face went out of focus, as though her own words had presented a question inside herself.

"Dave, can I see you?" Cisco said softly behind me.

I left Billy Holtzner's daughter and the man with the ponytail without saying goodbye. But they never noticed, their heads bent toward each other as they laughed over a private joke.

Cisco walked with me through the shade trees to my truck. He had slipped on a golf shirt with his gym shorts, and he kept pulling the cloth away from the dampness of his skin.

"I don't have choices about what people around me do sometimes," he said.

"Choose not to have them here, Cisco."

"I work in a bowl of piranhas. You think Billy Holtzner is off the wall? He twists noses. I can introduce you to people who blow heads."

"I didn't have probable cause on your friends. But they shouldn't take too much for granted."

"How many cops on a pad have you covered for? How many times have you seen a guy popped and a throw-down put on his body?"

"See you, Cisco."

"What am I supposed to feel, Dave? Like I just got visited by St. Francis of Assisi? In your ear."

I walked to my truck and didn't look back at him. I heard the woman braying loudly in the back yard.

When I went down to the bait shop to open up Monday morning, Cool Breeze Broussard was waiting for me at a spool table, the Cinzano umbrella ruffling over his head. The early sun was dark red through the trunks of the cypresses.

"It gonna be another hot one," he said.

"What's the haps, Breeze?"

"I got to talk . . . No, out here. I like to talk in the open space . . . How much of what I tell you other people got to learn about?"

"That depends."

He made a pained face and looked at the redness of the sun through the trees.

"I went to New Orleans Saturday. A guy up Magazine, Jimmy Fig, Tommy Figorelli's brother, the guy the Giacanos sawed up and hung in pieces from a ceiling fan? I figured Jimmy didn't have no love for the Giacanos 'cause of his brother, and, besides, me and Jimmy was in the Block together at Angola, see. So I t'ought he was the right man to sell me a cold piece," Cool Breeze said.

"You're buying unregistered guns?" I said.

"You want to hear me or not? . . . So he go, 'Willie, in your line of work, you don't need no cold piece.'

"I go, 'This ain't for work. I got in bad wit' some local guys, maybe you heard. But I ain't got no money right now, so I need you to front me the piece.'

"He say, 'You feeling some heat from somewhere, Breeze?' And he say it wit' this smart-ass grin on his face.

"I say, 'Yeah, wit' the same dudes who freeze-wrapped your brother's parts in his own butcher shop. I hear they drank eggnog while he was spinning round over their heads.'

"He say, 'Well, my brother had some sexual problems that got him into trouble. But it ain't Italians you got to worry about. The word is some peckerwoods got a contract to do a black blabbermouth in New Iberia. I just didn't know who it was.'

"I say, 'Blabbermouth, huh?'

"He go, 'You was ripping off the Giacanos and selling their own VCRs back to them? Then you snitch them off and come to New Orleans figuring somebody's gonna front you a piece? Breeze, nothing racial meant, but you people ought to stick to pimping and dealing rock.' "

"Who are these peckerwoods?" I asked.

"When I tole you the story about me and Ida, about how she wrapped that chain round her t'roat and drowned herself, I left somet'ing out."

"Oh?"

"A year after Ida died, I was working at the Terrebonne cannery, putting up sweet potatoes. Harpo Delahoussey run the security there for Mr. Terrebonne. We come to the end of the season and the cannery shut down, just like it do every winter, and everybody got laid off. So we went on down to the unemployment office and filed for unemployment insurance. Shouldn't have been no problem.

"Except three weeks go by and the state sends us a notice we ain't qualified for no checks 'cause we cannery workers, and 'cause the cannery ain't open, we ain't available to work.

"I went on down to see Mr. Terrebonne, but I never got past Harpo Delahoussey. He's sitting there at a big desk wit' his foot in the wastebasket, sticking a po'boy sandwich in his mout'. He go, 'It's been explained to you, Willie. Now, you don't want wait round here till next season, you go on down to New Orleans, get you a job, try to stay out of trouble for a while. But don't you come round here bothering Mr. Terrebonne. He been good to y'all.'

" 'Bout a week later they was a big fire at the cannery. You could smell sweet potatoes burning all the way down to Morgan City.

Harpo Delahoussey jumped out a second-story window wit' his clothes on fire. He'da died if he hadn't landed in a mud puddle."

"You set it?"

"Harpo Delahoussey had a nephew wit' his name. He use to be a city po-liceman in Franklin. Everybody called him Li'l Harpo."

"You think this is one of the peckerwoods?"

"Why else I'm telling you all this? Look, I ain't running no more."

"I think you're living inside your head too much, Breeze. The Giacanos use mechanics out of Miami or Houston."

"Jimmy Fig tole me I was a dumb nigger ought to be pimping and selling crack. What you saying ain't no different. I feel bad I come here."

He got up and walked down the dock toward his truck. He passed two white fishermen who were just arriving, their rods and tackle boxes gripped solidly in their hands. They walked around him, then glanced over their shoulders at his back.

"That boy looks like his old lady just cut him off," one of them said to me, grinning.

"We're not open yet," I said, and went inside the bait shop and latched the screen behind me.

EIGHT

You read the jacket on a man like Swede Boxleiter and dismiss him as one of those genetically defective creatures for whom psychologists don't have explanations and let it go at that.

Then he does or says something that doesn't fit the pattern, and you go home from work with boards in your head.

Early Monday morning I called Cisco Flynn's home number and got his answering service. An hour later he returned my call.

"Why do you want Swede's address? Leave him alone," he said.

"He's blackmailing you, isn't he?"

"I remember now. You fought Golden Gloves. Too many shots to the head, Dave."

"Maybe Helen Soileau and I should drop by the set again and talk to him there."

Boxleiter lived in a triplex built of green cinder blocks outside St. Martinville. When I turned into his drive he was throwing a golf ball against the cement steps on the side of the building, ricocheting it off two surfaces before he retrieved it out of the air again, his hand as fast as a snake's head, *click-click, click-click, click-click.* He wore blue Everlast boxing trunks and a gauzy see-through black shirt and white high-top gym shoes and leather gloves without fingers and a white bill cap that covered his shaved and stitched head like an inverted cook pan. He glanced at me over his shoulder, then began throwing the ball again.

"The Man," he said. The back yard had no grass and lay in deep shade, and beyond the tree trunks the bayou shimmered in the sunlight.

"I thought we'd hear from you," I said.

"How's that?"

"Civil suit, brutality charges, that kind of stuff."

"Can't ever tell."

"Give the golf game a break a minute, will you?"

His eyes smiled at nothing, then he flipped the ball out into the yard and waited, his sunken cheeks and small mouth like those of a curious fish.

"I couldn't figure the hold you had on Cisco," I said. "But it's that photo that began Megan's career, the one of the black man getting nailed in the storm drain, isn't it? You told the cops where he was coming out. Her big break was based on a fraud that cost a guy his life."

He cleaned an ear with his little finger, his eyes as empty of thought as glass.

"Cisco is my friend. I wouldn't hurt him for any reason in the world. Somebody try to hurt him, I'll cut them into steaks."

"Is that right?"

"You want to play some handball?"

"Handball?"

"Yeah, against the garage."

"No, I—"

"Tell the dyke I got no beef. I just didn't like the roust in front of all them people."

"Tell the dyke? You're an unusual man, Swede."

"I heard about you. You were in Vietnam. Anything on my sheet you probably did in spades."

Then, as though I were no longer there, he did a handstand in the yard and walked on stiffened arms through the shade, the bottoms of his gym shoes extended out like the shoulders of a man with no head.

C lete Purcel sat in the bow of the outboard and drained the foam out of a long-necked bottle of beer. He cast his Rapala between two willow trees and retrieved it back toward him, the sides of the lure flashing just below the surface. The sun was low on the western horizon and the canopy overhead was lit with fire, the water motionless, the mosquitoes starting to form in clouds over the islands of algae that extended out from the flooded cypress trunks.

A bass rose from the silt, thick-backed, the black-green dorsal fin glistening when it broke the water, and knocked the Rapala into the air without taking the treble hook. Clete set his rod on the bow and slapped the back of his neck and looked at the bloody smear on his palm.

"So this guy Cool Breeze is telling you a couple of crackers got the whack on him? One of them is maybe the guy who did these two brothers out in the Atchafalaya Basin?" he said.

"Yeah, that's about it."

"But you don't buy it?"

"When did the Giacanos start using over-the-hill peckerwoods for button men?"

"I wouldn't mark it off, mon. This greaseball in Igor's was complaining to me about how the Giacano family is falling apart, how they've lost their self-respect and they're running low-rent action like porno joints and dope in the projects. I say, 'Yeah, it's a shame. The world's really going to hell,' and he says, 'You telling me, Purcel? It's so bad we got a serious problem with somebody, we got to outsource.'

"I say, 'Outsource?'

"He goes, 'Yeah, niggers from the Desire, Vietnamese lice-heads, crackers who spit Red Man in Styrofoam cups at the dinner table.'

"It's the Dixie Mafia, Dave. There's a nest of them over on the Mississippi coast."

I drew the paddle through the water and let the boat glide into a cove that was freckled with sunlight. I cast a popping bug with yellow feathers and red eyes on the edge of the hyacinths. A solitary blue heron lifted on extended wings out of the grass and flew through an opening in the trees, dimpling the water with its feet.

"But you didn't bring me out here to talk about wiseguy bullshit, did you?" Clete said.

I watched a cottonmouth extend its body out of the water, curling around a low branch on a flooded willow, then pull itself completely into the leaves.

"I don't know how to say it," I said.

"I'll clear it up for both of us. I like her. Maybe we got something going. That rubs you the wrong way?"

"A guy gets involved, he doesn't see things straight sometimes," I said.

" 'Involved,' like in the sack? You're asking me if I'm in the sack with Megan?"

"You're my friend. You carried me down a fire escape when that kid opened up on us with a .22. Something stinks about the Flynn family."

Clete's face was turned into the shadows. The back of his neck was the color of Mercurochrome.

"On my best day I kick in some poor bastard's door for Nig Rosewater. Last week a greaseball tried to hire me to collect the vig for a couple of his shylocks. Megan's talking about getting me on as head of security with a movie company. You think that's bad?"

I looked at the water and the trapped air bubbles that chained to the surface out of the silt. I heard Clete's weight turn on the vinyl cushion under him.

"Say it, Dave. Any broad outside of a T&A joint must have an angle if she'd get involved with your podjo. I'm not sensitive. But lay off Megan."

I disconnected the sections of my fly rod and set them in the bottom of the boat. When I lifted the outboard and yanked the starter rope, the dry propeller whined like a chain saw through the darkening swamp. I didn't speak again until we were at the dock. The air was hot, as though it had been baked on a sheet of tin, the current yellow and dead in the bayou, the lavender sky thick with birds.

Up on the dock, Clete peeled off his shirt and stuck his head under a water faucet. The skin across his shoulders was dry and scaling.

"Come on up for dinner," I said.

"I think I'm going back to New Orleans tonight." He took his billfold out of his back pocket and removed a five-dollar bill and pushed it into a crack in the railing. "I owe for the beer and gas," he said, and walked with his spinning rod and big tackle box to his car, his love handles aching with fresh sunburn.

The next night, under a full moon, two men wearing hats drove a pickup truck down a levee in Vermilion Parish. On either side of them marshlands and saw grass seemed to flow like a wide green river into the Gulf. The two men stopped their truck on the levee and crossed a plank walkway that oozed sand and water under their combined weight. They passed a pirogue that was tied to the walkway, then stepped on ground that was like sponge under their western boots. Ahead, inside the fish camp, someone walked across the glare of a Coleman lantern and made a shadow on the window. Mout' Broussard's dog raised its head under the shack, then padded out into the open air on its leash, its nose lifted into the wind.

NINE

Mout' stood in the doorway of the shack and looked at the two white men. Both were tall and wore hats that shadowed their faces. The dog, a yellow-and-black mongrel with scars on its ears, growled and showed its teeth.

"Shut up, Rafe!" Mout' said.

"Where's Willie Broussard at?" one of the men said. The flesh in his throat was distended and rose-colored, and gray whiskers grew on his chin.

"He gone up the levee to the sto'. Coming right back. Wit' some friends to play bouree. What you gentlemens want?" Mout' said.

"Your truck's right yonder. What'd he drive in?" the second man said. He wore a clear plastic raincoat and his right arm held something behind his thigh.

"A friend carried him up there."

"We stopped there for a soda. It was locked up. Where's your outboard, old man?" the man with whiskers said.

"Ain't got no outboa'd."

"There's the gas can yonder. There's the cut in the cattails where it was tied. Your boy running a trot line?"

"What y'all want to bother him for? He ain't done you nothing."

"You don't mind if we come inside, do you?" the man in the raincoat said. When he stepped forward, the dog lunged at his ankle. He kicked his boot sideways and caught the dog in the mouth, then pulled the screen and latch out of the doorjamb.

"You stand over in the corner and stay out of the way," the man with whiskers said.

The man in the raincoat lifted the Coleman lantern by the bail and walked into the back yard with it. He came back in and shook his head.

The man with whiskers bit off a corner on a tobacco plug and worked it into his jaw. He picked up an empty coffee can out of a trash sack and spit in it.

"I told you we should have come in the a.m. You wake them up and do business," the man in the raincoat said.

"Turn off the lantern and move the truck."

"I say mark it off. I don't like guessing who's coming through a door."

The man with whiskers looked at him meaningfully.

"It's your rodeo," the man in the raincoat said, and went back out the front door.

The wind blew through the screens into the room. Outside, the moonlight glittered like silver on the water in the saw grass.

"Lie down on the floor where I can watch you. Here, take this pillow," the man with whiskers said.

"Don't hurt my boy, suh."

"Don't talk no more. Don't look at my face either."

"What's I gonna do? You here to kill my boy."

"You don't know that. Maybe we just want to talk to him . . . Don't look at my face."

"I ain't lying on no flo'. I ain't gonna sit by while y'all kill my boy. What y'all t'ink I am?"

"An old man, just like I'm getting to be. You can have something to eat or put your head down on the table and take a nap. But don't mix in it. You understand that? You mix in it, we gonna forget you're an old nigra don't nobody pay any mind to."

The man in the raincoat came back through the door, a sawed-off over-and-under shotgun in his right hand.

"I'm burning up. The wind feels like it come off a desert," he said, and took off his coat and wiped his face with a handkerchief. "What was the old man talking about?"

"He thinks the stock market might take a slide."

"Ask him if there's any stray pussy in the neighborhood."

The man with whiskers on his chin leaned over and spit tobacco juice into the coffee can. He wiped his lips with his thumb.

"Bring his dog in here," he said.

"What for?"

"Because a dog skulking and whimpering around the door might indicate somebody kicked it."

"I hadn't thought about that. They always say you're a thinking man, Harpo."

The man with the whiskers spit in the can again and looked hard at him.

The man who had worn the raincoat dragged the dog skittering through the door on its leash, then tried to haul it into the air. But the dog's back feet found purchase on the floor and its teeth tore into the man's hand.

"Oh, shit!" he yelled out, and pushed both his hands between his thighs.

"Get that damn dog under control, old man, or I'm gonna shoot both of you," the man with whiskers said.

"Yes, suh. He ain't gonna be no trouble. I promise," Mout' said.

"You all right?" the man with whiskers asked his friend.

His friend didn't answer. He opened an ice chest and found a bottle of wine and poured it on the wound. His hand was strung with blood, his fingers shaking as though numb with cold. He tied his handkerchief around the wound, pulling it tight with his teeth, and sat down in a wood chair facing the door, the shotgun across his knees.

"This better come out right," he said.

. . .

M out' sat in the corner, on the floor, his dog between his thighs. He could hear mullet splash out in the saw grass, the drone of a distant boat engine, dry thunder booming over the Gulf. He wanted it to rain, but he didn't know why. Maybe if it rained, no, stormed, with lightning all over the sky, Cool Breeze would take shelter and not try to come back that night. Or if it was thundering real bad, the two white men wouldn't hear Cool Breeze's outboard, hear him lifting the crab traps out of the aluminum bottom, hefting up the bucket loaded with catfish he'd unhooked from the trot line.

"I got to go to the bat'room," he said.

But neither of the white men acknowledged him.

"I got to make water," he said.

The man with whiskers stood up from his chair and straightened his back.

"Come on, old man," he said, and let Mout' walk ahead of him out the back door.

"Maybe you a good man, suh. Maybe you just ain't giving yourself credit for being a good man," Mout' said.

"Go ahead and piss."

"I ain't never give no trouble to white people. Anybody round New Iberia tell you that. Same wit' my boy. He worked hard at the bowling alley. He had him a li'l sto'. He tried to stay out of trouble but wouldn't nobody let him."

Then Mout' felt his caution, his lifetime of deference and obsequiousness and pretense slipping away from him. "He had him a wife, her name was Ida, the sweetest black girl in Franklin, but a white man said she was gonna cook for him, just like that, or her husband was gonna go to the penitentiary. Then he took her out in the shed and made her get down on her knees and do what he want. She t'rowed up and begged him not to make her do it again, and every t'ree or fo' nights he walked her out in the shed and she tole herself it's gonna be over soon, he gonna get tired of me and then me and Cool Breeze gonna be left alone, and when he got finished wit' her and made her hate herself and hate my boy, too, another white man come along and give her presents and took her to his bed and tole her t'ings to tell Cool Breeze so he'd know he wasn't nothing but a

nigger and a nigger's wife is a white man's jelly roll whenever
he want it."

"Shake it off and zip up your pants," the man with whiskers said.

"You cain't get my boy fair. He'll cut yo' ass."

"You better shut up, old man."

"White trash wit' a gun and a big truck. Seen y'all all my life. Got
to shove niggers round or you don't know who you are."

The man with whiskers pushed Mout' toward the shack, surprised
at the power and breadth of muscle in Mout's back.

"I might have underestimated you. Don't take that as good news,"
he said.

M out' woke just before first light. The dog lay in his lap, its coat
stiff with mud. The two white men sat in chairs facing the
front door, their shoulders slightly rounded, their chins dropping to
their chests. The man with the shotgun opened his eyes suddenly, as
though waking from a dream.

"Wake up," he said.

"What is it?"

"Nothing. That's the point. I don't want to drive out of here in
sunlight."

The man with whiskers rubbed the sleep out of his face.

"Bring the truck up," he said.

The man with the shotgun looked in Mout's direction, as if asking
a question.

"I'll think about it," the man with whiskers said.

"It's mighty loose, Harpo."

"Every time I say something, you got a remark to make."

The man with the shotgun rewrapped the bloody handkerchief on
his hand. He rose from the chair and threw the shotgun to his friend.
"You can use my raincoat if you decide to do business," he said, and
went out into the dawn.

Mout' waited in the silence.

"What do you think we ought to do about you?" the man with
whiskers asked.

"Don't matter what happen here. One day the devil gonna come for y'all, take you where you belong."

"You got diarrhea of the mouth."

"My boy better than both y'all. He outsmarted you. He know y'all here. He out there now. Cool Breeze gonna come after you, Mr. White Trash."

"Stand up, you old fart."

Mout' pushed himself to his feet, his back against the plank wall. He could feel his thighs quivering, his bladder betraying him. Outside, the sun had risen into a line of storm clouds that looked like the brow of an angry man.

The man with whiskers held the shotgun against his hip and fired one barrel into Mout's dog, blowing it like a bag of broken sticks and torn skin into the corner.

"Get a cat. They're a lot smarter animals," he said, and went out the door and crossed the board walkway to the levee where his friend sat on the fender of their pickup truck, smoking a cigarette.

TEN

"Cool Breeze run out of gas. That's why he didn't come back to the camp," Mout' said.

It was Wednesday afternoon, and Helen and I sat with Mout' in his small living room, listening to his story.

"What'd the Vermilion Parish deputies say?" Helen asked.

"Man wrote on his clipboa'd. Said it was too bad about my dog. Said I could get another one at the shelter. I ax him, 'What about them two men?' He said it didn't make no sense they come into my camp to kill a dog. I said, 'Yeah, it don't make no sense 'cause you wasn't listening to the rest of it.' "

"Where's Cool Breeze, Mout'?"

"Gone."

"Where?"

"To borrow money."

"Come on, Mout'," I said.

"To buy a gun. Cool Breeze full of hate, Mr. Dave. Cool Breeze don't show it, but he don't forgive. What bother me is the one he don't forgive most is himself."

. . .

Back at my office, I called Special Agent Adrien Glazier at the FBI office in New Orleans.

"Two white men, one with the first name of Harpo, tried to clip Willie Broussard at a fish camp in Vermilion Parish," I said.

"When was this?"

"Last night."

"Is there a federal crime involved here?"

"Not that I know of. Maybe crossing a state line to commit a felony."

"You have evidence of that?"

"No."

"Then why are you calling, Mr. Robicheaux?"

"His life's in jeopardy."

"We're not unaware of the risk he's incurred as a federal witness. But I'm busy right now. I'll have to call you back," she said.

"You're busy?"

The line went dead.

A uniformed deputy picked up Cool Breeze in front of a pawn-shop on the south side of New Iberia and brought him into my office.

"Why the cuffs?" I said.

"Ask him what he called me when I told him to get in the cruiser," the deputy replied.

"Take them off, please."

"By all means. Glad to be of service. You want anything else?" the deputy said, and turned a tiny key in the lock on the cuffs.

"Thanks for bringing him in."

"Oh, yeah, anytime. I always had aspirations to be a bus driver," he said, and went out the door, his eyes flat.

"Who you think is on your side, Breeze?" I said.

"Me."

"I see. Your daddy says you're going to get even. How you going to do that? You know who these guys are, where they live?"

He was sitting in the chair in front of my desk now, looking out the window, his eyes downturned at the corners.

"Did you hear me?" I said.

"You know how come one of them had a raincoat on?" he said.

"He didn't want the splatter on his clothes."

"You know why they left my daddy alive?"

I didn't reply. His gaze was still focused out the window. His hands looked like black starfish on his thighs.

"Long as Mout's alive, I'll probably be staying at his house," he said. "Mout' don't mean no more to them than a piece of nutria meat tied in a crab trap."

"You didn't answer my question."

"Them two men who killed the white boys out in the Basin? They ain't did that in St. Mary Parish without permission. Not to no white boys, they didn't. And it sure didn't have nothing to do with any black girl they raped in New Iberia."

"What are you saying?"

"Them boys was killed 'cause of something they done right there in St. Mary."

"So you think the same guys are trying to do you, and you're going to find them by causing some trouble over in St. Mary Parish? Sounds like a bad plan, Breeze."

His eyes fastened on mine for the first time, his anger unmasked. "I ain't said that. I was telling you how it work round here. Blind hog can find an ear of corn if you t'row it on the ground. But you tell white folks grief comes down from the man wit' the money, they ain't gonna hear that. You done wit' me now, suh?"

Late that same afternoon, an elderly priest named Father James Mulcahy called me from St. Peter's Church in town. He used to have a parish made up of poor and black people in the Irish Channel, and had even known Clete Purcel when Clete was a boy, but he had been transferred by the Orleans diocese to New Iberia, where he did little more than say Mass and occasionally hear confessions.

"There's a lady here. I thought she came for reconciliation. But I'm not even sure she's Catholic," he said.

"I don't understand, Father."

"She seems confused, I think in need of counseling. I've done all I can for her."

"You want me to talk to her?"

"I suspect so. She won't leave."

"Who is she?"

"Her name is Lila Terrebonne. She says she lives in Jeanerette."

Helen Soileau got in a cruiser with me and we drove to St. Peter's. The late sun shone through the stained glass and suffused the interior of the church with a peculiar gold-and-blue light. Lila Terrebonne sat in a pew by the confessional boxes, immobile, her hands in her lap, her eyes as unseeing as a blind person's. An enormous replication of Christ on the cross hung on the adjacent wall.

At the vestibule door Father Mulcahy placed his hand on my arm. He was a frail man, his bones as weightless as a bird's inside his skin.

"This lady carries a deep injury. The nature of her problem is complex, but be assured it's of the kind that destroys people," he said.

"She's an alcoholic, Father. Is that what we're talking about here?" Helen said.

"What she told me wasn't in a sacramental situation, but I shouldn't say any more," he replied.

I walked up the aisle and sat in the pew behind Lila.

"You ever have a guy try to pick you up in church before?" I asked.

She turned and stared at me, her face cut by a column of sunshine. The powder and down on her cheeks glowed as though illuminated by klieg lights. Her milky green eyes were wide with expectation that seemed to have no source.

"I was just thinking about you," she said.

"I bet."

"We're all going to die, Dave."

"You're right. But probably not today. Let's take a ride."

"It's strange I'd end up sitting here under the Crucifixion. Do you know the Hanged Man in the Tarot?"

"Sure," I said.

"That's the death card."

"No, it's St. Sebastian, a Roman soldier who was martyred for his faith. It represents self-sacrifice," I said.

"The priest wouldn't give me absolution. I'm sure I was baptized Catholic before I was baptized Protestant. My mother was a Catholic," she said.

Helen stood at the end of Lila's pew, chewing gum, her thumbs hooked in her gunbelt. She rested three fingers on Lila's shoulders.

"How about taking us to dinner?" she said.

An hour later we crossed the parish line into St. Mary. The air was mauve-colored, the bayou dimpled with the feeding of bream, the wind hot and smelling of tar from the highway. We drove up the brick-paved drive of the Terrebonne home. Lila's father stood on the portico, a cigar in his hand, his shoulder propped against a brick pillar.

I pulled the cruiser to a stop and started to get out.

"Stay here, Dave. I'm going to take Lila to the door," Helen said.

"That isn't necessary. I'm feeling much better now. I shouldn't have had a drink with that medication. It always makes me a bit otherworldly," Lila said.

"Your father doesn't like us, Lila. If he wants to say something, he should have the chance," Helen said.

But evidently Archer Terrebonne was not up to confronting Helen Soileau that evening. He took a puff from his cigar, then walked inside and closed the heavy door audibly behind him.

The portico and brick parking area were deep in shadow now, the gold and scarlet four-o'clock flowers in full bloom. Helen walked toward the portico with her arm around Lila's shoulders, then watched her go in the house and close the door. Helen continued to look at the door, working the gum in her jaw, the flat of one hand pushed down in the back of her gunbelt.

She opened the passenger door and got in.

"I'd say leapers and vodka," I said.

"No odor, fried terminals. Yeah, that sounds right. Great combo for a coronary," she replied.

I turned around in front of the house and drove toward the service road and the bridge over the bayou. Helen kept looking over the seat through the rear window.

"I wanted to kick her old man's ass. With a baton, broken teeth and bones, a real job," she said. "Not good, huh, bwana?"

"He's one of those guys who inspire thoughts like that. I wouldn't worry about it."

"I had him made for a child molester. I was wrong. That woman's been raped, Dave."

ELEVEN

The next morning I called Clete Purcel in New Orleans, signed out of the office for the day, and drove across the elevated highway that spanned the chain of bays in the Atchafalaya Basin, across the Mississippi bridge at Baton Rouge, then down through pasture country and the long green corridor through impassable woods that tapered into palmettos and flooded cypress on the north side of Lake Pontchartrain. Then I was at the French Quarter exit, with the sudden and real urban concern of having to park anywhere near the Iberville Welfare Project.

I left my truck off Decatur, two blocks from the Cafe du Monde, and crossed Jackson Square into the shade of Pirates Alley between the lichen-stained garden of the Cathedral and the tiny bookstore that had once been the home of William Faulkner. Then I walked on down St. Ann, in sunlight again, to a tan stucco building with an arched entrance and a courtyard and a grilled balcony upstairs that dripped bougainvillea, where Clete Purcel kept his private investigative agency and sometimes lived.

"You want to take down Jimmy Fig? How hard?" he said.

"We don't have to bounce him off the furniture, if that's what you mean."

Clete wore a pressed seersucker suit with a tie, and his hair had just been barbered and parted on the side and combed straight down on his head so that it looked like a little boy's.

"Jimmy Figorelli is a low-rent sleaze. Why waste time on a shit bag?" he said.

"It's been a slow week."

He looked at me with the flat, clear-eyed pause that always indicated his unbelief in what I was saying. Through the heavy bubbled yellow glass in his doors, I saw Megan Flynn walk down the stairs in blue jeans and a T-shirt and carry a box through the breezeway to a U-Haul trailer on the street.

"She's helping me move," Clete said.

"Move where?"

"A little cottage between New Iberia and Jeanerette. I'm going to head security at that movie set."

"Are you crazy? That director or producer or whatever he is, Billy Holtzner, is the residue you pour out of spittoons."

"I ran security for Sally Dio at Lake Tahoe. I think I can handle it."

"Wait till you meet Holtzner's daughter and boyfriend. They're hypes, or at least she is. Come on, Clete. You were the best cop I ever knew."

Clete turned his ring on his finger. It was made of gold and silver and embossed with the globe and anchor of the U.S. Marine Corps.

"Yeah, 'was' the best cop. I got to change and help Megan. Then we'll check out Jimmy Fig. I think we're firing in the well, though," he said.

After he had gone upstairs I looked out the back window at the courtyard, the dry wishing well that was cracked and never retained water, the clusters of untrimmed banana trees, Clete's rust-powdered barbells that he religiously pumped and curled, usually half full of booze, every afternoon. I didn't hear Megan open the door to the breezeway behind me.

"What'd you say to get him upset?" she asked. She was perspiring from her work and her T-shirt was damp and shaped against her breasts. She stood in front of the air-conditioning unit and lifted the hair off the back of her neck.

"I think you're sticking tacks in his head," I said.

"Where the hell you get off talking to me like that?"

"Your brother's friends are scum."

"Two-thirds of the world is. Grow up."

"Boxleiter and I had a talk. The death photo of the black guy in the drainpipe was a setup."

"You're full of shit, Dave."

We stared at each other in the refrigerated coolness of the room, almost slit-eyed with antagonism. Her eyes had a reddish-brown cast in them like fire inside amber glass.

"I think I'll wait outside," I said.

"You know what homoeroticism is? Guys who aren't quite gay but who've got a yen they never deal with?" she said.

"You'd better not hurt him."

"Oh, yeah?" she said, and stepped toward me, her hands shoved in her back pockets like a baseball manager getting in an umpire's face. Her neck was sweaty and ringed with dirt and her upper lip was beaded with moisture. "I'm not going to take your bullshit, Dave. You go fuck yourself." Then her face, which was heart-shaped and tender to look at and burning with anger at the same time, seemed to go out of focus. *"Hurt* him? My father was nailed alive to a board wall. You lecture me on hurting people? Don't you feel just a little bit embarrassed, you self-righteous sonofabitch?"

I walked outside into the sunshine. Sweat was running out of my hair; the backdraft of a passing sanitation truck enveloped me with dust and the smell of decaying food. I wiped my forehead on my sleeve and was repelled by my own odor.

Clete and I drove out of the Quarter, crossed Canal, and headed up Magazine in his convertible. He had left the top down while the car had been parked on the street and the seats and metal surfaces were like the touch of a clothes iron. He drove with his left hand, his right clenched around a can of beer wrapped in a paper sack.

"You want to forget it?" I asked.

"No, you want to see the guy, we see the guy."

"I heard Jimmy Fig wasn't a bad kid before he was at Khe Sanh."

"Yeah, I heard that story. He got wounded and hooked on morphine. Makes great street talk. I'll tell you another story. He was the wheelman on a jewelry store job in Memphis. It should have been an easy in-and-out, smash-and-grab deal, except the guys with him decided they didn't want witnesses, so they executed an eighty-year-old Jew who had survived Bergen-Belsen."

"I apologize to you and Megan for what I said back there."

"I've got hypertension, chronic obesity, and my own rap sheet at NOPD. What do guys like us care about stuff like that?"

He pressed his aviator glasses against his nose, hiding his eyes. Sweat leaked out of his porkpie hat and glistened on his flexed jaw.

Jimmy Figorelli ran a sandwich shop and cab stand on Magazine just below Audubon Park. He was a tall, kinetic, wired man, with luminous black eyes and black hair that grew in layers on his body.

He was chopping green onions in an apron and never missed a beat when we entered the front door and stood under the bladed ceiling fan that turned overhead.

"You want to know who put a hit on Cool Breeze Broussard? You come to my place of business and ask me a question like that, like you need the weather report or something?" He laughed to himself and raked the chopped onions off the chopping board onto a sheet of wax paper and started slicing a boned roast into strips.

"The guy doesn't deserve what's coming down on him, Jimmy. Maybe you can help set it right," I said.

"The guys you're interested in don't fax me their day-to-day operations," he replied.

Clete kept lifting his shirt up from his shoulders with his fingers.

"I got a terrible sunburn, Jimmy. I want to be back in the air-conditioning with a vodka and tonic, not listening to a shuck that might cause a less patient person to come around behind that counter," Clete said.

Jimmy Figorelli scratched an eyebrow, took off his apron and picked up a broom and began sweeping up green sawdust from around an ancient Coca-Cola cooler that sweated with coldness.

"What I heard is the clip went to some guys already got it in for Broussard. It's nigger trouble, Purcel. What else can I tell you? *Semper fi,*" he said.

"I heard you were in the First Cav at Khe Sanh," I said.

"Yeah, I was on a Jolly Green that took a RPG through the door. You know what I think all that's worth?"

"You paid dues lowlifes don't. Why not act like it?" I said.

"I got a Purple Heart with a *V* for valor. If I ever find it while I'm cleaning out my garage, I'll send it to you," he said.

I could hear Clete breathing beside me, almost feel the oily heat his skin gave off.

"You know what they say about the First Cav patch, Jimmy. 'The horse they couldn't ride, the line they couldn't cross, the color that speaks for itself,' " Clete said.

"Yeah, well, kiss my ass, you Irish prick, and get out of my store."

"Let's go," I said to Clete.

He stared at me, his face flushed, the skin drawn back against the eye sockets. Then he followed me outside, where we stood under an oak and watched one of Jimmy Fig's cabs pick up a young black woman who carried a red lacquered purse and wore a tank top and a miniskirt and white fishnet stockings.

"You didn't like what I said?" Clete asked.

"Why get on the guy's outfit? It's not your way."

"You got a point. Let me correct that."

He walked back inside, his hands at his sides, balled into fists as big as hams.

"Hey, Jimmy, I didn't mean anything about the First Cav. I just can't take the way you chop onions. It irritates the hell out of me," he said.

Then he drove his right fist, lifting his shoulder and all his weight into the blow, right into Jimmy Figorelli's face.

Jimmy held on to the side of the Coca-Cola box, his hand trembling uncontrollably on his mouth, his eyes dilated with shock, his fingers shining with blood and bits of teeth.

Three days later it began to rain, and it rained through the Labor Day weekend and into the following week. The bayou by the dock rose above the cattails and into the canebrake, my rental boats filled with water, and moccasins crawled into our yard. On Saturday night, during a downpour, Father James Mulcahy knocked on our front door.

He carried an umbrella and wore a Roman collar and a rain-flecked gray suit and a gray fedora. When he stepped inside he tried not to breathe into my face.

"I'm sorry for coming out without calling first," he said.

"We're glad you dropped by. Can I offer you something?" I said.

He touched at his mouth and sat down in a stuffed chair. The rain was blowing against the gallery, and the tin roof of the bait shop quivered with light whenever thunder was about to roll across the swamp.

"Would you like a drink, sir?" I asked.

"No, no, that wouldn't be good. Coffee's fine. I have to tell you about something, Mr. Robicheaux. It bothers me deeply," he said.

His hands were liver-spotted, ridged with blue veins, the skin as thin as parchment on the bones. Bootsie brought coffee and sugar and hot milk on a tray from the kitchen. When the priest lifted the cup to his mouth his eyes seemed to look through the steam at nothing, then he said, "Do you believe in evil, Mr. Robicheaux? I don't mean the wicked deeds we sometimes do in a weak moment. I mean evil in the darkest theological sense."

"I'm not sure, Father. I've seen enough of it in people not to look for a source outside of ourselves."

"I was a chaplain in Thailand during the Vietnam War. I knew a young soldier who participated in a massacre. You might have seen the pictures. The most unforgettable was of a little boy holding his grandmother's skirts in terror while she begged for their lives. I spent many hours with that young soldier, but I could never remove the evil that lived in his dreams."

"I don't understand how—" I began.

He raised his hand. "Listen to me," he said. "There was another man, a civilian profiteer who lived on the air base. His corporation made incendiary bombs. I told him the story of the young soldier who had machine-gunned whole families in a ditch. The profiteer's rejoinder was to tell me about a strafing gun his company had patented. In thirty seconds it could tear the sod out of an entire football field. In that moment I think that man's eyes were the conduit into the abyss."

Bootsie's face wore no expression, but I saw her look at me, then back at the priest.

"Please have dinner with us," she said.

"Oh, I've intruded enough. I really haven't made my point either. Last night in the middle of the storm a truck stopped outside the rectory. I thought it was a parishioner. When I opened the door a man in a slouch hat and raincoat was standing there. I've never felt the presence of evil so strongly in my life. I was convinced he was there to kill me. I think he would have done it if the housekeeper and Father Lemoyne hadn't walked up behind me.

"He pointed his arm at me and said, 'Don't you break the seal.' Then he got back in his truck and drove away with the lights off."

"You mean divulge the content of a confession?" I asked.

"He was talking about the Terrebonne woman. I'm sure of it. But what she told me wasn't under the seal," he replied.

"You want to tell me about Lila, Father?" I said.

"No, it wouldn't be proper. A confidence is a confidence. Also, she wasn't entirely coherent and I might do her a great disservice," he said. But his face clouded, and it was obvious his own words did little to reassure him.

"This man in the truck, Father? If his name is Harpo, we want to be very careful of him," I said.

"His eyes," the priest said.

"Sir?"

"They were like the profiteer's. Without moral light. A man like that speaking of the confessional seal. It offends something in me in a way I can't describe."

"Have dinner with us," I said.

"Yes, that's very kind of you. Your home seems to have a great warmth to it. From outside it truly looked like a haven in the storm. Could I have that drink after all?"

He sat at the table with a glass of cream sherry, his eyes abstract, feigning attention, like those of people who realize that momentary refuge and the sharing of fear with others will not relieve them of the fact that death may indeed have taken up residence inside them.

Monday morning I drove down Bayou Teche through Jeanerette into the little town of Franklin and talked to the chief of police. He was a very light mulatto in his early forties who wore sideburns and a gold ring in his ear and a lacquered-brim cap on the back of his head.

"A man name of Harpo? There used to be a Harpo Delahoussey. He was a sheriff's deputy, did security at the Terrebonne cannery," the police chief said.

"That's not the one. This guy was maybe his nephew. He was a Franklin police officer. People called him Little Harpo," I said.

He fiddled with a pencil and gazed out the window. It was still raining, and a black man rode a bicycle down the sidewalk, his body framed against the smoky neon of a bar across the street.

"When I was a kid there was a cop round here name of H. Q. Scruggs." He wet his lips. "When he come into the quarters we knew to call him Mr. H.Q. Not Officer. That wasn't enough for this gentleman. But I remember white folks calling him Harpo sometimes. As I recall, he'd been a guard up at Angola, too. If you want to talk about him, I'll give you the name and address of a man might hep you."

"You don't care to talk about him?"

He laid the pencil flat on his desk blotter. "I don't like to even remember him. Fortunately today I don't have to," he said.

. . .

Clem Maddux sat on his gallery, smoking a cigarette, in a sway-back deer-hide chair lined with a quilt for extra padding. One of his legs was amputated at the torso, the other above the knee. His girth was huge, his stomach pressing in staggered layers against the oversized ink-dark blue jeans he wore. His skin was as pink and un-blemished as a baby's, but around his neck goiters hung from his flesh like a necklace of duck's eggs.

"You staring at me, Mr. Robicheaux?" he asked.

"No, sir."

"It's Buerger's Disease. Smoking worsens it. But I got diabetes and cancer of the prostate, too. I got diseases that'll outlive the one that kills me," he said, then laughed and wiped spittle off his lips with his wrist.

"You were a gun bull at Angola with Harpo Scruggs?"

"No, I was head of farm machinery. I didn't carry a weapon. Harpo was a tower guard, then a shotgun guard on horseback. That must have been forty years ago."

"What kind of hack was he?"

"Piss-poor in my opinion. How far back you go?"

"You talking about the Red Hat gang and the men buried under the levee?"

"There was this old fart used to come off a corn-whiskey drunk meaner than a razor in your shoe. He'd single out a boy from his gang and tell him to start running. Harpo asked to get in on it."

"Asked to kill someone?"

"It was a colored boy from Laurel Hill. He'd sassed the field boss at morning count. When the food truck come out to the levee at noon, Harpo pulled the colored boy out of the line and told him he wasn't eating no lunch till he finished sawing a stump out of the river bottom. Harpo walked him off into some gum trees by the water, then I seen the boy starting off on his own, looking back uncertain-like while Harpo was telling him something. Then I heard it, *pow, pow,* both barrels. Double-ought bucks, from not more than eight or ten feet."

Maddux tossed his cigarette over the railing into the flower bed.

"What happened to Scruggs?" I asked.

"He done a little of this, a little of that, I guess."

"That's a little vague, cap."

"He road-ganged in Texas a while, then bought into a couple of whorehouses. What do you care anyway? The sonofabitch is probably squatting on the coals."

"He's squatting—"

"He got burned up with a Mexican chippy in Juárez fifteen years ago. Wasn't nothing left of him except a bag of ash and some teeth. Damn, son, y'all ought to update and get you some computers."

TWELVE

Two days later I sat at my desk, sifting through the Gypsy fortune-telling deck called the Tarot. I had bought the deck at a store in Lafayette, but the instruction book that accompanied it dealt more with the meaning of the cards than with the origins of their iconography. Regardless, it would be impossible for anyone educated in a traditional Catholic school not to recognize the historical associations of the imagery in the Hanged Man.

The phone on my desk buzzed.

"Clete Purcel and Megan Flynn just pulled up," the sheriff said.

"Yeah?"

"Get him out of here."

"Skipper—"

He hung up.

A moment later Clete tapped on my glass and opened the door, then paused and looked back down the hall, his face perplexed.

"What happened, the john overflow in the waiting room again?" he said.

"Why's that?"

"A pall is hanging over the place every time I walk in. What do those guys do for kicks, watch snuff films? In fact, I asked the dispatcher that. Definitely no sense of humor."

He sat down and looked around my office, grinned at me for no reason, straightened his back, flexed his arms, bounced his palms up and down on the chair.

"Megan's with you?" I said.

"How'd you know that?"

"Uh, I think the sheriff saw y'all from his window."

"The sheriff? I get it. He told you to roll out the welcome wagon." His eyes roved merrily over my face. "How about we treat you to lunch at Lagniappe Too?"

"I'm buried."

"Megan gave you her drill instructor impersonation the other day?"

"It's very convincing."

He beat out a staccato with his hands on the chair arms.

"Will you stop that and tell me what's on your mind?" I said.

"This cat Billy Holtzner. I've seen him somewhere. Like from Vietnam."

"Holtzner?"

"So we had nasty little marshmallows over there, too. Anyway, I go, 'Were you in the Crotch?' He says, 'The Crotch?' I say, 'Yeah, the Marine Corps. Were you around Da Nang?' What kind of answer do I get? He sucks his teeth and goes back to his clipboard like I'm not there."

He waited for me to speak. When I didn't he said, *"What?"*

"I hate to see you mixed up with them."

"See you later, Streak."

"I'm coming with you," I said, and stuck the Hanged Man in my shirt pocket.

We ate lunch at Lagniappe Too, just down from The Shadows. Megan sat by the window with her hat on. Her hair was curved on her cheeks, and her mouth looked small and red when she took a piece of food off her fork. The light through the window seemed to frame her silhouette against the green wall of bamboo that grew in front of The Shadows. She saw me staring at her.

"Is something troubling you, Dave?" she asked.

"You know Lila Terrebonne?"

"The senator's granddaughter?"

"She comes to our attention on occasion. The other day we had to pick her up at the church, sitting by herself under a crucifix. Out of nowhere she asked me about the Hanged Man in the Tarot."

I slipped the card out of my shirt pocket and placed it on the tablecloth by Megan's plate.

"Why tell me?" she said.

"Does it mean something to you?"

I saw Clete lower his fork into his plate, felt his eyes fix on the side of my face.

"A man hanging upside down from a tree. The tree forms a cross," Megan said.

"The figure becomes Peter the Apostle, as well as Christ and St. Sebastian. Sebastian was tied to a tree and shot with darts by his fellow Roman soldiers. Peter asked to be executed upside down. You notice, the figure makes a cross with his legs in the act of dying?" I said.

Megan had stopped eating. Her cheeks were freckled with discoloration, as though an invisible pool of frigid air had burned her face.

"What is this, Dave?" Clete said.

"Maybe nothing," I said.

"Just lunch conversation?" he said.

"The Terrebonnes have had their thumbs in lots of pies," I said.

"Will you excuse me, please?" Megan said.

She walked between the tables to the rest room, her purse under her arm, her funny straw hat crimped across the back of her red hair.

"What the hell's the matter with you?" Clete said.

That evening I drove to Red Lerille's Health & Racquet Club in Lafayette and worked out with free weights and on the Hammer-Strength machines, then ran two miles on the second-story track that overlooked the basketball courts.

I hung my towel around my neck and did leg stretches on the handrail. Down below, some men were playing a pickup basketball game, thudding into one another clumsily, slapping one another's shoulders when they made a shot. But an Indonesian or Malaysian man at the end of the court, where the speed and heavy bags were hung, was involved in a much more intense and solitary activity. He wore sweats and tight red leather gloves, the kind with a metal dowel across the palm, and he ripped his fists into the heavy bag and sent it spinning on the chain, then speared it with his feet, hard enough to almost knock down a kid who was walking by.

He grinned at the boy by way of apology, then moved over to the speed bag and began whacking it against the rebound board, without rhythm or timing, slashing it for the effect alone.

"You were at Cisco's house. You're Mr. Robicheaux," a woman's voice said behind me.

It was Billy Holtzner's daughter. But her soapy blue eyes were focused now, actually pleasant, like a person who has stepped out of one identity into another.

"You remember me?" she asked.

"Sure."

"We didn't introduce ourselves the other day. I'm Geraldine Holtzner. The boxer down there is Anthony. He's an accountant for the studio. I'm sorry for our rudeness."

"You weren't rude."

"I know you don't like my father. Not many people do. We're not problem visitors here. If you have one, it's Cisco Flynn," she said.

"Cisco?"

"He owes my father a lot of money. Cisco thinks he can avoid his responsibilities by bringing a person like Swede Boxleiter around."

She gripped the handrail and extended one leg at a time behind her. Her wild, brownish-red hair shimmered with perspiration.

"You let that guy down there shoot you up?" I asked.

"I'm all right today. Sometimes I just have a bad day. You're a funny guy for a cop. You ever have a screen test?"

"Why not get rid of the problem altogether?"

But she wasn't listening now. "This area is full of violent people. It's the South. It lives in the woodwork down here. This black man who's coming after the Terrebonnes, why don't you do something about him?" she said.

"Which black man? Are you talking about Cool Breeze Broussard?"

"Which? Yeah, that's a good question. You know the story about the murdered slave woman, the children who were poisoned? If I had stuff like that in my family, I'd jump off a cliff. No wonder Lila Terrebonne's a drunk."

"It was nice seeing you," I said.

"Gee, why don't you just say fuck you and turn your back on people?"

Her skin was the color of milk that has browned in a pan, her blue eyes dancing in her face. She wiped her hair and throat with a towel and threw it at me.

"That kick-boxing stuff Anthony's doing? He learned it from me," she said.

Then she raised her face up into mine, her lips slightly parted, speckled with saliva, her eyes filled with anticipation and need.

On the way back home I stopped in the New Iberia city library and looked up a late-nineteenth-century reminiscence written about our area by a New England lady named Abigail Dowling, a nurse who came here during a yellow fever epidemic and was radicalized not by slavery itself and the misery it visited upon the black race but by what she called its dehumanizing effects on the white.

One of the families about which she wrote in detail was the Terrebonnes of St. Mary Parish.

Before the Civil War, Elijah Terrebonne had been a business partner in the slave trade with Nathan Bedford Forrest and later had ridden at Forrest's side during the battle of Brice's Crossing, where a minié shattered his arm and took him out of the war. But Elijah had also been below the bluffs at Fort Pillow when black troops who

begged on their knees were executed at point-blank range in retalia-
tion for a sixty-mile scorched-earth sweep by Federal troops into
northern Mississippi.

"He was of diminutive stature, with a hard, compact body. He sat
his horse with the rigidity of a clothes pin," Abigail Dowling wrote in
her journal. "His countenance was handsome, certainly, of a rosy hue,
and it exuded a martial light when he talked of the War. In consideration of his physical stature I tried to overlook his imperious manner.
In spite of his propensity for miscegenation, he loved his wife and their
twin girls and was unduly possessive about them, perhaps in part
because of his own romantic misdeeds.

"Unfortunately for the poor black souls on his plantation, the
lamps of charity and pity did not burn brightly in his heart. I have
been told General Forrest tried to stop the slaughter of negro soldiers
below the bluffs. I believe Elijah Terrebonne had no such redemptive
memory for himself. I believe the fits of anger that made him draw
human blood with a horse whip had their origins in the faces of dead
black men who journeyed nightly to Elijah's bedside, vainly begging
mercy from one who had murdered his soul."

The miscegenation mentioned by Abigail Dowling involved a
buxom slave woman named Lavonia, whose husband, Big Walter, had
been killed by a falling tree. Periodically Elijah Terrebonne rode to the
edge of the fields and called her away from her work, in view of the
other slaves and the white overseer, and walked her ahead of his horse
into the woods, where he copulated with her in an unused sweet
potato cellar. Later, he heard that the overseer had been talking freely
in the saloon, joking with a drink in his hand at the fireplace, stoking
the buried resentment and latent contempt of other landless whites
about the lust of his employer. Elijah laid open his face with a quirt
and adjusted his situation by moving Lavonia up to the main house as a
cook and a wet nurse for his children.

But when he returned from Brice's Crossing, with pieces of bone
still working their way out of the surgeon's incision in his arm, the
Teche country was occupied, his house and barns looted, the orchards
and fields reduced to soot blowing in the wind. The only meat on the

plantation consisted of seven smoked hams Lavonia had buried in the woods before the Federal flotilla had come up the Teche.

The Terrebonnes made coffee out of acorns and ate the same meager rations as the blacks. Some of the freed males on the plantation went to work on shares; others followed the Yankee soldiers marching north into the Red River campaign. When the food ran out, Lavonia was among a group of women and elderly folk who were assembled in front of their cabins by Elijah Terrebonne and then told they would have to leave.

She went to Elijah's wife.

Abigail Dowling wrote in the journal, "It was a wretched sight, this stout field woman without a husband, with no concept of historical events or geography, about to be cast out in a ruined land filled with night riders and drunken soldiers. Her simple entreaty could not have described her plight more adequately: 'I'se got fo' children, Missy. What's we gonna go? What's I gonna feed them with?' "

Mrs. Terrebonne granted her a one-month reprieve, either to find a husband or to receive help from the Freedmen's Bureau.

The journal continued: "But Lavonia was a sad and ignorant creature who thought guile could overcome the hardness of heart in her former masters. She put cyanide in the family's food, believing they would become ill and dependent upon her for their daily care.

"Both of the Terrebonne girls died. Elijah would have never known the cause of their deaths, except for the careless words of Lavonia's youngest child, who came to him, the worst choice among men, to seek solace. The child blurted out, 'My mama been crying, Mas'er. She got poison in a bottle under her bed. She say the devil give it to her and made her hurt somebody with it. I think she gonna take it herself.'

"By firelight Elijah dug up the coffins of his children from the wet clay and unwound the wrappings from their bodies. Their skin was covered with pustules the color and shape of pearls. He pressed his hand on their chests and breathed the air trapped in their lungs and swore it smelled of almonds.

"His rage and madness could be heard all the way across the fields to the quarters. Lavonia tried to hide with her children in the swamp, but to no avail. Her own people found her, and in fear of Elijah's wrath, they hanged her with a man's belt from a persimmon tree."

What did it all mean? Why did Geraldine Holtzner allude to the story at Red's Gym in Lafayette? I didn't know. But in the morning Megan Flynn telephoned me at the dock. Clete Purcel had been booked on a DWI and a black man had started a fire on the movie set in the Terrebonnes' front yard.

She wanted to talk.

"Talk? Clete's in the bag and you want to talk?" I said.

"I've done something terribly wrong. I'm just down the road. Will it bother you if I come by?"

"Yes, it will."

"Dave?"

"What?"

Then her voice broke.

THIRTEEN

egan sat at a back table in the bait shop with a cup of coffee and waited for me while I rang up the bill on two fishermen who had just finished eating at the counter. Her hat rested by her elbow and her hair blew in the wind from the fan, but there was a twisted light in her eyes, as though she could not concentrate on anything outside her skin.

I sat down across from her.

"Y'all had a fight?" I asked.

"It was over the black man who started the fire," she said.

"That doesn't make any sense," I said.

"It's Cool Breeze Broussard. It has to be. He was going to set fire to the main house but something scared him off. So he poured gasoline under a trailer on the set."

"Why should you and Clete fight over that?"

"I helped get Cool Breeze out of jail. I knew about all his trouble in St. Mary Parish and his wife's suicide and his problems with the Terrebonne family. I wanted the story. I pushed everything else out of my mind . . . Maybe I planted some ideas in him about revenge."

"You still haven't told me why y'all fought."

"Clete said people who set fires deserve to be human candles themselves. He started talking about some marines he saw trapped inside a burning tank."

"Breeze has always had his own mind about things. He's not easily influenced, Megan."

"Swede will kill him. He'll kill anybody he thinks is trying to hurt Cisco."

"That's it, huh? You think you're responsible for getting a black man into it with a psychopath?"

"Yes. And he's not a psychopath. You've got this guy all wrong."

"How about getting Clete into the middle of it? You think that might be a problem, too?"

"I feel very attached—"

"Cut it out, Megan."

"I have a deep—"

"He was available and you made him your point man. Except he doesn't have any idea of what's going on."

Her eyes drifted onto mine, then they began to film. I heard Batist come inside the shop, then go back out.

"Why'd you want to put him on that movie set?" I said.

"My brother. He's mixed up with bad people in the Orient. I think the Terrebonnes are in it, too."

"What do you know about the Terrebonnes?"

"My father hated them."

A customer came in and picked a package of Red Man off the wire rack and left the money on the register. Megan straightened her back and touched at one eye with her finger.

"I called the St. Mary Sheriff's Department. Clete will be arraigned at ten," I said.

"You don't hold me in very high regard, do you?"

"You just made a mistake. Now you've owned up to it. I think you're a good person, Meg."

"What do I do about Clete?"

"My father used to say never treat a brave man as less."

"I wish Cisco and I had never come back here."

But you always do, I thought. *Because of a body arched into wood planks, its blood pooling in the dust, its crusted wounds picked by chickens.*

"What did you say?" she asked.

"Nothing. I didn't say anything."

"I'm going. I'll be at Cisco's house for a spell."

She put a half dollar on the counter for the coffee and walked out the screen door. Then, just before she reached her automobile, she turned and looked back at me. She held her straw hat in her fingers, by her thigh, and with her other hand she brushed her hair back on her head, her face lifted into the sunlight.

Batist flung a bucket full of water across one of the spool tables.

"When they make cow eyes at you, it ain't 'cause they want to go to church, no," he said.

"What?"

"Her daddy got killed when she was li'l. She always coming round to talk to a man older than herself. Like they ain't no other man in New Iberia. You got to go to collitch to figure it out?" he said.

Two hours later Helen and I drove over to Mout' Broussard's house on the west side of town. A black four-door sedan with tinted windows and a phone antenna was parked in the dirt driveway, the back door open. Inside, we could see a man in a dark suit, wearing aviator glasses, unlocking the handcuffs on Cool Breeze Broussard.

Helen and I walked toward the car as Adrien Glazier and two male FBI agents got out with Cool Breeze.

"What's happenin', Breeze?" I said.

"They give me a ride to my daddy's," he replied.

"Your business here needs to wait, Mr. Robicheaux," Adrien Glazier said.

Out of the corner of my eye I saw one of the male agents touch Cool Breeze on the arm with one finger and point for him to wait on the gallery.

"What are you going to do with him?" I asked Adrien Glazier.

"Nothing."

"Breeze is operating out of his depth. You know that. Why are you leaving the guy out there?" I said.

"Has he complained to you? Who appointed you his special oversight person?" she replied.

"You ever hear of a guy named Harpo Scruggs?" I asked.

"No."

"I think he's got the contract on Breeze. Except he's supposed to be dead."

"Then you've got something to work on. In the meantime, we'll handle things here. Thanks for dropping by," the man who had uncuffed Cool Breeze said. He was olive-skinned, his dark blond hair cut short, his opaque demeanor one that allowed him to be arrogant without ever being accountable.

Helen stepped toward him, her feet slightly spread.

"Reality check, you pompous fuck, this is our jurisdiction. We go where we want. You try to run us off an investigation, you're going to be picking up the soap in our jail tonight," she said.

"She's the one busted up Boxleiter," the other male agent said, his elbow hooked over the top of the driver's door, a smile at the edge of his mouth.

"Yes?" she said.

"Impressive . . . Mean shit," he said.

"We're gone," Adrien Glazier said.

"Run this guy Scruggs. He was a gun bull at Angola. Maybe he's hooked up with the Dixie Mafia," I said.

"A dead man? *Right,*" she said, then got in her car with her two colleagues and drove away.

Helen stared after them, her hands on her hips.

"Broussard's the bait tied down under the tree stand, isn't he?" she said.

"That's the way I'd read it," I said.

Cool Breeze watched us from the swing on the gallery. His brogans were caked with mud and he spun a cloth cap on the tip of his index finger.

I sat down on the wood steps and looked out at the street.

"Where's Mout'?" I asked.

"Staying at his sister's."

"You're playing other people's game," I said.

"They gonna know when I'm in town."

"Bad way to think, podna."

I heard the swing creak behind me, then his brogans scuffing the boards under him as the swing moved back and forth. A young woman carrying a bag of groceries walked past the house and the sound of the swing stopped.

"My dead wife Ida, I hear her in my sleep sometimes. Talking to me from under the water, wit' that icy chain wrapped round her. I want to lift her up, out of the silt, pick the ice out of her mout' and eyes. But the chain just too heavy. I pull and pull and my arms is like lead, and all the time they ain't no air getting down to her. You ever have a dream like that?" he said.

I turned and looked at him, my ears ringing, my face suddenly cold.

"I t'ought so. You blame me for what I do?" he said.

That afternoon I made telephone calls to Juárez, Mexico, and to the sheriff's departments in three counties along the Tex-Mex border. No one had any information about Harpo Scruggs or his death. Then an FBI agent in El Paso referred me to a retired Texas Ranger by the name of Lester Cobb. His accent was deep down in his breathing passages, like heated air breaking through the top of oatmeal.

"You knew him?" I said into the receiver.

"At a distance. Which was as close as I wanted to get."

"Why's that?"

"He was a pimp. He run Mexican girls up from Chihuahua."

"How'd he die?"

"They say he was in a hot pillow joint acrost the river. A girl put one in his ear, then set fire to the place and done herself."

"They say?"

"He was wanted down there. Why would he go back into Juárez to get laid? That story never did quite wash for me."

"If he's alive, where would I look for him?"

"Cockfights, cathouses, pigeon shoots. He's the meanest bucket of shit with a badge I ever run acrost . . . Mr. Robicheaux?"

"Yes, sir?"

"I hope he's dead. He rope-drug a Mexican behind his Jeep, out through the rocks and cactus. You get in a situation with him . . . Oh, hell, I'm too damn old to tell another lawman his business."

It rained that evening, and from my lighted gallery I watched it fall on the trees and the dock and the tin roof of the bait shop and on the wide, yellow, dimpled surface of the bayou itself.

I could not shake the images of Cool Breeze's recurring dream from my mind. I stepped out into the rain and cut a half dozen roses from the bushes in the front garden and walked down the slope with them to the end of the dock.

Batist had pulled the tarp out on the guy wires and turned on the string of electric lights. I stood at the railing, watching the current drift southward toward West Cote Blanche Bay and eventually the Gulf, where many years ago my father's drilling rig had punched into an early pay sand, blowing the casing out of the hole. When the gas ignited, a black-red inferno ballooned up through the tower, all the way to the monkey board where my father worked as a derrick man. The heat was so great the steel spars burned and collapsed like matchsticks.

He and my murdered wife Annie and the dead men from my platoon used to speak to me through the rain. I found saloons by the water, always by the water, where I could trap and control light and all meaning inside three inches of Beam, with a Jax on the side, while the rain ran down the windows and rippled the walls with neon shadows that had no color.

Now, Annie and my father and dead soldiers no longer called me up on the phone. But I never underestimated the power of the rain or the potential of the dead, or denied them their presence in the world.

And for that reason I dropped the roses into the water and watched them float toward the south, the green leaves beaded with water as bright as crystal, the petals as darkly red as a woman's mouth turned toward you on the pillow for the final time.

On the way back up to the house I saw Clete Purcel's chartreuse Cadillac come down the dirt road and turn into the drive. The windows were streaked with mud, the convertible top as ragged as a layer of chicken feathers. He rolled down the window and grinned, in the same way that a mask grins.

"Got a minute?" he said.

I opened the passenger door and sat in the cracked leather seat beside him.

"You doing okay, Cletus?" I asked.

"Sure. Thanks for calling the bondsman." He rubbed his face. "Megan came by?"

"Yeah. Early this morning." I kept my eyes focused on the rain blowing out of the trees onto my lighted gallery.

"She told you we were quits?"

"Not exactly."

"I got no bad feelings about it. That's how it shakes out sometimes." He widened his eyes. "I need to take a shower and get some sleep. I'll be okay with some sleep."

"Come in and eat with us."

"I'm keeping the security gig at the set. If you see this guy Broussard, tell him not to set any more fires . . . Don't look at me like that, Streak. The trailer he burned had propane tanks on it. What if somebody had been in there?"

"He thinks the Terrebonnes are trying to have him killed."

"I hope they work it out. In the meantime, tell him to keep his ass off the set."

"You don't want to eat?"

"No. I'm not feeling too good." He looked out into the shadows and the water dripping out of the trees. "I got in over my head. It's my fault. I'm not used to this crap."

"She's got strong feelings for you, Clete."

"Yeah, my temp loves her cat. See you tomorrow, Dave."

I watched him back out into the road, then shift into low, his big head bent forward over the wheel, his expression as meaningless as a jack-o'-lantern's.

After Bootsie and Alafair and I ate dinner, I drove up the Loreauville road to Cisco Flynn's house. When no one answered the bell, I walked the length of the gallery, past the baskets of hanging ferns, and looked through the side yard. In back, inside a screened pavilion, Cisco and Megan were eating steaks at a linen-covered table with Swede Boxleiter. I walked across the grass toward the yellow circle of light made by an outside bug lamp. Their faces were warm, animated with their conversation, their movements automatic when one or the other wanted a dish passed or his silver wine goblet refilled. My loafer cracked a small twig.

"Sorry to interrupt," I said.

"Is that you, Dave? Join us. We have plenty," Cisco said.

"I wanted to see Megan a minute. I'll wait out in my truck," I said.

The three of them were looking out into the darkness, the tossed salad and pink slices of steak on their plates like part of a nineteenth-century French still life. In that instant I knew that whatever differences defined them today, the three of them were held together by a mutual experience that an outsider would never understand. Then Boxleiter broke the moment by picking up a decanter and pouring wine into his goblet, spilling it like drops of blood on the linen.

Ten minutes later Megan found me in the front yard.

"This morning you told me I had Boxleiter all wrong," I said.

"That's right. He's not what he seems."

"He's a criminal."

"To some."

"I saw pictures of the dude he shanked in the Canon City pen."

"Probably courtesy of Adrien Glazier. By the way, the guy you think he did? He was in the Mexican Mafia. He had Swede's cell partner drowned in a toilet . . . This is why you came out here?"

"No, I wanted to tell you I'm going to leave y'all alone. Y'all take your own fall, Megan."

"Who asked you to intercede on our behalf anyway? You're still pissed off about Clete, aren't you?" she said.

I walked across the lawn toward my truck. The wind was loud in the trees and made shadows on the grass. She caught up with me just as I opened the door to the truck.

"The problem is you don't understand your own thinking," she said. "You were raised in the church. You see my father's death as St. Sebastian's martyrdom or something. You believe in forgiving people for what's not yours to forgive. I'd like to take their eyes out."

"Their eyes. Who is *their,* Megan?"

"Every hypocrite in this—" She stopped, stepping back as though retreating from her own words.

"Ah, we finally got to it," I said.

I got in the truck and closed the door. I could hear her heated breathing in the dark, see her chest rise and fall against her shirt. Swede Boxleiter walked out of the side yard into the glow of light from the front gallery, an empty plate in one hand, a meat fork in the other.

FOURTEEN

The tall man who wore yellow-tinted glasses and cowboy boots and a weathered, smoke-colored Stetson made a mistake. While the clerk in a Lafayette pawnshop and gun store bagged up two boxes of .22 magnum shells for him, the man in the Stetson happened to notice a bolt-action military rifle up on the rack.

"That's an Italian 6.5 Carcano, ain't it? Hand it down here and I'll show you something," he said.

He wrapped the leather sling over his left arm, opened the bolt, and inserted his thumb in the chamber to make sure the gun was not loaded.

"This is the same kind Oswald used. Now, here's the mathematics. The shooter up in that book building had to get off three shots in five and a half seconds. You got a stopwatch?" he said.

"No," the clerk said.

"Here, look at my wristwatch. Now, I'm gonna dry-fire it three times. Remember, I ain't even aiming and Oswald was up six stories, shooting at a moving target."

"That's not good for the firing pin," the clerk said.

"It ain't gonna hurt it. It's a piece of shit anyway, ain't it?"

"I wish you wouldn't do that, sir."

The man in the Stetson set the rifle back on the glass counter and pinched his thumb and two fingers inside his Red Man pouch and put the tobacco in his jaw. The clerk's eyes broke when he tried to return the man's stare.

"You ought to develop a historical curiosity. Then maybe you wouldn't have to work the rest of your life at some little pissant job," the man said, and picked up his sack and started for the front door.

The clerk, out of shame and embarrassment, said to the man's back, "How come you know so much about Dallas?"

"I was there, boy. That's a fact. The puff of smoke on the grassy knoll?" He winked at the clerk and went out.

The clerk stood at the window, his face tingling, feeling belittled, searching in his mind for words he could fling out the door but knowing he would not have the courage to do so. He watched the man in the Stetson drive down the street to an upholstery store in a red pickup truck with Texas plates. The clerk wrote down the tag number and called the sheriff's department.

On Friday morning Father James Mulcahy rose just before dawn, fixed two sandwiches and a thermos of coffee in the rectory kitchen, and drove to Henderson Swamp, outside of the little town of Breaux Bridge, where a parishioner had given him the use of a motorized houseboat.

He drove along the hard-packed dirt track atop the levee, above the long expanse of bays and channels and flooded cypress and willows that comprised the swamp. He parked at the bottom of the levee, walked across a board plank to the houseboat, released the mooring ropes, and floated out from the willows into the current before he started the engine.

The clouds in the eastern sky were pink and gray, and the wind lifted the moss on the dead cypress trunks. Inside the cabin, he steered the houseboat along the main channel, until he saw a cove back in the trees where the bream were popping the surface along the edge of the hyacinths. When he turned into the cove and cut the engine, he heard an outboard coming hard down the main channel, the throttle full out, the noise like a chain saw splitting the serenity of the morning. The driver of the outboard did not slow his boat to prevent his wake from washing into the cove and disturbing the water for another fisherman.

Father Mulcahy sat in a canvas chair on the deck and swung the bobber from his bamboo pole into the hyacinths. Behind him, he heard the outboard turning in a circle, heading toward him again. He propped his pole on the rail, put down the sandwich he had just unwrapped from its wax paper, and walked to the other side of the deck.

The man in the outboard killed his engine and floated in to the cove, the hyacinths clustering against the bow. He wore yellow-tinted glasses, and he reached down in the bottom of his boat and fitted on a smoke-colored Stetson that was sweat-stained across the base of the crown. When he smiled his dentures were stiff in his mouth, the flesh of his throat red like a cock's comb. He must have been sixty-five, but he was tall, his back straight, his eyes keen with purpose.

"I'm fixing to run out of gas. Can you spare me a half gallon?" he said.

"Maybe your high speed has something to do with it," Father Mulcahy said.

"I'll go along with that." Then he reached out for an iron cleat on the houseboat as though he had already been given permission to board. Behind the seat was a paper bag stapled across the top and a one-gallon tin gas can.

"I know you," Father Mulcahy said.

"Not from around here you don't. I'm just a visitor, not having no luck with the fish."

"I've heard your voice."

The man stood up in his boat and grabbed the handrail and lowered his face so the brim of his hat shielded it from view.

"I have no gas to give you. It's all in the tank," Father Mulcahy said.

"I got a siphon. Right here in this bag. A can, too."

The man in the outboard put one cowboy boot on the edge of the deck and stepped over the rail, drawing a long leg behind him. He stood in front of the priest, his head tilted slightly as though he were examining a quarry he had placed under a glass jar.

"Show me where your tank's at. Back around this side?" he said, indicating the lee side of the cabin, away from the view of anyone passing on the channel.

"Yes," the priest said. "But there's a lock on it. It's on the ignition key."

"Let's get it, then, Reverend," the man said.

"You know I'm a minister?" Father Mulcahy said.

The man did not reply. He had not shaved that morning, and there were gray whiskers among the red and blue veins in his cheeks. His smile was twisted, one eye squinted behind the lens of his glasses, as though he were arbitrarily defining the situation in his own mind.

"You came to the rectory . . . In the rain," the priest said.

"Could be. But I need you to hep me with this chore. That's our number one job here."

The man draped his arm across the priest's shoulders and walked him inside the cabin. He smelled of deodorant and chewing tobacco, and in spite of his age his arm was thick and meaty, the crook of it like a yoke on the back of the priest's neck.

"Your soul will be forfeit," the priest said, because he could think of no other words to use.

"Yeah, I heard that one before. Usually when a preacher was trying to get me to write a check. The funny thing is, the preacher never wanted Jesus's name on the check."

Then the man in the hat pulled apart the staples on the paper bag he had carried on board and took out a velvet curtain rope and a roll of tape and a plastic bag. He began tying a loop in the end of the rope, concentrating on his work as though it were an interesting, minor task in an ordinary day.

The priest turned away from him, toward the window and the sun breaking through the flooded cypress, his head lowered, his fingers pinched on his eyelids.

The parishioner's sixteen-gauge pump shotgun was propped just to the left of the console. Father Mulcahy picked it up and leveled the barrel at the chest of the man in the Stetson hat and clicked off the safety.

"Get off this boat," he said.

"You didn't pump a shell into it. There probably ain't nothing in the chamber," the man said.

"That could be true. Would you like to find out?"

"You're a feisty old rooster, ain't you?"

"You sicken me, sir."

The man in yellow-tinted glasses reached in his shirt pocket with his thumb and two fingers and filled his jaw with tobacco.

"Piss on you," he said, and opened the cabin door to go back outside.

"Leave the bag," the priest said.

FIFTEEN

The priest called the sheriff's office in St. Martin Parish, where his encounter with the man in the Stetson had taken place, then contacted me when he got back to New Iberia. The sheriff and I interviewed him together at the rectory.

"The bag had a velvet cord and a plastic sack and a roll of tape in it?" the sheriff said.

"That's right. I left it all with the sheriff in St. Martinville," Father Mulcahy said. His eyes were flat, as though discussing his thoughts would only add to the level of degradation he felt.

"You know why he's after you, don't you, Father?" I said.

"Yes, I believe I do."

"You know what he was going to do, too. It would have probably been written off as a heart attack. There would have been no rope burns, nothing to indicate any force or violence," I said.

"You don't have to tell me that, sir," he replied.

"It's time to talk about Lila Terrebonne," I said.

"It's her prerogative to talk with you as much as she wishes. But not mine," he said.

"Hubris isn't a virtue, Father," I said.

His face flared. "Probably not. But I'll be damned if I'll be altered by a sonofabitch like the man who climbed on my boat."

"That's one way of looking at it. Here's my card if you want to put a net over this guy," I said.

When we left, rain that looked like lavender horse tails was falling across the sun. The sheriff drove the cruiser with the window down and ashes blew from his pipe onto his shirt. He slapped at them angrily.

"I want that guy in the hat on a respirator," he said.

"We don't have a crime on that houseboat, skipper. It's not even in our jurisdiction."

"The intended victim is. That's enough. He's a vulnerable old man. Remember when you lived through your first combat and thought you had magic? A dangerous time."

A half hour later a state trooper pulled over a red pickup truck with a Texas tag on the Iberia–St. Martin Parish line.

The sheriff and I stood outside the holding cell and looked at the man seated on the wood bench against the back wall. His western-cut pants were ironed with sharp creases, the hard points of his oxblood cowboy boots buffed to a smooth glaze like melted plastic. He played with his Stetson on his index finger.

The sheriff held the man's driver's license cupped in his palm. He studied the photograph on it, then the man's face.

"You're Harpo Scruggs?" the sheriff asked.

"I was when I got up this morning."

"You're from New Mexico?"

"Deming. I got a chili pepper farm there. The truck's a rental, if that's what's on your mind."

"You're supposed to be dead," the sheriff said.

"You talking about that fire down in Juárez? Yeah, I heard about that. But it wasn't me."

His accent was peckerwood, the Acadian inflections, if they had ever existed, weaned out of it.

"You terrorize elderly clergymen, do you?" I said.

"I asked the man for a can of gas. He pointed a shotgun at me."

"You mind going into a lineup?" the sheriff asked.

Harpo Scruggs looked at his fingernails.

"Yeah, I do. What's the charge?" he said.

"We'll find one," the sheriff said.

"I don't think y'all got a popcorn fart in a windstorm," he said.

He was right. We called Mout' Broussard's home and got no answer. Neither could we find the USL student who had witnessed the execution of the two brothers out in the Atchafalaya Basin. The father of the two brothers was drunk and contradictory about what he had seen and heard when his sons were lured out of the house.

It was 8 P.M. The sheriff sat in his swivel chair and tapped his fingers on his jawbone.

"Call Juárez, Mexico, and see if they've still got a warrant," he said.

"I already did. It was like having a conversation with impaired people in a bowling alley."

"Sometimes I hate this job," he said, and picked up a key ring off his desk blotter.

Ten minutes later the sheriff and I watched Harpo Scruggs walk into the parking lot a free man. He wore a shirt with purple and red flowers on it, and it swelled with the breeze and made his frame look even larger than it was. He fitted on his hat and slanted the brim over his eyes, took a small bag of cookies from his pocket and bit into one of them gingerly with his false teeth. He lifted his face into the breeze and looked with expectation at the sunset.

"See if you can get Lila Terrebonne in my office tomorrow morning," the sheriff said.

Harpo Scruggs's truck drove up the street toward the cemetery. A moment later Helen Soileau's unmarked car pulled into the traffic behind him.

That night Bootsie and I fixed ham and onion sandwiches and dirty rice and iced tea at the drainboard and ate on the breakfast table. Through the hallway I could see the moss in the oak trees glowing against the lights on the dock.

"You look tired," Bootsie said.

"Not really."

"Who's this man Scruggs working for?"

"The New Orleans Mob. The Dixie Mafia. Who knows?"

"The Mob letting one of their own kill a priest?"

"You should have been a cop, Boots."

"There's something you're not saying."

"I keep feeling all this stuff goes back to Jack Flynn's murder."

"The Flynns again." She rose from the table and put her plate in the sink and looked through the window into the darkness at the foot of our property. "Why always the Flynns?" she said.

I didn't have an adequate answer, not even for myself when I lay next to Bootsie later in the darkness, the window fan drawing the night air across our bed. Jack Flynn had fought at the battle of Madrid and at Alligator Creek on Guadalcanal; he was not one to be easily undone by company goons hired to break a farmworkers' strike. But the killers had kidnapped him out of a hotel room in Morgan City, beaten him with chains, impaled his broken body with nails as a lesson in terror to any poor white or black person who thought he could relieve his plight by joining a union. To this day not one suspect had been in custody, not one participant had spoken carelessly in a bar or brothel.

The Klan always prided itself on its secrecy, the arcane and clandestine nature of its rituals, the loyalty of its members to one another. But someone always came forward, out of either guilt or avarice, and told of the crimes they committed in groups, under cover of darkness, against their unarmed and defenseless victims.

But Jack Flynn's murderers had probably not only been protected, they had been more afraid of the people they served than Louisiana or federal law.

Jack Flynn's death was at the center of our current problems because we had never dealt with our past, I thought. And in not doing so, we had allowed his crucifixion to become a collective act.

I propped myself up on the mattress with one elbow and touched Bootsie's hair. She was sound asleep and did not wake. Her eyelids looked like rose petals in the moon's glow.

. . .

arly Saturday morning I turned into the Terrebonne grounds and drove down the oak-lined drive toward the house. The movie set was empty, except for a bored security guard and Swede Boxleiter, who was crouched atop a plank building, firing a nail gun into the tin roof.

I stood under the portico of the main house and rang the chimes. The day had already turned warm, but it was cool in the shade and the air smelled of damp brick and four-o'clock flowers and the mint that grew under the water faucets. Archer Terrebonne answered the door in yellow-and-white tennis clothes, a moist towel draped around his neck.

"Lila's not available right now, Mr. Robicheaux," he said.

"I'd very much like to talk to her, sir."

"She's showering. Then we're going to a brunch. Would you like to leave a message?"

"The sheriff would appreciate her coming to his office to talk about her conversation with Father James Mulcahy."

"Y'all do business in an extraordinary fashion. Her discussions with a minister are the subject of a legal inquiry?"

"This man was almost killed because he's too honorable to divulge something your daughter told him."

"Good day, Mr. Robicheaux," Terrebonne said, and closed the door in my face.

I drove back through the corridor of trees, my face tight with anger. I started to turn out onto the service road, then stopped the truck and walked out to the movie set.

"How's it hangin', Swede?" I said.

He fired the nail gun through the tin roof into a joist and pursed his mouth into an inquisitive cone.

"Where's Clete Purcel?" I asked.

"Gone for the day. You look like somebody pissed in your under-wear."

"You know the layout of this property?"

"I run power cables all over it."

"Where's the family cemetery?"

"Back in those trees."

He pointed at an oak grove and a group of whitewashed brick crypts with an iron fence around it. The grass within the fence was freshly mowed and clipped at the base of the bricks.

"You know of another burial area?" I asked.

"Way in back, a spot full of briars and palmettos. Holtzner says that's where the slaves were planted. Got to watch out for it so the local blacks don't get their ovaries fired up. What's the gig, man? Let me in on it."

I walked to the iron fence around the Terrebonne cemetery. The marble tablet that sealed the opening to the patriarch's crypt was cracked across the face from settlement of the bricks into the softness of the soil, but I could still make out the eroded, moss-stained calligraphy scrolled by a stone mason's chisel: *Elijah Boethius Terrebonne, 1831–1878, soldier for Jefferson Davis, loving father and husband, now brother to the Lord.*

Next to Elijah's crypt was a much smaller one in which his twin girls were entombed. A clutch of wildflowers, tied at the stems with a rubber band, was propped against its face. There were no other flowers in the cemetery.

I walked toward the back of the Terrebonne estate, along the edge of a coulee that marked the property line, beyond the movie set and trailers and sky-blue swimming pool and guest cottages and tennis courts to a woods that was deep in shade, layered with leaves, the tree branches wrapped with morning glory vines and cobweb.

The woods sloped toward a stagnant pond. Among the palmettos were faint depressions, leaf-strewn, sometimes dotted with mushrooms. Was the slave woman Lavonia, who had poisoned Elijah's daughters, buried here? Was the pool of black water, dimpled by dragonflies, part of the swamp she had tried to hide in before she was lynched by her own people?

Why did the story of the exploited and murdered slave woman hang in my mind like a dream that hovers on the edge of sleep?

I heard a footstep in the leaves behind me.

"I didn't mean to give you a start," Lila said.

"Oh, hi, Lila. I bet you put the wildflowers on the graves of the children."

"How did you know?"

"Did your father tell you why I was here?"

"No . . . He . . . We don't always communicate very well."

"A guy named Harpo Scruggs tried to kill Father Mulcahy."

The blood drained out of her face.

"We think it's because of something you told him," I said.

When she tried to speak, her words were broken, as though she could not form a sentence without using one that had already been spoken by someone else. "I told the priest? That's what you're saying?"

"He's taking your weight. Scruggs was going to suffocate him with a plastic bag."

"Oh, Dave—" she said, her eyes watering. Then she ran toward the house, her palms raised in the air like a young girl.

We had just returned from Mass on Sunday morning when the phone rang in the kitchen. It was Clete.

"I'm at a restaurant in Lafayette with Holtzner and his daughter and her boyfriend," he said.

"What are you doing in Lafayette?"

"Holtzner's living here now. He's on the outs with Cisco. They want to come by," he said.

"What for?"

"To make some kind of rental offer on your dock."

"Not interested."

"Holtzner wants to make his pitch anyway. Dave, the guy's my meal ticket. How about it?"

An hour later Clete rolled up to the dock in his convertible, with Holtzner beside him and the daughter and boyfriend following in a Lincoln. The four of them strolled down the dock and sat at a spool table under a Cinzano umbrella.

"Ask the waiter to bring everybody a cold beer," Holtzner said.

"We don't have waiters. You need to get it yourself," I said, standing in the sunlight.

"I got it," Clete said, and went inside the shop.

"We'll pay you a month's lease but we'll be shooting for only two or three days," Anthony, the boyfriend, said. He wore black glasses, and when he smiled the gap in his front teeth gave his face the imbecilic look of a Halloween pumpkin.

"Thanks anyway," I said.

"Thanks? That's it?" Holtzner said.

"He thinks we're California nihilists here to do a culture fuck on the Garden of Eden," Geraldine, the daughter, said to no one.

"You got the perfect place here for this particular scene. Geri's right, you think we're some kind of disease?" Holtzner said.

"You might try up at Henderson Swamp," I said.

Clete came back out of the bait shop screen carrying a round tray with four sweating long-neck bottles on it. He set them one by one on the spool table, his expression meaningless.

"Talk to him," Holtzner said to him.

"I don't mess with Streak's head," Clete said.

"I hear you got Cisco's father on the brain," Holtzner said to me. "His father's death doesn't impress me. My grandfather organized the first garment workers' local on the Lower East Side. They stuck his hands in a stamp press. Irish cops broke up his wake with clubs, took the ice off his body and put it in their beer. They pissed in my grandmother's sink."

"You have to excuse me. I need to get back to work," I said, and walked toward the bait shop. I could hear the wind ruffling the umbrella in the silence, then Anthony was at my side, grinning, his clothes pungent with a smell like burning sage.

"Don't go off in a snit, nose out of joint, that sort of thing," he said.

"I think you have a problem," I said.

"We're talking about chemical dependencies now, are we?"

"No, you're hard of hearing. No offense meant," I said, and went inside the shop and busied myself in back until all of them were gone except Clete, who remained at the table, sipping from his beer bottle.

"Why's Holtzner want to get close to you?" he asked.

"You got me."

"I remembered where I'd seen him. He was promoting USO shows in Nam. Except he was also mixed up with some PX guys who were selling stuff on the black market. It was a big scandal. Holtzner was kicked out of Nam. That's like being kicked out of Hell . . . You just going to sit there and not say anything?"

"Yeah, don't get caught driving with beer on your breath."

Clete pushed his glasses up on his head and drank from his bottle, one eye squinted shut.

That night, in a Lafayette apartment building on a tree-and-fern-covered embankment that overlooked the river, the accountant named Anthony mounted the staircase to the second-story landing and walked through a brick passageway toward his door. The underwater lights were on in the swimming pool, and blue strings of smoke from barbecue grills floated through the palm and banana fronds that shadowed the terrace. Anthony carried a grocery sack filled with items from a delicatessen, probably obscuring his vision, as evidently he never saw the figure that waited for him behind a potted orange tree.

The knife must have struck as fast as a snake's head, in the neck, under the heart, through the breastbone, because the coroner said Anthony was probably dead before the jar of pickled calf brains in his sack shattered on the floor.

SIXTEEN

Helen Soileau and I met Ruby Gravano and her nine-year-old boy at the Amtrak station in Lafayette Monday afternoon. The boy was a strange-looking child, with his mother's narrow face and black hair but with eyes that were set unnaturally far apart, as though they had been pasted on the skin. She held the boy, whose name was Nick, by one hand and her suitcase by the other.

"Is this gonna take long? Because I'm not feeling real good right now," she said.

"There's a female deputy in that cruiser over there, Ruby. She's going to take Nick for some ice cream, then we'll finish with business and take y'all to a bed-and-breakfast in New Iberia. Tomorrow you'll be back on your way," I said.

"Did you get the money bumped up? Houston's a lot more expensive than New Orleans. My mother said I can stay a week free, but then I got to pay her rent," she said.

"Three hundred is all we could do," I said.

Her forehead wrinkled. Then she said, "I don't feel too comfortable standing out here. I don't know how I got talked into this." She looked up and down the platform and fumbled in her bag for a pair of dark glasses.

"You wanted a clean slate in Houston. You were talking about a treatment program. Your idea, not ours, Ruby," Helen said.

The little boy's head rotated like a gourd on a stem as he watched the disappearing train, the people walking to their cars with their luggage, a track crew repairing a switch.

"He's autistic. This is all new to him. Don't look at him like that. I hate this shit," Ruby said, and pulled on the boy's hand as though she were about to leave us, then stopped when she realized she had no place to go except our unmarked vehicle, and in reality she didn't even know where that was.

We put Nick in the cruiser with the woman deputy, then drove to Four Corners and parked across the street from a sprawling red-and-white motel that looked like a refurbished eighteenth-century Spanish fortress.

"How do you know he's in the room?" Ruby said.

"One of our people has been watching him. In five minutes he's going to get a phone call. Somebody's going to tell him smoke is coming out of his truck. All you have to do is look through the binoculars and tell us if that's the john you tricked on Airline Highway," I said.

"You really got a nice way of saying it," she replied.

"Ruby, cut the crap. The guy in that room tried to kill a priest Friday morning. What do you think he'll do to you if he remembers he showed you mug shots of two guys he capped out in the Basin?" Helen said.

Ruby lowered her chin and bit her lip. Her long hair made a screen around her narrow face.

"It's not fair," she said.

"What?" I asked.

"Connie picked those guys up. But she doesn't get stuck with any of it. You got a candy bar or something? I feel sick. They wouldn't turn down the air-conditioning on the train."

She sniffed deep in her nose, then wiped her nostrils hard with a Kleenex, pushing her face out of shape.

Helen looked through the front window at one of our people in a phone booth on the corner.

"It's going down, Ruby. Pick up the binoculars," she said.

Ruby held the binoculars to her eyes and stared at the door to the room rented by Harpo Scruggs. Then she shifted them to an adjacent area in the parking lot. Her lips parted slightly on her teeth.

"What's going on?" she said.

"Nothing. What are you talking about?" I said.

"That's not the guy with the mug shots. I don't know that guy's name. We didn't ball him either," she said.

"Take the oatmeal out of your mouth," Helen said.

I removed the binoculars from her hands and placed them to my eyes.

"The guy out there in the parking lot. He came to the diner where the guy named Harpo and the other john were eating with us. He talks like a coon-ass. They went outside together, then he drove off," she said.

"You never told us this," I said.

"Why should I? You were asking about johns."

I put the binoculars back to my eyes and watched Alex Guidry, the fired Iberia Parish jailer who had cuckolded Cool Breeze Broussard, knock on empty space just as Harpo Scruggs ripped open the door and charged outside, barefoot and in his undershirt and western-cut trousers, expecting to see a burning truck.

L ater the same afternoon, when the sheriff was in my office, two Lafayette homicide detectives walked in and told us they were picking up Cool Breeze Broussard. They were both dressed in sport clothes, their muscles swollen with steroids. One of them, whose name was Daigle, lit a cigarette and kept searching with his eyes for an ashtray to put the burnt match in.

"Y'all want to go out to his house with us?" he asked, and dropped the match in the wastebasket.

"I don't," I said.

He studied me. "You got some kind of objection, something not getting said here?" he asked.

"I don't see how you make Broussard for this guy's, what's his name, Anthony Pollock's murder," I replied.

"He's got a hard-on for the Terrebonne family. There's a good possibility he started the fire on their movie set. He's a four-time loser. He shanked a guy on Camp J. He mangled a guy on an electric saw in your own jail. You want me to go on?" Daigle said.

"You've got the wrong guy," I said.

"Well, fuck me," he said.

"Don't use that language in here, sir," the sheriff said.

"What?" Daigle said.

"The victim was an addict. He had overseas involvements. He didn't have any connection with Cool Breeze. I think you guys have found an easy dartboard," I said.

"We made up all that stuff on Broussard's sheet?" the other detective said.

"The victim was stabbed in the throat, heart, and kidney and was dead before he hit the floor. It sounds like a professional yard job," I said.

"A yard job?" Daigle said.

"Talk to a guy by the name of Swede Boxleiter. He's on lend-lease from Canon City," I said.

"Swede who?" Daigle said, taking a puff off his cigarette with three fingers crimped on the paper.

The sheriff scratched his eyebrow.

"Get out of here," he said to the detectives.

A few minutes later the sheriff and I watched through the window as they got into their car.

"At least Pollock had the decency to get himself killed in Lafayette Parish," the sheriff said. "What's the status on Harpo Scruggs?"

"Helen said a chippy came to his room in a taxi. She's still in there."

"What's Alex Guidry's tie-in to this guy?"

"It has something to do with the Terrebonnes. Everything in St. Mary Parish does. That's where they're both from."

"Bring him in."

"What for?"

"Tell him he's cruel to animals. Tell him his golf game stinks. Tell him I'm just in a real pissed-off mood."

Tuesday morning Helen and I drove down Main, then crossed the iron drawbridge close by the New Iberia Country Club.

"You don't think this will tip our surveillance on Harpo Scruggs?" she said.

"Not if we do it right."

"When those two brothers were executed out in the Basin? One of the shooters had on a department uniform. It could have come from Guidry."

"Maybe Guidry was in it," I said.

"Nope, he stays behind the lines. He makes the system work for him."

"You know him outside the job?" I asked.

"He arrested my maid out on a highway at night when he was a deputy in St. Mary Parish. She's never told anyone what he did to her."

Helen and I parked the cruiser in front of the country club and walked past the swimming pool, then under a spreading oak to a practice green where Alex Guidry was putting with a woman and another man. He wore light brown slacks and two-tone golf shoes and a maroon polo shirt; his mahogany tan and thick salt-and-pepper hair gave him the look of a man in the prime of his life. He registered our presence in the corner of his eye but never lost his concentration. He bent his knees slightly and tapped the ball with a plop into the cup.

"The sheriff has invited you to come down to the department," I said.

"No, thank you," he said.

"We need your help with a friend of yours. It won't take long," Helen said.

The red flag on the golf pin popped in the wind. Leaves drifted out of the pecan trees and live oaks along the fairway and scudded across the freshly mowed grass.

"I'll give it some thought and ring y'all later on it," he said, and started to reach down to retrieve his ball from the cup.

Helen put her hand on his shoulder.

"Not a time to be a wise-ass, sir," she said.

Guidry's golf companions looked away into the distance, their eyes fixed on the dazzling blue stretch of sky above the tree line.

Fifteen minutes later we sat down in a windowless interview room. In the back seat of the cruiser he had been silent, morose, his face dark with anger when he looked at us. I saw the sheriff at the end of the hall just before I closed the door to the room.

"Y'all got some damn nerve," Guidry said.

"Someone told us you're buds with an ex-Angola gun bull by the name of Harpo Scruggs," I said.

"I know him. So what?" he replied.

"You see him recently?" Helen asked. She wore slacks and sat with one haunch on the corner of the desk.

"No."

"Sure?" I said.

"He's the nephew of a lawman I worked with twenty years ago. We grew up in the same town."

"You didn't answer me," I said.

"I don't have to."

"The lawman you worked with was Harpo Delahoussey. Y'all put the squeeze on Cool Breeze Broussard over some moonshine whiskey. That's not all you did either," I said.

His eyes looked steadily into mine, heated, searching for the implied meaning in my words.

"Harpo Scruggs tried to kill a priest Friday morning," Helen said.

"Arrest him, then."

"How do you know we haven't?" I asked.

"I don't. It's none of my business. I was fired from my job, thanks to your friend Willie Broussard," he said.

"Everyone else told us Scruggs was dead. But you know he's alive. Why's that?" Helen said.

He leaned back in the chair and rubbed his mouth, saying something in disgust against his hand at the same time.

"Say that again," Helen said.

"I said you damn queer, you leave me alone," he replied.

I placed my hand on top of Helen's before she could rise from the table. "You were in the sack with Cool Breeze's wife. I think you contributed to her suicide and helped ruin her husband's life. Does it give you any sense of shame at all, sir?" I said.

"It's called changing your luck. You're notorious for it, so lose the attitude, fucko," Helen said.

"I tell you what, when you're dead from AIDS or some other disease you people pass around, I'm going to dig up your grave and piss in your mouth," he said to her.

Helen stood up and massaged the back of her neck. "Dave, would you leave me and Mr. Guidry alone a minute?" she said.

B ut whatever she did or said after I left the room, it didn't work. Guidry walked past the dispatcher, used the phone to call a friend for a ride, and calmly sipped from a can of Coca-Cola until a yellow Cadillac with tinted windows pulled to the curb in front.

Helen and I watched him get in on the passenger side, roll down the window, and toss the empty can on our lawn.

"What bwana say now?" Helen said.

"Time to use local resources."

T hat evening Clete picked me up in his convertible in front of the house and we headed up the road toward St. Martinville.

"You call Swede Boxleiter a 'local resource'?" he said.

"Why not?"

"That's like calling shit a bathroom ornament."

"You want to go or not?"

"The guy's got electrodes in his temples. Even Holtzner walks around him. Are you listening?"

"You think he did the number on this accountant, Anthony Pollock?"

He thought about it. The wind blew a crooked part in his sandy hair.

"*Could* he do it? In a blink. Did he have motive? You got me, 'cause I don't know what these dudes are up to," he said. "Megan told me something about Cisco having a fine career ahead of him, then taking money from some guys in the Orient."

"Have you seen her?"

He turned his face toward me. It was flat and red in the sun's last light, his green eyes as bold as a slap. He looked at the road again.

"We're friends. I mean, she's got her own life. We're different kinds of people, you know. I'm cool about it." He inserted a Lucky Strike in his mouth.

"Clete, I'm—"

He pulled the cigarette off his lip without lighting it and threw it into the wind.

"What'd the Dodgers do last night?" he said.

We pulled into the driveway of the cinder-block triplex where Swede Boxleiter lived and found him in back, stripped to the waist, shooting marbles with a slingshot at the squirrels in a pecan tree.

He pointed his finger at me.

"I got a bone to pick with you," he said.

"Oh?"

"Two Lafayette homicide roaches just left here. They said you told them to question me."

"Really?" I said.

"They threw me up against the car in front of my landlord. One guy kicked me in both ankles. He put his hand in my crotch with little kids watching."

"Dave was trying to clear you as a suspect. These guys probably got the wrong signal, Swede," Clete said.

He pulled back the leather pouch on the slingshot, nests of veins popping in his neck, and fired a scarlet marble into the pecan limbs.

"I want to run a historical situation by you. Then you tell me what's wrong with the story," I said.

"What's the game?" he asked.

"No game. You're con-wise. You see stuff other people don't. This is just for fun, okay?"

He held the handle of the slingshot and whipped the leather pouch and lengths of rubber tubing in a circle, watching them gain speed.

"A plantation owner is in the sack with one of his slave women. He goes off to the Civil War, comes back home, finds his place trashed by the Yankees, and all his slaves set free. There's not enough food for everybody, so he tells the slave woman she has to leave. You with me?"

"Makes sense, yeah," Swede said.

"The slave woman puts poison in the food of the plantation owner's children, thinking they'll only get sick and she'll be asked to care for them. Except they die. The other black people on the plantation are terrified. So they hang the slave woman before they're all punished," I said.

Swede stopped twirling the slingshot. "It's bullshit," he said.

"Why?" I asked.

"You said the blacks were already freed. Why are they gonna commit a murder for the white dude and end up hung by Yankees themselves? The white guy, the one getting his stick dipped, he did her."

"You're a beaut, Swede," I said.

"This is some kind of grift, right?"

"Here's what it is," Clete said. "Dave thinks you're getting set up. You know how it works sometimes. The locals can't clear a case and they look around for a guy with a heavy sheet."

"We've got a shooter or two on the loose, Swede," I said. "Some guys smoked two white boys out in the Basin, then tried to clip a black guy by the name of Willie Broussard. I hate to see you go down for it."

"I can see you'd be broke up," he said.

"Ever hear of a dude named Harpo Scruggs?" I asked.

"No."

"Too bad. You might have to take his weight. See you around. Thanks for the help with that historical story," I said.

Clete and I walked back to the convertible. The air felt warm and moist, and the sky was purple above the sugarcane across the road. Out of the corner of my eye I saw Swede watching us from the middle of the drive, stretching the rubber tubes on his slingshot, his face jigsawed with thought.

We stopped at a filling station for gas down the road. The owner had turned on the outside lights and the oak tree that grew next to the building was filled with black-green shadows against the sky. Clete walked across the street and bought a sno'ball from a small wooden stand and ate it while I put in the gas.

"What was that plantation story about?" he asked.

"I had the same problem with it as Boxleiter. Except it's been bothering me because it reminded me of the story Cool Breeze told me about his wife's suicide."

"You lost me, big mon," Clete said.

"She was found in freezing water with an anchor chain wrapped around her. When they want to leave a lot of guilt behind, they use shotguns or go off rooftops."

"I'd leave it alone, Dave."

"Breeze has lived for twenty years with her death on his conscience."

"There's another script, too. Maybe he did her," Clete said. He bit into his sno'ball and held his eyes on mine.

■ ■ ■

Early the next morning Batist telephoned the house from the dock.

"There's a man down here want to see you, Dave," he said.

"What's he look like?"

"Like somebody stuck his jaws in a vise and busted all the bones. That ain't the half of it. While I'm mopping off the tables, he walks round on his hands."

I finished my coffee and walked down the slope through the trees. The air was cool and gray with the mist off the water, and molded pecan husks broke under my shoes.

"What's up, Swede?" I said.

He sat at a spool table, eating a chili dog with a fork from a paper plate.

"You asked about this guy Harpo Scruggs. He's an old fart, works out of New Mexico and Trinidad, Colorado. He freelances, but if he's doing a job around here, the juice is coming out of New Orleans."

"Yeah?"

"Something else. If Scruggs tried to clip a guy and blew it but he's still hanging around, it means he's working for Ricky the Mouse."

"Ricky Scarlotti?"

"There's two things you don't do with Ricky. You don't blow hits and you don't ever call him the Mouse. You know the story about the horn player?"

"Yes."

"That's his style."

"Would he have a priest killed?"

"That don't sound right."

"You ever have your IQ tested, Swede?"

"No, people who bone you five days a week don't give IQ tests."

"You're quite a guy anyway. You shank Anthony Pollock?"

"I was playing chess with Cisco. Check it out, my man. And don't send any more cops to my place. Believe it or not, I don't like some polyester geek getting his hand on my crank."

He rolled up his dirty paper plate and napkin, dropped them in a trash barrel, and walked down the dock to his car, snapping his fingers as though he were listening to a private radio broadcast.

■ ■ ■

Ricky Scarlotti wasn't hard to find. I went to the office, called NOPD, then the flower shop he owned at Carrollton and St. Charles.

"You want to chat up Ricky the Mouse with me?" I asked Helen.

"I don't think I'd go near that guy without a full-body condom on," she replied.

"Suit yourself. I'll be back this afternoon."

"Hang on. Let me get my purse."

We signed out an unmarked car and drove across the Atchafalaya Basin and crossed the Mississippi at Baton Rouge and turned south for New Orleans.

"So you're just gonna drop this Harpo Scruggs stuff in his lap?" Helen said.

"You bet. If Ricky thinks someone snitched him off, we'll know about it in a hurry."

"That story about the jazz musician true?" she said.

"I think it is. He just didn't get tagged with it."

The name of the musician is forgotten now, except among those in the 1950s who had believed his talent was the greatest since Bix Beiderbecke's. The melancholy sound of his horn hypnotized audiences at open-air concerts on West Venice beach. His dark hair and eyes and pale skin, the fatal beauty that lived in his face, that was like a white rose opening to black light, made women turn and stare at him on the street. His rendition of "My Funny Valentine" took you into a consideration about mutability and death that left you numb.

But he was a junky and jammed up with LAPD, and when he gave up the names of his suppliers, he had no idea that he was about to deal with Ricky Scarlotti.

Ricky had run a casino in Las Vegas, then a race track in Tijuana, before the Chicago Commission moved him to Los Angeles. Ricky didn't believe in simply killing people. He created living object lessons. He sent two black men to the musician's apartment in Malibu, where they pulled his teeth with pliers and mutilated his mouth. Later, the musician became a pharmaceutical derelict, went to prison in Germany, and died a suicide.

Helen and I drove through the Garden District, past the columned nineteenth-century homes shadowed by oaks whose root systems humped under sidewalks and cracked them upward like baked clay, past the iron green-painted streetcars with red-bordered windows clanging on the neutral ground, past Loyola University and Audubon Park, then to the levee where St. Charles ended and Ricky kept the restaurant, bookstore, and flower shop that supposedly brought him his income.

His second-story office was carpeted with a snow-white rug and filled with glass artworks and polished steel-and-glass furniture. A huge picture window gave onto the river and an enormous palm tree that brushed with the wind against the side of the building.

Ricky's beige pinstripe suit coat hung on the back of his chair. He wore a soft white shirt with a plum-colored tie and suspenders, and even though he was nearing sixty, his large frame still had the powerful muscle structure of a much younger man.

But it was the shape of his head and the appearance of his face that drew your attention. His ears were too large, cupped outward, the face unnaturally rotund, the eyes pouched with permanent dark bags, the eyebrows half-mooned, the black hair like a carefully scissored pelt glued to the skull.

"It's been a long time, Robicheaux. You still off the bottle?" he said.

"We're hearing some stuff that's probably all gas, Ricky. You know a mechanic, a freelancer, by the name of Harpo Scruggs?" I said.

"A guy fixes cars?" he said, and grinned.

"He's supposed to be a serious button man out of New Mexico," I said.

"Who's she? I've seen you around New Orleans someplace, right?" He was looking at Helen now.

"I was a patrolwoman here years ago. I still go to the Jazz and Heritage Festival in the spring. You like jazz?" Helen said.

"No."

"You ought to check it out. Wynton Marsalis is there. Great horn man. You don't like cornet?" she said.

"What is this, Robicheaux?"

"I told you, Ricky. Harpo Scruggs. He tried to kill Willie Brous-sard, then a priest. My boss is seriously pissed off."

"Tell him that makes two of us, 'cause I don't like out-of-town cops 'fronting me in my own office. I particularly don't like no bride of Frankenstein making an implication about a rumor that was put to rest a long time ago."

"Nobody has shown you any personal disrespect here, Ricky. You need to show the same courtesy to others," I said.

"That's all right. I'll wait outside," Helen said, then paused by the door. She let her eyes drift onto Ricky Scarlotti's face. "Say, come on over to New Iberia sometime. I've got a calico cat that just won't believe you."

She winked, then closed the door behind her.

"I don't provoke no more, Robicheaux. Look, I know about you and Purcel visiting Jimmy Figorelli. What kind of behavior is that? Purcel smashes the guy in the mouth for no reason. Now you're laying off some hillbilly *cafone* on me."

"I didn't say he was a hillbilly."

"I've heard of him. But I don't put out contracts on priests. What d'you think I am?"

"A vicious, sadistic piece of shit, Ricky."

He opened his desk drawer and removed a stick of gum and peeled it and placed it in his mouth. Then he brushed at the tip of one nostril with his knuckle, huffing air out of his breathing passage. He pushed a button on his desk and turned his back on me and stared out the picture window at the river until I had left the room.

That evening I drove to the city library on East Main. The spread-ing oaks on the lawn were filled with birds and I could hear the clumps of bamboo rattling in the wind, and fireflies were lighting in the dusk out on the bayou. I went inside the library and found the hardback collection of Megan's photography that had been published three years ago by a New York publishing house.

What could I learn from it? Maybe nothing. Maybe I only wanted to put off seeing her that evening, which I knew I had to do, even though I knew I was breaking an AA tenet by injecting myself into other people's relationships. But you don't let a friend like Clete Purcel swing in the gibbet.

The photographs in her collection were stunning. Her great talent was her ability to isolate the humanity and suffering of individuals who lived in our midst but who nevertheless remained invisible to most passersby. Native Americans on reservations, migrant farm-workers, mentally impaired people who sought heat from steam grates, they looked at the camera with the hollow eyes of Holocaust victims and made the viewer wonder what country or era the photo-graph had been taken in, because surely it could not have been our own.

Then I turned a page and looked at a black-and-white photo taken on a reservation in South Dakota. It showed four FBI agents in windbreakers taking two Indian men into custody. The Indians were on their knees, their fingers laced behind their heads. An AR-15 rifle lay in the dust by an automobile whose windows and doors were perforated with bullet holes.

The cutline said the men were members of the American Indian Movement. No explanation was given for their arrest. One of the agents was a woman whose face was turned angrily toward the cam-era. The face was that of the New Orleans agent Adrien Glazier.

I drove out to Cisco's place on the Loreauville road and parked by the gallery. No one answered the bell, and I walked down by the bayou and saw her writing a letter under the light in the gazebo, the late sun burning like a flare beyond the willow trees across the water. She didn't see or hear me, and in her solitude she seemed to possess all the self-contained and tranquil beauty of a woman who had never let the authority of another define her.

Her horn-rimmed glasses gave her a studious look that her careless and eccentric dress belied. I felt guilty watching her without her knowledge, but in that moment I also realized what it was that attracted men to her.

She was one of those women we instinctively know are braver and more resilient than we are, more long-suffering and more willing to be broken for the sake of principle. You wanted to feel tender toward Megan, but you knew your feelings were vain and presumptuous. She had a lion's heart and did not need a protector.

"Oh, Dave. I didn't hear you come up on me," she said, removing her glasses.

"I was down at the library looking at your work. Who were those Indians Adrien Glazier was taking down?"

"One of them supposedly murdered two FBI agents. Amnesty International thinks he's innocent."

"There were some other photos in there you took of Mexican children in a ruined church around Trinidad, Colorado."

"Those were migrant kids whose folks had run off. The church was built by John D. Rockefeller after his goons murdered the families of striking miners up the road at Ludlow."

"I mention it because Swede Boxleiter told me a hit man named Harpo Scruggs had a ranch around there."

"He should know. He and Cisco were placed in a foster home in Trinidad. The husband was a pederast. He raped Swede until he bled inside. Swede took it so the guy wouldn't start on Cisco next."

I sat down on the top step of the gazebo and tossed a pebble into the bayou.

"Clete's my longtime friend, Megan. He says he needs this security job with Cisco's company. I don't think that's why he's staying here," I said.

She started to speak but gave it up.

"Even though he says otherwise, I don't think he understands the nature of y'all's relationship," I said.

"Is he drinking?"

"Not now, but he will."

She rested her cheek on her hand and gazed at the bayou.

"What I did was rotten," she said. "I wake up every morning and feel like a bloody sod. I just wish I could undo it."

"Talk to him again."

"You want Cisco and me out of his life. That's the real agenda, isn't it?"

"The best cop New Orleans ever had has become a grunt for Billy Holtzner."

"He can walk out of that situation anytime he wants. How about my brother? Anthony Pollock worked for some nasty people in Hong Kong. Who do you think they're going to blame for his death?"

"To tell you the truth, it's a long way from Bayou Teche. I don't really care."

She folded her letter and put away her pen and walked up the green bank toward the house, her silhouette surrounded by the tracings of fireflies.

C isco filmed late that night and did not return home until after 2 A.M. The intruders came sometime between midnight and then. They were big, heavy men, booted, sure of themselves and unrelenting in their purpose. They churned and destroyed the flower beds, where they disabled the alarm system, and slipped a looped wire through a window jamb and released the catch from inside. Each went through the opening with one muscular thrust, because hardly any dirt was scuffed into the bricks below the jamb.

They knew where she slept, and unlike the men who admired Megan for her strength, these men despised her for it. Their hands fell upon her in her sleep, wrenched her from the bed, bound her eyes, hurled her through the door and out onto the patio and down the slope to the bayou. When she pulled at the tape on her eyes, they slapped her to her knees.

But while they forced her face into the water, none of them saw the small memo recorder attached to a key ring she held clenched in her palm. Even while her mouth and nostrils filled with mud and her lungs burned for air as though acid had been poured in them, she tried to keep her finger pressed on the "record" button.

Then she felt the bayou grow as warm as blood around her neck just as a veined, yellow bubble burst in the center of her mind, and she knew she was safe from the hands and fists and booted feet of the men who had always lived on the edge of her camera's lens.

SEVENTEEN

The tape on the small recorder had only a twenty-second capacity. Most of the voices were muffled and inaudible, but there were words, whole sentences, sawed out of the darkness that portrayed Megan's tormenters better than any photograph could:

"Hold her, damnit! This is one bitch been asking for it a long time. You cain't get her head down, get out of the way."

"She's bucking. When they buck, they're fixing to go under. Better pull her up unless we're going all the way."

"Let her get a breath, then give it to her again. Ain't nothing like the power of memory to make a good woman, son."

It was 2:30 A.M. now and the ambulance had already left with Megan for Iberia General. The light from the flashers on our parked cruisers was like a blue, white, and red net on the trees and the bayou's surface and the back of the house. Cisco paced back and forth on the lawn, his eyes large, his face dilated in the glare. Behind him I could see the sheriff squatted under the open window with a flashlight, peeling back the ruined flowers with one hand.

"You know who did it, don't you?" I said to Cisco.

"If I did, I'd have a gun down somebody's mouth," he replied.

"Give the swinging dick act a break, Cisco."

"I can't tell you who, I can only tell you why. It's payback for Anthony."

"Walk down to the water with me," I said, and cupped one hand on his elbow.

We went down the slope to the bayou, where the mudbank had been imprinted at the water's edge by Megan's bare knees and sliced by heavy boots that had fought for purchase while she struggled with at least three men. An oak tree sheltered us from the view of the sheriff and the uniformed deputies in the yard.

"Don't you lie to me. With these guys payback means dead. They want something. What is it?" I said.

"Billy Holtzner embezzled three-quarters of a million out of the budget by working a scam on our insurance coverage. But he put it on me. Anthony worked for the money people in Hong Kong. He believed what Billy told him. He started twisting my dials and ended up with big leaks in his arteries."

"Swede?"

"We were playing chess for a lot of the evening. I don't know if he did it or not. Swede's protective. Anthony was a prick."

"Protective? The victim was a prick? Great attitude."

"It's complicated. There's a lot of big finance involved. You're not going to understand it." He saw the look on my face. "I'm in wrong with some bad guys. The studio's going to file bankruptcy. They want to gut my picture and inflate its value on paper to liquidate their debts."

The current in the bayou was dead, hazed over with insects, and there was no air under the trees. He wiped his face with his hand.

"I'm telling the truth, Dave. I didn't think they'd go after Megan. Maybe there's something else involved. About my father, maybe. I don't understand it all either . . . Where you going?" he said.

"To find Clete Purcel."

"What for?"

"To talk to him before he hears about this from someone else."

"You coming to the hospital?" he asked, his fingers opened in front of him as though the words of another could be caught and held as physical guarantees.

It was still dark when I parked my truck by the stucco cottage Clete had rented outside Jeanerette. I pushed back the seat and slept through a rain shower and did not wake until dawn. When I woke, the rain had stopped and the air was heavy with mist, and I saw Clete at his mailbox in a robe, the *Morning Advocate* under his arm, staring curiously at my truck. I got out and walked toward him.

"What's wrong?" he said, lines breaking across his brow.

I told him of everything that happened at Cisco's house and of Megan's status at Iberia General. He listened and didn't speak. His face had the contained, heated intensity of a stainless-steel pan that had been left on a burner.

Then he said, "She's going to make it?"

"You bet."

"Come inside. I already have coffee on the stove." He turned away from me and pushed at his nose with his thumb.

"What are you going to do, Clete?"

"Go up to the hospital. What do you think?"

"You know what I mean."

"I'll fix eggs and sausage for both of us. You look like you got up out of a coffin."

Inside his kitchen I said, "Are you going to answer me?"

"I already heard about you and Helen visiting Ricky Scar. He's behind this shit, isn't he?"

"Where'd you hear about Scarlotti?"

"Nig Rosewater. He said Ricky went berserk after you left his office. What'd y'all do to jack him up like that?"

"Don't worry about it. You stay out of New Orleans."

He poured coffee in two cups and put a cinnamon roll in his mouth and looked out the window at the sun in the pine trees.

"Did you hear me?" I said.

"I got enough to do right here. I caught Swede Boxleiter in the Terrebonne cemetery last night. I think he was prizing bricks out of a crypt."

"What for?"

"Maybe he's a ghoul. You know what for. You planted all that Civil War stuff in his head. I'd love to tell Archer Terrebonne an ex-con meltdown is digging up his ancestors' bones."

But there was no humor in his face, only a tic at the corner of one eye. He went into the other room and called Iberia General, then came back in the kitchen, his eyes filled with private thoughts, and began beating eggs in a big pink bowl.

"Clete?"

"The Big Sleazy's not your turf anymore, Streak. Why don't you worry about how this guy Scruggs got off his leash? I thought y'all had him under surveillance."

"He lost the stakeout at the motel."

"You know the best way to deal with that dude? A big fat one between the eyes and a throw-down on the corpse."

"You might have your butt in our jail, if that's what it takes," I said.

He poured hot milk into my coffee cup. "Not even the perps believe that stuff anymore. You want to go to the hospital with me?" he said.

"You got it."

"The nurse said she asked for me. How about that? How about that Megan Flynn?"

I looked at the back of his thick neck and huge shoulders as he made breakfast and thought of warning NOPD before he arrived in New Orleans. But I knew that would only give his old enemies in the New Orleans Police Department a basis to do him even greater harm than Ricky Scarlotti might.

We drove back up the tree-lined highway to New Iberia in a corridor of rain.

■　■　■

At Iberia General I sat in the waiting room while Clete went in to see Megan first. Five minutes after we arrived I saw Lila Terrebonne walk down the hall with a spray of carnations wrapped in green tissue paper. She didn't see me. She paused at the open door to Megan's room, her eyelids blinking, her back stiff with apprehension. Then she turned and started hurriedly toward the elevator.

I caught her before she got on.

"You're not going to say hello?" I asked.

I could smell the bourbon on her breath, the cigarette smoke in her hair and clothes.

"Give these to Megan for me. I'll come back another time," she said.

"How'd you know she was here?"

"It was on the radio . . . Dave, get on the elevator with me." When the elevator door closed, she said, "I've got to get some help. I've had it."

"Help with what?"

"Booze, craziness . . . Something that happened to me, something I've never told anybody about except my father and the priest at St. Peter's."

"Why don't we sit in my pickup?" I said.

What follows is my reconstruction of the story she told me while the rain slid down the truck's windows and a willow tree by the bayou blew in the wind like a woman's hair.

She met the two brothers in a bar outside Morgan City. They were shooting pool, stretching across the table to make difficult shots, their sleeveless arms wrapped with green-and-red tattoos. They wore earrings and beards that were trimmed in neat lines along the jawbone, jeans that were so tight their genitalia were cupped to the smooth shape of a woman's palm. They sent a drink to her table, and one to an old man at the bar, and one to an oil-field roughneck who had used up his tab. But they made no overture toward her.

She watched them across the top of her gin ricky, the tawdry grace of their movements around the pool table, the lack of attention they showed anything except the skill of their game, the shots they speared into leather side pockets like junior high school kids.

Then one of them noticed her watching. He proffered the cue stick to her, smiling. She rose from her chair, her skin warm with gin, and wrapped her fingers around the cue's thickness, smiling back into the young man's face, seeing him glance away shyly, his cheeks color around the edges of his beard.

They played nine ball. Her father had taught her how to play billiards when she was a young girl. She could walk a cue ball down the rail, put reverse English on it and not leave an opponent an open shot, make a soft bank shot and drop the money balls—the one and the six and the nine—into the pocket with a tap that was no more than a whisper.

The two brothers shook their heads in dismay. She bought them each a bottle of beer and a gin ricky for herself. She played another game and beat them again. She noticed they didn't use profanity in her presence, that they stopped speaking in mid-sentence if she wished to interrupt, that they grinned boyishly and looked away if she let her eyes linger more than a few seconds on theirs.

They told her they built board roads for an oil company, they had been in the reformatory after their mother had deserted the family, they had been in the Gulf War, in a tank, one that'd had its treads blown off by an Iraqi artillery shell. She knew they were lying, but she didn't care. She felt a sense of sexual power and control that made her nipples hard, her eyes warm with toleration and acceptance.

When she walked to the ladies' room, the backs of her thighs taut with her high heels, she could see her reflection in the bar mirror and she knew that every man in the room was looking at the movement of her hips, the upward angle of her chin, the grace in her carriage that their own women would never possess.

The brothers did not try to pick her up. In fact, when the bar started to close, their conversation turned to the transmission on their truck, a stuck gear they couldn't free, their worry they could not make it the two miles to their father's fish camp. Rain streamed down the neon-lighted window in front.

She offered to follow them home. When they accepted, she experienced a strange taste in her throat, like copper pennies, like the wearing off of alcohol and the beginnings of a different kind of chemical reality. She looked at the faces of the brothers, the grins that looked incised in clay, and started to reconsider.

Then the bartender beckoned to her.

"Lady, taxicabs run all night. A phone call's a quarter. If they ain't got it, they can use mine free," he said.

"There's no problem. But thanks very much just the same. Thank you, truly. You're very nice," she replied, and hung her purse from her shoulder and let one of the brothers hold a newspaper over her head while they ran for her automobile.

They did it to her in an open-air tractor shed by a green field of sugarcane in the middle of an electric storm. One held her wrists while the other brother climbed between her legs on top of a worktable. After he came his body went limp and his head fell on her breast. His mouth was wet and she could feel it leaving a pattern on her blouse. Then he rose from her and put on his blue jeans and lit a cigarette before clasping her wrists so his brother, who simply unzipped his jeans without taking them off, could mount her.

When she thought it was over, when she believed there was nothing else they could take from her, she sat up on the worktable with her clothes crumpled in her lap. Then she watched one brother shake his head and extend his soiled hand toward her face, covering it like a surgeon's assistant pressing an ether mask on a patient, forcing her back down on the table, then turning her over, his hand shifting to the back of her neck, crushing her mouth into the wood planks.

She saw a bolt of lightning explode in the fork of a hardwood tree, saw it split the wood apart and tear the grain right through the heart of the trunk. Deep in her mind she thought she remembered a green felt pool table and a boyish figure shoving a cue like a spear through his bridged fingers.

Lila's face was turned slightly toward the passenger window when she finished her story.

"Your father had them killed?" I said.

"I didn't say that. Not at all."

"It's what happened, though, isn't it?"

"Maybe I had them killed. It's what they deserved. I'm glad they're dead."

"I think it's all right to feel that way," I said.

"What are you going to do with what I've told you?"

"Take you home or to a treatment center in Lafayette."

"I don't want to go into treatment again. If I can't do it with meetings and working the program, I can't do it at all."

"Why don't we go to a meeting after work? Then you go every day for ninety days."

"I feel like everything inside me is coming to an end. I can't describe it."

"It's called 'a world destruction fantasy.' It's bad stuff. Your heart races, you can't breathe, you feel like a piano wire is wrapped around your forehead. Psychologists say we remember the birth experience."

She pressed the heel of her hand to her forehead, then cracked the window as though my words had drawn the oxygen out of the air.

"Lila, I've got to ask you something else. Why were you talking about a Hanged Man?"

"I don't remember that. Not at all. That's in the Tarot, isn't it? I don't know anything about that."

"I see."

Her skin had gone white under her caked makeup, her eyelashes stiff and black and wide around her milky green eyes.

I walked through the rain into the hospital and rode up in the elevator with Lila's tissue-wrapped spray of carnations in my hand. Helen Soileau was in the waiting room.

"You get anything?" I asked.

"Not much. She says she thinks there were three guys. They sounded like hicks. One guy was running things," she replied.

"That's got to be Harpo Scruggs."

"I think we're going about this the wrong way. Cut off the head and the body dies."

"Where's the head?"

"Beats me," she said.

"Where's Purcel?"

"He's still in there."

I walked to the open door, then turned away. Clete was sitting on the side of Megan's bed, leaning down toward her face, his big arms and shoulders forming a tent over her. Her right hand rested on the back of his neck. Her fingers stroked his uncut hair.

The sky cleared that night, and Alafair and Bootsie and I cooked out in the back yard. I had told the sheriff about my conversation with Lila Terrebonne, but his response was predictable. We had established possible motivation for the execution of the two brothers. But that was all we had done. There was no evidence to link Archer Terrebonne, Lila's father, to the homicide. Second, the murders still remained outside our jurisdiction and our only vested interest in solving them was the fact that one of the shooters wore an Iberia Parish deputy sheriff's uniform.

I went with Lila to an AA meeting that night, then returned home.

"Clete called. He's in New Orleans. He said for you not to worry. What'd he mean?" Bootsie said.

EIGHTEEN

Ricky Scarlotti ate breakfast the next morning with two of his men in his restaurant by St. Charles and Carrollton. It was a fine morning, smelling of the wet sidewalks and the breeze off the river. The fronds of the palm trees on the neutral ground were pale green and lifting in the wind against a ceramic-blue sky; the streetcar was loading with passengers by the levee, the conductor's bell clanging. No one seemed to take notice of a chartreuse Cadillac convertible that turned off St. Charles and parked in front of the flower shop, nor of the man in the powder-blue porkpie hat and seersucker pants and Hawaiian shirt who sat behind the steering wheel with a huge plastic seal-top coffee mug in his hand.

The man in the porkpie hat inserted a dime in the parking meter and looked with interest at the display of flowers an elderly woman was setting out on the sidewalk under a canvas awning. He talked a moment with the woman, then entered the restaurant and stopped by the hot bar and wrapped a cold cloth around the handle of a heavy cast-iron skillet filled with chipped beef. He made his way unobtrusively between the checker-cloth-covered tables toward the rear of the restaurant, where Ricky Scarlotti had just patted his mouth with a napkin and had touched the wrist of one of the men at his side and nodded in the direction of the approaching figure in the porkpie hat.

The man at Ricky Scarlotti's side had platinum hair and a chemical tan. He put down his fork and got to his feet and stood flat-footed
like a sentinel in front of Ricky Scarlotti's table. His name was Benny
Grogan and he had been a professional wrestler before he had become
a male escort for a notorious and rich Garden District homosexual.
NOPD believed he had also been the backup shooter on at least two
hits for the Calucci brothers.

"I hope you're here for the brunch, Purcel," he said.

"Not your gig, Benny. Get off the clock," Clete said.

"Come on, make an appointment. Don't do this. Hey, you deaf?"
Then Benny Grogan reached out and hooked his fingers on the back
of Clete's shirt collar as Clete brushed past him.

Clete flung the chipped beef into Benny Grogan's face. It was
scalding hot and it matted his skin like a papier-mâché mask with slits
for the eyes. Benny's mouth was wide with shock and pain and an
unintelligible sound that rose out of his chest like fingernails grating
on a blackboard. Then Clete whipped the bottom of the skillet with
both hands across the side of Benny's head, and backswung it into the
face of the man who was trying to rise from his chair on the other side
of Ricky Scarlotti, the cast-iron cusp ringing against bone, bursting
the nose, knocking him backward on the floor.

Ricky Scarlotti was on his feet now, his mouth twisted, his finger
raised at Clete. But he never got the chance to speak.

"I brought you some of your own, Ricky," Clete said.

He jammed a pair of vise grips into Ricky Scarlotti's scrotum and
locked down the handles. Ricky Scarlotti's hands grabbed impotently
at Clete's wrists while his head reared toward the ceiling.

Clete began backing toward the front door, pulling Ricky
Scarlotti with him.

"Work with me on this. You can do it, Mouse. That a boy. Step
lively now. Coming through here, gangway for the Mouse!" Clete
said, pushing chairs and tables out of the way with his buttocks.

Out on the street he unhooked Scarlotti from the vise grips and
bounced him off the side of a parked car, then slapped his face with his
open hand, once, twice, then a third time, so hard the inside of
Scarlotti's mouth bled.

"I'm not carrying, Mouse. Free shot," Clete said, his hands palm up at his sides now.

But Scarlotti was paralyzed, his mouth hanging open, his lips like red Jell-O. Clete grabbed him by his collar and the back of his belt and flung him to the sidewalk, then picked him up, pushed him forward, and flung him down again, over and over, working his way down the sidewalk, clattering garbage cans along the cement. People stared from automobiles, the streetcar, and door fronts but no one intervened. Then, like a man who knows his rage can never be satiated, Clete lost it. He drove Scarlotti's head into a parking meter, smashing it repeatedly against the metal and glass. A woman across the street screamed hysterically and people began blowing car horns. Clete spun Scarlotti around by his bloodied shirtfront and threw him across a laddered display of flowers under the canvas awning.

"Tell these people why this is happening, Ricky. Tell them how you had a guy's teeth torn out, how you had a woman blindfolded and beaten and held underwater," Clete said, advancing toward him, his shoes crunching through the scattered potting soil.

Scarlotti dragged himself backward, his nose bleeding from both nostrils. But the elderly woman who had set the flowers out on the walk ran from the restaurant door and knelt beside him with her arms stretched across his chest, as though she were preventing him from rising. She screamed in Italian at Clete, her eyes serpentine and liquid.

Benny Grogan, the ex-wrestler, touched Clete on the elbow. Pieces of chipped beef still clung to his platinum hair. He held a ball-peen hammer in his hand, but he tossed it onto a sack of peat moss. For some reason, the elderly woman stopped screaming, as though a curtain had descended on a stage.

"You see a percentage in this, Purcel?" Benny Grogan said.

Clete looked at the elderly woman squatted by her son.

"You should go to church today, burn a candle, Mouse," he said.

He got in his convertible and drove to the corner, his tailpipe billowing white smoke, and turned down a shady side street toward St. Charles. He took his seal-top coffee mug off the dashboard and drank from it.

NINETEEN

It was early Saturday morning and Clete was changing a tire in my drive while he talked, spinning a lug wrench on a nut, his love handles wedging over his belt.

"So I took River Road and barrel-assed across the Huey Long and said goodbye to New Orleans for a while," he said. He squinted up at me and waited. "What?" he said.

"Scarlotti is a small player in this, Clete," I said.

"That's why you and Helen were pounding on his cage?" He got to his feet and threw his tools in the trunk. "I've got to get some new tires. I blew one coming off the bridge. What d' you mean, small player? That pisses me off, Dave."

"I think he and the Giancano family put the hit on Cool Breeze because he ratted them out to the Feds. But if you wanted to get even for Megan, you probably beat up on the wrong guy."

"The greaseballs are taking orders, even though they've run the action in New Orleans for a hundred years? Man, I learn something every day. Did you read that article in the *Star* about Hitler hiding out in Israel?"

His face was serious a moment, then he stuck an unlit cigarette in his mouth and the smile came back in his eyes and he twirled his porkpie hat on his finger while he looked at me, then at the sunrise behind the flooded cypresses.

I helped Batist at the bait shop, then drove to Cool Breeze's house on the west side of town and was told by a neighbor he was out at Mout's flower farm.

Mout' and a Hmong family from Laos farmed three acres of zinnias and chrysanthemums in the middle of a sugarcane plantation on the St. Martinville road, and each fall, when football season began, they cut and dug wagonloads of flowers that they sold to florists in Baton Rouge and New Orleans. I drove across a cattle guard and down a white shale road until I saw a row of poplars that was planted as a windbreak and Cool Breeze hoeing weeds out in the sunlight while his father sat in the shade reading a newspaper by a card table with a pitcher of lemonade on it.

I parked my truck and walked down the rows of chrysanthemums. The wind was blowing and the field rippled with streaks of brown and gold and purple color.

"I never figured you to take up farming, Breeze," I said.

"I give up on some t'ings. So my father made this li'l job for me, that's all," he said.

"Beg your pardon?"

"Getting even wit' people, t'ings like that. I ain't giving nobody reason to put me back in jail."

"You know what an exhumation order is?" I asked.

As with many people of color, he treated questions from white men as traps and didn't indicate an answer one way or another. He stooped over and jerked a weed and its root system out of the soil.

"I want to have a pathologist examine your wife's remains. I don't believe she committed suicide," I said.

He stopped work and rested his hands on the hoe handle. His hands looked like gnarled rocks around the wood. Then he put one hand inside the top of his shirt and rubbed his skin, his eyes never leaving mine.

"Say again?"

"I checked with the coroner's office in St. Mary Parish. No autopsy was done on Ida's body. It simply went down as a suicide."

"What you telling me?"

"I don't think she took her life."

"Didn't nobody have reason to kill her. Unless you saying I . . . Wait a minute, you trying to—"

"You're not a killer, Breeze. You're just a guy who got used by some very bad white people."

He started working the hoe between the plants again, his breath coming hard in his chest, his brow creased like an old leather glove. The wind was cool blowing across the field, but drops of sweat as big as marbles slid off his neck. He stopped his work again and faced me, his eyes wet.

"What we got to do to get this here order you talking about?" he asked.

When I got home a peculiar event was taking place. Alafair and three of her friends were in the front yard, watching a man with a flattop haircut stand erect on an oak limb, then topple into space, grab a second limb and hang from it by his knees.

I parked my pickup and walked across the yard while Boxleiter's eyes, upside down, followed me. He bent his torso upward, flipped his legs in the air, and did a half-somersault so that he hit the ground on the balls of his feet.

"Alafair, would you guys head on up to the house and tell Bootsie I'll be there in a minute?" I said.

"She's on the gallery. Tell her yourself," Alafair said.

"*Alf . . .*" I said.

She rolled her eyes as though the moment was more than her patience could endure, then she and her friends walked through the shade toward the house.

"Swede, it's better you bring business to my office," I said.

"I couldn't sleep last night. I always sleep, I mean dead, like stone.

But not last night. There's some heavy shit coming down, man. It's a feeling I get. I'm never wrong."

"Like what?"

"This ain't no ordinary grift." He fanned his hand at the air, as though sweeping away cobweb. "I never had trouble handling the action. You draw lines, you explain the rules, guys don't listen, they keep coming at you, you unzip their package. But that ain't gonna work on this one." He blotted the perspiration off his face with the back of his forearm.

"Sorry. You're not making much sense, Swede."

"I don't got illusions about how guys like me end up. But Cisco and Megan ain't like me. I was sleeping in the Dismas House in St. Louis after I finished my first bit. They came and got me. They see somebody jammed up, people getting pushed around, they make those people's problem their problem. They get that from their old man. That's why these local cocksuckers nailed him to a wall."

"You're going have to watch your language around my home, partner," I said.

His hand shot out and knotted my shirt in a ball.

"You're like every cop I ever knew. You don't listen. I can't stop what's going on."

I grabbed his wrist and thrust it away from me. He opened and closed his hands impotently.

"I hate guys like you," he said.

"Oh?"

"You go to church with your family, but you got no idea what life is like for two-thirds of the human race."

"I'm going inside now, Swede. Don't come around here anymore."

"What'd I do, use bad language again?"

"You cut up Anthony Pollock. I can't prove it, and it didn't happen in our jurisdiction, but you're an iceman."

"If I did it in a uniform, you'd be introducing me at the Kiwanis Club. I hear you adopted your kid and treated her real good. That's a righteous deed, man. But the rest of your routine is comedy. A guy with your brains ought to be above it."

He walked down the slope to the dirt road and his parked car. When he was out of the shade he stopped and turned around. His granny glasses were like ground diamonds in the sunlight.

"How many people did it take to crucify Megan and Cisco's old man and cover it up for almost forty years? I'm an iceman? Watch out one of your neighbors don't tack you up with a nail gun," he yelled up the slope while two fishermen unhitching a boat trailer stared at him openmouthed.

I raked and burned leaves that afternoon and tried not to think about Swede Boxleiter. But in his impaired way he had put his thumb on a truth about human behavior that eludes people who are considered normal. I remembered a story of years ago about a fourteen-year-old boy from Chicago who was visiting relatives in a small Mississippi town not far from the Pearl River. One afternoon he whistled at a white woman on the street. Nothing was said to him, but that night two Klansmen kidnapped him from the home of his relatives, shot and killed him, and wrapped his body in a net of bricks and wire and sank it in the river.

Everyone in town knew who had done it. Two local lawyers, respectable men not associated with the Klan, volunteered to defend the killers. The jury took twenty minutes to set them free. The foreman said the verdict took that long because the jury had stopped deliberations to send out for soda pop.

It's a story out of another era, one marked by shame and collective fear, but its point is not about racial injustice but instead the fate of those who bear Cain's mark.

A year after the boy's death a reporter from a national magazine visited the town by the Pearl River to learn the fate of the killers. At first they had been avoided, passed by on the street, treated at grocery or hardware counters as though they had no first or last names, then their businesses failed—one owned a filling station, the other a fertilizer yard—and their debts were called. Both men left town, and when asked their whereabouts old neighbors would only shake their heads as though the killers were part of a vague and decaying memory.

The town that had been complicit in the murder ostracized those who had committed it. But no one had been ostracized in St. Mary Parish. Why? What was the difference in the accounts of the black teenager's murder and Jack Flynn's, both of which seemed collective in nature?

Answer: The killers in Mississippi were white trash and economically dispensable.

Sunday afternoon I found Archer Terrebonne on his side patio, disassembling a spinning reel on a glass table top. He wore slippers and white slacks and a purple shirt that was embroidered with his initials on the pocket. Overhead, two palm trees with trunks that were as gray and smooth as elephant hide creaked against a hard-blue sky. Terrebonne glanced up at me, then resumed his concentration, but not in an unpleasant way.

"Sorry to bother you on Sunday, but I suspect you're quite busy during the week," I said.

"It's no bother. Pull up a chair. I wanted to thank you for the help you gave my daughter."

You didn't do wide end runs around Archer Terrebonne.

"It's wonderful to see her fresh and bright in the morning, unharried by all the difficulties she's had, all the nights in hospitals and calls from policemen," he said.

"I have a problem, Mr. Terrebonne. A man named Harpo Scruggs is running all over our turf and we can't get a net over him."

"Scruggs? Oh yes, quite a character. I thought he was dead."

"His uncle was a guy named Harpo Delahoussey. He did security work at y'all's cannery, the one that burned."

"Yes, I remember."

"We think Harpo Scruggs tried to kill a black man named Willie Broussard and almost drowned Jack Flynn's daughter."

He set down the tiny screwdriver and the exposed brass mechanisms of the spinning reel. The tips of his delicate fingers were bright with machine oil. The wind blew his white-gold hair on his forehead.

"But you use the father's name, not the daughter's. What inference should I gather from that, sir? My family has a certain degree of wealth and hence we should feel guilt over Jack Flynn's death?"

"Why do you think he was killed?"

"That's your province, Mr. Robicheaux, not mine. But I don't think Jack Flynn was a proletarian idealist. I think he was a resentful, envious troublemaker who couldn't get over the fact his family lost their money through their own mismanagement. Castle Irish don't do well when their diet is changed to boiled cabbage."

"He fought Franco's fascists in Spain. That's a peculiar way to show envy."

"What's your purpose here?"

"Your daughter is haunted by something in the past she can't tell anybody about. It's connected to the Hanged Man in the Tarot. I wonder if it's Jack Flynn's death that bothers her."

He curled the tips of his fingers against his palm, as though trying to rub the machinist's oil off them, looking at them idly.

"She killed her cousin when she was fifteen. Or at least that's what she's convinced herself," he said. He saw my expression change, my lips start to form a word. "We had a cabin in Durango at the foot of a mountain. They found the key to my gun case and started shooting across a snowfield. The avalanche buried her cousin in an arroyo. When they dug her out the next day, her body was frozen upright in the shape of a cross."

"I didn't know that, sir."

"You do now. I'm going in to eat directly. Would you care to join us?"

When I walked to my truck I felt like a man who had made an obscene remark in the midst of a polite gathering. I sat behind the steering wheel and stared at the front of the Terrebonne home. It was encased in shadow now, the curtains drawn on all the windows. What historical secrets, what private unhappiness did it hold? I wondered if I would ever know. The late sun hung like a shattered red flame in the pine trees.

TWENTY

I remember a Christmas dawn five years after I came home from Vietnam. I greeted it in an all-night bar built of slat wood, the floor raised off the dirt with cinder blocks. I walked down the wood steps into a deserted parking area, my face numb with alcohol, and stood in the silence and looked at a solitary live oak hung with Spanish moss, the cattle acreage that was gray with winter, the hollow dome of sky that possessed no color at all, and suddenly I felt the vastness of the world and all the promise it could hold for those who were still its children and had not severed their ties with the rest of the human family.

Monday morning I visited Megan at her brother's house and saw a look in her eyes that I suspected had been in mine on that Christmas morning years ago.

Had her attackers held her underwater a few seconds more, her body would have conceded what her will would not: Her lungs and mouth and nose would have tried to draw oxygen out of water and her chest and throat would have filled with cement. In that moment she knew the heartbreaking twilight-infused beauty that the earth can offer, that we waste as easily as we tear pages from a calendar, but neither would she ever forget or forgive the fact that her reprieve came from the same hands that did Indian burns on her skin and twisted her face down into the silt.

She was living in the guest cottage at the back of Cisco's house, and the French doors were open and the four-o'clocks planted as borders around the trees were dull red in the shade.

"What's that?" she said.

I lay a paper sack and the hard-edged metal objects inside it on her breakfast table.

"A nine-millimeter Beretta. I've made arrangements for some-body to give you instruction at the firing range," I said.

She slipped the pistol and the unattached magazine out of the sack and pulled back the slide and looked at the empty chamber. She flipped the butterfly safety back and forth.

"You have peculiar attitudes for a policeman," she said.

"When they deal the play, you take it to them with fire tongs," I said.

She put the pistol back in the sack and stepped out on the brick patio and looked at the bayou with her hands in the back pockets of her baggy khaki pants.

"I'll be all right after a while. I've been through worse," she said.

I stepped outside with her. "No, you haven't," I said.

"Excuse me?"

"It only gets so bad. You go to the edge, then you join a special club. A psychologist once told me only about three percent of the human family belongs to it."

"I think I'll pass on the honor."

"Why'd you come back?"

"I see my father in my sleep."

"You want the gun?"

"Yes."

I nodded and turned to go.

"Wait." She took her eyeglass case out of her shirt pocket and stepped close to me. There was a dark scrape at the corner of her eye, like dirty rouge rubbed into the grain. "Just stand there. You don't have to do anything," she said, and put her arms around me and her

head on my chest and pressed her stomach flat against me. She wore
doeskin moccasins and I could feel the instep of her foot on my ankle.

The top of her head moved under my chin and against my throat
and the wetness of her eyes was like an unpracticed kiss streaked on my
skin.

Rodney Loudermilk had lived two weeks on the eighth floor of
the old hotel that was not two blocks from the Alamo. The
elevator was slow and throbbed in the shaft, the halls smelled bad, the
fire escapes leaked rust down the brick sides of the building. But there
was a bar and grill downstairs and the view from his window was
magnificent. The sky was blue and salmon-colored in the evening, the
San Antonio River lighted by sidewalk restaurants and gondolas that
passed under the bridges, and he could see the pinkish stone front of
the old mission where he often passed himself off as a tour guide and
led college girls through the porticoed walkways that were hung with
grapevines.

He was blind in one eye from a childhood accident with a BB
gun. He wore sideburns and snap-button cowboy shirts with his
Montgomery Ward suits. He had been down only once, in Sugarland,
on a nickel-and-dime burglary beef that had gone sour because his fall
partner, a black man, had dropped a crowbar off the roof through the
top of a greenhouse.

But Rodney had learned his lesson: Stay off of roofs and don't try
to turn watermelon pickers into successful house creeps.

The three-bit on Sugarland Farm hadn't been a wash either. He
had picked up a new gig, one that had some dignity to it, that paid
better, that didn't require dealing with fences who took him off at
fifteen cents on the dollar. One week off the farm and he did his first
hit. It was much easier than he thought. The target was a rancher
outside Victoria, a loudmouth fat shit who drove a Cadillac with
longhorns for a hood ornament and who kept blubbering, "I'll give
you money, boy. You name the price. Look, my wife's gonna be back
from the store. Don't hurt her, okay . . . ," then had started to
tremble and messed himself like a child.

"That goes to show you, money don't put no lead in your pencil," Rodney was fond of telling his friends.

He also said the fat man was so dumb he never guessed his wife had put up the money for the hit. But Rodney let him keep his illusions. Why not? Business was business. You didn't personalize it, even though the guy was a born mark.

Their grief was their own, he said. They owed money, they stole it, they cheated on their wives. People sought justice in different ways. The state did it with a gurney and a needle, behind a viewing glass, while people watched like they were at an X-rated movie. Man, *that* was sick.

Rodney showered in the small tin stall and put on a fresh long-sleeve shirt, one that covered the tattooed chain of blue stars around his left wrist, then looked at his four suits in the closet and chose one that rippled with light like a sheet of buffed tin. He slipped on a new pair of black cowboy boots and fitted a white cowboy hat on his head, pulling the brim at an angle over his blind eye.

All you had to do was stand at the entrance to the Alamo and people came up and asked you questions. Clothes didn't make the person. Clothes *were* the person, he told people. You ever see a gun bull mounted on horseback without a hat and shades? You ever see a construction boss on a job without a clipboard and hard hat and a pocketful of ballpoints? You ever see a hooker that *ain't* made up to look like your own personal pinball machine?

Rodney conducted tours, gave directions around the city, walked tourists to their hotels so they wouldn't be mugged by what he called "local undesirables we're fixing to get rid of."

A buddy, a guy he'd celled with at Sugarland, asked him what he got out of it.

"Nothing. That's the point, boy. They got nothing I want."

Which wasn't true. But how did you explain to a pipehead that walking normals around, making them apprehensive one moment, relieving their fears another, watching them hang on his words about the cremation of the Texan dead on the banks of the river (an account he had memorized from a brochure) gave him a rush like a freight train loaded with Colombian pink roaring through the center of his head?

Or popping a cap on a slobbering fat man who thought he could bribe Rodney Loudermilk.

It was dusk when Rodney came back from showing two elderly nuns where Davy Crockett had been either bayoneted to death or captured against the barracks wall and later tortured. They both had seemed a little pale at the details he used to describe the event. In fact, they had the ingratitude to tell him they didn't need an escort back to their hotel, like he had BO or something. Oh, well. He had more important things on his mind. Like this deal over in Louisiana. He'd told his buddy, the pipehead, he didn't get into a new career so he could go back to strong-arm and B&E bullshit. That whole scene on the bayou had made him depressed in ways he couldn't explain, like somebody had stolen something from him.

She hadn't been afraid. When they're afraid, it proves they got it coming. When they're not afraid, it's like they're spitting in your face. Yeah, that was it. You can't pop them unless they're afraid, or they take part of you with them. Now he was renting space in his head to a hide (that's what he called women) he shouldn't even be thinking about. He had given her power, and he wanted to go back and correct the images that had left him confused and irritable and not the person he was when he gave guided tours in his western clothes.

He looked at the slip of paper he had made a note on when this crazy deal started. It read: *Meet H.S. in New Iberia. Educate a commonist?* A commonist? Republicans live in rich houses, not commonists. Any dumb shit knows that. Why had he gotten into this? He crumpled up the note in his palm and bounced it off the rim of the wastebasket and called the grill for a steak and baked potato, heavy on the cream and melted butter, and a green salad and a bottle of champale.

It was dusk and a purple haze hung on the rooftops when a man stepped out of a hallway window onto a fire escape, then eased one foot out on a ledge and worked his way across the brick side of the building, oblivious to the stares of two winos down in the alley eight floors below. When the ledge ended, he paused for only a moment, then with the agility of a cat, he hopped across empty space onto another ledge and entered another window.

Rodney Loudermilk had just forked a piece of steak into his mouth when the visitor seized him from behind and dragged him out of his chair, locking arms and wrists under Rodney's rib cage, lifting him into the air and simultaneously carrying him to the window, whose curtains swelled with the evening breeze. Rodney probably tried to scream and strike out with the fork that was in his hand, but a piece of meat was lodged like a stone in his throat and the arms of his visitor seemed to be cracking his ribs like sticks.

Then there was a rush of air and noise and he was out above the city, among clouds and rooftops and faces inside windows that blurred past him. He concentrated his vision on the dusky purple stretch of sky that was racing away from him, just like things had always raced away from him. It was funny how one gig led to another, then in seconds the rounded, cast-iron, lug-bolted dome of an ancient fire hydrant rose out of the cement and came at your head faster than a BB traveling toward the eye.

The account of Rodney Loudermilk's death was given us over the phone by a San Antonio homicide investigator named Cecil Hardin, who had found the crumpled piece of notepaper by the wastebasket in Loudermilk's hotel room. He also read us the statements he had taken from the two witnesses in the alley and played a taped recording of an interview with Loudermilk's pipehead friend.

"You got any idea who H.S. is?" Hardin asked.

"We've had trouble around here with an ex-cop by the name of Harpo Scruggs," I said.

"You think he's connected to Loudermilk's death?" he asked.

"The killer was an aerialist? My vote would go to another local, Swede Boxleiter. He's a suspect in a murder in Lafayette Parish."

"What are y'all running over there, a school for criminals? Forget I said that. Spell the name, please." Then he said, "What's the deal on this guy Boxleiter?"

"He's a psychopath with loyalties," I said.

"You a comedian, sir?"

I drove up the Loreauville road to Cisco's house. Megan was reading a book in a rocking chair on the gallery.

"Do you know where Swede was on Sunday?" I asked.

"He was here, at least in the morning. Why?"

"Just a little research. Does the name Rodney Loudermilk mean anything to you?"

"No. Who is he?"

"A guy with sideburns, blind in one eye?"

She shook her head.

"Did you tell Swede anything about your attackers, how they looked, what they said?"

"Nothing I didn't tell you. I was asleep when they broke in. They wound tape around my eyes."

I scratched the back of my neck. "Maybe Swede's not our man."

"I don't know what you're talking about, Dave."

"Sunday evening somebody canceled out a contract killer in a San Antonio hotel. He was probably one of the men who broke into your house."

She closed the book in her lap and looked out into the yard. "I told Swede about the blue stars on a man's wrist," she said.

"What?"

"One of them had a string of stars tattooed on his wrist. I told that to one of your deputies. He wrote it down."

"If he did, the sheriff and I never saw it."

"What difference does it make?"

"The guy in San Antonio, he was thrown out an eighth-floor window by somebody who knows how to leap across window ledges. He had a chain of blue stars tattooed around his left wrist."

She tried to hide the knowledge in her eyes. She took her glasses off and put them back on again.

"Swede was here that morning. He ate breakfast with us. I mean, everything about him was normal," she said, then turned her face toward me.

"Normal? You're talking about Boxleiter? Good try, Meg."

Helen and I drove to the movie set on the Terrebonne lawn.

"Sunday? I was at Cisco's. Then I was home. Then I went to a movie," Swede said. He dropped down from the back of a flatbed truck, his tool belt clattering on his hips. His gaze went up and down Helen's body. "We're not getting into that blackjack routine again, are we?"

"Which movie?" I asked.

"*Sense and Sensibility*. Ask at the theater. The guy'll remember me 'cause he says I plugged up the toilet."

"Sounds good to me. What about you, Helen?" I said.

"Yeah, I always figured him for a fan of British novels," she said.

"What am I supposed to have done?"

"Tossed a guy out a window in San Antonio. His head hit a fire hydrant at a hundred twenty miles per. Big mess," I said.

"Yeah? Who is this fucking guy I supposedly killed?"

"Would you try not to use profanity?" I said.

"Sorry. I forgot, Louisiana is an open-air church. I got a question for you. Why is it guys like me are always getting rousted whenever some barf bag gets marched off with the Hallelujah Chorus? Does Ricky the Mouse do time? Is Harpo Scruggs sitting in your jail? Of course not. You turned him loose. If guys like me weren't around, you'd be out of a job." He pulled a screwdriver from his belt and began tapping it across his palm, rolling his eyes, chewing gum, rotating his head on his neck. "Is this over? I got to get to work."

"We might turn out to be your best friends, Swede," I said.

"Yeah, shit goes great with frozen yogurt, too," he said, and walked away from us, his bare triangular back arched forward like that of a man in search of an adversary.

"You going to let him slide like that?" Helen said.

"Sometimes the meltdowns have their point of view."

"Just coincidence he stops up a toilet in a theater on the day he needs an alibi?"

"Let's go to the airport."

But if Swede took a plane to San Antonio or rented one, we could find no record of it.

That night the air was thick and close and smelled of chrysanthemums and gas, then the sky filled with lightning and swirls of black rain that turned to hail and clattered and bounced like mothballs on the tin roof of the bait shop.

Two days later I drove to St. Mary Parish with Cool Breeze Broussard to watch the exhumation of his wife's body from a graveyard that was being eaten daily by the Atchafalaya River.

At one time the graveyard had sat on dry ground, fringed by persimmon and gum trees, but almost twenty years ago the Atchafalaya had broken a levee and channeled an oxbow through the woods, flooding the grave sites, then had left behind a swampy knob of sediment strung with river trash. One side of the graveyard dipped toward the river, and each year the water cut more deeply under the bank, so that the top layer hung like the edge of a mushroom over the current.

Most of the framed and spiked name tags that served as markers had been knocked down or stepped on and broken by hunters. The dime-store vases and the jelly glasses used for flower jars lay embedded in sediment. The graduation and wedding and birth pictures wrapped in plastic had been washed off the graves on which they had been originally placed and were now spotted with mud, curled and yellowed by the sun so that the faces on them were not only anonymous but stared incongruously out of situations that seemed to have never existed.

The forensic pathologist and a St. Mary Parish deputy and the two black men hired as diggers and the backhoe operator waited.

"You know which one it is?" I asked Cool Breeze.

"That one yonder, wit' the pipe cross. I welded it myself. The shaft goes down t'ree feet," he said.

The serrated teeth on the bucket of the backhoe bit into the soft earth and lifted a huge divot of loam and roots and emerald-colored grass from the top of the grave. Cool Breeze's shoulder brushed against mine, and I could feel the rigidity and muted power in his body, like the tremolo that rises from the boiler room of a ship.

"We can wait on the levee until they're finished," I said.

"I got to look," he said.

"Beg your pardon?"

"Cain't have nobody saying later that ain't her."

"Breeze, she's been in the ground a long time."

"Don't matter. I'll know. What you t'ink I am anyway? Other men can look at my wife, but I'm scared to do it myself?"

"I think you're a brave man," I said.

He turned his head and looked at the side of my face.

The backhoe was bright yellow against the islands of willow trees between the graveyard and the main portion of the river. The loam in the grave turned to mud as the bucket on the backhoe dipped closer to the coffin. The day was blue-gold and warm and flowers still bloomed on the levee, but the air smelled of humus, of tree roots torn out of wet soil, of leaves that have gone acidic and brown in dead water. At five feet the two black diggers climbed into the hole with spades and began sculpting the coffin's shape, pouring water from a two-gallon can on the edges, wiping the surface and corners slick with rags.

They worked a canvas tarp and wood planks under it, then ran ropes tied to chains under the tarp, and we all lifted. The coffin came free more easily than I had expected, rocking almost weightlessly in the bottom of the canvas loop, a missing panel in one side blossoming with muddy fabric.

"Open it up," Cool Breeze said.

The pathologist looked at me. He wore red suspenders and a straw hat and had a stomach like a small pillow pushed under his belt. I nodded, and one of the diggers prized the lid loose with a blade screwdriver.

I had seen exhumations before. The view of mortality they present to the living is not easily dismissed. Sometimes the coffin fills with hair, the nails, particularly on the bare feet, grow into claws, the face puckers into a gray apple, the burial clothes contain odors that cause people to retch.

That is not what happened to Ida Broussard.

Her white dress had turned brown, like cheesecloth dipped in tea, but her skin had the smooth texture and color of an eggplant and her hair was shiny and black on her shoulders and there was no distortion in her expression.

Cool Breeze's hand reached out and touched her cheek. Then he walked away from us, without speaking, and stood on the edge of the graveyard and looked out at the river so we could not see his face.

"How do you explain it?" I said to the pathologist.

"An oil company buried some storage tanks around here in the 1930s. Maybe some chemical seepage got in the coffin," he replied.

He looked back into my eyes. Then he spoke again. "Sometimes I think they wait to tell us something. There's no need for you to pass on my observation."

TWENTY-ONE

Friday evening Bootsie and I dropped Alafair at the show in Lafayette, then ate dinner at a restaurant on the Vermilion River. But as soon as Alafair was not with us, Bootsie became introspective, almost formal when she spoke, her eyes lingering on objects without seeing them.

"What is it?" I said outside the restaurant.

"I'm just tired," she replied.

"Maybe we should have stayed home."

"Maybe we should have."

After Alafair went to bed, we were alone in the kitchen. The moon was up and the trees outside were full of shadows when the wind blew.

"Whatever it is, just say it, Boots."

"She was at the dock today. She said she couldn't find you at your office. She didn't bother to come up to the house. Of course, she's probably just shy."

"She?"

"You know who. She finds any excuse she can to come out here. She said she wanted to thank you for the shooting lessons you arranged for her. You didn't want to give them to her yourself?"

"Those guys almost killed her. They might pull it off the next time."

"Maybe it's her own fault."

"That's a rough thing to say, Boots."

"She hides behind adversity and uses it to manipulate other people."

"I'll ask her not to come here again."

"Not on my account, please."

"I give up," I said, and went out into the yard.

The cane in my neighbor's field was green and dented with channels like rivers when the wind blew, and beyond his tree line I could see lightning fork without sound out of the sky. Through the kitchen window I heard Bootsie clattering dishes into the dishwasher. She slammed the washer door shut, the cups and silverware rattling in the rack. I heard the washer start to hum, then her shadow went past the window and disappeared from view and the overhead light went off and the kitchen and the yard were dark.

We wanted Harpo Scruggs. But we had nothing to charge him with. He knew it, too. He called the dock on Sunday afternoon.

"I want to meet, talk this thing out, bring it to an end," he said.

"It's not a seller's market, Scruggs."

"What you got is your dick in your hand. I can clean the barn for you. There's an old nigra runs a barbecue joint next to a motel on State Road 70 north of Morgan City. Nine o'clock," he said, and hung up.

I went outside the bait shop and hosed down a rental boat a fisherman had just returned, then went back inside without chaining it up and called Helen Soileau at her home.

"You want to do backup on a meet with Harpo Scruggs?" I said.

"Make him come in."

"We don't have enough to charge him."

"There's still the college kid, the witness who saw the two brothers executed in the Basin."

"His family says he's on a walking tour of Tibet."

"He killed Mout's dog. Vermilion Parish can charge him with endangering."

"Mout' says he never got a good look at the guy's face."

"Dave, we need to work this guy. He doesn't bring the Feds into it, he doesn't plead out. We fit his head in a steel vise."

"So take a ride with me. I want you to bring a scoped rifle."

She was silent a moment. Then she said, "Tell the old man."

The barbecue place was a rambling, tin-roofed red building, with white trim and screen porches, set back in a grove of pines. Next door was a cinder-block motel that had been painted purple and fringed with Christmas lights that never came down. Through the screen on a side porch I saw Harpo Scruggs standing at the bar, a booted foot on the rail, his tall frame bent forward, his Stetson at an angle on his freshly barbered head. He wore a long-sleeve blue shirt with pink polka dots and an Indian-stitched belt and gray western slacks that flowed like water over the crook in his knee. He tilted back a shot glass of whiskey and sipped from a glass of beer.

I stood by a plank table at the edge of the clearing so he could see me. He put an unlit cigarette in his mouth and opened the screen door and lit the cigarette with a Zippo as he walked toward me.

"You got anybody with you?" he asked.

"You see anyone?"

He sat down at the plank table and smoked his cigarette, his elbows on the wood. The clouds above the pines were black and maroon in the sun's afterglow. He tipped his ashes carefully over the edge of the table so they wouldn't blow back on his shirt.

"I heard about a man got throwed out a window. I think one of two men done it. Swede Boxleiter or that bucket of whale sperm got hisself kicked off the New Orleans police force," he said.

"Clete Purcel?"

"If that's his name. You can tell them I didn't have nothing to do with hurting that woman."

"Tell them yourself."

"All this trouble we been having? It can end in one of two ways. That black boy, Broussard, don't testify against the dagos in New Orleans and some people gets paid back the money they're owed.

"The other way it ends is I get complete immunity as a government witness, all my real estate is sold and the proceeds are put in bearer bonds. Not one dollar of it gets touched by the IRS. Then I retire down in Guatemala. Y'all decide."

"Who the hell do you think you are?" I said.

A black man brought a bottle of Dixie beer on a metal tray to the table. Scruggs tipped him a quarter and wiped the lip of the bottle with his palm.

"I'm the man got something you want, son. Or you wouldn't be sitting here," he replied.

"You took money from Ricky Scarlotti, then fucked up everything you touched. Now you've got both the Mob and a crazoid like Boxleiter on your case," I said.

He drank out of the beer and looked into the pine trees, sucking his false teeth, his expression flat. But I saw the muted change in his eyes, the way heat glows when the wind puffs ash off a coal.

"You ain't so different from me," he said. "You want to bring them rich people down. I can smell it in you, boy. A poor man's got hate in his glands. It don't wash out. That's why nigras stink the way they do."

"You've caused a lot of trouble and pain for people around here. So we've decided in your case it should be a two-way street. I'd hoped you'd provoke a situation here."

"You got a hideaway on your ankle?"

"My partner has your face in the crosshairs of a scoped .30-06. She'd looked forward to this evening with great anticipation, sir. Enjoy your beer. We'll catch you down the road."

I walked out to the parking lot and waited for Helen to pull my truck around from the other side of the motel. I didn't look behind me, but I could feel his eyes on my back, watching. When Helen drew to a stop in front of me, the scoped, bolt-action rifle on the gun rack, the dust drifting off the tires, she cocked one finger like a pistol and aimed it out the window at Harpo Scruggs.

. . .

Tuesday morning the sheriff called me into his office.

"I just got the surveillance report on Scruggs," he said. "He took the Amtrak to Houston, spent the night in a Mexican hot pillow joint, then flew to Trinidad, Colorado."

"He'll be back."

"I think I finally figured out something about wars. A few people start them and the rest of us fight them. I'm talking about all these people who use our area for a bidet. I think this state is becoming a mental asylum, I really do." Something outside the window caught his attention. "Ah, my morning wouldn't be complete without it. Cisco Flynn just walked in the front door."

Five minutes later Cisco sat down in front of my desk.

"You got anything on these guys who attacked Megan?" he asked.

"Yeah. One of them is dead."

"Did you clear Swede on that deal?"

"You mean did I check out his alibi? He created a memorable moment at the theater. Water flowed out of the men's room into the lobby. At about five in the afternoon."

"From what I understand, that should put him home free."

"It might."

I watched his face. His reddish-brown eyes smiled at nothing.

"Megan felt bad that maybe she made a suspect out of Swede," he said.

"You can pretend otherwise, but he's a dangerous man, Cisco."

"How about the cowboy who went out the window? Would you call him a dangerous man?"

I didn't answer. We stared at each other across the desk. Then his eyes broke.

"Good seeing you, Dave. Thanks for giving Megan the gun," he said.

I watched silently as he opened the office door and went out into the hall.

I propped my forehead on my fingers and stared at the empty green surface of my desk blotter. Why hadn't I seen it? I had even used the term "aerialist" to the San Antonio homicide investigator.

I went out the side door of the building and caught Cisco at his car. The day was beautiful, and his suntanned face looked gold and handsome in the cool light.

"You called the dead man a cowboy," I said.

He grinned, bemused. "What's the big deal?" he said.

"Who said anything about how the guy was dressed?"

"I mean 'cowboy' like 'hit man.' That's what contract killers are called, aren't they?"

"You and Boxleiter worked this scam together, didn't you?"

He laughed and shook his head and got in his car and drove out of the lot, then waved from the window just before he disappeared in the traffic.

The forensic pathologist called me that afternoon.

"I can give it to you over the phone or talk in person. I'd rather do it in person," he said.

"Why's that?"

"Because autopsies can tell us things about human behavior I don't like to know about," he replied.

An hour later I walked into his office.

"Let's go outside and sit under the trees. You'll have to excuse my mood. My own work depresses the hell out of me sometimes," he said.

We sat in metal chairs behind the white-painted brick building that housed his office. The hard-packed earth stayed in shade almost year-round and was green with mold and sloped down to a ragged patch of bamboo on the bayou. Out in the sunlight an empty pirogue that had pulled loose from its mooring turned aimlessly in the current.

"There're abrasions on the back of her head and scrape marks on her shoulder, like trauma from a fall rather than a direct blow," he said. "Of course, you're more interested in cause of death."

"I'm interested in all of it."

"I mean, the abrasions on her skin could have been unrelated to her death. Didn't you say her husband knocked her around before she fled the home?"

"Yes."

"I found evidence of water in the lungs. It's a bit complicated, but there's no question about its presence at the time she died."

"So she was alive when she went into the marsh?"

"Hear me out. The water came out of a tap, not a swamp or marsh or brackish bay, not unless the latter contains the same chemicals you find in a city water supply."

"A faucet?"

"But that's not what killed her." He wore an immaculate white shirt, and his red suspenders hung loosely on his concave chest. He snuffed down in his nose and fixed his glasses. "It was heart failure, maybe brought on by suffocation."

"I'm not putting it together, Clois."

"You were in Vietnam. What'd the South Vietnamese do when they got their hands on the Vietcong?"

"Water poured on a towel?"

"I think in this case we're talking about a wet towel held down on the face. Maybe she fell, then somebody finished the job. But I'm in a speculative area now."

The image he had called up out of memory was not one I wanted to think about. I looked at the fractured light on the bayou, a garden blooming with blue and pink hydrangeas on the far bank. But he wasn't finished.

"She was pregnant. Maybe two months. Does that mean anything?" he said.

"Yeah, it sure does."

"You don't look too good."

"It's a bad story, Doc."

"They all are."

TWENTY-TWO

That evening Clete parked his convertible by the dock and hefted an ice chest up on his shoulder and carried it to a fish-cleaning table by one of the water faucets I had mounted at intervals on a water line that ran the length of the dock's handrail. He poured the ice and at least two dozen sac-a-lait out on the table, put on a pair of cloth gardener's gloves, and started scaling the sac-a-lait with a spoon and splitting open their stomachs and half-mooning the heads at the gills.

"You catch fish somewhere else and clean them at my dock?" I said.

"I hate to tell you this, the fishing's a lot better at Henderson. How about I take y'all to the Patio for dinner tonight?"

"Things aren't real cool at the house right now."

He kept his eyes flat, his face neutral. He washed the spooned fish scales off the board plank. I told him about the autopsy on Ida Broussard.

When I finished he said, "You like graveyard stories? How about this? I caught Swede Boxleiter going out of the Terrebonne cemetery last night. He'd used a trowel to take the bricks out of the crypt and pry open the casket. He took the rings from the corpse's fingers, and a pair of riding spurs and a silver picture frame that Archer Terrebonne says held a photo of some little girls a slave poisoned.

"I cuffed Boxleiter to a car bumper and went up to the house and told Terrebonne a ghoul had been in his family crypt. That guy must have Freon in his veins. He didn't say a word. He went down there with a light and lifted the bricks back out and dragged the casket out on the ground and straightened the bones and rags inside and put the stolen stuff back on the corpse, didn't blink an eye. He didn't even look at Boxleiter, like Boxleiter was an insect sitting under a glass jar."

"What'd you do with Boxleiter?"

"Fired him this morning."

"*You* fired him?"

"Billy Holtzner tends to delegate authority in some situations. He promised me a two-hundred-buck bonus, then hid in his trailer while I walked Boxleiter off the set. Have you told this Broussard guy his wife was murdered?"

"He's not home."

"Dave, I'll say it again. Don't let him come around the set to square a beef, okay?"

"He's not a bad guy, Clete."

"Yeah, they've got a lot of that kind on Camp J."

Early the next morning I sat with Cool Breeze on the gallery of his father's house and told him, in detail, of the pathologist's findings. He had been pushing the swing at an angle with one foot, then he stopped and scratched his hand and looked out at the street.

"The blow on the back of her head and the marks on her shoulders, could you have done that?" I said.

"I pushed her down on the steps. But her head didn't hit nothing but the screen."

"Was the baby yours?"

"Two months? No, we wasn't . . . It couldn't be my baby."

"You know where she went after she left your house, don't you?" I said.

"I do now."

"You stay away from Alex Guidry. I want your promise on that, Breeze."

He pulled on his fingers and stared at the street.

"I talked with Harpo Scruggs Sunday night," I said. "He's making noise about your testifying against the Giacanos and Ricky Scarlotti."

"Why ain't you got him in jail?"

"Sooner or later, they all go down."

"Ex-cop, ex-prison guard, man killed niggers in Angola for fun? They go down when God call 'em. What you done about Ida, it ain't lost on me. T'ank you."

Then he went back in the house.

I ate lunch at home that day. But Bootsie didn't sit at the kitchen table with me. Behind me, I heard her cleaning the drainboard, putting dishes in the cabinets, straightening canned goods in the cupboard.

"Boots, in all truth, I don't believe Megan Flynn has any romantic interest in an over-the-hill small-town homicide cop," I said.

"Really?"

"When I was a kid, my father was often drunk or in jail and my mother was having affairs with various men. I was alone a lot of the time, and for some reason I didn't understand I was attracted to people who had something wrong with them. There was a big, fat alcoholic nun I always liked, and a half-blind ex-convict who swept out Provost's Bar, and a hooker on Railroad Avenue who used to pay me a dollar to bring a bucket of beer to her crib."

"So?"

"A kid from a screwed-up home sees himself in the faces of excoriated people."

"You're telling me you're Megan Flynn's pet bête noire?"

"No, I'm just a drunk."

I heard her moving about in the silence, then she paused behind my chair and let the tips of her fingers rest in my hair.

"Dave, it's all right to call yourself that at meetings. But you're not a drunk to me. And she'd better not ever call you one either."

I felt her fingers trail off my neck, then she was gone from the room.

Two days later Helen and I took the department boat out on a wide bay off the Atchafalaya River where Cisco Flynn was filming a simulated plane crash. We let the bow of the boat scrape up onto a willow island, then walked out on a platform that the production company had built on pilings over the water. Cisco was talking to three other men, his eyes barely noting our presence.

"No, tell him to do it again," he said. "The plane's got to come in lower, right out of the sun, right across those trees. I'll do it with him if necessary. When the plane blows smoke, I want it to bleed into that red sun. Okay, everybody cool?"

It was impressive to watch him. Cisco used authority in a way that made others feel they shared in it. He was one of their own, obviously egalitarian in his attitudes, but he could take others across a line they wouldn't cross by themselves.

He turned to me and Helen.

"Watch the magic of Hollywood at work," he said. "This scene is going to take four days and a quarter of a million dollars to shoot. The plane comes in blowing black smoke, then we film a model crashing in a pond. We've got a tail section mounted on a mechanical arm that draws the wreckage underwater like a sinking plane, then we do the rescue dive in the LSU swimming pool. It edits down to two minutes of screen time. What d'you think about that?"

"I ran you through the National Crime Information Center. You and Swede Boxleiter took down a liquor store when you were seventeen," I said.

"Boy, the miracle of computers," he said. He glanced out at a boat that was moored in the center of the bay. It was the kind used for swamp tours, wide across the beam, domed with green Plexiglas, its white hull gleaming.

"Where were you Sunday evening, Cisco?" I said.

"Rented a pontoon plane and took a ride out on the Gulf."

"I have to pass on relevant information about you to a homicide investigator in San Antonio."

"So why tell me about it?"

"I try to do things in the daylight, at least when it involves people I used to trust."

"He's saying you're being treated better than you deserve," Helen said.

"The guy who soared on gilded wings out the hotel window? I think the Jersey Bounce was too easy. You saying I did it? Who cares?" Cisco replied.

"Rough words," I said.

"Yeah?" He picked up a pair of field glasses from a table and tossed them at me. "Check out the guys who are on that boat. That's reality out there. I wish it would go away, but I'm stuck with it. So give me a break on the wiseacre remarks."

I focused the glasses through an open window on a linen-covered table where Billy Holtzner and his daughter and two Asian men were eating.

"The two Chinese are the bean counters. When the arithmetic doesn't come out right, they count the numbers a second time on your fingers. Except your fingers aren't on your hands anymore," he said.

"I'd get into a new line of work," I said.

"Dave, I respect you and I don't want you to take this wrong. But don't bother me again without a warrant and in the meantime kiss my royal ass," Cisco said.

"You only try to get men to kiss your ass?" Helen said.

He walked away from us, both of his hands held in the air, as though surrendering to an irrational world, just as a twin-engine amphibian roared across the swamp at treetop level, a pipe in the stern blowing curds of black smoke across the sun.

. . .

That evening I jogged to the drawbridge on the dirt road while heat lightning veined the clouds and fireflies glowed and faded like wet matches above the bayou's surface. Then I did three sets each of push-ups, barbell curls, dead lifts, and military presses in the back yard, showered, and went to bed early.

On the edge of sleep I heard rain in the trees and Bootsie undressing in the bathroom, then I felt her weight next to me on the bed. She turned on her side so that her stomach and breasts were pressed against me, and put one leg across mine and her hand on my chest.

"You're drawn to people who have problems. My problem is I don't like other women making overtures to my husband," she said.

"I think that's a problem I can live with," I replied.

She raised her knee and hit me with it. Then her hand touched me and she lifted her nightgown and sat on my thighs and leaned over me and looked into my face.

Outside the window, I could see the hard, thick contours of an oak limb, wrapped with moonlight, glistening with rain.

The next day was Saturday. At false dawn I woke from a dream that lingered behind my eyes like cobweb. The dream was about Megan Flynn, and although I knew it did not signify unfaithfulness, it disturbed me just as badly, like a vapor that congeals around the heart.

In the dream she stood on a stretch of yellow hardpan, a treeless purple mountain at her back. The sky was brass, glowing with heat and dust. She walked toward me in her funny hat, her khaki clothes printed with dust, a tasseled red shawl draped around her shoulders.

But the red around her shoulders was not cloth. The wound in her throat had drained her face of blood, drenching her shirt, tasseling the ends of her fingers.

I went down to the dock and soaked a towel in the melted ice at the bottom of the cooler and held it to my eyes.

It was just a dream, I told myself. But the feeling that went with it, that was like toxin injected into the muscle tissue, wouldn't go away. I had known it in Vietnam, when I knew someone's death was at hand, mine or someone for whom I was responsible, and it had taken everything in me to climb aboard a slick that was headed up-country, trying to hide the fear in my eyes, the dryness in my mouth, the rancid odor that rose from my armpits.

But that had been the war. Since then I'd had the dream and the feelings that went with it only once—in my own house, the night my wife Annie was murdered.

Twenty years ago Alex Guidry had owned a steel-gray two-story frame house outside Franklin, with a staircase on the side and a second-floor screened porch where he slept in the hot months. Or at least this is what the current owner, an elderly man named Plo Castile, told me. His skin was amber, wizened, as hairless as a manikin's, and his eyes had the blue rheumy tint of oysters.

"I bought this property fo'teen years ago from Mr. Alex. He give me a good price, 'cause I already owned the house next do'," he said. "He slept right out yonder on that porch, at least when it wasn't cold, 'cause he rented rooms sometimes to oil-field people."

The yard was neat, with two palm trees in it, and flowers were planted around the latticework at the base of the main house and in a garden by a paintless barn and around a stucco building with a tin roof elevated above the walls.

"Is that a washhouse?" I said.

"Yes, suh, he had a couple of maids done laundry for them oil-field people. Mr. Alex was a good bidnessman."

"You remember a black woman named Ida Broussard, Mr. Plo?"

He nodded. "Her husband was the one been in Angola. He run a li'l sto'." His eyes looked at a cane field beyond the barbed-wire fence.

"She come around here?"

He took a package of tobacco and cigarette papers out of his shirt pocket. "Been a long time, suh."

"You seem like an honest man. I believe Ida Broussard was murdered. Did she come around here?"

He made a sound, as though a slight irritation had flared in his throat.

"Suh, you mean they was a murder here, that's what you saying?" But he already knew the answer, and his eyes looked into space and he forgot what he was doing with the package of tobacco and cigarette papers. He shook his head sadly. "I wish you ain't come here wit' this. I seen a fight. Yeah, they ain't no denying that. I seen it."

"A fight?"

"It was dark. I was working in my garage. She drove a truck into the yard and gone up the back stairs. I could tell it was Ida Broussard 'cause Mr. Alex had the floodlight on. But, see, it was cold wet'er then and he wasn't sleeping on the porch, so she started banging on the do' and yelling he better come out.

"I seen only one light go on. All them oil-field renters was gone, they was working seven-and-seven offshore back then. I didn't want to hear no kind of trouble like that. I didn't want my wife to hear it either. So I went in my house and turned on the TV.

"But the fighting stopped, and I seen the inside light go out, then the floodlight, too. I t'ought: Well, he ain't married, white people, colored people, they been doing t'ings together at night they don't do in the day for a long time now, it ain't my bidness. Later on, I seen her truck go down the road."

"You never told anyone this?"

"No, suh. I didn't have no reason to."

"After she was found dead in the swamp?"

"He was a policeman. You t'ink them other policemen didn't know he was carrying on wit' a colored woman, they had to wait for me to tell them about it?"

"Can I see the washhouse?"

The inside was cool and dank and smelled of cement and water. Duckboards covered the floor, and a tin washtub sat under a water spigot that extended from a vertical pipe in one wall. I placed my palm against the roughness of the stucco and wondered if Ida Broussard's cries or strangled breath had been absorbed into the dampness of these same walls.

"I boil crabs out here now and do the washing in my machine," Mr. Plo said.

"Are those wood stairs out there the same ones that were on the building twenty years ago?" I asked.

"I painted them. But they're the same."

"I'd like to take some slivers of wood from them, if you don't mind."

"What for?"

"If you see Alex Guidry, you can tell him I was here. You can also tell him I took evidence from your staircase. Mr. Plo, I appreciate your honesty. I think you're a good man."

He walked across his yard toward the front door, his face harried with his own thoughts, as wrinkled as a turtle's foot. Then he stopped and turned around.

"Her husband, the one run the li'l sto'? What happened to him?" he asked.

"He went back to prison," I answered.

Mr. Plo crimped his mouth and opened his screen door and went inside his house.

From his kitchen window Swede Boxleiter could see the bayou through the pecan trees in the yard. It was a perfect evening. A boy was fishing in a green pirogue with a bamboo pole among the lily pads and cattails; the air smelled like rain and flowers; somebody was barbecuing steak on a shady lawn. It was too bad Blimpo nailed him coming out of the graveyard. He liked being with Cisco and Megan again, knocking down good money on a movie set, working out every day, eating seafood and fixing tropical health drinks in the blender. Louisiana had its moments.

Maybe it was time to shake it. His union card was gold in Hollywood. Besides, in California nobody got in your face because you might be a little singed around the edges. Weirded out, your arms

stenciled with tracks, a rap sheet you could wallpaper the White
House with? That was the bio for guys who wrote six-figure scripts.
But he'd let Cisco call the shot. The problem was, the juice was just
too big on this one. Taking down punks like Rodney Loudermilk or
that accountant Anthony Whatever wasn't going to get anybody out
of Shitsville.

He loaded the blender with fresh strawberries, bananas, two raw
eggs, a peeled orange, and a can of frozen fruit cocktail, and flicked on
the switch. Why was that guy from the power company still messing
around outside?

"Hey, you! I told you, disconnect me again, your next job is
gonna be on the trash truck!" Swede said.

"That's my day job already," the utility man replied.

They sure didn't have any shortage of wise-asses around here,
Swede thought. How about Blimpo in his porkpie hat hooking him to
a car bumper and going up to the Terrebonne house and bringing this
guy back down to the crypt, like Swede's the pervert, a dog on a
chain, not this fuck Terrebonne crawling around on his hands and
knees, smoothing out the bones and rags in the casket, like he's pack-
ing up a rat's nest to mail it somewhere.

"What are you doing with my slingshot?" Swede said through the
window.

"I stepped on it. I'm sorry," the utility man said.

"Put it down and get out of here."

But instead the utility man walked beyond Swede's vision to the
door and knocked.

Swede went into the living room, shirtless and barefoot, and
ripped open the door.

"It's been a bad week. I don't need no more trouble. I pay my bill
through the super, so just pack up your shit and—" he said.

Then they were inside, three of them, and over their shoulders he
saw a neighbor painting a steak with sauce on a grill and he wanted to
yell out, to send just one indicator of his situation into the waning
light, but the door closed quickly behind the men, then the kitchen
window, too, and he knew if he could only change two seconds of his
life, revise the moment between his conversation with the utility man

at the window and the knock on the door, none of this would be happening, that's what two seconds could mean.

One of them turned on the TV, increasing the volume to an almost deafening level, then slightly lowering it. Were the three men smiling now, as though all four of them were involved in a mutually shameful act? He couldn't tell. He stared at the muzzle of the .25 automatic.

Man, in the bowl, big time, he thought.

But a fellow's got to try.

His shank had a four-inch blade, with a bone-and-brass handle, a brand called Bear Hunter, a real collector's item Cisco had given him. Swede pulled it from his right pocket, ticking the blade's point against the denim fabric, opening the blade automatically as he swung wildly at a man's throat.

It was a clean cut, right across the top of the chest, slinging blood in a diagonal line across the wall. Swede tried to get the second man with the backswing, perhaps even felt the knife arc into sinew and bone, but a sound like a Chinese firecracker popped inside his head, then he was falling into a black well where he should have been able to lie unmolested, looking up at the circle of peering faces far above him only if he wanted.

But they rolled him inside a rug and carried him to a place where he knew he did not want to go. He'd screwed up, no denying it, and they'd unzipped his package. But it should have been over. Why were they doing this? They were lifting him again now, out of a car trunk, over the top of the bumper, carrying him across grass, through a fence gate that creaked on a hinge, unrolling him now in the dirt, under a sky bursting with stars.

One of his eyes didn't work and the other was filmed with blood. But he felt their hands raising him up, molding him to a cruciform design that was foreign to his life, that should not have been his, stretching out his arms against wood. He remembered pictures from a Sunday school teacher's book, a dust-blown hill and a darkening sky and helmeted soldiers whose faces were set with purpose, whose fists clutched spikes and hammers, whose cloaks were the color of their work.

Hadn't a woman been there in the pictures, too, one who pressed a cloth against a condemned man's face? Would she do that for him, too? He wondered these things as he turned his head to the side and heard steel ring on steel and saw his hand convulse as though it belonged to someone else.

TWENTY-THREE

Helen and I walked through the clumps of banana trees and blackberry bushes to the north side of the barn, where a group of St. Mary Parish plainclothes investigators and uniformed sheriff's deputies and ambulance attendants stood in a shaded area, one that droned with iridescent green flies, looking down at the collapsed and impaled form of Swede Boxleiter. Swede's chest was pitched forward against the nails that held his wrists, his face hidden in shadow, his knees twisted in the dust. Out in the sunlight, the flowers on the rain trees were as bright as arterial blood among the leaves.

"It looks like we got joint jurisdiction on this one," a plainclothes cop said. His name was Thurston Meaux and he had a blond mustache and wore a tweed sports coat with a starched denim shirt and a striped tie. "After the photographer gets here, we'll take him down and send y'all everything we have."

"Was he alive when they nailed him up?" I asked.

"The coroner has to wait on the autopsy. Y'all say he took the head wound in his apartment?" he said.

"That's what it looks like," I replied.

"You found brass?"

"One casing. A .25."

"Why would somebody shoot a guy in Iberia Parish, then nail him to a barn wall in St. Mary?" Meaux said.

"Another guy died here in the same way forty years ago," I said.

"This is where that happened?"

"I think it's a message to someone," I said.

"We already ran this guy. He was a thief and a killer, a suspect in two open homicide cases. I don't see big complexities here."

"If that's the way you're going to play it, you won't get any-where."

"Come on, Robicheaux. A guy like that is a walking target for half the earth. Where you going?"

Helen and I walked back to our cruiser and drove through the weeds, away from the barn and between two water oaks whose leaves were starting to fall, then back out on the state road.

"I don't get it. What message?" Helen said, driving with one hand, her badge holder still hanging from her shirt pocket.

"If it was just a payback killing, the shooters would have left his body in the apartment. When we met Harpo Scruggs at the barbecue place? He said something about hating rich people. I think he killed Swede and deliberately tied Swede's murder to Jack Flynn's to get even with somebody."

She thought about it.

"Scruggs took the Amtrak to Houston, then flew back to Colo-rado," she said.

"So he came back. That's the way he operates. He kills people over long distances."

She looked over at me, her eyes studying my expression.

"But something else is bothering you, isn't it?" she said.

"Whoever killed Swede hung him up on the right side of where Jack Flynn died."

She shook a half-formed thought out of her face.

"I like working with you, Streak, but I'm not taking any walks inside your head," she said.

■ ■ ■

Alex Guidry was furious. He came through the front door of the sheriff's department at eight o'clock Monday morning, not slowing down at the information desk or pausing long enough to knock before entering my office.

"You're getting Ida Broussard's case reopened?" he said.

"You thought there was a statute of limitations on murder?" I replied.

"You took splinters out of my old house and gave them to the St. Mary Parish sheriff's office?" he said incredulously.

"That about sums it up."

"What's this crap about me suffocating her to death?"

I paper-clipped a sheaf of time sheets together and stuck them in a drawer.

"A witness puts you with Ida Broussard right before her death. A forensic pathologist says she was murdered, that water from a tap was forced down her nose and mouth. If you don't like what you're hearing, Mr. Guidry, I suggest you find a lawyer," I said.

"What'd I ever do to you?"

"Sullied our reputation in Iberia Parish. You're a bad cop. You bring discredit on everyone who carries a badge."

"You better get your own lawyer, you sonofabitch. I'm going to twist a two-by-four up your ass," he said.

I picked up my phone and punched the dispatcher's extension.

"Wally, there's a man in my office who needs an escort to his automobile," I said.

Guidry pointed one stiffened finger at me, without speaking, then strode angrily down the hallway. A few minutes later Helen came into my office and sat on the edge of my desk.

"I just saw our ex-jailer in the parking lot. Somebody must have spit on his toast this morning. He couldn't get his car door open and he ended up breaking off his key in the lock."

"Really?" I said.

Her eyes crinkled at the corners.

■ ■ ■

Four hours later our fingerprint man called. The shell casing found on the carpet of Swede Boxleiter's apartment was clean and the apartment contained no identifiable prints other than the victim's. That same afternoon the sheriff called Helen and me into his office.

"I just got off the phone with the sheriff's department in Trinidad, Colorado. Get this. They don't know anything about Harpo Scruggs, except he owns a ranch outside of town," he said.

"Is he there now?" Helen said.

"That's what I asked. This liaison character says, 'Why you interested in him?' So I say, 'Oh, we think he might be torturing and killing people in our area, that sort of thing.' " The sheriff picked up his leather tobacco pouch and flipped it back and forth in his fingers.

"Scruggs is a pro. He does his dirty work a long way from home," I said.

"Yeah, he also crosses state lines to do it. I'm going to call that FBI woman in New Orleans. In the meantime, I want y'all to go to Trinidad and get anything you can on this guy."

"Our travel budget is pretty thin, skipper," I said.

"I already talked to the Parish Council. They feel the same way I do. You keep crows out of a cornfield by tying a few dead ones on your fence wire. That's a metaphor."

Early the next morning our plane made a wide circle over the Texas panhandle, then we dropped through clouds that were pooled with fire in the sunrise and came in over biscuit-colored hills dotted with juniper and pine and pinyon trees and landed at a small windblown airport outside Raton, New Mexico.

The country to the south was as flat as a skillet, hazed with dust in the early light, the monotony of the landscape broken by an occasional mesa. But immediately north of Raton the land lifted into dry, pinyon-covered, steep-sided hills that rose higher and higher into a mountainous plateau where the old mining town of Trinidad, once home to the Earps and Doc Holliday, had bloomed in the nineteenth century.

We rented a car and drove up Raton Pass through canyons that were still deep in shadow, the sage on the hillsides silvered with dew. On the left, high up on a grade, I saw a roofless church, with a façade like that of a Spanish mission, among the ruins and slag heaps of an abandoned mining community.

"That church was in one of Megan's photographs. She said it was built by John D. Rockefeller as a PR effort after the Ludlow massacre," I said.

Helen drove with one hand on the steering wheel. She looked over at me with feigned interest in her eyes.

"Yeah?" she said, chewing gum.

I started to say something about the children and women who were suffocated in a cellar under a burning tent when the Colorado militia broke a miners' strike at Ludlow in 1914.

"Go on with your story," she said.

"Nothing."

"You know history, Streak. But it's still the good guys against the shit bags. We're the good guys."

She put her other hand on the wheel and looked at me and grinned, her mouth chewing, her bare upper arms round and tight against the short sleeves of her shirt.

We reached the top of the grade and came out into a wide valley, with big mountains in the west and the old brick and quarried rock buildings of Trinidad off to the right, on streets that climbed into the hills. The town was still partially in shadow, the wooded crests of the hills glowing like splinters of black-green glass against the early sun.

We checked in with the sheriff's department and were assigned an elderly plainclothes detective named John Nash as an escort out to Harpo Scruggs's ranch. He sat in the back seat of our rental car, a short-brim Stetson cocked on the side of his head, a pleasant look on his face as he watched the landscape go by.

"Scruggs never came to y'all's attention, huh?" I said.

"Can't say that he did," he replied.

"Just an ordinary guy in the community?"

"If he's what you say, I guess we should have taken better note of him." His face was sun-browned, his eyes as blue as a butane flame, webbed with tiny lines at the corners when he smiled. He looked back out the window.

"This definitely seems like a laid-back place, yessiree," Helen said, her eyes glancing sideways at me. She turned off the state highway onto a dirt road that wound through an arroyo layered with exposed rock.

"What do you plan to do with this fellow?" John Nash said.

"You had a shooting around here in a while?" Helen said.

John Nash smiled to himself and stared out the window again. Then he said, "That's it yonder, set back against that hill. It's a real nice spot here. Not a soul around. A Mexican drug smuggler pulled a gun on me down by that creek once. I killed him deader than hell."

Helen and I both turned around and looked at John Nash as though for the first time.

Harpo Scruggs's ranch was rail-fenced and covered with sage, bordered on the far side by low hills and a creek that was lined with aspens. The house was gingerbread late Victorian, gabled and paint-less, surrounded on four sides by a handrailed gallery. We could see a tall figure splitting firewood on a stump by the barn. Our tires thumped across the cattle guard. John Nash leaned forward with his arms on the back of my seat.

"Mr. Robicheaux, you're not hoping for our friend out there to do something rash, are you?" he said.

"You're an interesting man, Mr. Nash," I said.

"I get told that a lot," he replied.

We stopped the car on the edge of the dirt yard and got out. The air smelled like wet sage and wood smoke and manure and horses when there's frost on their coats and they steam in the sun. Scruggs paused in his work and stared at us from under the flop brim of an Australian bush hat. Then he stood another chunk of firewood on its edge and split it in half.

We walked toward him through the side yard. Coffee cans planted with violets and pansies were placed at even intervals along the edge of the gallery. For some reason John Nash separated himself from us and stepped up on the gallery and propped his hands on the rail and watched us as though he were a spectator.

"Nice place," I said to Scruggs.

"Who's that man up on my gallery?" he said.

"My boss man's brought the Feds into it, Scruggs. Crossing state lines. Big mistake," I said.

"Here's the rest of it. Ricky Scar is seriously pissed because a poor-white-trash peckerwood took his money and then smeared shit all over southwest Louisiana," Helen said.

"Plus you tied a current homicide to one that was committed forty years ago," I said.

"The real mystery is why the Mob would hire a used-up old fart who thinks bedding hookers will stop his johnson from dribbling in the toilet bowl three times a night. That Mexican hot pillow joint you visited in Houston? The girl said she wanted to scrub herself down with peroxide," Helen said. When Scruggs stared at her, she nodded affirmatively, her face dramatically sincere.

Scruggs leaned the handle of his ax against the stump and bit a small chew off a plug of tobacco, his shoulders and long back held erect inside his sun-faded shirt. He turned his face away and spit in the dirt, then rubbed his nose with the back of his wrist.

"You born in New Iberia, Robicheaux?" he asked.

"That's right."

"You think with what I know of past events, bodies buried in the levee at Angola, troublesome people killed in St. Mary Parish, I'm going down in a state court?"

"Times have changed, Scruggs," I said.

He hefted the ax in one hand and began splitting a chunk of wood into long white strips for kindling, his lips glazed with a brown residue from the tobacco in his jaw. Then he said, "If y'all going down to Deming to hurt my name there, it won't do you no good. I've lived a good life in the West. It ain't never been dirtied by nigra trouble and rich people that thinks they can make white men into nigras, too."

"You were one of the men who killed Jack Flynn, weren't you?" I said.

"I'm fixing to butcher a hog, then I got a lady friend coming out to visit. I'd like for y'all to be gone before she gets here. By the way, that man up on the gallery ain't no federal agent."

"We'll be around, Scruggs. I guarantee it," I said.

"Yeah, you will. Just like a tumblebug rolling shit balls."

We started toward the car. Behind me I heard his ax blade splitting a piece of pine with a loud snap, then John Nash called out from the gallery, "Mr. Scruggs, where's that fellow used to sell you cordwood, do your fence work and such, the one looks like he's got clap on his face?"

"He don't work for me no more," Scruggs said.

"I bet he don't. Being as he's in a clinic down in Raton with an infected knife wound," John Nash said.

I n the back seat of the car Nash took a notebook from his shirt pocket and folded back several pages.

"His name's Jubal Breedlove. We think he killed a trucker about six years ago over some dope but we couldn't prove it. I put him in jail a couple of times on drunk charges. Otherwise, his sheet's not remarkable," he said.

"You found this guy on your own?" I said.

"I started calling hospitals when you first contacted us. Wait till you see his face. People tend to remember it."

"Can you get on the cell phone and make sure Breedlove isn't allowed any phone calls in the next few minutes?" I said.

"I did that early this morning."

"You're a pretty good cop, Mr. Nash."

He grinned, then his eyes focused out the window on a snowshoe rabbit that was hopping through grass by an irrigation ditch. "By the way, I told you only what was on his sheet. About twenty years ago a family camping back in the hills was killed in their tents. The man done it was after the daughter. When I ran Jubal Breedlove in on a drunk charge, I found the girl's high school picture in his billfold."

Less than an hour later we were at the clinic in Raton. Jubal Breedlove lay in a narrow bed in a semiprivate room that was divided by a collapsible partition. His face was tentacled with a huge purple-and-strawberry birthmark, so that his eyes looked squeezed inside a mask. Helen picked up his chart from the foot of the bed and read it.

"Boxleiter put some boom-boom in your bam-bam, didn't he?" she said.

"What?" he said.

"Swede slung your blood all over the apartment. He might as well have written your name on the wall," I said.

"Swede who? I was robbed and stabbed behind a bar in Clayton," he said.

"That's why you waited until the wound was infected before you got treatment," I said.

"I was drunk for three days. I didn't know what planet I was on," he replied. His hair was curly, the color of metal shavings. He tried to concentrate his vision on me and Helen, but his eyes kept shifting to John Nash.

"Harpo wouldn't let you get medical help down in Louisiana, would he? You going to take the bounce for a guy like that?" I asked.

"I want a lawyer in here," he said.

"No, you don't," Nash said, and fitted his hand on Breedlove's jaws and gingerly moved his head back and forth on the pillow, as though examining the function of Breedlove's neck. "Remember me?"

"No."

He moved his hand down on Breedlove's chest, flattening it on the panels of gauze that were taped across Breedlove's knife wound.

"Mr. Nash," I said.

"Remember the girl in the tent? I sure do." John Nash felt the dressing on Breedlove's chest with his fingertips, then worked the heel of his hand in a slow circle, his eyes fixed on Breedlove's. Breedlove's mouth opened as though his lower lip had been jerked downward on a wire, and involuntarily his hands grabbed at Nash's wrist.

"Don't be touching me, boy. That'll get you in a lot of trouble," Nash said.

"Mr. Nash, we need to talk outside a minute," I said.

"That's not necessary," he replied, and gathered a handful of Kleenex from a box on the nightstand and wiped his palm with it. "Because everything is going to be just fine here. Why, look, the man's eyes glisten with repentance already."

■ ■ ■

We had one suspect in Trinidad, Colorado, now a second one
in New Mexico. I didn't want to think about the amount of
paperwork and the bureaucratic legal problems that might lie ahead of
us. After we dropped John Nash off at the sheriff's office, we ate lunch
in a cafe by the highway. Through the window we could see a storm
moving into the mountains and dust lifting out of the trees in a canyon
and flattening on the hardpan.

"What are you thinking about?" Helen asked.

"We need to get Breedlove into custody and extradite him back to
Louisiana," I said.

"Fat chance, huh?"

"I can't see it happening right now."

"Maybe John Nash will have another interview with him."

"That guy can cost us the case, Helen."

"He didn't seem worried. I had the feeling Breedlove knows
better than to file complaints about local procedure." When I didn't
reply, she said, "Wyatt Earp and his brothers used to operate around
here?"

"After the shoot-out at the O.K. Corral they hunted down some
other members of the Clanton gang and blew them into rags. I think
this was one of the places on their route."

"I wonder what kind of salary range they have here," she said.

I paid the check and got a receipt for our expense account.

"That story Archer Terrebonne told me about Lila and her cousin
firing a gun across a snowfield, about starting an avalanche?" I said.

"Yeah, you told me," Helen said.

"You feel like driving to Durango?"

We headed up through Walsenburg, then drove west into the
mountains and a rainstorm that turned to snow when we
approached Wolf Creek Pass. The juniper and pinyon trees and cinna-
mon-colored country of the southern Colorado plateau were behind
us now, and on each side of the highway the slopes were thick with

spruce and fir and pine that glistened with snow that began melting as
soon as it touched the canopy.

At the top of Wolf Creek we pulled into a rest stop and drank
coffee from a thermos and looked out on the descending crests of the
mountains. The air was cold and gray and smelled like pine needles
and wet boulders in a streambed and ice when you chop it out of a
wood bucket in the morning.

"Dave, I don't want to be a pill . . ." Helen began.

"About what?"

"It seems like I remember a story years ago about that avalanche, I
mean about Lila's cousin being buried in it and suffocating or freezing
to death," she said.

"Go on."

"I mean, who's to say the girl wasn't frozen in the shape of a cross?
That kind of stuff isn't in an old newspaper article. Maybe we're
getting inside our heads too much on this one."

I couldn't argue with her.

When we got to the newspaper office in Durango it wasn't hard to
find the story about the avalanche back in 1967. It had been featured
on the first page, with interviews of the rescuers and photographs of
the slide, the lopsided two-story log house, a barn splintered into
kindling, cattle whose horns and hooves and ice-crusted bellies pro-
truded from the snow like disembodied images in a cubist painting.
Lila had survived because the slide had pushed her into a creekbed
whose overhang formed itself into an ice cave where she huddled for
two days until a deputy sheriff poked an iron pike through the top and
blinded her with sunlight.

But the cousin died under ten feet of snow. The article made no
mention about the condition of the body or its posture in death.

"It was a good try and a great drive over," Helen said.

"Maybe we can find some of the guys who were on the search and
rescue team," I said.

"Let it go, Dave."

I let out my breath and rose from the chair I had been sitting in.
My eyes burned and my palms still felt numb from involuntarily tightening my hands on the steering wheel during the drive over Wolf

Creek Pass. Outside, the sun was shining on the nineteenth-century brick buildings along the street and I could see the thickly timbered, dark green slopes of the mountains rising up sharply in the background.

I started to close the large bound volume of 1967 newspapers in front of me. Then, like the gambler who can't leave the table as long as there is one chip left to play, I glanced again at a color photograph of the rescuers on a back page. The men stood in a row, tools in their hands, wearing heavy mackinaws and canvas overalls and stocking caps and cowboy hats with scarves tied around their ears. The snowfield was sunlit, dazzling, the mountains blue-green against a cloudless sky. The men were unsmiling, their clothes flattened against their bodies in the wind, their faces pinched with cold. I read the cutline below the photograph.

"Where you going?" Helen said.

I went into the editorial room and returned with a magnifying glass.

"Look at the man on the far right," I said. "Look at his shoulders, the way he holds himself."

She took the magnifying glass from my hand and stared through it, moving the depth of focus up and down, then concentrating on the face of a tall man in a wide-brim cowboy hat. Then she read the cutline.

"It says 'H. Q. Skaggs.' The reporter misspelled it. It's Harpo Scruggs," she said.

"Archer Terrebonne acted like he knew him only at a distance. I think he called him 'quite a character,' or something like that."

"Why would they have him at their cabin in Colorado? The Terrebonnes don't let people like Scruggs use their indoor plumbing," she said. She stared at me blankly, then said, as though putting her thoughts on index cards, "He did scut work for them? He's had something on them? Scruggs could be blackmailing Archer Terrebonne?"

"They're joined at the hip."

"Is there a Xerox machine out there?" she asked.

TWENTY-FOUR

We got back to New Iberia late the next day. I went to the office before going home, but the sheriff had already gone. In my mailbox he had left a note that read: "Let's talk tomorrow about Scruggs and the Feds."

That evening Bootsie and Alafair and I went to a restaurant, then I worked late at the dock with Batist. The moon was up and the water in the bayou looked yellow and high, swirling with mud, between the deep shadows of the cypress and willow trees along the banks.

I heard a car coming too fast on the dirt road, then saw Clete Purcel's convertible stop in front of the boat ramp, a plume of dust drifting across the canvas top. But rather than park by the ramp, he cut his lights and backed into my drive, so that the car tag was not visible from the road.

I went back into the bait shop and poured a cup of coffee. He walked down the dock, looking back over his shoulder, his print shirt hanging out of his slacks. He grinned broadly when he came through the door.

"Beautiful night. I thought I might get up early in the morning and do some fishing," he said.

"The weather's right," I said.

"How was Colorado?" he asked, then opened the screen door and looked back outside.

I started to pour him a cup of coffee, but he reached in the cooler and twisted the top off a beer and drank it at the end of the counter so he could see the far end of the dock.

"You mind if I sleep here tonight? I don't feel like driving back to Jeanerette," he said.

"What have you done, Clete?"

He ticked the center of his forehead with one fingernail and looked into space.

"A couple of state troopers almost got me by Spanish Lake. I'm not supposed to be driving except for business purposes," he said.

"Why would they be after you?"

"This movie gig is creeping me out. I went up to Ralph & Kacoo's in Baton Rouge," he said. "All right, here it is. But I didn't start it. I was eating oysters on the half-shell and having a draft at the bar when Benny Grogan comes up to me—you know, Ricky the Mouse's bodyguard, the one with platinum hair, the wrestler and part-time bone smoker.

"He touches me on the arm, then steps away like I'm going to swing on him or something. He says, 'We got a problem, Purcel. Ricky's stinking drunk in a back room.'

"I say, 'No, *we* don't got a problem. You got a problem.'

"He goes, 'Look, he's got some upscale gash in there he's trying to impress, so everything's gonna be cool. Long as maybe you go somewhere else. I'll pay your tab. Here's a hundred bucks. You're our guest somewhere else tonight.'

"I say, 'Benny, you want to wear food on your face again, just put your hand on my arm one more time.'

"He shrugs his shoulders and walks off and I thought that'd be the end of it. I was going to leave anyway, right after I took a leak. So I'm in the men's room, and they've got this big trough filled with ice in it, and of course people have been pissing in it all night, and I'm unzipping my pants and reading the newspaper that's under a glass up on the wall and I hear the door bang open behind me and some guy walking like the deck is tilting under his feet.

"He goes, 'I got something for you, Purcel. They say it hits your guts like an iron hook.'

"I'm not kidding you, Dave, I didn't think Ricky Scar could make my heart seize up, but that's what happened when I looked at what was in his hand. You ever see the current thread between the prongs on a stun gun? I go, 'Dumb move, Ricky. I was just leaving. I consider our troubles over.'

"He goes, 'I'm gonna enjoy this.'

"Just then this biker pushes open the door and brushes by Ricky like this is your normal, everyday rest-room situation. When Ricky turned his head I nailed him. It was a beaut, Dave, right in the eye. The stun gun went sailing under the stalls and Ricky fell backward in the trough. This plumber's helper was in the corner, one of these big, industrial-strength jobs for blowing out major toilet blockage. I jammed it over Ricky's face and shoved him down in the ice and held him under till I thought he might be more reasonable, but he kept kicking and flailing and frothing at the mouth and I couldn't let go.

"The biker says, 'The dude try to cop your stick or something?'

"I go, 'Find a guy named Benny Grogan in the back rooms. Tell him Clete needs some help. He'll give you fifty bucks.'

"The biker goes, 'Benny Grogan gives head, not money. You're on your own, Jack.'

"That's when Benny comes through the door and sticks a .38 behind my ear. He says, 'Get out of town, Purcel. Next time, your brains are coming out your nose.'

"I didn't argue, mon. I almost made the front door when I hear the Mouse come roaring out of the can and charge down the hallway at me, streaming ice and piss and toilet paper that was stuck all over his feet.

"Except a bunch of people in a side dining room fling open this oak door, it must be three inches thick with wrought iron over this thick yellow glass panel in it, and they slam it right into the Mouse's face, you could hear the metal actually ding off his skull.

"So while Ricky's rolling around on the carpet, I eased on outside and decided to cruise very copacetically out of Baton Rouge and leave the greaseballs alone for a while."

"Why were state troopers after you? Why were you out by Spanish Lake instead of on the four-lane?"

His eyes clicked sideways, as though he were seriously researching the question.

"Ummm, I kept thinking about begging off from the Mouse when he put his stun gun on snap, crackle, and pop. So out there in the parking lot were about eight or nine chopped-down Harleys. They belonged to the same bunch the Gypsy Jokers threatened to kill for wearing their colors. I still had all my repo tools in the trunk, so I found the Mouse's car and slim-jimmed the door and fired it up. Then I propped a board against the gas pedal, pointed it right into the middle of the Harleys, and dropped it into low.

"I cruised around for five minutes, then did a drive-by and watched it all from across the street. The bikers were climbing around on Ricky's car like land crabs, kicking windows out, slashing the seats and tires, tearing the wires out of the engine. It was perfect, Dave. When the cops got there, it was even better. The cops were throwing bikers in a van, Ricky was screaming in the parking lot, his broad trying to calm him down, Ricky swinging her around by her arm like she was a stuffed doll, people coming out every door in the restaurant like the place was on fire. Benny Grogan got sapped across the head with a baton. Anyway, it'll all cool down in a day or so. Say, you got any of those sandwiches left?"

"I just can't believe you," I said.

"What'd I do? I just wanted to eat some oysters and have a little peace and quiet."

"Clete, one day you'll create a mess you won't get out of. They're going to kill you."

"Scarlotti is a punk and a rodent and belongs under a sewer grate. Hey, the Bobbsey Twins from Homicide spit in their mouths and laugh it off, right? Quit worrying. It's only rock 'n' roll."

His eyes were green and bright above the beer bottle while he drank, his face flushed and dilated with his own heat.

■　■　■

Just after eight the next morning the sheriff came into my office. He stood at the window and propped his hands on the sill. His sleeves were rolled to his elbows, his forearms thick and covered with hair.

"I talked with that FBI woman, Glazier, about Harpo Scruggs. She's a challenge to whatever degree of civility I normally possess," he said.

"What'd she say?"

"She turned to an ice cube. That's what bothers me. He's supposed to be mixed up with the Dixie Mafia, but there's nothing in the NCIC computer on him. Why this general lack of interest?"

"Up until now his victims have been low profile, people nobody cared about," I said.

"That woman hates Megan Flynn. Why's it so personal with her?"

We looked at each other. "Guilt?" I said.

"Over what?"

"Good question."

I walked down to Helen's office, then we both signed out for New Orleans.

We drove to New Orleans and parked off Carondelet and walked over to the Mobil Building on Poydras Street. When we sat down in her office, she rose from her chair and opened the blinds, as though wishing to create an extra dimension in the room. Then she sat back down in a swivel chair and crossed her legs, her shoulders erect inside her gray suit, her ice-blue eyes fixed on something out in the hallway. But when I turned around, no one was there.

Then I saw it in her face, the dryness at the corner of the mouth, the skin that twitched slightly below the eye, the chin lifted as though to remove a tension in the throat.

"We thought y'all might want to help bring down this guy Scruggs. He's going back and forth across state lines like a Ping-Pong ball," I said.

"If you don't have enough grounds for a warrant, why should we?" she said.

"Every cop who worked with him says he was dirty. Maybe he even murdered convicts in Angola. But there's no sheet on him anywhere," I said.

"You're saying somehow that's our fault?"

"No, we're thinking Protected Witness Program or paid federal informant," Helen said.

"Where do you get your information? You people think—" she began.

"Scruggs is the kind of guy who would flirt around the edges of the Klan. Back in the fifties you had guys like that on the payroll," I said.

"You're talking about events of four decades ago," Adrien Glazier said.

"What if he was one of the men who murdered Jack Flynn? What if he committed that murder while he was in the employ of the government?" I said.

"You're not going to interrogate me in my own office, Mr. Robicheaux."

We stared mutely at each other, her eyes watching the recognition grow in mine.

"That's it, isn't it? You *know* Scruggs killed Megan Flynn's father. You've known it all along. That's why you bear her all this resentment."

"You'll either leave now or I'll have you removed from the building," she said.

"Here's a Kleenex. Your eyes look a little wet, ma'am. I can relate to your situation. I used to work for the NOPD and had to lie and cover up for male bozos all the time," Helen said.

We drove into the Quarter and had beignets and coffee and hot milk at the Cafe du Monde. While Helen bought some pralines for her nephew, I walked across the street into Jackson Square, past the sidewalk artists who had set up their easels along the piked fence that surrounded the park, past the front of St. Louis Cathedral where a string band was playing, and over to a small bookstore on Toulouse.

Everyone in AA knows that his survival as a wet drunk was due partly to the fact that most people fear the insane and leave them alone. But those who are cursed with the gift of Cassandra often have the same fate imposed upon them. Gus Vitelli was a slight, bony Sicilian ex-horse trainer and professional bouree player whose left leg had been withered by polio and who had probably read almost every book in the New Orleans library system. He was obsessed with what he called "untold history," and his bookstore was filled with material on conspiracies of every kind.

He told anyone who would listen that the main players in the assassinations of both John Kennedy and Martin Luther King came from the New Orleans area. Some of the names he offered were those of Italian gangsters. But if the Mob was bothered by his accusations, they didn't show it. Gus Vitelli had long ago been dismissed in New Orleans as a crank.

The problem was that Gus was a reasonable and intelligent man. At least in my view.

He was wearing a T-shirt that exclaimed "I Know Jack Shit," and wrote prices on used books while I told him the story about the murder of Jack Flynn and the possible involvement of an FBI informant.

"It wouldn't surprise me that it got covered up. Hoover wasn't any friend of pinkos and veterans of the Lincoln Brigade," he said. He walked to a display table and began arranging a pile of paperback books, his left leg seeming to collapse and then spring tight again with each step. "I got a CIA manual here that was written to teach the Honduran army how to torture people. Look at the publication date, 1983. You think people are gonna believe that?" He flipped the manual at me.

"Gus, have you heard anything about a hit on a black guy named Willie Broussard?"

"Something involving the Giacanos or Ricky Scarlotti?"

"You got it."

"Nothing about a hit. But the word is Ricky Scar's sweating ball bearings 'cause he might have to give up some Asian guys. The truth is, I'm not interested. People like Ricky give all Italians a bad name. My great-grandfather sold bananas and pies out of a wagon. He raised thirteen kids like that. He got hung from a streetlamp in 1890 when the police commissioner was killed."

I thanked him for his time and started to leave.

"The guy who was crucified against the barn wall?" he said. "The reason people don't buy conspiracy theories is they think 'conspiracy' means everybody's on the same program. That's not how it works. Everybody's got a different program. They just all want the same guy dead. Socrates was a gadfly, but I bet he took time out to screw somebody's wife."

I had worried that Cool Breeze Broussard might go after Alex Guidry. But I had not thought about his father.

Mout' and two of his Hmong business partners bounced their stake truck loaded with cut flowers into the parking lot of the New Iberia Country Club. Mout' climbed down from the cab and asked the golf pro where he could find Alex Guidry. It was windy and bright, and Mout' wore a suit coat and a small rainbow-colored umbrella that clamped on his head like an elevated hat.

He began walking down the fairway, his haystack body bent forward, his brogans rising and falling as though he were stepping over plowed rows in a field, a cigar stub in the side of his mouth, his face expressionless.

He passed a weeping willow that was turning gold with the season, and a sycamore whose leaves looked like flame, then stopped at a polite distance from the green and waited until Alex Guidry and his three friends had putted into the cup.

"Mr. Guidry, suh?" Mout' said.

Guidry glanced at him, then turned his back and studied the next fairway.

"Mr. Guidry, I got to talk wit' you about my boy," Mout' said.

Guidry pulled his golf cart off the far slope of the green. But his friends had not moved and were looking at his back now.

"Mr. Guidry, I know you got power round here. But my boy ain't coming after you. Suh, please don't walk away," Mout' said.

"Does somebody have a cell phone?" Guidry asked his friends.

"Alex, we can go over here and have a smoke," one of them said.

"I didn't join this club to have an old nigger follow me around the golf course," Guidry replied.

"Suh, my boy blamed himself twenty years for Ida's death. I just want you to talk wit' me for five minutes. I apologize to these gentlemen here," Mout' said.

Guidry began walking toward the next tee, his golf cart rattling behind him.

For the next hour Mout' followed him, perspiration leaking out of the leather brace that held his umbrella hat in place, the sun lighting the pink-and-white discoloration that afflicted one side of his face.

Finally Guidry sliced a ball into the rough, speared his club angrily into his golf bag, walked to the clubhouse, and went into the bar.

It took Mout' twenty minutes to cover the same amount of ground and he was sweating and breathing heavily when he came inside the bar. He stood in the center of the room, amid the felt-covered card tables and click of poker chips and muted conversation, and removed his umbrella hat and fixed his blue, cataract-frosted eyes on Guidry's face.

Guidry kept signaling the manager with one finger.

"Mr. Robicheaux say you held a wet towel over Ida's nose and mout' and made her heart stop. He gonna prove it, so that mean my boy don't have to do nothing, he ain't no threat to you," Mout' said.

"Somebody get this guy out of here," Guidry said.

"I'm going, suh. You can tell these people here anyt'ing you want. But I knowed you when you was buying black girls for t'ree dol'ars over on Hopkins. So you ain't had to go after Ida. You ain't had to take my boy's wife, suh."

The room was totally quiet. Alex Guidry's face burned like a red lamp. Mout' Broussard walked back outside, his body bent forward at the middle, his expression as blank as the grated door on a woodstove.

TWENTY-FIVE

Late Friday afternoon I received a call from John Nash in Trinidad.

"Our friend Jubal Breedlove checked out of the clinic in Raton and is nowhere to be found," he said.

"Did he hook up with Scruggs?" I asked.

"It's my feeling he probably did."

The line was silent.

"Why do you feel that, Mr. Nash?" I asked.

"His car's at his house. His clothes seem undisturbed. He didn't make a withdrawal from his bank account. What does that suggest to you, Mr. Robicheaux?"

"Breedlove's under a pile of rock?"

"Didn't Vikings put a dog at the foot of a dead warrior?" he asked.

"Excuse me?"

"I was thinking about the family he murdered in the campground. The father put up a terrific fight to protect his daughter. I hope Breedlove's under a pile of rock by that campground."

. . .

After work I had to go after a boat a drunk smashed into a stump and left with a wrenched propeller on a sandbar. I tilted the engine's housing into the stern of the boat and was about to slide the hull back into the water when I saw why the drunk had waded through the shallows to dry land and walked back to his car: the aluminum bottom had a gash in it like a twisted smile.

I wedged a float cushion into the leak so I could pull the boat across the bayou into the reeds and return with a boat trailer to pick it up. Behind me I heard an outboard come around the corner and then slow when the man in the stern saw me standing among the flooded willows.

"I hope you don't mind my coming out here. The Afro-American man said it would be all right," Billy Holtzner said.

"You're talking about Batist?"

"Yes, I think that's his name. He seems like a good fellow."

He cut his engine and let his boat scrape up on the sandbar. When he walked forward the boat rocked under him and he automatically stooped over to grab the gunnels. He grinned foolishly.

"I'm not very good at boats," he said.

My experience has been that the physical and emotional transformation that eventually comes aborning in every bully never takes but one form. The catalyst is fear and its effects are like a flame on candle wax. The sneer around the mouth and the contempt and disdain in the eyes melt away and are replaced by a self-effacing smile, a confession of an inconsequential weakness, and a saccharine affectation of goodwill in the voice. The disingenuousness is like oil exuded from the skin; there's an actual stink in the clothes.

"What can I do for you?" I said.

He stood on the sandbar in rolled denim shorts and tennis shoes without socks and a thick white shirt sewn with a half dozen pockets. He looked back down the bayou, listening to the drone of an outboard engine, his soft face pink in the sunset.

"Some men might try to hurt my daughter," he said.

"I think your concern is for yourself, Mr. Holtzner."

When he swallowed, his mouth made an audible click.

"They've told me I either pay them money I don't have or they'll hurt Geri. These men take off heads. I mean that literally," he said.

"Come down to my office and make a report."

"What if they find out?" he asked.

I had turned to chain the damaged hull to the back of my outboard. I straightened up and looked into his face. The air itself seemed fouled by his words, his self-revelation hanging in the dead space between us like a dirty flag. His eyes went away from me.

"You can call me during office hours. Whatever you tell me will be treated confidentially," I said.

He sat down in his boat and began pushing it awkwardly off the sandbar by shoving a paddle into the mud.

"Did we meet somewhere before?" he asked.

"No. Why?"

"Your hostility. You don't hide it well."

He tried to crank his engine, then gave it up and drifted with the current toward the dock, his shoulders bent, the hands that had twisted noses splayed on his flaccid thighs, his chest indented as though it had been stuck with a small cannonball.

I didn't like Billy Holtzner or the group he represented. But in truth some of my feelings had nothing to do with his or their behavior.

In the summer of 1946 my father was in the Lafayette Parish Prison for punching out a policeman who tried to cuff him in Antlers Pool Room. That was the same summer my mother met a corporal from Fort Polk named Hank Clausson.

"He was at Omaha Beach, Davy. That's when our people was fighting Hitler and run the Nazis out of Europe. He got all kind of medals he gonna show you," she said.

Hank was lean and tall, his face sun-browned, his uniform always starched and pressed and his shoes and brass shined. I didn't know he was sleeping over until I walked in on him in the bathroom one morning and caught him shaving in his underwear. The back of his right shoulder was welted with a terrible red scar, as though someone had dug at the flesh with a spoon. He shook his safety razor in the stoppered lavatory water and drew another swath under his chin.

"You need to get in here?" he asked.

"No," I said.

"That's where a German stuck a bayonet in me. That was so kids like you didn't end up in an oven," he said, and crimped his lips together and scraped the razor under one nostril.

He put a single drop of hair tonic on his palms and rubbed them together, then rubbed the oil into his scalp and drew his comb back through his short-cropped hair, his knees bending slightly so he could see his face fully in the mirror.

Hank took my mother and me to the beer garden and bowling alley out on the end of East Main. We sat at a plank table in a grove of oak trees that were painted white around the trunks and hung with speakers that played recorded dance music. My mother wore a blue skirt that was too small for her and a white blouse and a pillbox hat with an organdy veil pinned up on top. She was heavy-breasted and thick-bodied, and her sexuality and her innocence about it seemed to burst from her clothes when she jitterbugged, or, even a moment later, slow-danced with Hank, her face hot and breathless, while his fingers slipped down the small of her back and kneaded her rump.

"Hank's in a union for stagehands in the movie business, Davy. Maybe we going out to Hollywood and start a new life there," she said.

The loudspeakers in the trees were playing "One O'Clock Jump," and through the windows in the bar I could see couples jitterbugging, spinning, flinging each other back and forth. Hank tipped his bottle of Jax beer to his lips and took a light sip, his eyes focused on nothing. But when a blond woman in a flowered dress and purple hat walked across his gaze, I saw his eyes touch on her body like a feather, then go empty again.

"But maybe you gonna have to stay with your aunt just a little while," my mother said. "Then I'm gonna send for you. You gonna ride the Sunset Limited to Hollywood, you."

My mother went inside the bowling alley to use the rest room.

The trees were glowing with the white flood lamps mounted on the branches, the air roaring with the music of Benny Goodman's orchestra. The blond woman in the flowered dress and purple hat walked to our table, a small glass of beer in one hand. The butt of her cigarette was thick with lipstick.

"How's the war hero?" she said.

He took another sip from his bottle of Jax and picked up a package of Lucky Strikes from the table and removed a cigarette gingerly by the tip and placed it in his mouth, never looking at the woman.

"My phone number's the same as it was last week. I hope nothing's been hard in your life," she said.

"Maybe I'll call you sometime," he replied.

"No need to call. You can come whenever you want," she said. When she grinned there was a red smear on her teeth.

"I'll keep it in mind," he said.

She winked and walked away, the cleft in her buttocks visible through the thinness of her dress. Hank opened a penknife and began cleaning his nails.

"You got something to say?" he asked me.

"No, sir."

"That woman there is a whore. You know what a whore is, Davy?"

"No." There was a glaze of starch on his khaki thigh. I could smell an odor like heat and soap and sweat that came from inside his shirt.

"It means she's not fit to sit down with your mother," he said. "So I don't want you talking about what you just heard. If you do, you'd best be gone when I come over."

Three days later my aunt and I stood on the platform at the train station and watched my mother and Hank climb aboard the Sunset Limited. They disappeared through the vestibule, then she came back and hugged me one more time.

"Davy, it ain't gonna be long. They got the ocean out there and movie stars and palm trees everywhere. You gonna love it, you," she said. Then Hank pulled her hand, and the two of them went into the observation car, their faces opaque now, like people totally removed from anything recognizable in their lives. Behind my mother's head I could see mural paintings of mesas and flaming sunsets.

But she didn't send for me, nor did she write or call. Three months later a priest telephoned collect from Indio, California, and asked my father if he could wire money for my mother's bus ticket back to New Iberia.

For years I dreamed of moonscape and skeletal trees along a railroad bed where white wolves with red mouths lived among the branches. When the Sunset Limited screamed down the track, the wolves did not run. They ate their young. I never discussed the dream with anyone.

TWENTY-SIX

A psychologist would probably agree that unless a person is a sociopath, stuffed guilt can fill him with a level of neurotic anxiety that is like waiting for a headsman in a cloth hood to appear at the prison door.

I didn't know if Alex Guidry was a sociopath or not, but on Monday Helen and I began tightening a couple of dials on his head.

We parked the cruiser at the entrance to his home and watched him walk from his bunkerlike brick house to the garage and open the garage door, simultaneously looking in our direction. He drove down the long shell drive to the parish road and slowed by the cruiser, rolling down his window on its electric motor. But Helen and I continued talking to each other as though he were not there. Then we made a U-turn and followed him to the finance company his wife's family owned in town, his eyes watching us in the rearview mirror.

Decades back the wife's father had made his way through the plantation quarters every Saturday morning, collecting the half-dollar payments on burial policies that people of color would give up food, even prostitute themselves, in order to maintain. The caskets they were buried in were made out of plywood and cardboard and crepe paper, wrapped in dyed cheesecloth and draped with huge satin bows. The plots were in Jim Crow cemeteries and the headstones had all the dignity of Hallmark cards. But as gaudy and cheap and sad as it all was, the spaded hole in the ground and the plastic flowers and the satin ribbons that decorated the piled dirt did not mark the entrance to the next world but the only level of accomplishment the dead could achieve in this one.

The Negro burial insurance business had passed into history and the plantation quarters were deserted, but the same people came with regularity to the finance company owned by the wife's family and signed papers they could not read and made incremental loan payments for years without ever reducing the principal. A pawnshop stood next door, also owned by the wife's family. Unlike most businesspeople, Guidry and his in-laws prospered most during economic recession.

We parked behind his car and watched him pause on the sidewalk and stare at us, then go inside.

A moment later a brown Honda, driven by a tall man in a gray suit, pulled to the curb, on the wrong side of the street, and parked bumper to bumper in front of Guidry's car. The driver, who was a DEA agent named Minos Dautrieve, got out and met us on the sidewalk in front of the finance company's glass doors. His crew-cut blond hair was flecked with white threads now, but he still had the same tall, angular good looks that sports photographers had loved when he played forward for LSU and was nicknamed "Dr. Dunkenstein" after he sailed through the air and slammed the ball so hard through the rim he shattered the backboard like hard candy.

"How's the fishing?" he said.

"They've got your name on every fin," I said.

"I'll probably come out this evening. How you doin', Helen?"

"Just fine. Lovely day, isn't it?" she replied.

"Do we have our friend's attention?" he asked, his back to the glass doors.

"Yep," I said.

He took a notebook out of his pocket and studied the first page of it.

"Well, I have to pick up a couple of things for my wife, then meet her and her mother in Lafayette. We'll see you-all," he said. He put the notebook back in his pocket, then walked to the front doors of the finance company, cupped his hands around his eyes to shield them from the sun, and peered through the tinted glass.

After he had driven away, Alex Guidry came out on the sidewalk.

"What are you people doing?" he said.

"You're an ex-cop. Guess," Helen said.

"That man's a federal agent of some kind," Guidry said.

"The guy who just left? He's an ex-jock. He was all-American honorable mention at LSU. That's a fact," I said.

"What is this?" he said.

"You're in the shithouse, Mr. Guidry. That's what it is," Helen said.

"This is harassment and I won't put up with it," he said.

"You're naive, sir. You're the subject of a murder investigation. You're also tied in with Harpo Scruggs. Scruggs has asked for immunity. You know where that leaves his friends? I'd get a parachute," I said.

"Fuck you," he said, and went back inside.

But his shirtsleeve caught on the door handle. When he pulled at it he ripped the cloth and hit a matronly white woman between the shoulder blades with his elbow.

Two hours later Guidry called the office.

"Scruggs is getting immunity for what?" he asked.

"I didn't say he was 'getting' anything."

I could hear him breathing against the receiver.

"First guy in line doesn't do the Big Sleep," I said.

"Same answer. Do your worst. At least I didn't flush my career down the bowl because I couldn't keep a bottle out of my mouth," he said.

"Ida Broussard was carrying your baby when you killed her, Mr. Guidry."

He slammed down the phone.

. . .

Three days later, in the cool of the evening, Lila Terrebonne and
Geraldine Holtzner came down the dirt road in Clete Purcel's
chartreuse Cadillac, the top down, and pulled into the drive. Alafair
and I were raking leaves and burning them on the edge of the road.
The leaves were damp and black, and the smoke from the fire twisted
upward into the trees in thick yellow curds and smelled like marijuana
burning in a wet field. Both Lila and Geraldine seemed delighted with
the pink-gray loveliness of the evening, with our activity in the yard,
with themselves, with the universe.

"What are you guys up to?" I said.

"We're going to a meeting. You want to tag along?" Geraldine
said from behind the wheel.

"It's a thought. What are you doing with Clete's car?" I said.

"Mine broke down. He lent me his," Geraldine said. "I went back
to Narcotics Anonymous, in case you're wondering. But I go to AA
sometimes, too."

Lila was smiling, a wistful, unfocused beam in her eye. "Hop in,
good-looking," she said.

"Did y'all make a stop before you got here?" I asked.

"Dave, I bet you urinated on radiators in elementary school," Lila
said.

"I might see y'all up there later. Y'all be careful about Clete's tires.
The air is starting to show through," I said.

"This is a lovely car. You drive it and suddenly it's 1965. What a
wonderful time that was, just before everything started to change," she
said.

"Who could argue, Lila?" I said.

Unless you were black or spent '65 in Vietnam, I thought as they
drove away.

The AA meeting that evening was held in the upstairs rooms of an
old brick church out on West Main. The Confederates had used
the church for a hospital while they tried to hold back the Federals on

the Teche south of town; then, after the town had been occupied and looted and the courthouse torched, the Federals inverted half the pews and filled them with hay for their horses. But most of the people in the upper rooms this evening cared little about the history of the building. The subject of the meeting was the Fifth Step of AA recovery, which amounts to owning up, or confessing, to one's past.

There are moments in Fifth Step meetings that cause the listeners to drop their eyes to the floor, to lose all expression in their faces, to clench their hands in their laps and wince inwardly at the knowledge that the barroom they had entered long ago had only one exit, and it opened on moral insanity.

Lila Terrebonne normally listened and did not speak at meetings. Tonight was different. She sat stiffly on a chair by the window, a tree silhouetted by a fiery sunset behind her head. The skin of her face had the polished, ceramic quality of someone who has just come out of a windstorm. Her hands were hooked together like those of an opera singer.

"I think I've had a breakthrough with my therapist," she said. "I've always had this peculiar sensation, this sense of guilt, I mean, a fixation I guess with crucifixes." She laughed self-deprecatingly, her eyes lowered, her eyelashes as stiff as wire. "It's because of something I saw as a child. But it didn't have anything to do with me, right? I mean, it's not part of the program to take somebody else's inventory. All I have to do is worry about what I've done. As people say, clean up my side of the street. Who am I to judge, particularly if I'm not in the historical context of others?"

No one had any idea of what she was talking about. She rambled on, alluding to her therapist, using terms most blue-collar people in the room had no understanding of.

"It's called psychoneurotic anxiety. It made me drink. Now I think most of that is behind me," she said. "Anyway, I didn't leave my panties anywhere today. That's all I have."

After the meeting I caught her by Clete's car. The oak tree overhead was filled with fireflies, and there was a heavy, wet smell in the air like sewer gas.

"Lila, I've never spoken like this to another AA member before, but what you said in there was total bullshit," I said.

She fixed her eyes on mine and blinked her eyelashes coyly and said nothing.

"I think you're stoned, too," I said.

"I have a prescription. It makes me a little funny sometimes. Now stop beating up on me," she said, and fixed my collar with one hand.

"You know who murdered Jack Flynn. You know who executed the two brothers in the swamp. You can't conceal knowledge like that from the law and expect to have any serenity."

"Marry me in our next incarnation," she said, and pinched my stomach. Then she made a sensual sound and said, "Not bad, big stuff."

She got in the passenger seat and looked at herself in her compact mirror and waited for Geraldine Holtzner to get behind the wheel. Then the two of them cruised down a brick-paved side street, laughing, the wind blowing their hair, like teenage girls who had escaped into a more innocent, uncomplicated time.

Two days passed, then I received another phone call from Alex Guidry, this time at the dock. His voice was dry, the receiver held close to his mouth.

"What kind of deal can I get?" he said.

"That depends on how far you can roll over."

"I'm not doing time."

"Don't bet on it."

"You're not worried about a dead black woman or a couple of shit bags who got themselves killed out in the Basin. You want the people who nailed up Jack Flynn."

"Give me a number. I'll call you back," I said.

"Call me back?"

"Yeah, I'm busy right now. I've already reached my quotient for jerk-off behavior today."

"I can give you Harpo Scruggs tied hand and foot on a barbecue spit," he said.

I could hear him breathing through his nose, like a cat's whisker scraping across the perforations. Then I realized the source of his fear.

"You've talked to Scruggs, haven't you?" I said. "You called him about his receiving immunity. Which means he knows you're in communication with us. You dropped the dime on yourself . . . Hello?"

"He's back. I saw him this morning," he said.

"You're imagining things."

"He's got an inoperable brain tumor. The guy's walking death. That's his edge."

"Better come in, Mr. Guidry."

"I don't give a deposition until he's in custody. I want the sheriff's guarantee on that."

"You won't get it."

"One day I'm going to make you suffer. I promise it." He eased the phone down into the cradle.

On Monday, Adrien Glazier knocked on my office door. She was dressed in blue jeans and hiking shoes and a denim shirt, and she carried a brown cloth shoulder bag scrolled with Mexican embroidery. The ends of her ash-blond hair looked like they had been brushed until they crawled with static electricity, then had been sprayed into place.

"We can't find Willie Broussard," she said.

"Did you try his father's fish camp?"

"Why do you think I'm dressed like this?"

"Cool Breeze doesn't report in to me, Ms. Glazier."

"Can I sit down?"

Her eyes met mine and lingered for a moment, and I realized her tone and manner had changed, like heat surrendering at the end of a burning day.

"An informant tells us some people in Hong Kong have sent two guys to Louisiana to clip off a troublesome hangnail or two," she said. "I don't know if the target is Willie Broussard or Ricky Scarlotti or a couple of movie producers. Maybe it's all of the above."

"My first choice would be Scarlotti. He's the only person who has reason to give up some of their heroin connections."

"If they kill Willie Broussard, they take the squeeze off Scarlotti. Anyway, I'm telling you what we know."

I started to bring up the subject of Harpo Scruggs again and the possibility of his having worked for the government, but I let it go.

She dropped a folder on my desk. Clipped to two xeroxed Mexico City police memorandums was a grainy eight-by-ten photograph that had been taken in an open-air fruit market. The man in the photo stood at a stall, sucking a raw oyster out of its shell.

"His name is Rubén Esteban. He's one of the men we think Hong Kong has sent here."

"He looks like a dwarf."

"He is. He worked for the Argentine Junta. Supposedly he interrogated prisoners by chewing off their genitals."

"What?"

"The Triads always ruled through terror. The people they hire create living studies in torture and mutilation. Call Amnesty International in Chicago and see what they have to say about Esteban."

I picked up the photo and looked at it again. "Where's the material on the other guy?" I asked.

"We don't know who he is. Mr. Robicheaux, I'm sorry for having given you a bad time in some of our earlier conversations."

"I'll survive," I said, and tried to smile.

"My father was killed in Korea while people like Jack Flynn were working for the Communist Party."

"Flynn wasn't a Red. He was a Wobbly."

"You could fool me. He was lucky a House committee didn't have him shipped to Russia."

Then she realized she had said too much, that she had admitted looking at his file, that she was probably committed forever to being the advocate for people whose deeds were indefensible.

"You ever sit down and talk with Megan? Maybe y'all are on the same side," I said.

"You're too personal, sir."

I raised my hands by way of apology.

She smiled slightly, then hung her bag from her shoulder and walked out of the office, her eyes already assuming new purpose, as though she were burning away all the antithetical thoughts that were like a thumbtack in her brow.

A t eight-thirty that night Bootsie and I were washing the dishes in the kitchen when the phone rang on the counter.

"This is what you've done, asshole. My reputation's ruined. My job is gone. My wife has left me. You want to hear more?" the voice said.

"Guidry?" I said.

"There's a rumor going around I'm the father of a halfwit mulatto I sold to a cathouse in Morgan City. The guy who told me that said he heard it from your buddy Clete Purcel."

"Either you're in a bar or you've become irrational. Either way, don't call my home again."

"Here it is. I'll give you the evidence on Flynn's murder. I said *evidence,* not just information. I'll give you the shooters who did the two brothers, I'll give you the guys who almost drowned Megan Flynn, I'll give you the guy who's been writing the checks. What's on your end of the table?"

"The Iberia prosecutor will go along with aiding and abetting. We'll work with St. Mary Parish. It's a good deal. You'd better grab it."

He was quiet a long time. Outside, the heat lightning looked like silver plate through the trees.

"Are you there?" I said.

"Scruggs threatened to kill me. You got to bring this guy in."

"Give us the handle to do it."

"It was under your feet the whole time and you never saw it, you arrogant shithead."

I waited silently. The receiver felt warm and moist in my hand.

"Go to the barn where Flynn died. I'll be there in forty-five minutes. Leave the muff diver at home," he said.

"You don't make the rules, Guidry. Another thing, call her that again and I'm going to break your wagon."

I hung up, then dialed Helen's home number.

"You don't want to check in with the St. Mary sheriff's office first?" she said.

"They'll get in the way. Are you cool on this?" I said.

"What do you mean?"

"We take Guidry down clean. No scratches on the freight."

"The guy who said he'd dig up my grave and piss in my mouth? To tell you the truth, I wouldn't touch him with a baton. But maybe you'd better get somebody else for backup, bwana."

"I'll meet you at the end of East Main in twenty minutes," I said.

I went into the bedroom and took my holstered 1911 model U.S. Army .45 from the dresser drawer and clipped it onto my belt. I wiped my palms on my khakis unconsciously. Through the screen window the oak and pecan trees seemed to tremble in the heat lightning that leaped between the clouds.

"Streak?" Bootsie said.

"Yes?"

"I overheard your conversation. Don't worry about Helen. It's you that man despises," she said.

Helen and I drove down the two-lane through Jeanerette, then turned off on an oak-lined service road that led past the barn with the cratered roof and sagging walls where Jack Flynn died. The moon had gone behind a bank of storm clouds, and the landscape was dark, the blackberry bushes in the pasture humped against the lights of a house across the bayou. The leaves of the oaks along the road flickered with lightning, and I could smell rain and dust in the air.

"Guidry's going to do time, isn't he?" Helen said.

"Some anyway."

"I partnered with a New Orleans uniform who got sent up to Angola. First week down a Big Stripe cut his face. He had himself put in lockdown and every morning the black boys would spit on him when they went to breakfast."

"Yeah?"

"I was just wondering how many graduates of the parish prison will be in Guidry's cell house."

Helen turned the cruiser off the road and drove past the water oaks through the weeds and around the side of the barn. The wind was up now and the banana trees rattled and swayed against the barn. In the headlights we could see clusters of red flowers in the rain trees and dust swirling off the ground.

"Where is he?" Helen said. But before I could speak she pointed at two pale lines of crushed grass where a car had been driven out in the pasture. Then she said, "I got a bad feeling, Streak."

"Take it easy," I said.

"What if Scruggs is behind this? He's been killing people for forty years. I don't plan to walk blindfolded into the Big Exit." She cut the lights and unsnapped the strap on her nine-millimeter Beretta.

"Let's walk the field. You go to the left, I go to the right . . . Helen?"

"What?"

"Forget it. Scruggs and Guidry are both pieces of shit. If you feel in jeopardy, take them off at the neck."

We got out of the cruiser and walked thirty yards apart through the field, our weapons drawn. Then the moon broke behind the edge of a cloud and we could see the bumper and front fender of an automobile that was parked close behind a blackberry thicket. I circled to the right of the thicket, toward the rear of the automobile, then I saw the tinted windows and buffed, soft-yellow exterior of Alex Guidry's Cadillac. The driver's door was partly open and a leg in gray pants and a laced black shoe was extended into the grass. I clicked on the flashlight in my left hand.

"Put both hands out the window and keep them there," I said.

But there was no response.

"Mr. Guidry, you will put your hands out the window, or you will be in danger of being shot. Do you hear me?" I said.

Helen moved past a rain tree and was now at an angle to the front of the Cadillac, her Beretta pointed with two hands straight in front of her.

Guidry rose from the leather seat, pulling himself erect by hooking his arm over the open window. But in his right hand I saw the nickel-plated surfaces of a revolver.

"Throw it away!" I shouted. "Now! Don't think about it! Guidry, throw the piece away!"

Then lightning cracked across the sky, and out of the corner of his vision he saw Helen take up a shooter's position against the trunk of the rain tree. Maybe he was trying to hold the revolver up in the air and step free of the car, beyond the open door, so she could see him fully, but he stumbled out into the field, his right arm pressed against the wound in his side and the white shirt that was sodden with blood.

But to Helen, looking into the glare of my flashlight, Guidry had become an armed silhouette.

I yelled or think I yelled, *He's already hit,* but it was too late. She fired twice, *pop, pop,* the barrel streaking the darkness. The first round hit him high in the chest, the second in the mouth.

But Guidry's night in Gethsemane was not over. He stumbled toward the barn, his lower face like a piece of burst fruit, and swung his pistol back in Helen's direction and let off one shot that whined away across the bayou and made a sound like a hammer striking wood.

She began firing as fast as her finger could pull the trigger, the ejected shells pinging off the trunk of the rain tree, until I came behind her and fitted my hands on both her muscular arms.

"He's down. It's over," I said.

"No, he's still there. He let off another round. I saw the flash," she said, her eyes wild, the tendons in her arms jumping as though she were cold.

"No, Helen."

She swallowed, breathing hard through her mouth, and wiped the sweat off her nose with her shoulder, never releasing the two-handed grip on the Beretta. I shined the light out across the grass onto the north side of the barn.

"Oh, shit," she said, almost like a plea.

"Call it in," I said.

"Dave, he's lying in the same, I mean like, his arms are out like—"

"Get on the radio. That's all you have to do. Don't regret any-thing that happened here tonight. He dealt the play a long time ago."

"Dave, he's on the left side of where Flynn died. I can't take this stuff. I didn't know the guy was hit. Why didn't you yell at me?"

"I did. I think I did. Maybe I didn't. He should have thrown away the piece."

We stood there like that, in the blowing wind and dust and the raindrops that struck our faces like marbles, the vault of sky above us exploding with sound.

TWENTY-SEVEN

The Argentine dwarf who called himself Rubén Esteban could not have been more unfortunate in his choice of a hotel.

Years ago in Lafayette, twenty miles from New Iberia, a severely retarded, truncated man named Chatlin Ardoin had made his living as a newspaper carrier who delivered newspapers to downtown businesses or sold them to train passengers at the Southern Pacific depot. His voice was like clotted rust in a sewer pipe; his arms and legs were stubs on his torso; his face had the expression of baked corn bread under his formless hat. Street kids from the north side baited him; an adman, the nephew of the newspaper's publisher, delighted in calling him Castro, driving him into an emotional rage.

The two-story clapboard hotel around the corner from the newspaper contained a bar downstairs where newsmen drank after their deadline. It was also full of hookers who worked the trade through the late afternoon and evening, except on Fridays, when the owner, whose name was Norma Jean, served free boiled shrimp for family people in the neighborhood. Every afternoon Chatlin brought Norma Jean a free newspaper, and every afternoon she gave him a frosted schooner of draft beer and a hard-boiled egg. He sat at the end of the bar under the air-conditioning unit, his canvas bag of rolled newspapers piled on the stool next to him, and peeled and ate the egg and drank the beer and stared at the soap operas on the TV with an intensity that made some believe he comprehended far more of the world than his appearance indicated. Norma Jean was thoroughly corrupt and allowed her girls no latitude when it came to pleasing their customers, but like most uneducated and primitive people, she intuitively felt, without finding words for the idea, that the retarded and insane were placed on earth to be cared for by those whose souls might otherwise be forfeit.

A beer and a hard-boiled egg wasn't a bad price for holding on to a bit of your humanity.

Fifteen years ago, during a hurricane, Chatlin was run over by a truck on the highway. The newspaper office was moved; the Southern Pacific depot across from the hotel was demolished and replaced by a post office; and Norma Jean's quasi-brothel became an ordinary hotel with a dark, cheerless bar for late-night drinkers.

Ordinary until Rubén Esteban checked into the hotel, then came down to the bar at midnight, the hard surfaces of his face glowing like corn bread under the neon. Esteban climbed on top of a stool, his Panama hat wobbling on his head. Norma Jean took one look at him and began screaming that Chatlin Ardoin had escaped from the grave.

Early Wednesday morning Helen and I were at the Lafayette Parish Jail. It was raining hard outside and the corridors were streaked with wet footprints. The homicide detective named Daigle took us up in the elevator. His face was scarred indistinctly and had the rounded, puffed quality of a steroid user's, his black hair clipped short across the top of his forehead. His collar was too tight for him and he kept pulling at it with two fingers, as though he had a rash.

"You smoked a guy and you're not on the desk?" he said to Helen.

"The guy already had a hole in him," I said. "He also shot at a police officer. He also happened to put a round through someone's bedroom wall."

"Convenient," Daigle said.

Helen looked at me.

"What's Esteban charged with?" I asked.

"Disturbing the peace, resisting. Somebody accidentally knocked him off the barstool when Norma Jean started yelling about dead people. The dwarf got off the floor and went for the guy's crotch. The uniform would have cut him loose, except he remembered y'all's bulletin. He said getting cuffs on him was like trying to pick up a scorpion," Daigle said. "What's the deal on him, again?"

"He sexually mutilated political prisoners for the Argentine Junta. They were buds with the Gipper," I said.

"The what?" he said.

Rubén Esteban sat on a wood bench by himself in the back of a holding cell, his Panama hat just touching the tops of his jug ears. His face was triangular in shape, dull yellow in hue, the eyes set at an oblique angle to his nose.

"What are you doing around here, podna?" I said.

"I'm a chef. I come here to study the food," he answered. His voice sounded metallic, as though it came out of a resonator in his throat.

"You have three different passports," I said.

"That's for my cousins. We're a—how you call it?—we're a team. We cook all over the world," Esteban said.

"We know who you are. Stay out of Iberia Parish," Helen said.

"Why?" he asked.

"We have an ordinance against people who are short and ugly," she replied.

His face was wooden, impossible to read, the eyes hazing over under the brim of his hat. He touched an incisor tooth and looked at the saliva on the ball of his finger.

"Governments have protected you in the past. That won't happen here. Am I getting through to you, Mr. Esteban?" I said.

"Me cago en la puta de tu madre," he answered, his eyes focused on the backs of his square, thick hands, his mouth curling back in neither a sneer nor a grimace but a disfigurement like the expression in a corpse's face when the lips wrinkle away from the teeth.

"What'd he say?" Daigle asked.

"He probably doesn't have a lot of sentiment about Mother's Day," I said.

"That's not all he don't have. He's got a tube in his pants. No penis," Daigle said, and started giggling.

Outside, it was still raining hard when Helen and I got in our cruiser.

"What'd Daigle do before he was a cop?" Helen asked.

"Bill collector and barroom bouncer, I think."

"I would have never guessed," she said.

Rubén Esteban paid his fine that afternoon and was released.

That night I sat in the small office that I had fashioned out of a storage room in the back of the bait shop. Spread on my desk were xeroxed copies of the investigator's report on the shooting and death of Alex Guidry, the coroner's report, and the crime scene photos taken in front of the barn. The coroner stated that Guidry had already been hit in the rib cage with a round from a .357 magnum before Helen had ever discharged her weapon. Also, the internal damage was massive and probably would have proved fatal even if Helen had not peppered him with her nine-millimeter.

One photo showed the bloody interior of Guidry's Cadillac and a bullet hole in the stereo system and another in the far door, including a blood splatter on the leather door panel, indicating the original shooter had fired at least twice and the fatal round had hit Guidry while he was seated in the car.

Another photo showed tire tracks in the grass that were not the Cadillac's.

Two rounds had been discharged from Guidry's .38, one at Helen, the other probably at the unknown assailant.

The photo of Guidry, like most crime scene photography, was stark in its black and white contrasts. His back lay propped against the barn wall, his spine curving against the wood and the earth. His hands and lower legs were sheathed in blood, his shattered mouth hanging open, narrowing his face like a tormented figure in a Goya painting.

The flood lamps were on outside the bait shop, and the rain was blowing in sheets on the bayou. The water had overflowed the banks, and the branches of the willows were trailing in the current. The body of a dead possum floated by under the window, its stomach yellow and swollen in the electric glare, the claws of feeding blue-point crabs affixed to its fur. I kept thinking of Guidry's words to me in our last telephone conversation: *It was under your feet the whole time and you never saw it.*

What was under my feet? Where? By the barn? Out in the field where Guidry was hit with the .357?

Then I saw Megan Flynn's automobile park by the boat ramp and Megan run down the dock toward the bait shop with an umbrella over her head.

She came inside, breathless, shaking water out of her hair. Unconsciously, I looked up the slope through the trees at the lighted gallery and living room of my house.

"Wet night to be out," I said.

She sat down at the counter and blotted her face with a paper napkin.

"I got a call from Adrien Glazier. She told me about this guy Rubén Esteban," she said.

Not bad, Adrien, I thought.

"This guy's record is for real, Dave. I heard about him when I covered the Falklands War," she said.

"He was in custody on a misdemeanor in Lafayette this morning. He doesn't blend into the wallpaper easily."

"We should feel better? Why do you think the Triads sent a walking horror show here?"

Megan wasn't one to whom you gave facile assurances.

"We don't know who his partner is. While we're watching Esteban, the other guy's peddling an ice-cream cart down Main Street," I said.

"Thank you," she said, and dried the back of her neck with another napkin. Her skin seemed paler, her mouth and her hair a darker shade of red under the overhead light. I glanced away from her eyes.

"You and Cisco want a cruiser to park by your house?" I asked.

"I have a bad feeling about Clete. I can't shake it," she said.

"Clete?" I said.

"Geri Holtzner is driving his car all around town. Look, nobody is going to hurt Billy Holtzner. You don't kill the people who owe you money. You hurt the people around them. These guys put bombs in people's automobiles."

"I'll talk to him about it."

"I already have. He doesn't listen. I hate myself for involving him in this," she said.

"I left my Roman collar up at the house, Meg."

"I forgot. Swinging dicks talk in deep voices and never apologize for their mistakes."

"Why do you turn every situation into an adversarial one?" I asked.

She raised her chin and tilted her head slightly. Her mouth reminded me of a red flower turning toward light.

Bootsie opened the screen door and came in holding a raincoat over her head.

"Oh, excuse me. I didn't mean to walk into the middle of something," she said. She shook her raincoat and wiped the water off it with her hand. "My, what a mess I'm making."

The next afternoon we executed a search warrant on the property where Alex Guidry was shot. The sky was braided with thick gray and metallic-blue clouds, and the air smelled like rain and wood pulp and smoke from a trash fire.

Thurston Meaux, the St. Mary Parish plainclothes, came out of the barn with a rake in his hand.

"I found two used rubbers, four pop bottles, a horseshoe, and a dead snake. That any help to y'all?" he said.

"Pretty clever," I said.

"Maybe Alex Guidry was just setting you up, podna. Maybe you're lucky somebody popped him first. Maybe there was never anything here," Meaux said.

"Tell me, Thurston, why is it nobody wants to talk about the murder of Jack Flynn?"

"It was a different time. My grandfather did some things in the Klan, up in nort' Louisiana. He's an old man now. It's gonna change the past to punish him now?"

I started to reply but instead just walked away. It was easy for me to be righteous at the expense of another. The real problem was I didn't have any idea what we were looking for. The yellow crime scene tape formed a triangle from the barn to the spot where Guidry's Cadillac had been parked. Inside the triangle we found old shotgun and .22 shells, pig bones, a plowshare that groundwater had turned into rusty lace, the stone base of a mule-operated cane grinder overgrown with morning glory vine. A deputy sheriff swung his metal detector over a desiccated oak stump and got a hot reading. We splintered the stump apart and found a fan-shaped ax head, one that had been hand-forged, in the heart of the wood.

At four o'clock the uniformed deputies left. The sun came out and I watched Thurston Meaux sit down on a crate in the lee of the barn and eat a sandwich, let the wax paper blow away in the wind, then pull the tab on a soda can and drop it in the dirt.

"You're contaminating the crime scene," I said.

"Wrong," he replied.

"Oh?"

"Because we're not wasting any more time on this bullshit. You've got some kind of obsession, Robicheaux." He brushed the crumbs off his clothes and walked to his automobile.

Helen didn't say anything for a long time. Then she lifted a strand of hair out of her eye and said, "Dave, we've walked every inch of the field and raked all the ground inside and around the barn. You want to start over again, that's okay with me, but—"

"Guidry said, 'It was under your feet, you arrogant shithead.' Whatever he was talking about, it's physical, maybe something we walked over, something he could pick up and stick in my face."

"We can bring in a Cat and move some serious dirt."

"No, we might destroy whatever is here."

She let out her breath, then began scraping a long divot with a mattock around the edges of the hardpan.

"You're a loyal friend, Helen," I said.

"Bwana has the keys to the cruiser," she said.

I stood in front of the barn wall and stared at the weathered wood, the strips of red paint that were flaking like fingernail polish, the dust-sealed nail holes where Jack Flynn's wrists had been impaled. Whatever evidence was here had been left by Harpo Scruggs, not Alex Guidry, I thought. It was something Scruggs knew about, had deliberately left in place, had even told Guidry about. But why?

To implicate someone else. Just as he had crucified Swede Boxleiter in this spot to tie Boxleiter's death to Flynn's.

"Helen, if there's anything here, it's right by where Jack Flynn died," I said.

She rested the mattock by her foot and wiped a smear of mud off her face with her sleeve.

"If you say so," she said.

"Long day, huh?"

"I had a dream last night. Like I was being pulled back into history, into stuff I don't want to have anything to do with."

"You told me yourself, we're the good guys."

"When I kept shooting at Guidry? He was already done. I just couldn't stop. I convinced myself I saw another flash from his weapon. But I knew better."

"He got what he deserved."

"Yeah? Well, why do I feel the way I do?"

"Because you still have your humanity. It's because you're the best."

"I want to make this case and lock the file on it. I mean it, Dave."

She put down her mattock and the two of us began piercing the hardpan with garden forks, working backward from the barn wall, turning up the dirt from six inches below the surface. The subsoil was black and shiny, oozing with water and white worms. Then I saw a coppery glint and a smooth glass surface wedge out of the mud while Helen was prizing her fork against a tangle of roots.

"Hold it," I said.

"What is it?"

"A jar. Don't move the fork."

I reached down and lifted a quart-size preserve jar out of the mud and water. The top was sealed with both rubber and a metal cap. I squatted down and dipped water out of the hole and rinsed the mud off the glass.

"An envelope and a newspaper clipping? What's Scruggs doing, burying a time capsule?" Helen said.

We walked to the cruiser and wiped the jar clean with paper towels, then set it on the hood and unscrewed the cap. I lifted the newspaper clipping out with two fingers and spread it on the hood. The person who had cut it out of the *Times-Picayune* had carefully included the strip at the top of the page which gave the date, August 8, 1956. The headline on the story read: "Union Organizer Found Crucified".

Helen turned the jar upside down and pulled the envelope out of the opening. The glue on the flap was still sealed. I slipped my pocketknife in the corner of the flap and sliced a neat line across the top of the envelope and shook three black-and-white photos out on the hood.

Jack Flynn was still alive in two of them. In one, he was on his hands and knees while men in black hoods with slits for eyes swung blurred chains on his back; in the other, a fist clutched his hair, pulling his head erect so the camera could photograph his destroyed face. But in the third photo his ordeal had come to an end. His head lay on his shoulder; his eyes were rolled into his head, his impaled arms stretched out on the wood of the barn wall. Three men in cloth hoods were looking back at the camera, one pointing at Flynn as though indicating a lesson to the viewer.

"This doesn't give us squat," Helen said.

"The man in the middle. Look at the ring finger on his left hand. It's gone, cut off at the palm," I said.

"You know him?"

"It's Archer Terrebonne. His family didn't just order the murder. He helped do it."

"Dave, there's no face to go with the hand. It's not a felony to have a missing finger. Look at me. A step at a time and all that jazz, right? You listening, Streak?"

TWENTY-EIGHT

I t was an hour later. Terrebonne had not been at his home, but a maid had told us where to find him. I parked the cruiser under the oaks in front of the restaurant up the highway and cut the engine. The water dripping out of the trees steamed on the hood.

"Dave, don't do this," Helen said.

"He's in Iberia Parish now. I'm not going to have these pictures lost in a St. Mary Parish evidence locker."

"We get them copied, then do it by the numbers."

"He'll skate."

"You know a lot of rich guys working soybeans in Angola? That's the way it is."

"Not this time."

I went inside the foyer, where people waited in leather chairs for an available table. I opened my badge on the maître d'.

"Archer Terrebonne is here with a party," I said.

The maître d's eyes locked on mine, then shifted to Helen, who stood behind me.

"Is there a problem?" he asked.

"Not yet," I said.

"I see. Follow me, please."

We walked through the main dining room to a long table at the
rear, where Terrebonne was seated with a dozen other people. The
waiters had just taken away their shrimp cocktails and were now serving the gumbo off of a linen-covered cart.

Terrebonne wiped his mouth with a napkin, then waited for a
woman in a robin's-egg-blue suit to stop talking before he shifted his
eyes to me.

"What burning issue do you bring us tonight, Mr. Robicheaux?"
he asked.

"Harpo Scruggs pissed in your shoe," I said.

"Sir, would you not—" the maître d' began.

"You did your job. Beat it," Helen said.

I lay the three photographs down on the tablecloth.

"That's you in the middle, Mr. Terrebonne. You chain-whipped
Jack Flynn and hammered nails through his wrists and ankles, then let
your daughter carry your guilt. You truly turn my stomach, sir," I
said.

"And you're way beyond anything I'll tolerate," he said.

"Get up," I said.

"What?"

"Better do what he says," Helen said behind me.

Terrebonne turned to a silver-haired man on his right. "John,
would you call the mayor's home, please?" he said.

"You're under arrest, Mr. Terrebonne. The mayor's not going to
help you," I said.

"I'm not going anywhere with you, sir. You put your hand on my
person again and I'll sue you for battery," he said, then calmly began
talking to the woman in a robin's-egg-blue suit on his left.

Maybe it was the long day, or the fact the photos had allowed me
to actually see the ordeal of Jack Flynn, one that time had made an
abstraction, or maybe I simply possessed a long-buried animus toward
Archer Terrebonne and the imperious and self-satisfied arrogance that
he and his kind represented. But long ago I had learned that anger, my
old enemy, had many catalysts and they all led ultimately to one
consequence, an eruption of torn red-and-black color behind the

eyes, an alcoholic blackout without booze, then an adrenaline surge that left me trembling, out of control, and possessed of a destructive capability that later filled me with shame.

I grabbed him by the back of his belt and hoisted him out of the chair, pushed him facedown on the table, into his food, and cuffed his wrists behind him, hard, ratcheting the curved steel tongues deep into the locks, crimping the veins like green string. Then I walked him ahead of me, out the foyer, into the parking area, pushing past a group of people who stared at us openmouthed. Terrebonne tried to speak, but I got the back door of the cruiser open and shoved him inside, cutting his scalp on the jamb.

When I slammed the door I turned around and was looking into the face of the woman in the robin's-egg-blue suit.

"You manhandle a sixty-three-year-old man like that? My, you must be proud. I'm so pleased we have policemen of your stature protecting us from ourselves," she said.

The sheriff called me into his office early the next morning. He rubbed the balls of his fingers back and forth on his forehead, as though the skin were burned, and looked at a spot six inches in front of his face.

"I don't know where to begin," he said.

"Terrebonne was kicked loose?"

"Two hours after you put him in the cage. I've had calls from a judge, three state legislators, and a U.S. congressman. You locked him in the cage with a drag queen and a drunk with vomit all over his clothes?"

"I didn't notice."

"I bet. He says he's going to sue."

"Let him. He's obstructed and lied in the course of a murder investigation. He's dirty from the jump, skipper. Put that photo and his daughter in front of a grand jury and see what happens."

"You're really out to burn his grits, aren't you?"

"You don't think he deserves it?" I said.

"The homicide was in St. Mary Parish. Dave, this guy had to have stitches in his head. Do you know what his lawyers are going to do with that?"

"We've been going after the wrong guys. Cut off the snake's head and the body dies," I said.

"I called my insurance agent about an umbrella policy this morning, you know, the kind that protects you against losing your house and everything you own. I'll give you his number."

"Terrebonne skates?"

The sheriff picked up a pink memo slip in the fingers of each hand and let them flutter back to his ink blotter.

"You've figured it out," he said.

L ate that afternoon, just as the sun dipped over the trees, Cisco Flynn walked down the dock where I was cleaning the barbecue pit, and sat on the railing and watched me work.

"Megan thinks she caused some trouble between you and your wife," he said.

"She's right," I said.

"She's sorry about it."

"Look, Cisco, I'm kind of tired of y'all's explanations about various things. What's the expression, 'Get a life'?"

"That guy who got thrown out the hotel window in San Antonio? Swede did it, but I helped set up the transportation and the alibi at the movie theater."

"Why tell me?"

"He's dead, but he was a good guy. I'm not laying off something I did on a friend."

"You got problems with your conscience about the hotel flyer, go to San Antone and turn yourself in."

"What's with you, man?"

"Archer Terrebonne, the guy who has money in your picture, killed your father. Come down to the office and check out the photos. I made copies before I turned the originals over to St. Mary Parish. The downside of the story is I can't touch him."

His face looked empty, insentient, as though he were winded, his lips moving without sound. He blinked and swallowed. "Archer Terrebonne? No, there's something wrong. He's been a guest in my home. What are you saying?" he said.

I went inside the bait shop and didn't come back out until he was gone.

That night the moon was down and leaves were blowing in the darkness outside, rattling against the trunks of the oak and pecan trees. When I went into the bedroom the light was off and Bootsie was sitting in front of her dresser in her panties and a T-shirt, looking out the window into the darkness.

"You eighty-sixed Cisco?" she said.

"Not exactly. I just didn't feel like talking to him anymore."

"Was this over Megan?"

"When she comes out here, we have trouble," I said.

The breeze ginned the blades in the window fan and I could hear leaves blowing against the screen.

"It's not her fault, it's mine," Bootsie said.

"Beg your pardon?"

"You take on other people's burdens, Dave. It's just the way you are. That's why you're the man I married."

I put my hand on her shoulder. She looked at our reflection in the dresser mirror and stood up, still facing the mirror. I slipped my arms around her waist, under her breasts, and put my face in her hair. Her body felt muscular and hard against mine. I moved my hand down her stomach, and she arched her head back against mine and clasped the back of my neck. Her stiffening breasts, the smoothness of her stomach and the taper of her hips, the hardness of her thighs, the tendons in her back, the power in her upper arms, when I embraced all these things with touch and mind and eye, it was like watching myself become one with an alabaster figure who had been infused with the veined warmth of a new rose.

Then I was between her thighs on top of the sheet and I could hear a sound in my head like wind in a conch shell and feel her press me deeper inside, as though both of us were drawing deeper into a cave beneath the sea, and I knew that concerns over winged chariots and mutability and death should have no place among the quick, even when autumn thudded softly against the window screen.

In Vietnam I had anxieties about toe-poppers and booby-trapped 105 duds that made the skin tighten around my temples and the blood veins dilate in my brain, so that during my waking hours I constantly experienced an unrelieved pressure band along one side of my head, just as though I were wearing a hat. But the visitor who stayed on in my nightmares, long after the war, was a pajama-clad sapper by the name of Bedcheck Charlie.

Bedcheck Charlie could cross rice paddies without denting the water, cut crawl paths through concertina wire, or tunnel under claymores if he had to. He had beaten the French with resolve and a shovel rather than a gun. But there was no question about what he could do with a bolt-action rifle stripped off a dead German or Sudanese Legionnaire. He waited for the flare of a Zippo held to a cigarette or the tiny blue flame from a heat tab flattening on the bottom of a C-rat can, then he squeezed off from three hundred yards out and left a wound shaped like a keyhole in a man's face.

But I doubt if Ricky Scarlotti ever gave much thought to Vietnamese sappers. Certainly his mind was focused on other concerns Saturday morning when he sat outside the riding club where he played polo sometimes, sipping from a glass of burgundy, dipping bread in olive oil and eating it, punching his new girlfriend, Angela, in the ribs whenever he made a point. Things were going to work out. He'd gotten that hillbilly, Harpo Scruggs, back on the job. Scruggs would clip that snitch in New Iberia, the boon, what was his name, the one ripping off the Mob's own VCRs and selling them back to them, Broussard was his name, clip him once and for all and take the weight off Ricky so he could tell that female FBI agent to shove her Triad bullshit up her nose with chopsticks.

In fact, he and Angela and the two bodyguards had tickets for the early flight to Miami Sunday morning. Tomorrow he'd be sitting on the beach behind the Doral Hotel, with a tropical drink in his hand, maybe go out to the trotters or the dog track later, hey, take a deep-sea charter and catch a marlin and get it mounted. Then call up some guys in Hallandale who he'd pay for each minute they had that fat shit Purcel begging on videotape. Ricky licked his lips when he thought about it.

A sno'ball truck drove down the winding two-lane road through the park that bordered the riding club. Ricky took off his pilot's glasses and wiped them with a Kleenex, then put them back on again. What's a sno'ball truck doing in the park when no kids are around? he thought. The sno'ball truck pulled into the oak trees and the driver got out and watched the ducks on the pond, then disappeared around the far side of the truck.

"Go see what that guy's doing," Ricky said to one of his bodyguards.

"He's lying in the shade, taking a nap," the bodyguard replied.

"Tell him this ain't Wino Row, go take his naps somewhere else," Ricky said.

The bodyguard walked across the road, into the trees, and spoke to the man on the ground. The man sat up and yawned, looked in Ricky's direction while the bodyguard talked, then started his truck and drove away.

"Who was he?" Ricky asked the bodyguard.

"A guy sells sno'balls."

"Who *was* he?"

"He didn't give me his fucking name, Ricky. You want I should go after him?"

"Forget it. We're out of drinks here. Get the waiter back."

An hour later Ricky's eyes were red with alcohol, his skin glazed with sweat from riding his horse hard in the sun. An ancient green milk truck, with magnetized letters on the side, drove down the two-lane road through the park, exited on the boulevard, then made a second pass through the park and stopped in the trees by the duck pond.

Benny Grogan, the other bodyguard, got up from Ricky's table. He wore a straw hat with a multicolored band on his platinum hair.

"Where you going?" Ricky said.

"To check the guy out."

"He's a knife grinder. I seen that truck all over the neighborhood," Ricky said.

"I thought you didn't want nobody hanging around, Ricky," Benny said.

"He's a midget. How's he reach the pedals? Bring the car around. Angela, you up for a shower?" Ricky said.

The milk truck was parked deep in the shade of the live oaks. The rear doors opened, flapping back on their hinges, and revealed a prone man in a yellow T-shirt and dark blue jeans. His long body was stretched out behind a sandbag, the sling of the scoped rifle twisted around his left forearm, the right side of his face notched into the rifle's stock.

When he squeezed off, the rifle recoiled hard against his shoulder and a flash leaped off the muzzle, like an electrical short, but there was no report.

The bullet tore through the center of Ricky's throat. A purple stream of burgundy flowed from both corners of his mouth, then he began to make coughing sounds, like a man who can neither swallow nor expel a chicken bone, while blood spigoted from his wound and spiderwebbed his chest and white polo pants. His eyes stared impotently into his new girlfriend's face. She pushed herself away from the table, her hands held out in front of her, her knees close together, like someone who did not want to be splashed by a passing car.

The shooter slammed the back doors of the milk truck and the driver drove the truck through the trees and over the curb onto the boulevard. Benny Grogan ran down the street after it, his .38 held in the air, automobiles veering to each side of him, their horns blaring.

It was Monday when Adrien Glazier gave me all the details of Scarlotti's death over the phone.

"NOPD found the truck out by Lake Pontchartrain. It was clean," she said.

"You got anything on the shooter?"

"Nothing. It looks like we've lost our biggest potential witness against the boys from Hong Kong," she said.

"I'm afraid people in New Orleans won't mourn that fact," I said.

"You can't tell. Greaseball wakes are quite an event. Anyway, we'll be there."

"Tell the band to play 'My Funny Valentine,' " I said.

TWENTY-NINE

That evening I drove down to Clete's cottage outside Jeanerette. He was washing his car in the side yard, rubbing a soapy sponge over the hood.

"I think I'm going to get it restored, drive it around like a classic instead of a junk heap," he said. He wore a pair of rubber boots and oversized swimming trunks, and the hair on his stomach was wet and plastered to his skin.

"Megan thinks the guys who did Ricky Scar might try to hurt Holtzner by going through his daughter. She thinks you shouldn't let her drive your car around," I said.

"When those guys want to pop somebody, they don't do it with car bombs. It's one on one, like Ricky Scar got it."

"Have you ever listened to me once in your life about anything?"

"On the perfecta that time at Hialeah. I lost three hundred bucks."

"Archer Terrebonne killed Cisco Flynn's father. I told Cisco that."

"Yeah, I know. He says he doesn't believe you." Clete moved the sponge slowly back and forth on the car hood, his thoughts sealed behind his face, the water from the garden hose sluicing down on his legs.

"What's bothering you?" I asked.

"Terrebonne's a major investor in Cisco's film. If Cisco walks out, his career's a skid mark on the bowl. I just thought he might have more guts. I bet a lot of wrong horses."

He threw the bucket of soapy water into a drainage ditch. The sun looked like a smoldering fire through the pine trees.

"You want to tell me what's really bothering you?" I said.

"I thought Megan and me might put it back together. That's why I scrambled Ricky Scar's eggs, to look like big shit, that simple, mon. Megan's life is international, I mean, all this local stuff is an asterisk in her career." He blew his breath out. "I got to stop drinking. I've got a buzz like a bad neon sign in my head."

"Let's put a line in the water," I said.

"Dave, those pictures Harpo Scruggs buried in the ground? That dude's got backup material somewhere. Something that can put a thumb in Terrebonne's eye."

"Yeah, but I can't find Scruggs. The guy's a master at going in and out of the woodwork," I said.

"Remember what that retired Texas Ranger in El Paso told you? About looking for him in cathouses and at pigeon shoots and dogfights?"

His skin was pink in the fading light, the hair on his shoulders ruffling in the breeze.

"Dogfights? No, it was something else," I said.

The cockfights were held in St. Landry Parish, in a huge, rambling wood-frame nightclub, painted bright yellow and set back against a stand of green hardwoods. The shell parking lot could accommodate hundreds of automobiles and pickup trucks, and the patrons (blue-collar people, college students, lawyers, professional gamblers) who came to watch the birds blind and kill each other with metal spurs and slashers did so with glad, seemingly innocent hearts.

The pit was railed, enclosed with chicken wire, the dirt hard-packed and sprinkled with sawdust. The rail, which afforded the best view, was always occupied by the gamblers, who passed thousands of dollars in wagers from hand to hand, with neither elation nor resentment, as though the matter of exchanging currency were impersonal and separate from the blood sport taking place below.

It was all legal. In Louisiana fighting cocks are classified as fowl and hence are not protected by the laws that govern the treatment of most animals. In the glow of the scrolled neon on the lacquered yellow pine walls, under the layers of floating cigarette smoke, in the roar of noise that rattled windows, you could smell the raw odor of blood and feces and testosterone and dried sweat and exhaled alcohol that I suspect was very close to the mix of odors that rose on a hot day from the Roman arena.

Clete and I sat at the end of the bar. The bartender, who was a Korean War veteran named Harold who wore black slacks and a short-sleeve white shirt and combed his few strands of black hair across his pate, served Clete a vodka collins and me a Dr Pepper in a glass filled with cracked ice. Harold leaned down toward me and put a napkin under my glass.

"Maybe he's just late. He's always been in by seven-thirty," he said.

"Don't worry about it, Harold," I said.

"We gonna have a public situation here?" he said.

"Not a chance," Clete said.

We didn't have long to wait. Harpo Scruggs came in the side door from the parking lot and walked to the rail around the cockpit. He wore navy blue western-cut pants with his cowboy boots and hat, and a silver shirt that tucked into his Indian-bead belt as tightly as tin. He made a bet with a well-known cockfighter from Lafayette, a man who when younger was both a pimp and a famous barroom dancer.

The cocks rose into the air, their slashers tearing feathers and blood from each other's bodies, while the crowd's roar lifted to the ceiling. A few minutes later one of the cocks was dead and Scruggs gently pulled a sheaf of hundred-dollar bills from between the fingers of the ex-pimp he had made his wager with.

"I think I'm experiencing Delayed Stress Syndrome. There was a place just like this in Saigon. The bar girls were VC whores," Clete said.

"Has he made us?" I asked.

"I think so. He doesn't rattle easy, does he? Oh-oh, here he comes."

Scruggs put one hand on the bar, his foot on the brass rail, not three feet from us.

"Has that worm talked to you yet?" he said to Harold.

"He's waiting right here for you," Harold said, and lifted a brown bottle of mescal from under the bar and set it before Scruggs, with a shot glass and a saucer of chicken wings and a bottle of Tabasco.

Scruggs took a twenty-dollar bill from a hand-tooled wallet and inserted it under the saucer, then poured into the glass and drank from it. His eyes never looked directly as us but registered our presence in the same flat, lidless fashion an iguana's might.

"You got a lot of brass," I said to him.

"Not really. Since I don't think your bunch could drink piss out of a boot with the instructions printed on the heel," he replied. He unscrewed the cork in the mescal bottle with a squeak and tipped another shot into his glass.

"Some out-of-town hitters popped Ricky Scar. That means you're out of the contract on Willie Broussard and you get to keep the front money," I said.

"I'm an old man. I'm buying quarter horses to take back to Deming. Why don't y'all leave me be?" he said.

"You use vinegar?" Clete said.

This time Scruggs looked directly at him. "Say again."

"You must have got it on your clothes. When you scrubbed the gunpowder residue off after you smoked Alex Guidry. Those .357s leave powder residue like you dipped your hand in pig shit," Clete said.

Scruggs laughed to himself and lit a cigarette and smoked it, his back straight, his eyes focused on his reflection in the bar mirror. A man came up to him, made a bet, and walked away.

"We found the photos you buried in the jar. We want the rest of it," I said.

"I got no need to trade. Not now."

"We'll make the case on you eventually. I hear you've got a carrot growing in your brain. How'd you like to spend your last days in the jail ward at Charity?" I said.

He emptied the mescal bottle and shook the worm out of the bottom into the neck. It was thick, whitish green, its skin hard and leathery. He gathered it into his lips and sucked it into his mouth. "Is it true the nurse's aides at Charity give blow jobs for five dollars?" he asked.

Clete and I walked out into the parking lot. The air was cool and smelled of the fields and rain, and across the road the sugarcane was bending in the wind. I nodded to Helen Soileau and a St. Landry Parish plainclothes who sat in an unmarked car.

An hour later Helen called me at the bait shop, where I was helping Batist clean up while Clete ate a piece of pie at the counter. Scruggs had rented a house in the little town of Broussard.

"Why's he still hanging around here?" I asked Clete.

"A greedy piece of shit like that? He's going to put a soda straw in Archer Terrebonne's jugular."

On Wednesday afternoon I left the office early and worked in the yard with Alafair. The sun was gold in the trees, and red leaves drifted out of the branches onto the bayou. We turned on the soak hoses in the flower beds and spaded out the St. Augustine grass that had grown through the brick border, and the air, which was unseasonably cool, smelled of summer, like cut lawns and freshly turned soil and water from a garden hose, rather than autumn and shortening days.

Lila Terrebonne parked a black Oldsmobile with darkly tinted windows by the boat ramp and rolled down the driver's window and waved. Someone whom I couldn't see clearly sat next to her. The trunk was open and filled with cardboard boxes of chrysanthemums. She got out of the Oldsmobile and crossed the road and walked into the pecan trees, where Alafair and I were raking up pecan husks and leaves that had gone black with water.

Lila wore a pale blue dress and white pumps and a domed straw hat, one almost like Megan's. For the first time in years her eyes looked clear, untroubled, even happy.

"I'm having a party tomorrow night. Want to come?" she said.

"I'd better pass, Lila."

"I did a Fifth Step, you know, cleaning house. With an ex-hooker, can you believe it? It took three hours. I think she wanted a drink when it was over."

"That's great. I'm happy for you."

Lila looked at Alafair and waited, as though an unstated expectation among us had not been met.

"Oh, excuse me. I think I'll go inside. Talk on the phone. Order some drugs," Alafair said.

"You don't need to go, Alf," I said.

"Bye-bye," she said, jittering her fingers at us.

"I've made peace with my father, Dave," Lila said, watching Alafair walk up the steps of the gallery. Then: "Do you think your daughter should talk to adults like that?"

"If she feels like it."

Her eyes wandered through the trees, her long lashes blinking like black wire. "Well, anyway, my father's in the car. He'd like to shake hands," she said.

"You've brought your—"

"Dave, I've forgiven him for the mistakes he made years ago. Jack Flynn was in the Communist Party. His friends were union terrorists. Didn't you do things in war you regretted?"

"*You've* forgiven him? Goodbye, Lila."

"No, he's been good enough to come out here. You're going to be good enough to face him."

I propped my rake against a tree trunk and picked up two vinyl bags of leaves and pecan husks and carried them out to the road. I hoped that somehow Lila would simply drive away with her father.

Instead, he got out of the Oldsmobile and approached me, wearing white trousers and a blue sports coat with brass buttons.

"I'm willing to shake hands and start over again, Mr. Robicheaux. I do this out of gratitude for the help you've given my daughter. She has enormous respect for you," he said.

He extended his hand. It was manicured and small, the candy-striped French cuff lying neatly across the wrist. It did not look like a hand that possessed the strength to whip a chain across a man's back and sunder his bones with nails.

"I'm offering you my hand, sir," he said.

I dropped the two leaf bags on the roadside and wiped my palms on my khakis, then stepped back into the shade, away from Terrebonne.

"Scruggs is blackmailing you. You need me, or someone like me, to pop a cap on him and get him out of your life. That's not going to happen," I said.

He tapped his right hand gingerly on his cheek, as though he had a toothache.

"I tried. Truly I have. Now, I'll leave you alone, sir," he said.

"You and your family pretend to gentility, Mr. Terrebonne. But your ancestor murdered black soldiers under the bluffs at Fort Pillow and caused the deaths of his twin daughters. You and your father brought grief to black people like Willie Broussard and his wife and killed anyone who threatened your power. None of you are what you seem."

He stood in the center of the road, not moving when a car passed, the dust swirling around him, his face looking at words that seemed to be marching by in front of his eyes.

"I congratulate you on your sobriety, Mr. Robicheaux. I suspect for a man such as yourself it was a very difficult accomplishment," he said, and walked back to the Oldsmobile and got inside and waited for his daughter.

I turned around and almost collided into Lila.

"I can't believe what you just did. How dare you?" she said.

"Don't you understand what your father has participated in? He crucified a living human being. Wake up, Lila. He's the definition of evil."

She struck me across the face.

I stood in the road, with the ashes of leaves blowing around me, and watched their car disappear down the long tunnel of oaks.

"I hate her," Alafair said behind me.

"Don't give them power, Alf," I replied.

But I felt a great sorrow. Inside all of Lila's alcoholic madness she had always seen the truth about her father's iniquity. Now, the restoration of light and the gift of sobriety in her life had somehow made her morally blind.

I put my arm on Alafair's shoulder, and the two of us walked into the house.

THIRTY

isco Flynn was in my office the next morning. He sat in
a chair in front of my desk, his hands opening and closing on his thighs.

"Out at the dock, when I told you to look at the photos? I was
angry," I said, holding the duplicates of the three photographs from
the buried jar.

"Just give them to me, would you?" he said.

I handed the photographs across the desk to him. He looked at
them slowly, one by one, his face never changing expression. But I
saw a twitch in his cheek under one eye. He lay the photos back on
the desk and straightened himself in the chair.

His voice was dry when he spoke. "You're sure that's Terrebonne,
the dude with the missing finger?"

"Every road we take leads to his front door," I said.

"This guy Scruggs was there, too?"

"Put it in the bank."

He stared out the window at the fronds of a palm tree swelling in
the wind.

"I understand he's back in the area," Cisco said.

"Don't have the wrong kind of thoughts, partner."

"I always thought the worst people I ever met were in Hollywood. But they're right here."

"Evil doesn't have a zip code, Cisco."

He picked up the photos and looked at them again. Then he set them down and propped his elbows on my desk and rested his forehead on his fingers. I thought he was going to speak, then I realized he was weeping.

A t noon, when I was on my way to lunch, Helen caught up with me in the parking lot.

"Hang on, Streak. I just got a call from some woman named Jessie Rideau. She says she was in the hotel in Morgan City the night Jack Flynn was kidnapped," she said.

"Why's she calling us now?"

We both got in my truck. I started the engine. Helen looked straight ahead, as though trying to rethink a problem she couldn't quite define.

"She says she and another woman were prostitutes who worked out of the bar downstairs. She says Harpo Scruggs made the other woman, someone named Lavern Viator, hide a lockbox for him."

"A lockbox? Where's the Viator woman?"

"She joined a cult in Texas and asked Rideau to keep the lockbox. Rideau thinks Scruggs killed her. Now he wants the box."

"Why doesn't she give it to him?"

"She's afraid he'll kill her after he gets it."

"Tell her to come in."

"She doesn't trust us either."

I parked the truck in front of the cafeteria on Main Street. The drawbridge was up on Bayou Teche and a shrimp boat was passing through the pilings.

"Let's talk about it inside," I said.

"I can't eat. Before Rideau got panicky and hung up on me, she said the killers were shooting craps in the room next to Jack Flynn. They waited till he was by himself, then dragged him down a back stairs and tied him to a post on a dock and whipped him with chains.

She said that's all that was supposed to happen. Except Scruggs told the others the night was just beginning. He made the Viator woman come with them. She held Jack Flynn's head in a towel so the blood wouldn't get on the seat."

Helen pressed at her temple with two fingers.

"What is it?" I said.

"Rideau said you can see Flynn's face on the towel. Isn't that some bullshit? She said there're chains and a hammer and handcuffs in the box, too. I got to boogie, boss man. The next time this broad calls, I'm transferring her to your extension," she said.

I spent the rest of the day with the paperwork that my file drawer seemed to procreate from the time I closed it in the afternoon until I opened it in the morning. The paperwork all concerned the Pool, that comic Greek chorus of miscreants who are always in the wings, upstaging our most tragic moments, flatulent, burping, snickering, catcalling at the audience. It has been my long-held belief as a police officer that Hamlet and Ophelia might command our respect and admiration, but Sir Toby Belch and his minions usually consume most of our energies.

Here are just a few random case file entries in the lives of Pool members during a one-month period.

A pipehead tries to smoke Drāno crystals in a hookah. After he recovers from destroying several thousand brain cells in his head, he dials 911 and dimes his dealer for selling him bad dope.

A man steals a blank headstone from a funeral home, engraves his mother's name on it, and places it in his back yard. When confronted with the theft, he explains that his wife poured his mother's ashes down the sink and the man wished to put a marker over the septic tank where his mother now resides.

A woman who has fought with her common-law husband for ten years reports that her TV remote control triggered the electronically operated door on the garage and crushed his skull.

Two cousins break into the back of a liquor store, then can't start their car. They flee on foot, then report their car as stolen. It's a good plan. Except they don't bother to change their shoes. The liquor store's floor had been freshly painted and the cousins track the paint all over our floors when they file their stolen car report.

That evening Clete and I filled a bait bucket with shiners and took my outboard to Henderson Swamp and fished for sac-a-lait. The sun was dull red in the west, molten and misshaped as though it were dissolving in its own heat among the strips of lavender cloud that clung to the horizon. We crossed a wide bay, then let the boat drift in the lee of an island that was heavily wooded with willow and cypress trees. The mosquitoes were thick in the shadows of the trees, and you could see bream feeding among the lily pads and smell an odor like fish roe in the water.

I looked across the bay at the levee, where there was a paintless, tin-roofed house that had not been there three weeks ago.

"Where'd that come from?" I said.

"Billy Holtzner just built it. It's part of the movie," Clete said.

"You're kidding. That guy's like a disease spreading itself across the state."

"Check it out."

I reached into the rucksack where I had packed our sandwiches and a thermos of coffee and my World War II Japanese field glasses. I adjusted the focus on the glasses and saw Billy Holtzner and his daughter talking with a half dozen people on the gallery of the house.

"Aren't you supposed to be out there with them?" I asked Clete.

"They work what they call a twelve-hour turnaround. Anyway, I go off the clock at five. Then he's got some other guys to boss around. They'll be out there to one or two in the morning. Dave, I'm going to do my job, but I think that guy's dead meat."

"Why?"

"You remember guys in Nam you knew were going to get it? Walking fuckups who stunk of fear and were always trying to hang on to you? Holtzner's got that same stink on him. It's on his breath, in his clothes, I don't even like looking at him."

A few drops of rain dimpled the water, then the sac-a-lait started biting. Unlike bream or bass, they would take the shiner straight down, pulling the bobber with a steady tension into the water's darkness. They would fight hard, pumping away from the boat, until they broke the surface, when they would turn on their side and give it up.

We layered them with crushed ice in the cooler, then I took our ham-and-onion sandwiches and coffee thermos out of the rucksack and lay them on the cooler's top. In the distance, by the newly constructed movie set, I saw two figures get on an airboat and roar across the bay toward us.

The noise of the engine and fan was deafening, the wake a long, flat depression that swirled with mud. The pilot cut the engine and let the airboat float into the lee of the island. Billy Holtzner sat next to him, a blue baseball cap on his head. He was smiling.

"You guys on the job?" he said.

"No. We're just fishing," I said.

"Get out of here," he said, still smiling.

"We fish this spot a lot, Billy. We're both off the clock," Clete said.

"Oh," Holtzner said, his smile dying.

"Everything copacetic?" Clete said.

"Sure," Holtzner said. "Want to come up and watch us shoot a couple of scenes?"

"We're heading back in a few minutes. Thanks just the same," I said.

"Sure. My daughter's with me," he said, as though there were a logical connection between her presence and his invitation. "I mean, maybe we'll have a late-night dinner later."

Neither Clete nor I responded. Holtzner touched the boat pilot on the arm, and the two of them roared back across the bay, their backdraft showering the water's surface with willow leaves.

"How do you read that?" I said.

"The guy's on his own, probably for the first time in his life. It must be rough to wake up one morning and realize you're a gutless shit who doesn't deserve his family," Clete said, then bit into his sandwich.

. . .

The next day two uniformed city cops and I had to arrest a parolee from Alabama by the swimming pool at City Park. Even with cuffs on, he spit on one cop and kicked the other one in the groin. I pushed him against the side of the cruiser and tried to hold him until I could get the back door open, then the cop who had been spit on Maced him and sprayed me at the same time.

I spent the next ten minutes rinsing my face and hair in the lavatory inside the recreation building. When I came back outside, wiping the water off my neck with a paper towel, the parolee and the city cops were on their way to the jail and Adrien Glazier was standing by my pickup truck. Out on the drive, among the oak trees, I saw a dark blue waxed car with two men in suits and shades standing by it. Leaves were swirling in eddies around their car.

"The sheriff told us you were here. How's that stuff feel?" she said.

"Like somebody holding a match to your skin."

"We just got a report from Interpol on the dwarf. He's enjoying himself on the Italian Riviera."

"Glad to hear it," I said.

"So maybe the shooter who did Ricky Scar left with him."

"You believe that?" I asked.

"No. Take a walk with me."

She didn't wait for a reply. She turned and began walking slowly through the trees toward the bayou and the picnic tables that were set under tin sheds by the waterside.

"What's going on, Ms. Glazier?" I said.

"Call me Adrien." She rested her rump against a picnic table and folded her arms across her chest. "Did Cisco Flynn confess his involvement in a homicide to you?"

"Excuse me?"

"The guy who got chucked out a hotel window in San Antonio? I understand his head hit a fire hydrant. Did Cisco come seeking absolution at your bait shop?"

"My memory's not as good as it used to be. Y'all have a tap on his phone or a bug in his house?"

"We're giving you a free pass on this one. That's because I acted like a pisspot for a while," she said.

"It's because you know Harpo Scruggs was a federal snitch when he helped crucify Jack Flynn."

"You should come work for us. I never have any real laughs these days."

She walked off through the trees toward the two male agents who waited for her, her hips undulating slightly. I caught up with her.

"What have you got on the dwarf's partner?" I asked.

"Nothing. Watch your ass, Mr. Robicheaux," she replied.

"Call me Dave."

"Not a chance," she said. Then she grinned and made a clicking goodbye sound in her jaw.

T hat night I watched the ten o'clock news before going to bed. I looked disinterestedly at some footage about a State Police traffic check, taken outside Jeanerette, until I saw Clete Purcel on the screen, showing his license to a trooper, then being escorted to a cruiser.

Back in the stew pot, I thought, probably for violating the spirit of his restricted permit, which allowed him to drive only for business purposes.

But that was Clete, always in trouble, always out of sync with the rest of the world. I knew the trooper was doing his job and Clete had earned his night in the bag, but I had to pause and wonder at the illusionary cell glue that made us feel safe about the society we lived in.

Archer Terrebonne, who would murder in order to break unions, financed a movie about the travail and privation of plantation workers in the 1940s. The production company helped launder money from the sale of China white. The FBI protected sociopaths like Harpo Scruggs and let his victims pay the tab. Harpo Scruggs worked for the state of Louisiana and murdered prisoners in Angola. The vested interest of government and criminals and respectable people was often the same.

In my scrapbook I had an inscribed photograph that Clete had given me when we were both in uniform at NOPD. It had been taken by an Associated Press photographer at night on a Swift Boat in Vietnam, somewhere up the Mekong, in the middle of a firefight. Clete was behind a pair of twin fifties, wearing a steel pot and a flack vest with no shirt, his youthful face lighted by a flare, tracers floating away into the darkness like segmented neon.

I could almost hear him singing, "I got a freaky old lady name of Cocaine Katie."

I thought about calling the jail in Jeanerette, but I knew he would be back on the street in the morning, nothing learned, deeper in debt to a bondsman, trying to sweep the snakes and spiders back in their baskets with vodka and grapefruit juice.

He made me think of my father, Aldous, whom people in the oil field always called Big Al Robicheaux, as though it were one name. It took seven Lafayette cops in Antlers Pool Room to put him in jail. The fight wrecked the pool room from one end to the other. They hit him with batons, broke chairs on his shoulders and back, and finally got his mother to talk him into submission so they didn't have to kill him.

But jails and poverty and baton-swinging cops never broke his spirit. It took my mother's infidelities to do that. The Amtrak still ran on the old Southern Pacific roadbed that had carried my mother out to Hollywood in 1946, made up of the same cars from the original Sunset Limited she had ridden in, perhaps with the same desert scenes painted on the walls. Sometimes when I would see the Amtrak crossing through winter fields of burned cane stubble, I would wonder what my mother felt when she stepped down on the platform at Union Station in Los Angeles, her pillbox hat slanted on her head, her purse clenched in her small hand. Did she believe the shining air and the orange trees and the blue outline of the San Gabriel Mountains had been created especially for her, to be discovered in exactly this moment, in a train station that echoed like a cathedral? Did she walk into the green roll of the Pacific and feel the water balloon her dress out from her thighs and fill her with a sexual pleasure that no man ever gave her?

What's the point?

Hitler and George Orwell already said it. History books are written by and about the Terrebonnes of this world, not jarheads up the Mekong or people who die in oil-well blowouts or illiterate Cajun women who believe the locomotive whistle on the Sunset Limited calls for them.

THIRTY-ONE

drien Glazier called Monday morning from New Orleans.

"You remember a hooker by the name of Ruby Gravano?" she asked.

"She gave us the first solid lead on Harpo Scruggs. She had an autistic son named Nick," I said.

"That's the one."

"We put her on the train to Houston. She was getting out of the life."

"Her career change must have been short-lived. She was selling out of her pants again Saturday night. We think she tricked the shooter in the Ricky Scar gig. Unlucky girl."

"What happened?"

"Her pimp is a peckerwood named Beeler Grissum. Know him?"

"Yeah, he's a Murphy artist who works the Quarter and Airline Highway."

"He worked the wrong dude this time. He and Ruby Gravano tried to set up the outraged-boyfriend skit. The john broke Grissum's neck with a karate kick. Ruby told NOPD she'd seen the john a week or so ago with a dwarf. So they thought maybe he was the shooter on the Scarlotti hit and they called us."

"Who's the john?"

"All she could say was he has a Canadian passport, blond or gold hair, and a green-and-red scorpion tattooed on his left shoulder. We'll send the composite through, but it looks generic—egg-shaped head, elongated eyes, sideburns, fedora with a feather in it. I'm starting to think all these guys had the same mother."

"Where's Ruby now?"

"At Charity."

"What'd he do to her?"

"You don't want to know."

A few minutes later the composite came through the fax machine and I took it out to Cisco Flynn's place on the Loreauville road. When no one answered the door, I walked around the side of the house toward the patio in back. I could hear the voices of both Cisco and Billy Holtzner, arguing furiously.

"You got a taste, then you put your whole face in the trough. Now you swim for the shore with the rats," Holtzner said.

"You ripped them off, Billy. I'm not taking the fall," Cisco said.

"This fine house, this fantasy you got about being a southern gentleman, where you think it all comes from? You made your money off of me."

"So I'm supposed to give it back because you burned the wrong guys? That's the way they do business in the garment district?"

Then I heard their feet shuffling, a piece of iron furniture scrape on brick, a slap, like a hand hitting a body, and Cisco's voice saying, "Don't embarrass yourself on top of it, Billy."

A moment later Holtzner came around the back corner of the house, walking fast, his face heated, his stare twisted with his own thoughts. I held up the composite drawing in front of him.

"You know this guy?" I asked.

"No."

"The FBI thinks he's a contract assassin."

Holtzner's eyes were dilated, red along the rims, his skin filmed with an iridescent shine, a faint body odor emanating from his clothes, like a man who feels he's about to slide down a razor blade.

"So you bring it out to Cisco Flynn's house? Who you think is the target for these assholes?" he said.

"I see. You are."

"You got me made for a coward. It doesn't bother me. I don't care what happens to me anymore. But my daughter never harmed anybody except herself. All pinhead back there has to do is mortgage his house and we can make a down payment on our debt. I'm talking about my daughter's life here. Am I getting through to you?"

"You have a very unpleasant way of talking to people, Mr. Holtzner," I said.

"Go fuck yourself," he said, and walked across the lawn to his automobile, which he had parked under a shade tree.

I followed him and propped both my hands on the edge of his open window just as he turned the ignition. He looked up abruptly into my face. His leaded eyelids made me think of a frog's.

"Your daughter's been threatened? Explicitly?" I said.

"Explicitly? I can always spot a thinker," he said. He dropped the car into reverse and spun two black tracks across the grass to the driveway.

I went back up on the gallery and knocked again. But Megan came to the door instead of Cisco. She stepped outside without inviting me in, a brown paper bag in her hand.

"I'm returning your pistol," she said.

"I think you should hang on to it for a while."

"Why'd you show Cisco those photos of my father?"

"He came to my office. He asked to see them."

"Take the gun. It's unloaded," she said. She pushed the bag into my hands.

"You're worried he might go after Archer Terrebonne?"

"You shouldn't have shown him those photos. Sometimes you're unaware of the influence you have over others, Dave."

"I tell you what. I'm going to get all the distance I can between me and you and Cisco. How's that?"

She stepped closer to me, her face tilted up into mine. I could feel her breath on my skin. For a moment I thought she was being flirtatious, deliberately confrontational. Then I saw the moisture in her eyes.

"You've never read the weather right with me. Not on anything. It's not Cisco who might do something to Archer Terrebonne," she said. She continued to stare into my face. There were broken veins in the whites of her eyes, like pieces of red thread.

That evening I saw Clete's chartreuse convertible coming down the dirt road toward the dock, with Geraldine Holtzner behind the wheel, almost unrecognizable in a scarf and dark glasses, and Clete padding along behind the car, in scarlet trunks, rotted T-shirt, and tennis shoes that looked like pancakes on his feet.

Geraldine Holtzner braked to a stop by the boat ramp and Clete opened the passenger door and took a bottle of diet Pepsi out of the cooler and wiped the ice off with his palm. He breathed through his mouth, sweat streaming out of his hair and down his chest.

"You trying to have a heart attack?" I said.

"I haven't had a drink or a cigarette in two days. I feel great. You want some fried chicken?" he said.

"They pulled your license altogether?" I said.

"Big time," he said.

"Clete—" I said.

"So beautiful women drive me around now. Right, Geri?"

She didn't respond. Instead, she stared at me from behind her dark glasses, her mouth pursed into a button. "Why are you so hard on my father?" she said.

I looked at Clete, then down the road, in the shadows, where a man in a ribbed undershirt was taking a fishing rod and tackle box out of his car trunk.

"I'd better get back to work," I said.

"I'll take a shower in the back of the bait shop and we'll go to a movie or something. How about it, Geri?" Clete said.

"Why not?" she said.

"I'd better pass," I said.

"I've got a case of 12-Step PMS today, you know, piss, moan, and snivel. Don't be a sorehead," Geraldine said.

"Come back later. We'll take a boat ride," I said.

"I can't figure what Megan sees in you," Geraldine said.

I went back down the dock to the bait shop, then turned and watched Clete padding along behind the convertible, like a trained bear, the dust puffing around his dirty tennis shoes.

A few minutes later I walked up to the house and ate supper in the kitchen with Alafair and Bootsie. The phone rang on the counter. I picked it up.

"Dave, this probably don't mean nothing, but a man was axing about Clete right after you went up to eat," Batist said.

"Which man?"

"He was fishing on the bank, then he come in the shop and bought a candy bar and started talking French. Then he ax in English who own that convertible that was going down the road. I tole him the only convertible I seen out there was for Clete Purcel. Then he ax if the woman driving it wasn't in the movies.

"I tole him I couldn't see through walls, no, so I didn't have no idea who was driving it. He give me a dol'ar tip and gone back out and drove away in a blue car."

"What kind of French did he speak?" I asked.

"I didn't t'ink about it. It didn't sound no different from us."

"I'll mention it to Clete. But don't worry about it."

"One other t'ing. He only had an undershirt on. He had a red-and-green tattoo on his shoulder. It look like a, what you call them t'ings, they got them down in Mexico, it ain't a crawfish, it's a—"

"Scorpion?" I said.

I called Clete at his cottage outside Jeanerette.

"The Scarlotti shooter may be following you. Watch for a blond guy, maybe a French Canadian—" I began.

"Guy with a tattoo on his shoulder, driving a blue Ford?" Clete said.

"That's the guy."

"Geri and I stopped at a convenience store and I saw him do a U-turn down the street and park in some trees. I strolled on down toward a pay phone, but he knew I'd made him."

"You get his tag number?" I asked.

"No, there was mud on it."

"Can you get hold of Holtzner?"

"If I have to. The guy's wiring is starting to spark. I smelled crack in his trailer today."

"Where's Geraldine?"

"Where's any hype? In her own universe. That broad's crazy, Dave. After I told her we were being followed by the guy with the tattoo, she accused me of setting her up. Every woman I meet is either unattainable or nuts . . . Anyway, I'll try to find Holtzner for you."

An hour later he called me back.

"Holtzner just fired me," he said.

"Why?"

"I got him on his cell phone and told him the Canadian dude was in town. He went into a rage. He asked me why I didn't take down this guy when I had the chance. I go, 'Take down, like cap the guy?'

"He goes, '*What,* an ex-cop kicked off the police force for killing a federal witness has got qualms?'

"I say, 'Yeah, as a matter of fact I do.'

"He goes, 'Then sign your own paychecks, Rhino Boy.'

"*Rhino Boy?* How'd I ever get mixed up with these guys, Dave?"

"Lots of people ask themselves that question," I said.

The ex-prostitute named Jessie Rideau, who claimed to have been present when Jack Flynn was kidnapped, called Helen Soileau's extension the next day. Helen had the call transferred to my office.

"Come talk to us, Ms. Rideau," I said.

"You giving out free coffee in lockup?" she said.

"We want to put Harpo Scruggs away. You help us, we help you."

"Gee, where I heard that before?" I could hear her breath flattening on the receiver, as though she were trying to blow the heat out of a burn. "You ain't gonna say nothing?"

"I'll meet you somewhere else."

"St. Peter's Cemetery in ten minutes."

"How will I recognize you?" I asked.

"I'm the one that's not dead."

I parked my truck behind the cathedral and walked over to the old cemetery, which was filled with brick-and-plaster crypts that had settled at broken angles into the earth. She sat on the seat of her paint-blistered gas-guzzler, the door open, her feet splayed on the curb, her head hanging out in the sunlight as I approached her. She had coppery hair that looked like it had been waved with an iron, and brown skin and freckles like a spray of dull pennies on her face and neck. Her shoulders were wide, her breasts like watermelons inside her blue cotton shirt, her turquoise eyes fastened on me, as though she had no means of defending herself against the world once it escaped her vision.

"Ms. Rideau?"

She didn't reply. A fire truck passed and she never took her eyes off my face.

"Give us a formal statement on Scruggs, enough to get a warrant for his arrest. That's when your problems start to end," I said.

"I need money to go out West, somewhere he cain't find me," she said.

"We don't run a flea market. If you conceal evidence in a criminal investigation, you become an accomplice after the fact. You ever do time?"

"You a real charmer."

I looked at my watch.

"Maybe I'd better go," I said.

"Harpo Scruggs gonna kill me. I had that box hid all them years for him. Now he gonna kill me over it. That's what y'all ain't hearing."

"Why does he want the lockbox now?" I asked.

"Him and me run a house toget'er. Fo' years ago I found out he killed Lavern Viator in Texas. Lavern was the other girl that was in Morgan City when they beat that man wit' chains. So I moved the box to a different place, one he ain't t'ought about."

"Let's try to be honest here, Jessie. Did you move it because you knew he was blackmailing someone with it and you thought it was valuable?"

Raindrops were falling out of the sunlight. There were blue tattoos of hearts and dice inside Jessie Rideau's forearms. She stared at the crypts in the cemetery, her eyes recessed, her face like that of a person who knows she will never have any value to anyone other than use.

"I gonna be wit' them dead people soon," she said.

"Where'd you do time?"

"A year in St. John the Baptist. Two years in St. Gabriel."

"Let us help you."

"Too late." She pulled the car door shut and started the engine. The exhaust pipe and muffler were rusted out, and smoke billowed from under the car frame.

"Why does he want the lockbox now?" I said.

She shot me the finger and gunned the car out into the street, the roar of her engine reverberating through the crypts.

There are days that are different. They may look the same to everyone else, but on certain mornings you wake and know with absolute certainty you've been chosen as a participant in a historical script, for reasons unknown to you, and your best efforts will not change what has already been written.

On Wednesday the false dawn was bone-white, just like it had been the day Megan came back to New Iberia, the air brittle, the wood timbers in our house aching with cold. Then hailstones clattered on the tin roof and through the trees and rolled down the slope onto the dirt road. When the sun broke above the horizon the clouds in the eastern sky trembled with a glow like the reflection of a distant forest fire. When I walked down to the dock, the air was still cold, crisscrossed with the flight of robins, more than I had seen in years. I started cleaning the congealed ash from the barbecue pit, then rinsed my hands in an oaken bucket that had been filled with rainwater the night before. But Batist had cleaned a nutria in it for crab bait, and when I poured the water out it was red with blood.

At the office I called Adrien Glazier in New Orleans.

"Anything on the Scarlotti shooter?" I said.

"You figured out he's a French Canadian. You're ahead of us. What's the matter?" she said.

"Matter? He's going to kill somebody."

"If it will make you feel better, I already contacted Billy Holtzner and offered him Witness Protection. He goes, 'Where, on an ice floe at the South Pole?' and hangs up."

"Send some agents over here, Adrien."

"Holtzner's from Hollywood. He knows the rules. You get what you want when you come across. I told him the G's casting couch is nongender-specific. Try to have a few laughs with this stuff. You worry too much."

It began to rain just after sunset. The light faded in the swamp and the air was freckled with birds, then the rain beat on the dock and the tin roof of the bait shop and filled the rental boats that were chained up by the boat ramp. Batist closed out the cash register and put on his canvas coat and hat.

"Megan's daddy, the one got nailed to the barn? You know how many black men been killed and nobody ever been brought to cou't for it?" he said.

"Doesn't make it right," I said.

"Makes it the way it is," he replied.

After he had gone I turned off the outside lights so no late customers would come by, then began mopping the floor. The rain on the roof was deafening and I didn't hear the door open behind me, but I felt the cold blow across my back.

"Put your mop up. I got other work for you," the voice said.

I straightened up and looked into the seamed, rain-streaked face of Harpo Scruggs.

THIRTY-TWO

His face was bloodless, shriveled like a prune, glistening under the drenched brim of his hat. His raincoat dripped water in a circle on the floor. A blue-black .22 Ruger revolver, with ivory grips, on full cock, hung from his right hand.

"I got a magnum cylinder in it. The round will go through both sides of your skull," he said.

"What do you want, Scruggs?"

"Fix me some coffee and milk in one of them big glasses yonder." He pointed with one finger. "Put about four spoons of honey in it."

"Have you lost your mind?"

He propped the heel of his hand against the counter for support. The movement caused him to pucker his mouth and exhale his breath. It touched my face, like the raw odor from a broken drain line.

"You're listing," I said.

"Fix the coffee like I told you."

A moment later he picked up the glass with his left hand and drank from it steadily until it was almost empty. He set the glass on the counter and wiped his mouth with the back of his wrist. His whiskers made a scraping sound against his skin.

"We're going to Opelousas. You're gonna drive. You try to hurt me, I'll kill you. Then I'll come back and kill your wife and child. A man like me don't give it no thought," he said.

"Why me, Scruggs?"

" 'Cause you got an obsession over the man we stretched out on that barn wall. You gonna do right, no matter who you got to mess up. It ain't a compliment."

We took his pickup truck to the four-lane and headed north toward Lafayette and Opelousas. He didn't use the passenger seat belt but instead sat canted sideways with his right leg pushed out in front of him. His raincoat was unbuttoned and I could see the folds of a dark towel that were tied with rope across his side.

"You leaking pretty bad?" I said.

"Hope that I ain't. I'll pop one into your brisket 'fore I go under."

"I'm not your problem. We both know that."

With his left hand he took a candy bar from the dashboard and tore the paper with his dentures and began to eat the candy, swallowing as though he hadn't eaten in days. He held the revolver with his other hand, the barrel and cylinder resting across his thigh, pointed at my kidney.

The rain swept in sheets against the windshield. We passed through north Lafayette, the small, wood, galleried houses on each side of us whipped by the rain. Outside the city the country was dark green and sodden and there were thick stands of hardwoods on both sides of the four-lane and by the exit to Grand Coteau I saw emergency flares burning on the road and the flashers of emergency vehicles. A state trooper stood by an overturned semi, waving the traffic on with his flashlight.

"Was you ever a street cop?" Scruggs said.

"NOPD," I said.

"I was a gun bull at Angola, city cop, and road-gang hack, too. I done it all. I got no quarrel with you, Robicheaux."

"You want me to bring down Archer Terrebonne, don't you?"

"When I was a gun bull at Angola? That was in the days of the

Red Hat House. The lights would go down all over the system and ole Sparky would make fire jump off their tailbone. There was this white boy from Mississippi put a piece of glass in my food once. A year later he cut up two other convicts for stealing a deck of cards from his cell. Guess who got to walk him into the Red Hat House?

"Lightning was crawling all over the sky that night and the current didn't work right. That boy was jolting in the straps for two minutes. The smell made them reporters hold handkerchiefs to their mouths. They was falling over themselves to get outside. I laughed till I couldn't hardly stand up."

"What's the point?"

"I'm gonna have my pound of flesh from Archer Terrebonne. You gonna be the man cut it out for me."

He straightened his tall frame inside his raincoat, his face draining with the effort. He saw me watching him and raised the barrel of the Ruger slightly, so that it was aimed upward at my armpit. He put his hand on the towel tied across his side and looked at it, then wiped his hand on his pants.

"Terrebonne paid my partner to shoot my liver out. I didn't think my partner would turn on me. I'll be damned if you can trust anybody these days," he said.

"The man who helped you kill the two brothers out in the Atchafalaya Basin?"

"That's him. Or was. I wouldn't eat no pigs that was butchered around here for a while . . . Take that exit yonder."

We drove for three miles through farmland, then followed a dirt road through pine trees, past a pond that was green with algae and covered with dead hyacinths, to a two-story yellow frame house whose yard was filled with the litter of dead pecan trees. The windows had been nailed over with plywood, the gallery stacked with hay bales that had rotted.

"You recognize it?" he asked.

"It was a brothel," I said.

"The governor of Lou'sana used to get laid there. Walk ahead of me."

We crossed through the back yard, past a collapsed privy and a cistern, with a brick foundation, that had caved outward into dis-jointed slats. The barn still had its roof, and through the rain I could hear hogs snuffing inside it. A tree of lightning burst across the sky and Scruggs jerked his face toward the light as though loud doors had been thrown back on their hinges behind him.

He saw me watching him and pointed the revolver at my face.

"I told you to walk ahead of me!" he said.

We went through the rear door of the house into a gutted kitchen that was illuminated by the soft glow of a light at the bottom of a basement stairs.

"Where is Jessie Rideau?" I said.

Lightning crashed into a piney woods at the back of the property.

"Keep asking questions and I'll see you spend some time with her," he said, and pointed at the basement stairs with the barrel of the gun.

I walked down the wood steps into the basement, where a rechargeable Coleman lantern burned on the cement floor. The air was damp and cool, like the air inside a cave, and smelled of water and stone and the nests of small animals. Behind an old wooden icebox, the kind with an insert at the top for a block of tonged ice, I saw a woman's shoe and the sole of a bare foot. I walked around the side of the icebox and knelt down by the woman's side and felt her throat.

"You sonofabitch," I said to Scruggs.

"Her heart give out. She was old. It wasn't my fault," Scruggs said. Then he sat down in a wood chair, as though all his strength had drained through the bottoms of his feet. He stared at me dully from under the brim of his hat and wet his lips and swallowed before he spoke again.

"Yonder's what you want," he said.

In the corner, amidst a pile of bricks and broken mortar and plaster that had been prized from the wall with a crowbar, was a steel box that had probably been used to contain dynamite caps at one time. The lid was bradded and painted silver and heavy in my hand when I lifted it back on its hinges. Inside the box were a pair of handcuffs, two lengths of chain, a bath towel flattened inside a plastic bag, and a big hammer whose handle was almost black, as though stove soot and grease had been rubbed into the grain.

"Terrebonne's prints are gonna be on that hammer. The print will hold in blood just like in ink. Forensic man done told me that," Scruggs said.

"You've had your hands all over it. So have the women," I replied.

"The towel's got Flynn's blood all over it. So do them chains. You just got to get the right lab man to lift Terrebonne's prints."

His voice was deep in his throat, full of phlegm, his tongue thick against his dentures. He kept straightening his shoulders, as though resisting an unseen weight that was pushing them forward.

I removed the towel from the plastic bag and unfolded it. It was stiff and crusted, the fibers as pointed and hard as young thorns. I looked at the image in the center of the cloth, the black lines and smears that could have been a brow, a chin, a set of jawbones, eye sockets, even hair that had been soaked with blood.

"Do you have any idea of what you've been part of? Don't any of you understand what you've done?" I said to him.

"Flynn stirred everybody up. I know what I done. I was doing a job. That's the way it was back then."

"What do you see on the towel, Scruggs?"

"Dried blood. I done told you that. You carry all this to a lab. You gonna do that or not?"

He breathed through his mouth, his eyes seeming to focus on an insect an inch from the bridge of his nose. A terrible odor rose from his clothes.

"I'm going for the paramedics now," I said.

"A .45 ball went all the way through my intestines. I ain't gonna live wired to machines. Tell Terrebonne I expect I'll see him. Tell him Hell don't have no lemonade springs."

He fitted the Ruger's barrel under the top of his dentures and pulled the trigger. The round exited from the crown of his head and patterned the plaster on the brick wall with a single red streak. His head hung back on his wide shoulders, his eyes staring sightlessly at the ceiling. A puff of smoke, like a dirty feather, drifted out of his mouth.

THIRTY-THREE

Two days later the sky was blue outside my office, a balmy wind clattering the palm trees on the lawn. Clete stood at the window, his porkpie hat on his head, his hands on his hips, surveying the street and the perfection of the afternoon. He turned and propped his huge arms on my desk and stared down into my face.

"Blow it off. Prints or no prints, rich guys don't do time," he said.

"I want to have that hammer sent to an FBI lab," I said.

"Forget it. If the St. Landry Parish guys couldn't lift them, nobody else is going to either. You even told Scruggs he was firing in the well."

"Look, Clete, you mean well, but—"

"The prints aren't what's bothering you. It's that damn towel."

"I saw the face on it. Those cops in Opelousas acted like I was drunk. Even the skipper down the hall."

"So fuck 'em," Clete said.

"I've got to get back to work. Where's your car?"

"Dave, you saw that face on the towel because you believe. You expect guys with jock rash of the brain to understand what you're talking about?"

"Where's your car, Clete?"

"I'm selling it," he said. He was sitting on the corner of my desk now, his upper arms scaling with dried sun blisters. I could smell salt water and sun lotion on his skin. "Leave Terrebonne alone. The guy's got juice all the way to Washington. You'll never touch him."

"He's going down."

"Not because of anything we do." He tapped his knuckles on the desk. "There's my ride."

Through the window I saw his convertible pull up to the curb. A woman in a scarf and dark glasses was behind the wheel.

"Who's driving?" I asked.

"Lila Terrebonne. I'll call you later."

A t noon I met Bootsie in City Park for lunch. We spread a checkered cloth on a table under a tin shed by the bayou and set out the silverware and salt and pepper shakers and a thermos of iced tea and a platter of cold cuts and stuffed eggs. The camellias were starting to bloom, and across the bayou we could see the bamboo and flowers and the live oaks in the yard of The Shadows.

I could almost forget about the events of the last few days.

Until I saw Megan Flynn park her car on the drive that wound through the park and stand by it, looking in our direction.

Bootsie saw her, too.

"I don't know why she's here," I said.

"Invite her over and find out," Bootsie said.

"That's what I have office hours for."

"You want me to do it?"

I set down the stack of plastic cups I was unwrapping and walked across the grass to the spreading oak Megan stood under.

"I didn't know you were with anyone. I wanted to thank you for all you've done and say goodbye," she said.

"Where are you going?"

"Paris. Rivages, my French publisher, wants me to do a collection on the Spaniards who fled into the Midi after the Spanish Civil War. By the way, I thought you'd like to know Cisco walked out on the film. It's probably going to bankrupt him."

"Cisco's stand-up."

"Billy Holtzner doesn't have the talent to finish it by himself. His backers are going to be very upset."

"That composite I gave you of the Canadian hit man, you and Cisco have no idea who he is?"

"No, we'd tell you."

We looked at each other in the silence. Leaves gusted from around the trunks of the trees onto the drive. Her gaze shifted briefly to Bootsie, who sat at the picnic table with her back to us.

"I'm flying out tomorrow afternoon with some friends. I don't guess I'll see you for some time," she said, and extended her hand. It felt small and cool inside mine.

I watched her get in her car, drawing her long khaki-clad legs and sandaled feet in after her, her dull red hair thick on the back of her neck.

Is this the way it all ends? I thought. Megan goes back to Europe, Clete eats aspirins for his hangovers and labors through all the sweaty legal mechanisms of the court system to get his driver's license back, the parish buries Harpo Scruggs in a potter's field, and Archer Terrebonne fixes another drink and plays tennis at his club with his daughter.

I walked back to the tin shed and sat down next to Bootsie.

"She came to say goodbye," I said.

"That's why she didn't come over to the table," she replied.

That evening, which was Friday, the sky was purple, the clouds in the west stippled with the sun's last orange light. I raked stream trash out of the coulee and carried it in a washtub to the compost pile, then fed Tripod, our three-legged coon, and put fresh water in his bowl. My neighbor's cane was thick and green and waving in the field, and flights of ducks trailed in long V formations across the sun.

The phone rang inside, and Bootsie carried the portable out into the yard.

"We've got the Canadian identified. His name is Jacques Poitier, a real piece of shit," Adrien Glazier said. "Interpol says he's a suspect in at least a dozen assassinations. He's worked the Middle East, Europe, both sides in Latin America. He's gotten away with killing Israelis."

"We're not up to dealing with guys like this. Send us some help," I said.

"I'll see what I can do Monday," she said.

"Contract killers don't keep regular hours."

"Why do you think I'm making this call?" she said.

To feel better, I thought. But I didn't say it.

That evening I couldn't rest. But I didn't know what it was that bothered me.

Clete Purcel? His battered chartreuse convertible? Lila Terrebonne?

I called Clete's cottage.

"Where's your Caddy?" I asked.

"Lila's got it. I'm signing the title over to her Monday. Why?"

"Geraldine Holtzner's been driving it all over the area."

"Streak, the Terrebonnes might hurt themselves, but they don't get hurt by others. What does it take to make you understand that?"

"The Canadian shooter is a guy named Jacques Poitier. Ever hear of him?"

"No. And if he gives me any grief, I'm going to stick a .38 down his pants and blow his Jolly Roger off. Now, let me get some sleep."

"Megan told you she's going to France?"

The line was so quiet I thought it had gone dead. Then he said, "She must have called while I was out. When's she going?"

Way to go, Robicheaux, I thought.

■ ■ ■

The set that had been constructed on the levee at Henderson Swamp was lighted with the haloed brilliance of a phosphorus flare when Lila Terrebonne drove Clete's convertible along the dirt road at the top of the levee, above the long, wind-ruffled bays and islands of willow trees that were turning yellow with the season. The evening was cool, and she wore a sweater over her shoulders, a dark scarf with roses stitched on it tied around her head. She found her father with Billy Holtzner, and the three of them ate dinner on a cardboard table by the water's edge and drank a bottle of nonalcoholic champagne that had been chilled in a silver bucket.

When she left, she asked a grip to help her fasten down the top on her car. He was the only one to notice the blue Ford that pulled out of a fish camp down the levee and followed her toward the highway. He did not think it significant and did not mention the fact to anyone until later.

The man in the blue Ford followed her through St. Martinville and down the Loreauville road to Cisco Flynn's house. When she turned into Cisco's driveway, a lawn party was in progress and the man in the Ford parked on the swale and opened his hood and appeared to onlookers to be at work on his engine.

On the patio, behind the house, Lila Terrebonne called Cisco Flynn a lowborn, treacherous sycophant, picked up his own mint julep from the table, and flung it in his face.

But on the front lawn a jazz combo played atop an elevated platform, and the guests wandered among the citrus and oak trees and the drink tables and the music that seemed to charm the pink softness of the evening into their lives. Megan wore her funny straw hat with an evening dress that clung to her figure like ice water, and was talking to a group of friends, people from New York and overseas, when she noticed the man working on his car.

She stood between two myrtle bushes, on the edge of the swale, and waited until he seemed to feel her eyes on his back. He straightened up and smiled, but the smile came and went erratically, as though the man thought it into place.

He wore a form-fitting long-sleeve gold shirt and blue jeans that were so tight they looked painted on his skin. A short-brim fedora with a red feather in the band rested on the fender. His hair was the color of his shirt, waved, and cut long and parted on the side so it combed down over one ear.

"It's a battery cable. I'll have it started in a minute," he said in a French accent.

She stared at him without speaking, a champagne glass resting in the fingers of both hands, her chest rising and falling.

"I am a big fan of American movies. I saw a lady turn in here. Isn't she the daughter of a famous Hollywood director?" he said.

"I'm not sure who you mean," Megan said.

"She was driving a Cadillac, a convertible," he said, and waited. Then he smiled, wiping his hands on a handkerchief. "Ah, I'm right, aren't I? Her father is William Holtzner. I love all his films. He is wonderful," the man said.

She stepped backward, once, twice, three times, the myrtle bushes brushing against her bare arms, then stood silently among her friends. She looked back at the man with gold hair only after he had restarted his car and driven down the road. Five minutes later Lila Terrebonne backed the Cadillac down the drive, hooking one wheel over the slab into a freshly watered flower bed, then shifted into low out on the road and floored the accelerator toward New Iberia. Her radio was blaring with rock 'n' roll from the 1960s, her face energized with vindication inside the black scarf, stitched with roses, that was tied tightly around her head.

The man named Jacques Poitier caught up with her on the two-lane road that paralleled Bayou Teche, only one mile from her home. Witnesses said she tried to outrun him, swerving back and forth across the highway, blowing her horn, waving desperately at a group of blacks on the side of the road. Others said he passed her and they heard a gunshot. But we found no evidence of the latter, only a thread-worn tire that had exploded on the rim before the Cadillac skidded sideways, showering sparks off the pavement, into an oncoming dump truck loaded with condemned asbestos.

THIRTY-FOUR

I
f there was any drama at the crime scene later, it was not in our
search for evidence or even in the removal of Lila's body from
under the crushed roof of the Cadillac. Archer Terrebonne arrived at the scene twenty minutes after the crash, and was joined a few
minutes later by Billy Holtzner. Terrebonne immediately took charge,
as though his very presence and the slip-on half-top boots and red
flannel shirt and quilted hunting vest and visor cap he wore gave him a
level of authority that none of the firemen or paramedics or sheriff's
deputies possessed.

They all did his bidding or sought sanction or at a minimum gave
an explanation to him for whatever they did. It was extraordinary
to behold. His attorney and family physician were there; also a
U.S. congressman and a well-known movie actor. Terrebonne
wore his grief like a patrician who had become a man of the people.
A three-hundred-pound St. Mary Parish deputy, his mouth full of
Red Man, stood next to me, his eyes fixed admiringly on Terrebonne.

"That ole boy is one brave sonofabuck, ain't he?" he said.

The paramedics covered Lila's body with a sheet and wheeled it
on the gurney to the back of an ambulance, the strobe lights of TV

cameras flowing with it, passing across Terrebonne's and Holtzner's stoic faces.

Helen Soileau and I walked through the crowd until we were a few feet from Terrebonne. Red flares burned along the shoulder of the road, and mist clung to the bayou and the oak trunks along the bank. The air was cold, but my face felt hot and moist with humidity. His eyes never registered our presence, as though we were moths outside a glass jar, looking in upon a pure white flame.

"Your daughter's death is on you, Terrebonne. You didn't intend for it to happen, but you helped bring the people here who killed her," I said.

A woman gasped; the scattered conversation around us died.

"You hope this will destroy me, don't you?" he replied.

"Harpo Scruggs said to tell you he'd be expecting you soon. I think he knew what he was talking about," I said.

"Don't you talk to him like that," Holtzner said, rising on the balls of his feet, his face dilating with the opportunity that had presented itself. "I'll tell you something else, too. Me and my new co-director are finishing our picture. And it's going to be dedicated to Lila Terrebonne. You can take your dirty mouth out of here."

Helen stepped toward him, her finger lifted toward his face.

"He's a gentleman. I'm not. Smart off again and see what happens," she said.

We walked to our cruiser, past the crushed, upside-down shell of Clete's Cadillac, the eyes of reporters and cops and passersby riveted on the sides of our faces.

I heard a voice behind me, one I didn't recognize, yell out, "You're the bottom of the barrel, Robicheaux."

Then others applauded him.

Early the next morning Helen and I began re-creating Lila Terrebonne's odyssey from the movie set on the levee, where she had dinner with her father and Billy Holtzner, to the moment she must have realized her peril and tried to outrun the contract assassin named Jacques Poitier. We interviewed the stage grip who saw the

blue Ford pull out of the fish camp and follow her back down the
levee; an attendant at a filling station in St. Martinville, where she
stopped for gasoline; and everyone we could find from the Flynns'
lawn party.

The New York and overseas friends of Megan and Cisco were
cooperative and humble to a fault, in large part because they never
sensed the implications of what they told us. But after talking with
three guests from the lawn party, I had no doubt as to what transpired
during the encounter between Megan and the French Canadian
named Poitier.

Helen and I finished the last interview at a bed-and-breakfast
across from The Shadows at three o'clock that afternoon. It was warm
and the trees were speckled with sunlight, and a few raindrops were
clicking on the bamboo in front of The Shadows and drying as soon as
they struck the sidewalks.

"Megan's plane leaves at three-thirty from Acadiana Regional.
See if you can get a hold of Judge Mouton at his club," I said.

"A warrant? We might be on shaky ground. There has to be
intent, right?"

"Megan never did anything in her life without intending to."

Our small local airport had been built on the site of the old U.S.
Navy air base outside of town. As I drove down the state road
toward the hangars and maze of runways, under a partially blue sky
that was starting to seal with rain clouds, my heart was beating in a
way that it shouldn't, my hands sweating black prints on the steering
wheel.

Then I saw her, with three other people, standing by a hangar, her
luggage next to her, while a Learjet taxied around the far side of a
parking area filled with helicopters. She wore her straw hat and a pink
dress with straps and lace around the hem, and when the wind began
gusting she held her hat to her head with one hand in a way that made
me think of a 1920s flapper.

She saw me walking toward her, like someone she recognized
from a dream, then her eyes fixed on mine and the smile went out of

her face and she glanced briefly toward the horizon, as though the wind and the churning treetops held a message for her.

I looked at my watch. It was 3:25. The door to the Lear opened and a man in a white jacket and dark blue pants lowered the steps to the tarmac. Her friends picked up their luggage and drifted toward the door, glancing discreetly in her direction, unsure of the situation.

"Jacques Poitier stopped his car on the swale in front of your party. Your guests heard you talking to him," I said.

"He said his car was broken. He was working on it," she replied.

"He asked you if the woman driving Clete's Cadillac was Holtzner's daughter."

She was silent, her hair ruffling thickly on her neck. She looked at the open door of the plane and the attendant who waited for her.

"You let him think it was Geraldine Holtzner," I said.

"I didn't tell him anything, Dave."

"You knew who he was. I gave you the composite drawing."

"They're waiting for me."

"Why'd you do it, Meg?"

"I'm sorry for Lila Terrebonne. I'm not sorry for her father."

"She didn't deserve what happened to her."

"Neither did my father. I'm going now, unless you're arresting me. I don't think you can either. If I did anything wrong, it was a sin of omission. That's not a crime."

"You've already talked to a lawyer," I said, almost in amazement.

She leaned down and picked up her suitcase and shoulder bag. When she did, her hat blew off her head and bounced end over end across the tarmac. I ran after it, like a high school boy would, then walked back to her, brushing it off, and placed it in her hands.

"I won't let this rest. You've contributed to the death of an innocent person. Just like the black guy who died in your lens years ago. Somebody else has paid your tab. Don't come back to New Iberia, Meg," I said.

Her eyes held on mine and I saw a great sadness sweep through her face, like that of a child watching a balloon break loose from its string and float away suddenly on the wind.

EPILOGUE

That afternoon the wind dropped and there was a red tint like dye in the clouds, and the water was high and brown in the bayou, the cypress and willows thick with robins. It should have been a good afternoon for business at the bait shop and dock, but it wasn't. The parking area was empty; there was no whine of boat engines out on the water, and the sound of my footsteps on the planks in the dock echoed off the bayou as though I were walking under a glass dome.

A drunk who had given Batist trouble earlier that day had broken the guardrail on the dock and fallen to the ramp below. I got some lumber and hand tools and an electric saw from the tin shed behind the house to repair the gap in the rail, and Alafair clipped Tripod's chain on his collar and walked him down to the dock with me. I heard the front screen door bang behind us, and I turned and saw Bootsie on the gallery. She waved, then went down into the flower bed with a trowel and a plastic bucket and began working on her knees.

"Where is everybody?" Alafair said out on the dock.

"I think a lot of people went to the USL game today," I replied.

"There's no sound. It makes my ears pop."

"How about opening up a couple of cans of Dr Pepper?" I said.

She went inside the bait shop, but did not come back out right away. I heard the cash register drawer open and knew the subterfuge that was at work, one that she used to mask her charity, as though somehow it were a vice. She would pay for the fried pie she took from the counter, then cradle Tripod in one arm and hand-feed it to him whether he wanted it or not, while his thick, ringed tail flipped in the air like a spring.

I tried to concentrate on repairing the rail on the dock and not see the thoughts that were as bright and jagged as shards of glass in the center of my mind. I kept touching my brow and temple with my arm, as though I were wiping off sweat, but that wasn't my trouble. I could feel a band of pressure tightening across the side of my head, just as I had felt it on night trails in Vietnam or when Bedcheck Charlie was cutting through our wire.

What was it that bothered me? The presence of men like Archer Terrebonne in our midst? But why should I worry about his kind? They had always been with us, scheming, buying our leaders, deceiving the masses. No, it was Megan, and Megan, and Megan, and her betrayal of everything I thought she represented: Joe Hill, the Wobblies, the strikers murdered at Ludlow, Colorado, Woody Guthrie, Dorothy Day, all those faceless working people whom historians and academics and liberals alike treat with indifference.

I ran the electric saw through a two-by-four and ground the blade across a nail. The board seemed to explode, the saw leaping from my hand, splinters embedding in my skin like needles. I stepped backward from the saw, which continued to spin by my foot, then ripped the cord loose from the socket in the bait-shop wall.

"You all right, Dave?" Alafair said through the screen.

"Yeah, I'm fine," I said, holding the back of my right hand.

Through the trees next to the bayou I saw a mud-splattered stake truck loaded with boxes of chrysanthemums coming down the road. The truck pulled at an angle across the boat ramp, and Mout' Broussard got out on the passenger's side and a tiny Hmong woman in a conical straw hat with a face like a withered apple got down from the other. Mout' put a long stick across his shoulders, and the woman loaded wire-bailed baskets of flowers on each end of it, then picked up a basket herself and followed him down the dock.

"You sell these for us, we gonna give you half, you," Mout' said.

"I don't seem to have much business today, Mout'," I said.

"Season's almost over. I'm fixing to give them away," he said.

"Put them under the eave. We'll give it a try," I said.

He and the woman lay the flowers in yellow and brown and purple clumps against the bait-shop wall. Mout' wore a suit coat with his overalls and was sweating inside his clothes. He wiped his face with a red handkerchief.

"You doing all right?" he said to me.

"Sure," I said.

"That's real good. Way it should be," he said. He replaced the long stick across his shoulders and extended his arms on it and walked with the Hmong woman toward the truck, their bodies lit by the glow of the sun through the trees.

Why look for the fires that burn in western skies? I thought. The excoriated symbol of difference was always within our ken. You didn't have to see far to find it—an elderly black man who took pride in the fact he shined Huey Long's and Harry James's shoes or a misplaced and wizened Hmong woman who had fought the Communists in Laos for the French and the CIA and now grew flowers for Cajuns in Louisiana. The story was ongoing, the players changing only in name. I believe Jack Flynn understood that and probably forgave his children when they didn't.

I sat on a bench by the water faucet and tried to pick the wood splinters out of the backs of my hands. The wind came up and the robins filled the air with a sound that was almost deafening, their wings fluttering above my head, their breasts the color of dried blood.

"Are we still going to the show tonight?" Alafair said.

"You better believe it, you," I said, and winked.

She flipped Tripod up on her shoulder like a sack of meal, and the three of us went up the slope to find Bootsie.